"This will be the last time I ask you. What have you done with the children?"

Grenly looked up at her, and there were tears streaming down his grizzled cheek. "Done? We ain't done nothin', and that's the problem. First the navy came and took all our boys into conscript. We did nothing. Then not two days ago, a biomancer came and took all our girls. And *still* we did nothing." His fists were clenched and his whole body shook with suppressed rage. "My own Kapany. That monster in white took her and God knows what he will do with her. And when he loaded them all up on his ship, he left behind a chest of money as recompense. Like any amount of money could replace my sweet little Kapany." The man was openly weeping now, his breath hissing through clenched yellow teeth.

"Two days?" asked Hope, the ice in her stomach softening. "Where was it heading?"

"What?" Grenly blinked back tears, looking bewildered by her question.

"It would help if I knew the direction the ship was heading. And if you can remember, the number of masts and guns as well."

Grenly frowned. "But why?"

"So that we can run it down and free your daughters," said Hope.

"But...didn't you hear me?" he asked. "There's a *biomancer* on board that ship."

"This here is Dire Bane you're talking to," Filler said quietly. "And there ain't a biomancer alive can scare her."

Also by Jon Skovron

THE EMPIRE OF STORMS
Hope and Red

Bane and Shadow

Struts & Frets

Misfit

Man Made Boy

This Broken Wondrous World

BANE
AND
SHADOW

THE EMPIRE OF STORMS: BOOK TWO

JON SKOVRON

www.orbitbooks.net

Copyright © 2017 by Jon Skovron
Excerpt from *The Empire of Storms: Book Three* copyright © 2017 by Jon Skovron
Excerpt from *The Dragon Lords: Fool's Gold* copyright © 2016 by Jon Hollins
Map copyright © 2017 by Tim Paul

Cover design by Lauren Panepinto
Cover illustration/photo by Bastien Lecouffe Deharme
Cover copyright © 2017 by Hachette Book Group, Inc.

Orbit
Hachette Book Group
1290 Avenue of the Americas
New York, NY 10104
orbitbooks.net

First Edition: February 2017

Orbit is an imprint of Hachette Book Group.
The Orbit name and logo are trademarks of Little, Brown Book Group Limited.

The publisher is not responsible for websites (or their content) that are not owned by the publisher.

The Hachette Speakers Bureau provides a wide range of authors for speaking events. To find out more, go to www.hachettespeakersbureau.com or call (866) 376-6591.

ISBNs: 978-0-316-26814-1 (mass market), 978-0-316-26817-2 (ebook)

Printed in the United States of America

OPM

10 9 8 7 6 5 4 3 2 1

*In memory of Eve Reinhardt Caripedes,
bravest of warriors*

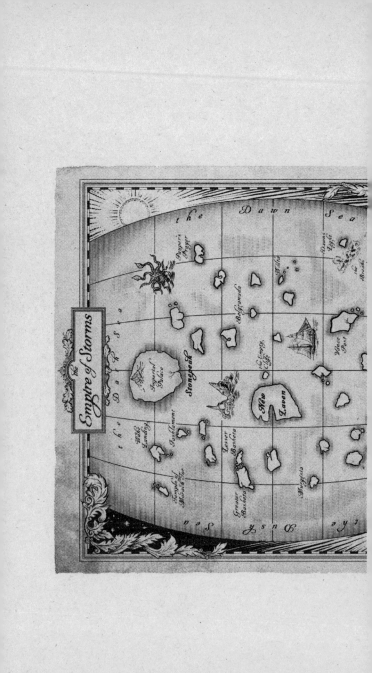

The Empire of Storms

the Dawn Sea

the Dark Sea

the Quiet Sea

the Southern Isles

Galwych

Gaster

a. The Docks
b. Rain Gate
c. Broken remains of the Thunder Gate
d. Wind Gate
e. Call to Arms Inn
f. Ifmish's Tinsmithy
g. Blagely's Fine Furniture
h. Thunder and Gale Tavern
i. Lightning Gate
j. Wheelhouse Tavern
k. South Market

Sunset Point

Stonyrea

PART ONE

It is neither fate nor chance alone that controls our destiny. Rather, it is the clash of those two terrible powers that gives violent and savage birth to our lives, and our legacy.

And what of choice? I have never seen compelling proof that it makes the slightest difference.

—from the secret writings of
the Dark Mage

1

*I*t wasn't Brice Vaderton's first tour of duty, but it felt near enough, because this was his first time captaining an imperial frigate. The *Guardian* was a newly constructed, three-masted, square-rigged warship with forty-two cannons. It was half again as large as his last ship, and with twice the firepower.

Captain Vaderton's quarters were big enough to hold a desk, a full-sized bunk, and a sofa. Had he been married, it would have been spacious enough to bring a wife. The cabin was positioned in the stern beneath the raised poop deck. It had several large portholes that offered a view of bright, cloudless blue skies and rippling dark green water as far as the eye could see. They'd had uncommonly good weather for the western edge of the empire, especially this time of year. As late summer gave way to fall, this region was usually raked with sudden, capricious blusters and sheets of icy rain. Instead, they'd had clear skies and a steady, manageable wind. Vaderton didn't expect it to last, but he'd run with it as long as he could.

The captain sat at his desk, catching up on his logbooks. He was meticulous in his record keeping, something his superiors told him was one of the reasons they felt confident entrusting him with one of the greatest ships in the empire, despite his age.

Vaderton had just celebrated his fortieth year and was now the youngest officer to be given command of an imperial war frigate. He intended to prove that their trust in him was not misplaced. As part of the grand imperial inspection, his orders were to sail down the western edge of the empire until he reached the straights that separated the Southern Isles from the rest of the empire, then head east to Vance Post. Along the way, he was to stop in all ports of call, partly to gather the annual census reports, and partly to show the new, resplendent might of the imperial navy. As simple as this tour was, Vaderton intended to do it by the book, no exceptions.

He checked his watch. Nine o'clock. Time for his mid-morning deck inspection. He stood and pulled on his heavy white coat. Despite the late-summer heat that still hung in the air, he liked the weight of it. The stiffness of the gold brocade in the front and the gold epaulets on his shoulders made him feel as if he was protected by the might of the entire imperial navy. He smoothed back his short, navy regulation–cut brown hair, then took his captain's hat, also white with gold detail, and placed it securely on his head. He'd seen other captains wear their hat tilted back on the head. It cut a dashing figure, but it was terribly impractical. The first big gust of wind would fling it out to sea. Back at the academy, some of his classmates had teased him about obsessing over such minor details. However, none of them had yet been given command of a frigate, so he felt confident that his was the correct course.

Vaderton opened the door and stepped out onto the quarterdeck.

"Captain on deck!" called Midshipman Kellert.

Anyone on deck who could stop what they were doing did so, and gave Captain Vaderton a sharp salute. Only a month at sea, and they were already shaping up to be a fine crew. Counting the cannon-eers, the *Guardian* had approximately two hundred crew, more than three times the number of his last ship. In the past, he'd always made a point of learning every name. That was impossible now, but as he scanned the deck, he gave them each a moment of eye contact. It was as important to acknowledge good behavior as it was to punish bad.

"Take your ease," he said gravely, and they went back to their tasks. He turned to Kellert, who looked smart in his own white imperial officer's jacket. That had been a point of contention between them when they first set out. By nature, Kellert was a slov-enly, unkempt sort. Vaderton had suggested that if Kellert didn't wish to look like a proper officer, he was welcome to the less-formal accommodations of the crew. A few nights sleeping in a hammock and eating with the men had straightened him out. One of Vaderton's responsibilities was to groom his officers to one day serve the empire as a captain on their own ship. He took that duty as seriously as any other.

"Report, Mr. Kellert," he said as he scanned the deck, watching the men work.

"All clear, Captain." Kellert gave a slight smile and said, "Well, except the ghost ship."

Captain Vaderton did not return the smile. "What do you mean by 'ghost ship,' Mr. Kellert?"

"Oh, it's nothing, sir. Young Jillen, who takes the night watch in the crow's nest, thought he saw a ship in the distance a little before sunrise. But when he called down to me, I couldn't see anything with the glass. He'd probably just been dozing off for a min-ute, but the men started teasing him that he'd seen a ghost ship. You know, to frighten the poor boy."

"He still maintains that he saw a ship?" Captain Vaderton asked.

Kellert looked a little uncomfortable now. "I suppose, sir."

"You *suppose*? Did you not question him further? Perhaps for details on this ship he saw?"

"The boy's only twelve years old. It could have been anything, sir." Kellert was beginning to look nervous.

"*Anything* includes pirates, Mr. Kellert."

Kellert blanched. "Yes, sir. Would you like me to question him now?"

"Send him to me. I will question him myself."

"Yes, sir," said Kellert meekly.

Captain Vaderton nodded, then watched the midshipman hurry off. He decided his charge still had a long way before him.

Vaderton walked unhurriedly across the quarterdeck, then down to the main deck. As he went, he watched the crew move around him with tight precision. It made him marvel that these men—none of them interesting or remarkable on their own—could be combined to perform the daunting task of sailing one of the most powerful ships in the empire.

He climbed the short ladder up to the forecastle, where he stood and looked out across the rippling green water to where it met the smooth blue sky on the horizon. In general, Captain Vaderton kept his thoughts and feelings close. But the sight of the open sea before him and the smell of salt wind in his lungs always softened his grip, if only a little.

"You wanted to see me, sir?" asked a light voice.

Captain Vaderton turned and regarded Jillen. The boy was an odd one, which was probably why Vaderton remembered him. He was uncommonly short and slight of build, even for one so young. He spoke with the slurring cadence of someone born to the slums of New Laven, but he was surprisingly intelligent for such humble beginnings. Vaderton had even noticed him examining books and notes, as if he had some rudimentary knowledge of letters.

"Mr. Kellert informs me that you saw something on midnight watch?" he asked the boy.

"I did, sir. Off the port stern. Looked like a ship, sir."

"Can you describe this ship?"

"Two masts crowded with sail. Heading toward us. And it didn't have any imperial flags. Least, none that I could see."

"And did you report this to Mr. Kellert?"

"I did, sir."

"And he didn't think it worth bringing to my immediate attention?"

"As I understand it, sir, he thought I must have dreamed it. Because by the time he took a look, it had disappeared."

"A disappearing ship? That is your report?" Vaderton asked gravely.

"I suppose so, sir." Jillen gave the captain a nervous look. "I know it sounds slippy, but that's what I saw. Sir."

Captain Vaderton understood why Kellert had not been eager to report this. The midshipman thought it impossible. Vaderton might have made the same mistake himself when he was younger. But if the last few years had taught him anything, it was never to count on something being impossible.

"Young Mr. Jillen," said the captain. "Tell me what a ship is."

"Sir?" Jillen seemed even more nervous, his eyes darting around like he was looking for an escape.

"You're not in trouble, boy," said the captain. "Just tell me, in plain words, what you think constitutes a ship."

"It's a wooden vessel that floats and has sails that catch the wind to make it go."

Captain Vaderton nodded. "Not bad. But a ship is

more than the vessel. It's also the people on it. They are a part of the ship as well. Each has his job, which he must carry out for the good of the whole. If any of those parts stops working, the entire ship suffers."

"Like bees," said Jillen.

"Bees?" asked Vaderton, caught off guard.

"Sure, it takes hundreds of bees to make a beehive and keep it going. Each bee has his or her job. The queen bee is in charge, but even she has a job to do. That's how a hive works." Jillen beamed up at him, then added, "Sir."

"Yes," said Vaderton, wondering at how this New Laven street urchin could have such knowledge. "And do any of the bees ever decide that perhaps they won't perform all their duties and hope the queen won't notice or mind?"

"Of course not, sir. If the bees stop working, the whole hive might die."

"Indeed," said Vaderton. "What if a person on a ship decided not to perform all his duties? Let us say he took it upon himself to determine if something was possible or not, instead of bringing it to the captain for him to decide. That crew member might well put the entire ship in jeopardy."

Jillen's eyes went wide. "But, Captain, I told—"

Captain Vaderton raised his hand and Jillen immediately went silent. Smart boy. "As I said before, young Mr. Jillen, you are not in trouble. But I want you to keep what I have said fixed firmly in your mind while you witness Midshipman Kellert receive ten lashes."

"Y-yes, sir," said Jillen, looking no less frightened.

———

All hands were called to witness Kellert receive his lashes at midday. The sun blazed brightly overhead, gleaming off the blood and sweat that ran down the midshipman's back as he clung to the mainmast. No doubt some of the men thought the captain too harsh, especially Kellert's fellow officers, who tended to think themselves above such punishment. But by such a public show, the captain made it clear that he would tolerate no shoddy work, be they crew or officers. Furthermore, this lesson also benefited Kellert. For all its great ships and fierce fighting men, it was the iron resolve of the officer class that kept the imperial navy afloat. And it was Captain Vaderton's solemn duty to make sure that the captains of the future were just as resilient and exacting, tempered by the fires of experience and discipline so that they had iron wills of their own.

Captain Vaderton took no pleasure in it, though. In fact, he was pleased to note that Kellert didn't cry out. Even as he was led away to the officers' quarters to recover, Kellert walked steadily, back straight, head high. He might not be the most reliable officer, but at least he could take a beating.

Once the ordeal was over, and the men sent back to their posts, Captain Vaderton set a double watch at all hours, with orders to report anything they saw, no matter how minor or strange, directly to him. Then he took a turn at the helm. It wasn't necessary, of course. The *Guardian* had several helmsmen. But Captain Vaderton liked the feel of the hard wooden wheel in his hands now and then, especially after performing some of his more distasteful duties. The late afternoon sun sent sparkles skittering across the white-flecked sea. He took in a slow breath and allowed himself to savor the steady pull of the wheel against his hands—the surge of the ocean itself. To his mind, there was nothing more grand in all the world.

Gradually, Captain Vaderton became aware of a presence standing respectfully nearby.

"Mr. Jillen," he said. "Something on your mind?"

"Begging your pardon, Captain." Jillen squinted up at him in the hard sun.

There was something almost pretty about the boy's delicate features. Vaderton knew if the boy didn't toughen up, his peers would soon be giving him hells. But it was not Vaderton's duty to instruct the regular crew. That was the bosun's responsibility. So Vaderton said nothing about it. "Out with it, Mr. Jillen. You've already disturbed my serene repose."

"Well, sir." Jillen looked up at him earnestly. "I just wanted to know what you think it was I saw. The disappearing ship, I mean."

"I don't know," said the captain. "But there are stranger things in this world than ships that seem to vanish, I can assure you. I have seen weather that gave no warning. I have seen oarfish the length of this deck. And once, off in the distance, I saw a giant ship encased in metal."

"A ship of *metal*, sir? How did it not sink?"

"Perhaps some sailing art not yet known to us. Perhaps by biomancery."

"Biomancers, sir?" Jillen hesitated for a moment. "The men say you know one, sir. A biomancer, I mean. Is it true?"

"I'm not sure any normal man can *know* a biomancer. But I did serve one for a time, and he was pleased with my service." Vaderton knew that many of his peers whispered that this was the real reason he had been given a frigate at such a young age. The favor of biomancers held sway in both the navy and the imperial court.

"Are they really sorcerers, sir?" asked Jillen. "It's not just tricks?"

The captain smiled faintly. "Did you know, young Mr. Jillen, that we are not the only large and deadly thing in these seas called the Guardian?"

"I thought no two ships could have the same name."

"Oh, but it isn't a ship," said Vaderton. "It's a great sea beast created by the biomancers to protect the northern borders of the empire against invaders. I saw it myself, once, while I was in service to the biomancers. A terrible kraken as big as an island that can crush a ship in one of its massive tentacles as easily as you crack an egg."

"It sounds incredible, sir." Jillen's eyes were as wide and round as whirlpools.

"Think of the power of that kraken. Then imagine the power it must have taken to create such a thing. And *that* is the power of the biomancers."

Jillen shivered.

"You'll find, young Mr. Jillen, that the world is full of wonders and terrors far beyond our humble expectations. Like as not, you'll see some before the end of this tour."

Jillen looked frightened, but also thrilled. "I hope so, sir."

Vaderton smiled. "It is ever the prerogative of youth to seek adventure. But most have their fill sooner than they expect."

"Not me, sir," Jillen said, his thin face confident. "I'll seek until the end of my days."

Captain Vaderton nodded. "May it always be so for you, young Mr. Jillen."

———

It was near twilight when a shout went up from the crow's nest. Captain Vaderton was back in his quarters, dining alone, as was his wont. A fist pounded frantically at his door. "We're under attack, Captain!"

Captain Vaderton grabbed his coat and hat, then

threw open the door. "How many?" he demanded of the ashen-faced officer. "Is it pirates?"

The officer shook his head, his words stuttering as he tried to get them out. "Ghost ship!"

"Get ahold of yourself." Vaderton shoved the officer aside, sending the young man sprawling. He strode across the quarterdeck as he pulled on his coat. Hecker stood at the helm, his knuckles white as he gripped the wheel.

"Report," snapped the captain.

"Coming up on the port stern, sir."

"Give me your glass."

Hecker handed it to him. "You won't need it, though, sir."

The captain frowned as he made his way astern and climbed the ladder to the poop deck. From that height, he could see plainly what Hecker meant. A ship bore down on them, its two masts crammed with as much canvas as they could hold, plus the jibs and trysail. What made it unusual was that the entire vessel, from hull to royals, glowed an eerie phosphorescent green, the sort he'd seen emanating from jellyfish beneath the surface of the ocean on a calm night. Even taking into account the amount of sail and the advantage of wind, it was coming at them impossibly fast. Evasion was out of the question. Not that he had any intention of running.

"All hands!" he bellowed. "Beat to quarters!"

The word went down the ship as the drums began to pound. Soon the mess hall was empty and the deck was crawling with men. The captain returned to Hecker at the helm. The cannon master, Mr. Frain, had just arrived, looking disheveled, his eyes wide with concern.

"Frain, tuck in your shirts. Hecker, bring us about and give them a look at our broadside. Ghost or not, we'll make driftwood of them."

Frain immediately began putting himself together, his expression calming. Hecker nodded and spun the wheel. "Aye, Captain."

Often that was all it took. Show a bit of courage, and the men would find their own.

The *Guardian* turned slowly, its massive bulk driving against the prevailing current.

"Reporting for duty, sir." Midshipman Kellert stood at attention, looking pale but steady, his uniform spotless and wrinkle-free.

Captain Vaderton had given him leave to rest after his lashing, and was pleased to see the young officer had declined. He put his hand on Kellert's shoulder and nodded. "Very good, Mr. Kellert. We'll make a man of you yet. Tell Mr. Bitlow to ready the bow chasers in case they try to come about suddenly."

"Aye, sir." Kellert saluted again and hurried off.

The *Guardian* had completed its turn so that the port side faced the oncoming ship.

"Mr. Frain, show them what they're in for," Vaderton called to the cannon master.

"Port-side cannons at the ready!" called Frain down to the gun deck below.

Vaderton heard the sound of twenty cannons slamming into position, their iron muzzles bristling from the hull. He could almost feel the destructive potential of the ship vibrating in the deck beneath his feet.

"She don't seem intent on coming about, sir," said Hecker.

The captain frowned. "A head-on charge at our broadside is suicide. Even at their speed, they'll most likely be torn to pieces before they get close enough to ram or grapple. Surely their captain must see that." He trained his glass on them, but it was difficult to make out details of the hazy green ship. He could see no men, no flags or markings. He felt in his bones there was some other trick at work here, but he had no idea what it was. He couldn't show that to the men, of course.

"Maybe it's because they're already dead, sir," said Hecker. "Could be our shot will pass right through them."

"If that's true, they'll pass right through us as well. Either way, we'll find out soon enough," Vaderton said grimly. "Mr. Frain, fire as soon as we're in range."

"Aye, Captain."

A stillness fell on the crew as every man watched the approaching luminous ship.

"Fire!" called Frain.

The line of cannons roared like thunder, sending up a thick cloud of smoke. Their aim was true and the shot struck the approaching ship square in the bow. But instead of merely taking on damage, the entire ship exploded silently into tiny glowing pieces that sprayed out in all directions before slowly sinking into the sea.

"What in all hells...," said Frain.

A roar of cannon fire came from the starboard, and the *Guardian* bucked furiously from the impact. Captain Vaderton spun around, struggling to keep his footing on the swaying deck. He stared in disbelief at the ship that had suddenly appeared on the other side. It looked exactly the same as the first one, except it wasn't hazy and glowing. This ship was all too real, and had just unloaded a volley of shot into their starboard hull at point-blank range.

"Captain," said Frain, his voice pinched with fear. "Look at that flag."

The flag that flew from this ship's main had a white background on which had been painted a black oval with eight black lines trailing down from it. It was the sign of the biomancers, which Vaderton knew all too well. But cutting across that symbol was a thick, bloodred *X*. That, he had never seen. But he'd heard about it in all the old stories.

"The flag of the *Kraken Hunter*," whispered Hecker. "It's Dire Bane."

"No," said Captain Vaderton, his voice faltering for the first time. "It can't be. He was slain some forty years ago by Vinchen hand. Dire Bane is dead!"

A sailor ran up from the gun deck and said something quietly to Frain, who flinched at the news, then turned to the captain. "She's taken out most of our starboard cannons, sir."

"Are we taking on water?" demanded Vaderton.

Frain shook his head.

"There's that, at least," said Vaderton, his voice steadying. He watched as the *Kraken Hunter* cut across the stern and came around to their port side. "They caught us in a neat trick, but this fight is far from over, gentlemen. I don't know who is flying the flag of Dire Bane, but it's time to show them what an imperial warship can do. Mr. Frain, how long until the port cannons are reloaded?"

"Should only be a minute or two," said Frain. "We'll be ready well before they are."

"Excellent. Have them fire when ready."

The *Kraken Hunter* came about fast and closed rapidly. But before the *Guardian* could fire a single shot, the *Kraken Hunter* unloaded another volley, this time at their port side. The ship shook again, and Vaderton could hear the screams of the dead and dying cannoneers below.

"How could they reload that fast?" Frain shook his head in disbelief. "I swear, Captain. It's not possible."

"Clearly, it is." Vaderton watched as the *Kraken Hunter* hewed closer. The distance was still too great to throw a grapple, but they would likely cut across

the bow and close for a grapple on the other side,
now that they had no fear of cannon fire.

But instead they fired a third volley. This time, it
was grapeshot that scattered across the main deck,
tearing apart men and rigging with equal ferocity.

"How are they reloading so fast!" yelled Frain.

The *Kraken Hunter* continued on its trajectory
across their bow.

"Where's my bow chasers!" roared Captain Vaderton. He trained his glass on the bow and saw that
the third shot had been concentrated near the forecastle. It had claimed fewer lives than if it had gone
across the waist, but now there was no one manning
the guns. Among the dead and dying, Vaderton saw
Kellert lying dead across one of the guns, as if shield-
ing it with his body. A cluster of shot had taken off
the side of his skull, and his brains were spilled onto
the iron bore.

Meanwhile, the *Kraken Hunter* had come about
on the starboard side again. It was still too wide
to board, and Vaderton thought it might unload a
fourth volley. He bellowed, "Hit the decks!" and the
entire crew threw themselves down, including the
captain.

But instead of the roar of cannon fire, he heard
two pops, like springs snapping. He jumped to his
feet in time to see two grappling hooks latch on to
the *Guardian*'s starboard gunwale. The line went
taut and the *Kraken Hunter* reeled itself in close.

"All hands on starboard side to be boarded!"

The crew stumbled to their feet, grabbing swords,
pikes, and pistols as they hurried to the starboard
side.

Before they reached it, four figures rose up from
the *Kraken Hunter*.

On the far left was a tall, powerfully built man in
a black vest. He had close-cropped dark hair and

beard, his tan face grimy with soot. One leg was encased in a steel frame, and he held a heavy mace in his thick hand. His expression was calm. Almost disinterested.

On the far right was a woman with curly dark hair. She wore a short wool coat and breeches tucked into tall leather boots. In her hands was a strange weapon. It looked like a length of fine chain, but there was a heavy weight on one end, and a knife blade on the other. Her dark eyes glittered even more sharply than her chainblade, a slight snarl on her rich burgundy lips.

Next to her was the tallest woman Vaderton had ever seen. She stood erect, almost regal, in a tight white gown that flared out into long, billowing sleeves. A deep white hood hid most of her face. It reminded Vaderton alarmingly of those worn by biomancers. All that could be seen framed between locks of straight black hair was the lower half of her calm face, lips painted bright red.

The final figure was a woman with the pale skin and blond hair of someone from the Southern Isles. She wore black leather Vinchen armor and had a sword in place of her right hand. When she turned her cold blue eyes on the captain, they struck a chill in his heart.

"Surrender now, and there need not be any more bloodshed," she said, her voice ringing across the ship.

"You have some surprises, I'll grant you," said Vaderton. "But you're no Dire Bane, just a woman. And you're outnumbered besides. I'll see you dead before sunrise." Then he drew his pistol and fired at her.

She flicked her sword arm. The blade gave an eerie hum as it swiveled around on a hinge at her wrist and slapped the bullet away. At the same time, the woman in white lifted her arms, the long white sleeves swirling as she splayed her fingers. Then every loaded gun on the deck suddenly exploded. Men screamed as they clutched at powder-burned hands and faces.

No one but a Vinchen could knock a bullet out of the air. And who else but a biomancer could make guns spontaneously explode? But Vaderton knew for a fact that women were forbidden in both the Vinchen and biomancer orders. So what was he dealing with?

The woman dressed as a Vinchen pointed her sword at Captain Vaderton. Then she kept her eyes locked on his as she hacked her way slowly through the now-disorderly chaos of wounded, frightened men. Mixed with the cries of pain was her sword's dark, mournful song.

Her companions jumped into the fray as well. The man laid about him with his mace, caving in skulls almost casually, or sweeping men off their feet with his steel leg. The woman on the other side darted in and out, snapping her chainblade into a sailor's throat, then another's eye, all the while using the weighted end to defend herself from attack. The biomancer woman stood back from the rest, her hands weaving in front of her constantly, as if dancing. Wherever she pointed, death sprang up. Some men caught fire; others crumbled to dust. Still others clawed at their own skin and shrieked as if their blood was boiling them alive.

All too soon, the Vinchen woman gained the quarterdeck, leaving headless and limbless bodies in her wake. The air was thick with the smell of blood.

Captain Vaderton drew his sword, but his hand shook despite his best efforts to still it.

The Vinchen woman's gaze was as ferocious and unfathomable as the sea. "Captain Vaderton, known servant of the biomancer council. Surrender, or die."

"A captain never surrenders his ship," said Vaderton, his voice shaking as badly as his hands. "I will do my duty or die trying."

She nodded. "Perhaps there's still some honor left in you after all. I'll make it quick." She brought her sword down.

"No!"

The boy Jillen threw his own slight body between Vaderton and the sword.

The Vinchen woman twisted her arm, and the blade swiveled to the side. She glared at the boy. "Move aside, or I will be forced to kill you, too."

Vaderton could feel Jillen's entire body quivering in terror, but he shook his head and didn't move.

The woman nodded, her face sad. "I understand, and commend you for your bravery." Then she raised her sword again.

"Captain, wait!"

The Vinchen paused and waited patiently as the woman with the chainblade ran over to them.

She stared at Jillen. "Little Bee? Is that you?"

It was a question that made Jillen shrink back when even a sword hadn't.

"Filler!" called the woman with the chain.

The man turned his head toward her.

"Come here!"

He calmly brained the man he'd been fighting, then stomped slowly over, his metal leg clanking. "What is it, Nettie?"

The woman named Nettie pointed wordlessly at Jillen.

Filler's eyes widened. "Jilly? What are you doing on an imp ship?"

Jillen moved forward cautiously. "Filler? Is that really you?"

"Of course it is, Bee. And why are you dressed like a boy?"

"She's posing as a sailor, obviously," said Nettie.

"But *why*?" asked Filler.

Jillen (or was it Jilly?) looked up at Filler like she wanted to move closer, but didn't want to leave Vaderton undefended. "I'm looking for my mom. She enlisted, remember?"

Filler's face fell. He touched something on his metal leg so that the knee bent and he knelt down in front of her. "I'm sorry, Little Bee. Red and I let you believe what that imp soldier said about your mom signing up for the navy. The truth is, she was taken by the biomancers."

"No."

"I knew your mom," he said quietly. "There was no way she'd ever enlist in the navy. Fact is, she *hated* ships and imps both. I'm sorry, Jilly."

The two stared at each other, Jilly's face a battleground of emotions.

"I'll just kill the rest of them myself, shall I?" called the biomancer woman. Then she made a sailor's skull cave in with a gesture.

"Yes, thank you, Brigga Lin," the Vinchen woman said absently, her eyes still on Jilly. "A friend of Red's is a friend of mine. You are welcome to join my crew, Jilly."

"I'm a part of *this* crew, though," said Jilly.

"Are you?" asked the Vinchen.

Jilly turned to the captain, who had remained silent during this entire exchange. His expression had shifted slowly from shock, to horror, to outrage.

"Captain?"

"Deceiving an officer about your gender," he said in a strangled voice, "is punishable by death."

"Listen, you cunt-dropping," said Nettie. "This girl just saved your life."

Captain Vaderton drew himself up, his anger finally stilling his hands and burning courage into his heart. "I would rather die than be beholden to some...capricious New Laven pixie!"

"That is all I needed..." Nettie began coiling her chain around her fist.

"Stop," the Vinchen woman said softly. "Nettles, go assist Brigga Lin with cleanup, then help Alash disable any remaining cannons, cut the rigging, and recover any shot or powder. Filler, go to the captain's quarters and get the money chest."

The two left without another word.

Jilly looked nervously between the Vinchen and Captain Vaderton. "What are you going to do with him?"

"I'm going to let him live, whether he likes it or not." She turned her deep blue eyes back to Vaderton. "We will cast you adrift on your 'guardian,' with a crew of the dead men you were supposed to protect. If you somehow survive, you will tell everyone you meet about me."

"Who in all hells are you?" demanded Vaderton.

"I am Dire Bane. And I will purge this empire of the Council of Biomancery, even if I have to dismantle it, ship by ship."

2

*W*illmont Pavi frequently lost track of time. This was particularly true when he was in the middle of a big project. His friends had grown so accustomed to it, they generally didn't even comment when he showed up at the Wheelhouse Tavern late, looking disheveled and unshaven.

But he knew that *tonight's* meeting was different and he absolutely could not be late. So that entire afternoon, he forced himself to look up from his work at regular intervals and check the large clock that ticked solemnly on the shelf. When the sun finally began to drop behind the building tops and Mr. Blagely locked the front door of the furniture shop, Willmont was the first apprentice to finish packing up his work. Old Blagely gave him a surprised look when he saw the cleared worktable.

"You meeting a girl, Willy?" Blagely had no hair on the top of his head, and as he gazed speculatively at Willmont, the furrows of his brow went all the way up to the beginning of his smooth, spotted scalp.

"Just meeting some friends, Mr. Blagely." Willmont was unaccustomed to lying, but it was only a partial lie.

"Make sure you aren't rushing that piece you're working on, is all, Willy."

"I won't rush, Mr. Blagely."

"I don't need to remind you how important it is to you, and me, and everyone in this shop?"

"No, sir," said Willmont.

"Good boy." Blagely patted him on the shoulder. "On your way, then."

"Thank you, sir." Willmont hurried out the back entrance, where they received deliveries of wood from Lesser Basheta, as well as jars of stain, crates of nails, and other things necessary for making fine furniture. Mr. Blagely's shop was well known to nobles and rich merchants for producing some of the highest-quality pieces in Stonepeak. But that didn't seem to be good enough for Blagely anymore. He'd set his sights higher, and was counting on Willmont to make it happen.

Willmont followed the narrow alley behind the shop out to the main thoroughfare of Artisan Way. He walked past fabric shops, glass-blowing shops, and other handcrafts. This was a popular block for nobles to shop, so elegant carriages frequently rattled past, and Willmont shared the sidewalk with neatly dressed servants, their arms loaded with packages.

As Willmont continued toward the tavern, he thought back, with equal parts pleasure and anxiety, on the day he'd been commissioned for this new piece that Blagely felt was so important.

Two young men had come into the shop. It was a large shop with four worktables, an apprentice at each one. His table was closest to the door, and Mr. Blagely was always urging him to make more of an effort to greet customers courteously when they came in, even if they were interrupting his work. Willmont had suggested he could move to one of the tables at the back of the store instead, and one of the other apprentices could make the effort of being courteous to customers. But Blagely had refused.

"You're my prize apprentice, Willy, and I

want customers to see your work first," he'd said. "I just wish you'd mind your manners better." Then he'd sighed with a weary resignation. "I suppose that's what I get for taking on the son of a stonemason."

It was true that Willmont's father was a stonemason, and not one to soften his words with courtesy or manners. Oddly enough, the reason that Willmont had taken an apprenticeship in Blagely's furniture shop was because his father deemed him altogether too delicate and sensitive to follow his older brothers in the family business. His father blamed the indulgence of a mother toward her youngest child, God rest her soul. Willmont felt it was more her untimely death than her parenting that made him a little emotional, but his father wasn't the sort of man one could talk to about such things. And his father had been right about the choice of shops. The fine crafting of furniture was much better suited to Willmont's temperament than the hard chisel and scrape of stonework. Mr. Blagely was far kinder than his father. Willmont even got along well with craftsmen from other shops, and soon enough had a small circle of friends. But there was a big difference between the simple, earnest talk of tradesmen, and the fine, lacy speech of the upper classes. Whenever he spoke with palace folk, a tiny version of his father awoke within him.

On the day the two young men came into the shop, Willmont was finishing some decorative detail work for the back of a chair. It was his favorite part of furniture making. Something he looked forward to during the earlier, simpler stages of the project. So when the two men came in and waited expectantly, he ignored them.

After a few minutes, one of them cleared his throat, and said in a clear voice, "I say there, fronzie."

"Yeah?" said Willmont, still not looking up from his work.

"I was wondering who made that exquisite dove carving that currently sits in the windowsill of your shop."

Willmont stopped his work and looked at them carefully for the first time. The speaker wore a bright blue frock coat, and his long dark hair was carefully curled. He had a light dusting of the orange powder on his face that many rich young people applied. To Willmont, he looked like any other customer. The other young man, however, was a bit unusual. He had a fine linen shirt, cravat, and soft leather boots like his companion. But instead of a frock coat, he wore a brown leather longcoat that looked like it had been to several different hells and back. He also wore fingerless leather gloves, and glasses that had been tinted so dark, his eyes were hidden behind them.

"I made the dove," Willmont said finally.

"It's a splendid piece," said the man with the curly hair.

"It's not for sale," said Willmont.

The man smiled. "Naturally not. I'd imagine it holds far too much sentimental value to part with."

"No," said Willmont. "It's just not what we sell here. We sell furniture."

"Oh. I see." The man was starting to get that mixture of confusion and frustration that Willmont often seemed to inspire in customers. When he saw that look, he was supposed to go get Mr. Blagely. But Mr. Blagely was out on an errand. So Willmont just went back to his work.

In his peripheral vision, Willmont could see the curly-haired man shift his weight back and forth a few times. He heard him take in a breath, as if he was about to say something, but then didn't. The whole thing made Willmont uncomfortable. He tried to ignore them as best he could and went back to his chair detailing.

Then the man with the dark glasses stepped forward. "It's like this, my wag," he said in a cheerful, easy voice. "We wanted to know if you'd be willing to make a similar piece. But instead of a dove, it would be a..." He looked at the curly-haired man.

"A falcon," said the man.

"Right. A falcon," said the man with dark glasses. "Just as sunny as the one you made, but a different bird, keen?"

"That would take a long time," said Willmont.

"Of course it would, old pot," said the man. "We wouldn't dream of rushing your artistry, if you don't mind me calling it that. And naturally, you'd be well paid."

"I don't know..." Willmont didn't particularly care for falcons or other birds of prey. They tended to eat the birds he *did* like.

Then the door opened and Mr. Blagely came bustling in. "Hello, honorable sirs!" He made his way around them to stand next to Willmont. "My name is Honus Blagely, owner of this shop. Sorry if Willy's said anything terrible. He's a damn fine craftsman, but not much good when it comes to..." When he got his first real look at the men, his eyes went wide and he bowed low. "Your Highness! My apologies for not recognizing you sooner!" He glanced over and saw Willmont wasn't bowing, so he reached up and yanked him down as well.

Forced to remain bowing, Willmont craned his head up to look at the curly-haired man, who seemed a little embarrassed as he smiled. "It's quite alright, Mr. Blagely. This is my first time out of the palace without a full escort. Apparently, Lord Pastinas here is as deadly as an entire troop of soldiers, and somewhat less conspicuous."

Lord Pastinas grinned in what Willmont thought was a very unlordly way. "I do my best, Your Highness."

"We are completely at your disposal, Your Highness." Blagely slowly rose, letting Willmont come up with him. "How may we serve you today?"

"I really admire your apprentice's dove carving and hope he is willing to make a falcon for me."

"He'd be delighted and honored, Your Highness!" said Blagely.

"Excellent," said Prince Leston. "Thank you… Willy, is it?"

"Yes, Your Highness," said Blagely, because Willmont was strictly forbidden from speaking when his boss was in the middle of negotiating a commission. Otherwise, he would have told them that he preferred to go by his full name.

"Willy here expressed some concern about the time it would take to make it," said Lord Pastinas.

"Oh, don't you worry about him." Blagely gave an uncomfortable laugh.

"I *do* want to make certain he is adequately compensated for his time," said Prince Leston. "Would fifty gold be sufficient, do you think?"

Blagely's eyes went wide. "Your Highness is most generous."

"Marvelous." The prince nodded to Lord Pastinas, who opened a pouch at his waist and began to count out fifty pieces.

Once Blagely held the fifty gold pieces in his apron, he bowed again to the prince. "I'll deliver it straight to the palace as soon as he finishes, Your Highness."

"I look forward to it, Mr. Blagely," said Prince Leston. Then he turned and left, with Lord Pastinas close behind.

Once they were gone, Blagely let out a sigh. "Thank God I came in when I did!"

"It's going to take a long time to make a falcon," said Willmont. "I won't be making any chairs for a while."

Blagely put his hands on Willmont's shoulders and grinned. "Piss on chairs! This could be our future, boy!"

"Making falcons?" asked Willmont.

"High-end decorative pieces for the nobility! Just imagine! If your falcon pleases the prince, he will have it on display somewhere in the palace. And all those fawning lords and ladies will admire it and ask him where he got it, and he will tell them about our shop. You know how those lacies all copy each other. They'll all want some bird or other animal and they'll all pay a great deal more than they would for a simple chair. If we play this right, we could become rich ourselves!"

Nothing was the same after that. Willmont stopped making chairs and spent every day working on the falcon for His Imperial Highness. It wasn't that Willmont preferred making chairs. In fact, he loved coming into the shop every day and sitting down with the falcon that was slowly emerging from the thick piece of wood on his table. What he didn't necessarily like were the things that came with it. Mr. Blagely hovered constantly, checking his progress, asking how it was going, how he was feeling, was he eating enough, and a hundred more questions that, when taken all together, made Willmont terribly anxious. The other thing the falcon brought was the Godly Naturalists.

Willmont had of course told his friends about his new imperial commission. A few weeks later, one of them, Kiptich, had asked if he wanted to help make the empire a better place. Of course Willmont said yes. Who didn't want the empire to be better? So Kiptich had taken him to a tavern called the Thunder and Gale. It was much dirtier and smellier than the Wheelhouse. There they had met a droopy-faced man named Hannigan. Kiptich had to do a lot of talking to convince Hannigan that Willmont could be trusted. Then Hannigan asked Willmont a lot of strange questions about what he thought of the prince, the emperor, and even Lord Pastinas. He also asked what he thought about biomancers for some reason. Eventually Hannigan agreed that Willmont could attend the next meeting of the Godly Naturalists.

That was the meeting he hurried to now. The meeting Kiptich told him he absolutely could not be late to.

Willmont walked down the clean, wide streets of Stonepeak with the confidence of someone who had lived there his whole life. He knew there were many people who came and went, but he had never understood that. After all, Stonepeak was the largest island in the empire. It was also the richest and most powerful, since it was the capital. As far as Willmont knew, it was the greatest place in the world. Why would anyone want to leave?

In the north part of the island was the black mountain after which the city was named. Its base took nearly a quarter of the island. All the main streets extended out from the mountain like spokes on a wheel. Or more accurately, one third of a wheel. The buildings were generally two or three stories, with flat roofs and brick walls covered in a uniform beige plaster. Many cities had grown up haphazardly for one reason or another. But Stonepeak was a city that had been carefully planned right from the beginning. When Emperor Cremalton first united the islands, he chose Stonepeak as his capital because it had the highest mountain in the empire. He then built his palace into the side of the mountain so that he could look down upon his entire empire. There had been a small city at the base of the mountain before, but the emperor had it burned to the ground so he could start fresh. In its place, he and his chief biomancer, Burness Vee, designed a city worthy of His Imperial Majesty. Emperor Cremalton didn't live to see it completed. But biomancers lived unnaturally long lives, so Burness Vee was present when the last brick was put in place. He died the next day, as if he had staved off death for that sole purpose.

It was just after sunset now, and the beige walls of the buildings were tinted gold by the last rays of light when Willmont arrived at the Thunder and Gale. He stepped inside, wrinkling his nose at the stench of sweat and stale beer. The tavern wasn't crowded, which didn't surprise Willmont. Who would come to a smelly, dimly lit place like this by choice?

Willmont walked to the bar at the back, as Kiptich had instructed him. Next to the bar was a hatch in the floor that led to the cellar. The bartender watched with seeming disinterest as Willmont lifted the hatch and climbed down.

The cellar ceiling was high enough for Willmont to stand up straight. Neat rows of barrels and crates were stacked on the soft dirt floor. It was almost entirely dark, but there was one light far at the end. He walked nervously toward it, trying not to think of all the spiders and rats that could be lurking in the darkness around him.

When he reached the light, he saw five men sitting around a table with a lantern placed in the center. One of the men was Kiptich. Another was Hannigan. He also recognized a silversmith who had a shop down the street from the furniture shop. Judging by their aprons and calloused hands, the other two were fellow craftsmen as well.

"You made it on time!" The light of the lantern

showed relief on Kiptich's gaunt face. He was a glass-blower by trade, and claimed the fumes from melted glass never left him with much of an appetite.

"I promised I would," said Willmont. "I always keep my promises."

"I'm glad to hear that." The skin around Hannigan's eyes drooped low like an old dog's, but the look behind them was clear and alert. "Have a seat, Willmont, and we'll tell you why we've invited you here tonight."

Willmont took the empty seat at the foot of the table. The two men he didn't know sat on the left, the silversmith and Kiptich on the right, and Hannigan at the head.

"Firstly, let me tell you why the Godly Naturalists formed," said Hannigan. "It's because we see there is a problem with the empire."

"A problem?" asked Willmont.

"You would agree that Emperor Martarkis, as a direct descendant of Cremalton, was chosen by God to rule, wouldn't you?"

"Of course."

"It may alarm you to learn, then, that in his old age, the emperor is being controlled by the biomancers."

"Controlled how?"

"Biomancers have ways, you know. And old men can be easily fooled. The fact is, the emperor has lived an unnaturally long time, hasn't he?"

"Over a hundred now," said Willmont. "No normal man has ever lived so long. I thought it was God keeping him alive for some great purpose."

Kiptich shook his head. "Don't you see, Willmont? It's the biomancers that are keeping him alive. Because they know that if Emperor Martarkis died, the rightful ruler, Prince Leston, would take over. So instead, they keep old Martarkis alive, just barely, prop him up once a year at the imperial pronouncement, and make him talk like a puppet."

"But why don't they want the prince to rule?" asked Willmont. "He seems pretty nice for a noble."

"That's the whole problem," said one of the men Willmont didn't know. "We all love the prince, and when he's in charge, he won't let the biomancers take our good, honest people to experiment on anymore. He'll put a stop to such an outrage."

"It's even worse for other islands," said the silversmith. "I hear the biomancers commandeer ships from the imperial navy and take them off to some small island on the outskirts of the empire and experiment on an entire population."

Hannigan nodded. "Those biomancers mean to make something terrible and unnatural of the entire empire."

"What do we do?" asked Willmont, who loved Stonepeak and did not want to see it turned into something terrible and unnatural.

"That's where you come in, my wag," said Kiptich. "We need to get word to the prince. Explain to him what's really going on out there in the world. Those biomancers keep him so isolated, he probably has no idea. We tried approaching him in the street once, but his soldiers wouldn't let us anywhere near him."

"He doesn't have soldiers anymore," said Willmont. "Just one man."

"That one with the dark glasses?" sneered the silversmith. "Who knows why he wears those. Probably could kill you just by looking at you if he wanted."

"Or maybe he ain't even got eyes," said the other man.

"He didn't seem that bad to me," said Willmont. "At least he could talk regularly."

"Point is," said Hannigan, "we can't chance it. We need to be smart. So we've come up with a plan to write the prince a letter. And then you're going to smuggle it to him inside that falcon you're making."

"You mean like make a secret compartment?"

"Exactly!" said Kiptich. "It has to be hidden enough so that nobody else sees it, but not so well hidden that the prince doesn't find it once he gets it."

Willmont thought about it. "I suppose I could make a small slit in the base that the note could be slipped into. Then I could glue a panel over the slit to cover it. If I watered down the glue a little, it would only hold for a few days. Hopefully by then, it would be safely in the prince's possession."

Hannigan grinned at Kiptich. "You were right. This boy's a gem."

"Told you," said Kiptich.

Hannigan turned back to Willmont. "Welcome to the Godly Naturalists, my wag."

"Thank you," said Willmont, looking around the table. "So is it just us?"

Hannigan laughed. "Oh no. There's a few different groups. We're the tradesmen group, but believe it or not, it was all started by a group of lords at the palace who were tired of watching the biomancers infect the empire with their unnatural ways. And there's some wags over by the South Market, too. Mostly farmers, cooks, a few vintners, and the like. The way I see it, we all got a stake in—"

Suddenly, small blades protruded from Hannigan's eyes. He shuddered, as blood oozed from his ruined eye sockets, then fell forward. Willmont had never seen someone killed before, and for a moment, his shocked mind could only stare uncomprehendingly at the dead man who had just been talking to him.

Then Kiptich whimpered a pathetic "piss'ell" and the spell was broken. Panic rose inside Willmont like a wave as he looked around at the other men at the table.

The silversmith stared blankly, as if in a trance. Then he slowly tipped forward onto the table. Another blade protruded from the base of his skull.

Willmont turned to the two men on the left that he didn't know. They leaned into each other, their eyes staring and mouths slack.

"Kiptich," whispered Willmont. "What's going on?"

Kiptich shook his head, his gaunt face looking frightened in the lantern light. "Let's get the hells out of here before we're next."

The two stumbled to their feet. Kiptich stepped away from the table and out of the light.

"Wait, let's take the lantern!" Willmont picked it up and shone it toward Kiptich. He saw his friend again for a moment. Then a dark shape moved quickly past, blocking his view. When he saw Kiptich again, his friend was clutching his ribs, blood seeping between his fingers. He gave Willmont a terrified look as he gasped for air that didn't seem to come. Then he dropped to the dirt.

Willmont stood alone. The tremors in his hand made the lantern light flicker. Even though his mind screamed at him to move, to run for the hatch, his feet stayed where they were, locked in place with fear.

Then he felt a sharp pain in his wrist. He yelped and dropped the lantern.

He clutched at his now-bleeding wrist and squinted into the darkness. Above his own harsh gasps for breath, he heard a noise and jerked his head around. At the edge of the light, he saw a shadowy form dressed in gray.

Then Willmont felt a white-hot stab of pain in his throat. He tried to cry out, but there was only a gurgle. Something warm and wet spilled down his chest as he watched the shadowy form melt back into the darkness.

The last thing to enter Willmont's mind before he died was that the falcon would never be finished. Mr. Blagely would be so disappointed.

3

Jilly stood at the rail and watched the disabled *Guardian* recede into the distance. The *Kraken Hunter* was a fast little brig, but Jilly still had a hard time understanding how the ship had beaten one three times her size with four times the number of guns.

"Mr. Finn?"

The old wrink stood nearby, his hands firm on the wheel, his one eye squinting in the late afternoon sun. "Aye, Jilly?" he asked in the comforting cadence of someone from Paradise Circle.

"How'd you do it?"

"What's that?"

"Take the *Guardian* with a lesser ship and fewer people?"

He smiled. "I did very little. Only steered her around in a circle a few times."

"You know what I mean."

"How do *you* think we done it?"

"Captain Vaderton said a crew is part of the ship. So if the vessel herself wasn't the reason, it must have been the people on her."

"Yes, I suppose that's true. And the captain most important of all. A battle can be lost or won on the strength of the captain alone."

Jilly turned to the forecastle, where the woman

who called herself Dire Bane stood and gazed out at the horizon. Her arms were at her back, her left hand holding the strange clamp at the end of her right wrist. Her loose blond hair whipped in the wind like a flag.

Jilly ran her fingers through her own short brown hair. For the last two years, she'd had to keep it short so she could pass as a boy. Maybe she'd grow it long again, now that she was on Dire Bane's ship, where such things seemed acceptable.

"I never heard of a molly captain before," she said to Missing Finn. "I didn't think it was allowed."

The old wrink grinned. "I think you'll find a great many things on this ship that are not, strictly speaking, allowed."

"How can she be Dire Bane? I mean, I thought Dire Bane was a tom. And that he'd been killed."

"Dire Bane is a name she took on."

"Like a title?" asked Jilly.

"More like a promise," said Finn. "And I think you'll find that Captain Bane is someone who takes her promises very seriously."

She certainly looked serious to Jilly. Almost frightening in her cool fierceness.

The woman who stood next to Captain Bane was just as intimidating, although in a different way. She wore a flowing white gown with a hood that was now thrown back to reveal her long black hair. She was nearly a head taller than Captain Bane, and had an imperious manner about her, like a lacy who was used to getting her own way.

"Who is the fine lady next to the captain?" Jilly asked Finn. "I saw her doing things that looked like magic. How can she do that?"

"She used to be a biomancer, before they kicked her out of their order."

"Why'd they do that?"

"As I understand it, because she's a molly."

Jilly thought about that awhile as she stared at the two women. Then she asked, "Why's it so bad to be a molly?"

Missing Finn looked at her sharply. "It ain't bad at all. Some of my best wags are mollies."

"Then why are there so many things we're not allowed to do? We're not supposed to be sailors or soldiers or captains or I guess biomancers, even. But it's not like we *can't* do those things, is it?"

"You have only to look around this ship to know the answer to that."

"Then why are we not *supposed* to be those things?" she asked.

"Just lacy nonsense, you ask me," said Finn. "You know as well as I, we don't worry about such balls and pricks in Paradise Circle."

They stood without talking for a little while, the ship beneath them cutting across the endless sea. After a few minutes, Missing Finn began to hum softly to himself. Jilly couldn't remember the name of the tune, but it was something she'd heard as a child in Paradise Circle. Back when she'd been called Little Bee. How did it go...?

Sail away, my wag. Sail away.
Before the night turns to day.
Or they'll drag you down
To rotten old Keystown
So away, my wag. Sail away.

A sudden homesickness welled up in her. But that was strange, because it almost felt like her childhood home was on this ship. There was Filler, whom she'd tortured endlessly with questions and gossip and whatever else popped into her head when she'd been bored and her mother wasn't at home, which had been often. He'd put on some more muscle. He looked a little older and hairier, and something had happened to his leg. But he was still the same tall, quiet presence that had given her so much comfort. He now sat peering down at a large sheet of paper with drawings and calculations of some kind spread across a barrel top. Next to him was a man who looked so much like Red, she'd almost thought it was, until she got a good look at his eyes. Filler had introduced him as Alash, Red's lacy cousin from Hollow Falls.

Nettles sat nearby, polishing her chain. She looked even more beautiful than Jilly remembered, with her thick curly hair, full lips, and smoldering eyes. Jilly had been so mad at her for taking nearly all of Red's time that last month before Jilly had gone to live with her aunt in Hammer Point.

And back in the stern was the infamous Sadie the Goat, one of the boldest and craziest wags the Circle had ever produced. She was a legend. Jilly had to admit, though, that she didn't look much like a legend as she lounged on the deck, snoring, her thin white hair fluttering in the breeze, a fishing line held loosely in her hand. But Sadie had been Red's mentor. Red, who had taught Jilly to pick a lock, to read, and at the very end, after an extended bout of pleading, how to throw a knife. If not for those three skills, Jilly didn't know if she would have survived the last few years.

"Mr. Finn? What happened to Red?"

"The biomancers have him." He saw the look of horror on her face and quickly added, "But don't worry. They won't harm him. Brigga Lin and Captain Bane are certain of it. Apparently they need him for something special."

"And we're going to rescue him, right?"

"That's the idea. Although it won't be a simple

thing, I'm afraid. Those biomancers are as fearsome as people say. Maybe even more so. We have to be smart and patient and do it right."

"But we *are* going to do it?"

"Captain Bane swore it."

Jilly turned again to Captain Bane. She looked so strong and confident. Jilly wondered if she'd ever be near as impressive.

"How's about a turn at the wheel?" said Finn.

"Me?" asked Jilly. "But—"

"Don't be so grave. This ain't the navy, you know. And we've got a nice stretch in front of us. Nothing to it but to keep her straight."

"But I don't know *how.*"

"That's why I'm going to teach you," said Finn. "Come now. Every hand needs to make themselves useful. Time you did, too."

———

Bleak Hope stood on the forecastle and stared north at the empty stretch of sea in the last red light of day. She wished she could look across the miles to see Stonepeak. It had taken them nearly a year to refit the *Lady's Gambit* into the battle-worthy *Kraken Hunter*, and perfect their strategy. They'd begun with small imperial sloops—one-masted ships with few cannons. Then they had moved on to larger two-masted schooners and brigs. They'd learned from one of those captains about Brice Vaderton, a man recently given command of an imperial frigate as a reward for his service to the biomancers. The *Guardian* had been the first fully armed frigate that they'd taken, and they'd spent more than a week planning and trailing the ship before they'd made their move. She knew these were all steps toward Red's rescue, but she felt a constant, low tickle of frustration that she wasn't closer.

The months after the attack on Stonepeak had been some of the hardest in her life. Loss had been her constant companion. She would sit in her quarters, reading or studying a map, and she would imagine she heard him call her name. It sounded so real, she would even turn, in spite of herself, knowing she would not see those glinting, mischievous red eyes.

Sometimes in those early months, she would also forget she had lost her hand. She would instinctively reach for a cup, only to knock it aside with her clamp. Back then, she was able to picture her missing hand vividly. Every line and freckle. The scar from when she'd burned herself while cooking for the brothers. The roughness of the knuckles from years of striking wooden boards. The creases in her palm that her mother told her meant she would have a long life and one great love. Back then, she had been able to see that hand as if it were right there in front of her. Sometimes, it had even felt like it was there. It would ache or itch, or tingle in an odd way.

But slowly, month by month, she adapted to her new hand, crafted by Alash, Filler, and Brigga Lin. Finally there came a day when she realized that she couldn't remember her old hand clearly anymore. The details had slipped away, like morning mist lifting off the surface of the sea. Now, when she tried to picture her old hand, she saw nothing more than a ghostly outline.

She dreaded the day when she would only be able to picture that much of Red.

"What do you think he's doing right now?" she asked Brigga Lin, who stood silently at her side.

"There's no way of knowing." Brigga Lin had little inclination toward sentimentality.

"Probably getting into trouble," said Hope. "He has a knack for that."

"When we do finally free him, he may not be the man you remember," said Brigga Lin.

"So you've said."

"The biomancers have techniques that can change the inside of a person as well as the outside."

"If they've done something like that to him, we'll just have to find a way to undo it." Hope massaged her forearm above the clamp. "One problem at a time."

Brigga Lin nodded, watching Hope continue to massage her arm. "It's getting worse, isn't it?"

"It's getting more intense," said Hope. "I still say it's too early to tell if it's good or bad."

"The Song of Sorrows is a centuries-old weapon forged by biomancery arts that are unfamiliar even to me. Every time you attach it to your clamp, there is a direct, unfiltered link between that blade and your nervous system. We have no idea what kind of effect it's having on your body."

"Which is why you shouldn't jump to conclusions that it's bad."

"I'm not jumping to conclusions. I'm being cautious. Let me at least temporarily disconnect the wires that are fused to your tendons."

"Absolutely not. That's what gives me the level of control I need."

They were silent for a while, the wind pulling at their hair, and at Brigga Lin's dress.

"What does it feel like?" Brigga Lin asked. "Is it painful?"

Hope thought about it for a moment, her hand working its way past her elbow to massage her upper arm. Finally, she said, "When I was a girl, my teacher, Hurlo the Cunning, told me that there was no logical explanation for the Song of Sorrows to make the sound that it does. He said that *his* teacher, Shilgo the Wise, told him that the blade remembers every life that it takes, and that the sound we hear is it mourning for the loss of those lives." She traced a line with her finger from her arm to her shoulder, and across her chest to her heart. "That is what it's like. As if I, too, am feeling its grief with every life I take."

"It sounds awful," said Brigga Lin.

"It's instructive." Hope gave Brigga Lin a pointed look and said, "And nothing for you to worry about. Now, let's go talk to Alash. He said there was some trouble with the new revolving cannon mechanism."

Brigga Lin's thin black eyebrow rose. "I thought it worked beautifully."

"Apparently, we were lucky our whole ship didn't explode."

Brigga Lin sighed with exasperation. "I still don't know about all his mechanical contrivances. You wouldn't get that level of unpredictability from *my* arts."

"Your phosphorescent moss replica was flawless," agreed Hope.

"As was the water mirage that cloaked us."

"Please don't rub it in. You know how sensitive Alash is."

Hope walked back to the main deck, where Alash and Filler were examining the designs for the mechanism they had created. It looked to Hope a lot like the rotating cylinders in the revolver pistols she'd seen imperial soldiers use, only much larger, and with three chambers instead of six. Loading a regular cannon took at least two people per cannon, three if you wanted it done swiftly. But Hope's skeleton crew was needed elsewhere during a battle. Alash's mechanism allowed them to preload three shots for each cannon before the battle. Then, when they were engaged, only Alash was needed to pull the cords that fired each round. All in all, Hope thought it was a very clever design. But not if it might blow up the ship.

"Well, my wags?" She put her hand on Alash's shoulder and rested her clamp on Filler's. "Do you have good news for me?"

"Yes and no, Captain," said Alash.

"We know what happened and why," said Filler. "Just not how to stop it from happening or being worse next time."

"You see," said Alash, his brow furrowed as he pointed out various parts of the diagram. "The first shot goes off without a hitch. But after that, the remains of the percussion cap have a tendency to cling to the firing pin. When that happens, the second shot may potentially ignite an external spark, in addition to the internal spark in the muzzle bore. If that external spark lands on the third, unfired chamber, the entire cannon might explode. And if *that* happens, then, in addition to grievously injuring the cannoneer, it could also set off a chain reaction that detonates every cannon on the lower deck, most likely taking the upper deck and a good portion of the hull with it." He smiled up at her in satisfaction, as if he were not talking about a catastrophic incident. Hope had noticed that when Alash was focused on a highly technical problem, he tended to think so abstractly that the reality escaped him.

"That sounds bad," she said.

His face fell. "Well, yes, it is, of course."

"There were a great many 'ifs' and 'potentiallys' in that explanation," said Brigga Lin disdainfully. "How likely do you think it is something like this could actually happen?"

"Oh, uh, not particularly likely, Ms. Lin." Alash looked down at his designs, nervously smoothing out the corners. Brigga Lin was an imposing presence, and nearly everyone responded to that. But Alash seemed barely able to make eye contact with her.

"Yet you said it nearly happened today," pressed Hope.

"The percussion cap remains *did* spark on the second shot," said Alash. "That's how I discovered the flaw. The sparks just happened to not land in the third chamber this time. The important thing to remember is if we continue to use these cannons, even an unlikely scenario is bound to happen eventually."

"What if you covered the back of the two chambers not currently in the bore?" suggested Brigga Lin.

"I'm not sure that's possible," said Alash.

"No, it might work." Filler tapped the drawing with one of his thick, calloused fingers. "If we made stationary plates on the base that didn't travel with the chambers."

"I suppose..." Alash examined the diagram doubtfully.

"Perhaps you don't like the suggestion because it came from me?" asked Brigga Lin.

"What?" Alash looked alarmed. "Of course not."

Her eyes narrowed. "Do you still not trust me because I was a biomancer?"

"Don't be silly," said Alash, wringing his hands.

"Oh, I'm just a silly woman, is that it?" snapped Brigga Lin.

"No, I don't think of you like that at all!" Alash looked almost panicked.

"You don't think of me as a woman?"

"No, please! You've got it all wrong!"

"I don't care if you take my suggestion or not," said Brigga Lin. "I hope your stupid cannons *do* blow you up!" She spun on her heel, her white gown swirling, and stalked off.

Alash stared after her, looking pale. "I, uh, think I might lie down for a bit." He hurried off in the opposite direction.

Hope rubbed her temple. It was becoming increasingly clear that there was something more than a rivalry of methodology going on between them. So far, she'd just ignored it, but it looked like she wouldn't have that luxury much longer.

But as she'd just told Brigga Lin earlier, one problem at a time. It seemed like she reminded herself that a lot, these days.

"Filler?" she asked wearily.

Filler gazed down at the design, scratching his bushy beard. "Get me to a smithy, and I'll make the chamber covers for you."

Hope gave him a grateful smile. "You have been my rock this past year, Filler."

"I'm no mechanical genius or biomancer. Not even much of a sailor. But I always helped Red as best I could, and I know he wants me to help you the same while he's gone."

Hope absently massaged her forearm as she stared north across the sea again. "We *will* get him back, Fill."

"Of course we will, Captain."

———

They reached the island of High Guster late the following morning. Missing Fin steered them into a secluded cove a little ways from the village. They'd taken down the *Kraken Hunter* flag, but there was always the potential that the ship itself could be recognized in port. They were there to find Filler a smithy, not to start a meaningless skirmish with the local imperial outpost. High Guster was a tiny island with no strategic value. Little could be gained by direct conflict, and the imperial presence was likely to be small. Ideally, they would slip in, bribe the local smithy for access to his tools, and be on their way without incident, as they'd done several times before on other islands.

Initially, Hope decided only she and Filler would go ashore, but at the last minute changed her mind and brought Jilly along as well. A child would help them blend in the small, domestically focused village.

As Filler rowed the dingy ashore, Hope noticed Jilly glance at her clamp, then hurriedly look away.

"Did you want to ask me something, Jilly?"

"Oh." Jilly looked guiltily back at the clamp, then at Hope. "Captain, would you tell me what happened to your hand?"

Hope smiled faintly. "If Red were here, I'm sure he would spin you an epic tale, but I don't have his gift of storytelling. So I'll just say that I cut it off myself."

Jilly's eyes grew wide. *"Why?"*

"A biomancer had poisoned it. The poison was spreading and I had to make the choice. My hand or my life."

Jilly stared at her in awe.

"Don't ever tell Red," said Filler as he pulled smoothly on the oars, "but sometimes I prefer your plainer style, Captain."

"He would be crushed to hear it," said Hope.

When they landed on the beach, the three of them dragged the dingy into a sparse thicket, and covered it with some seaweed. Then they entered the strip of forest that separated them from the village. As they walked between the trees, the quiet sounds of the woodlands were broken by the rhythmic squeak of Filler's metal leg frame. Hope was glad they weren't trying to sneak into town. Even so, she worried it might draw attention to them.

"What happened to your leg, Filler?" Jilly asked.

"Shot at the Battle of Three Cups," he said. "That story, Red does tell fine."

"You were at the battle?" asked Jilly.

"Of course. Couldn't stand the idea of one of our own selling us out to the biomancers like that." Filler looked down at her. "Were you still in Hammer Point then?"

Jilly nodded. "I wanted to join, but our neighborhood was under Sharn, and she said none of her people could go."

"I always wondered why she stayed behind," said Hope. "She was the only one who did."

"People say she struck a deal with the biomancers instead," said Jilly.

Filler looked at her sharply. "You believe it?"

"I don't now," said Jilly. "Sharn always seemed a fine molly to me, but it was crystal that people started going missing after the battle."

"Did your aunt go missing?" asked Filler.

Jilly's face went dark. She shook her head. "No, not her. Not likely ever. But all those people going missing, it was one of the reasons I cut my hair and joined the navy to look for my mom. Didn't realize them biomancers had already taken her, too."

"They've taken a great many people," said Hope.

"Why does the emperor let it happen?" asked Jilly. "Aren't we all his people?"

Hope put her hand on Jilly's thin shoulder. "The next time I break into his palace, I plan to ask him."

———

The village of High Guster was no more than a hundred buildings. All the roads were dirt, and rutted with ancient wagons that trundled slowly past. The buildings themselves seemed to be a mixture of stone and wood, which made sense, given the large number of trees on the island.

As they made their way down the dusty road through town, Hope noticed that they were drawing even more attention than she'd expected. But the townspeople weren't staring at her, with her missing hand and black Vinchen armor, or Filler, with his intimidating height and clanking leg. They stared at Jilly.

Hope glanced down at Jilly, who walked at her left. She didn't notice their singular interest in her. Instead she seemed fascinated by the town itself.

"Awfully small, ain't it?" she asked. "I can *see* from one end to the other."

Hope smiled. "I grew up on an island even smaller than this, down in the Southern Isles."

"Do they all have yellow hair like yours in the south?"

"Most do. The families who have lived there since before the empire was formed. But occasionally other people have come down from the north to live a simpler life, far from the politics and violence of places like Stonepeak and New Laven. High Guster is not so far south, but perhaps it's small enough and far enough from the capital to enjoy a similar peace."

"You sure about that?" asked Filler. "Don't feel exactly peaceful to me."

"I know what you mean." Hope hadn't been here since she sailed under Carmichael. Everything looked as it had then, but something felt different. Perhaps it was the people, who carried themselves more timidly than she remembered.

It wasn't long before they found the smithy, a large squat building wisely free of wood. Inside was an older man, much shorter than Filler, but with arms and a chest nearly twice as thick. He was hard at work shaping a small hand plow when they entered the hot, dim room, but he stopped the moment he saw them. Or rather, when he saw Jilly. He mopped his face and neck with a thick cloth as he stepped out from behind his anvil.

"Name's Grenly. What can I do for you folks?" he asked.

"Mr. Grenly," said Hope. "My smith would like to use your forge for a few hours."

He squinted at her, then at Filler. "I'm accustomed to doing my own work. If you need something made, I can make most things."

"I'm sure you can," said Hope. "But our needs are specific and unusual. I would prefer my own smith do the work. I can assure you, he is skilled and unlikely to damage your tools. But as a precaution, I would like you to accept this money, in case there are any minor reparations you discover need to be made later."

She took a small bag from her belt filled with more gold than the smith probably received in a year. But when he saw it, he scowled.

"Money ain't so interesting to me these days."

Hope glanced questioningly at Filler. They'd made similar offers in other villages, always with success.

"We don't mean no disrespect to your skill," said Filler. "The thing is, the less you know about us or what we want, the safer you are."

Grenly spat. "Safe from who?"

Filler seemed just as surprised by the hostility as Hope. There was more going on here in High Guster. Something to do with the timidity that had come over the townspeople.

"When we first came in, you stared at our girl." Hope put her hand on Jilly's head. "Her hair is a little short, but otherwise, she's not particularly remarkable. Yet everyone in this village looks at her as if she was some rare creature."

Grenly's mouth was set hard. He stared down at his thick, scarred hands. "Just wasn't expecting to see someone so young is all."

An icy dread started to form in Hope's stomach. "I haven't seen any children since we arrived. Where are they?"

The smith remained silent, continuing to stare down at his hands.

Hope snapped the clamp onto her sword and said in a flat, hard voice. "This will be the last time I ask you. What have you done with the children?"

Grenly looked up at her, and there were tears streaming down his grizzled cheek. "Done? We ain't done nothin', and that's the problem. First the navy came and took all our boys into conscript. We did nothing. Then not two days ago, a biomancer came and took all our girls. And *still* we did nothing." His fists were clenched and his whole body shook with suppressed rage. "My own Kapany. That monster in white took her and God knows what he will do with her. And when he loaded them all up on his ship, he left behind a chest of money as recompense. Like any amount of money could replace my sweet little Kapany." The man was openly weeping now, his breath hissing through clenched yellow teeth.

"Two days?" asked Hope, the ice in her stomach softening. "Where was it heading?"

"What?" Grenly blinked back tears, looking bewildered by her question.

"It would help if I knew the direction the ship was heading. And, if you can remember, the number of masts and guns as well."

Grenly frowned. "But why?"

"So that we can run it down and free your daughters," said Hope.

"But...didn't you hear me?" he asked. "There's a *biomancer* on board that ship."

"This here is Dire Bane you're talking to," Filler said quietly. "And there ain't a biomancer alive can scare her."

"*The* Dire Bane?" Grenly gave her an unsure look. "Well, whoever you are, if you bring back my Kapany, I'll let your man here have free rein of my shop as long and as often as you like."

Hope smiled grimly. "I'll hold you to that, Mr. Grenly."

4

"Lord Pastinas, perhaps you would care to eat now?"

Red woke slowly. Reluctantly. Another restless night of dimly recalled dreams. They were always dark and violent, leaving him oddly sore, as if his whole body had been tense while he slept.

He opened his eyes and saw Hume, one of the palace servants, standing patiently with a covered silver tray. The gaf had to be at least as old as Sadie, but he had a full head of iron-gray hair pulled back in a tight ponytail. His posture was straight as a rod, and no matter what Red did or said, he hadn't been able to get the man to even crack a smile.

"Oh, Humey, my wag, you know I don't go in for breakfast and the like."

"Of course, my lord. That is why I have brought you lunch."

"Already?"

Hume looked at him gravely. "Midday is the traditional time for serving lunch, my lord."

"Midday? Piss'ell, but I've been a late riser recently."

"Indeed, my lord," agreed Hume.

"I've just been sleeping terrible these past few weeks," said Red as he accepted the tray from Hume.

"Perhaps your lordship has a lot on his mind."

Red shrugged as he lifted the cover on his tray. He still wasn't used to being called *lord*. He'd asked Hume to just call him Red, but Hume had said— very apologetically—that His Highness had directly commanded him to show Red all due propriety and respect as befitted his station as Lord Pastinas of Hollow Falls.

Part of Red's discomfort with the title was due to how neatly the biomancers had arranged it all. They wanted to keep Red at the palace without making their connection obvious. But without a title, Red's presence would have been restricted to the lower floors. So they had Emperor Martarkis declare Alash an outlaw and strip him of all claim to his inheritance. Then they had the emperor legitimize Red as heir. Red appreciated the irony that *he* was now the noble and his cousin the outlaw, but it stopped being funny a few days later when word reached the palace that old man Pastinas had died in his sleep, making Red the new Lord Pastinas of Hollow Falls. It was one thing to mess around with meaningless titles. It was something else entirely to kill a defenseless old wrink, cock-dribble though he was. It was too late to save his grandfather, but Red promised himself that he would find a way to set Alash up as the proper lord of the manor. In the meantime, he tried to think of the whole thing as one great big con.

He looked down at the steaming dish of lamb, rice, and broccoli, all coated in some sort of cheese shavings. The endless supply of good food was one thing he had no trouble adjusting to. Well, that wasn't completely true. His stomach had a hard time getting used to all the butter and cheese at first. But with a concerted effort, he got past all that within the first month. So much so that he might have been in danger of getting fat, if not for his intense training regimen overseen by the biomancers. They pushed him hard. So hard that there were days when the only thing that got him through it was thinking about how he would one day turn all their training against them. He really looked forward to that day.

"His Highness has requested the pleasure of your company after you have finished eating, my lord," said Hume.

"Where is the old princey?" asked Red.

"At the cliff gardens, my lord."

"Of course he is."

Red ate quickly, then handed the tray to Hume. He climbed out of the big feather bed and opened his wardrobe.

"Do you require assistance getting dressed, my lord?"

"Humey, old pot, if I ever get so lacy I need someone to dress me, I expect you to shoot me right between the eyes, keen?"

"As you wish, my lord."

Red pulled on breeches, boots, and a linen shirt, then turned toward the door.

"My lord, you seem to have forgotten your cravat and jacket," said Hume, his face still unmarked by emotion.

"Oh, no, Humey. Just don't feel like wearing them today."

Hume's eyebrow flickered for just a moment. "How very...provocative of you, my lord."

Red slapped him on the shoulder. "That's the idea, my wag." Then he turned and left his apartments.

He got some odd looks as he strode cheerfully down the hallway. People at the palace generally didn't walk around outside their apartments without a jacket and cravat. Red knew this. He could have followed the rules and truly blended. But part of his con was to use his unusual background and circumstances to make himself a novelty item. It seemed to be working so far. He found that even though lacies gripped tightly to their propriety, they were fascinated by his wonton disregard for it. He wasn't sure how long they'd put up with him, but he planned to enjoy it while it lasted.

Red's apartments were on the thirty-fifth floor of the palace. There were a total of fifty floors, the top thirty of which were only accessible to the nobility. Of course, they couldn't be expected to climb all those steps. A lift platform had been constructed along with the rest of the palace. It was operated by a team of palace soldiers who worked in shifts so that it was available at any time, day or night. Except it wasn't usually available for Red. Ammon Set, head of the biomancer council, had instructed the lift operation team that Red was only allowed in it when he was in the company of other nobles. When he was alone, Ammon Set expected him to utilize the steps as part of his strength and endurance training.

Red walked past the lift entrance and nodded to the soldier who stood out front. The gaf nodded back respectfully. If any of them thought Red's ban was strange, they didn't let on. Red suspected that servants and soldiers in the palace were used to taking seemingly arbitrary orders from biomancers. Or else, they were just really good at hiding it. Maybe that's how it was here. Each place had its own work culture. Because of his title, Red was shut out of that at the palace, and he didn't like it. The few awkward attempts he'd made to let people know he wasn't really a lacy had been met with polite indulgence. The kind you gave to rich lacies who were a little embarrassed by their own wealth. Obviously, none of them believed him.

It was probably for the best. If he had brought any of them in on his con, and the biomancers found out, those poor saltheads would disappear, true as trouble. And Red didn't want that on his conscience. It meant he was frequently alone, though, even in a crowd of nobles all vying for his attention. The only true wag he'd made was, oddly enough, Prince Leston.

Perhaps it wasn't so odd, though. Leston suffered from the same problem of feeling lonely in a crowded room. For the prince, though, it was because not a single one of the ass-licking, bird-faced cunt-droppings spoke to him like a real person. As far as Red could tell, they didn't even like him. He was just the tom who filled their bucket.

Red jogged the fifteen flights down to the twentieth floor, which was the level of the cliff gardens. Then he walked boldly through the hall toward the west garden entrance. As he passed a group of nobles pretending like they weren't staring at his open shirt collar and flapping sleeves, he winked at them, sending them scurrying off like a pack of perfumed rats. That put a smile on his face. He slipped on his tinted glasses and threw open the door.

Prince Leston came to the cliff gardens often, usually when he was restless and needed concrete proof that there was a world beyond the confines of the palace. The cliff gardens were set into a ledge carved into the side of the mountain that wrapped all the way around to the east side of the palace. Red wasn't sure if it was irrigated by some mysterious biomancer process or some feat of engineering, but either way, having a lush green space this high up and open to the air was impressive. And even more impressive was the view. For a palace built into the side of a mountain, there were precious few places with a decent view. Most of the windows showed nothing other than clouds and sky. The cliff gardens was one of the few places you could actually look out and see the entire city of Stonepeak stretched out below you.

"Your Highness, I have come, once again, to save you from your habitual melancholy brooding!" Red declared as he stepped out onto the gardens.

The prince had been slouched on a stone bench, staring down at the city, a lock of his carefully curled hair dangling in front of his solemn face. But he brightened when he heard Red's voice, and laughed when he saw him.

"My Lord Pastinas, without your jacket and cravat you look like a brigand!"

Red bowed low, then sauntered over and dropped down next to him on the bench. "Did I ever tell you about the time I sailed under Captain Sadie the Pirate Queen, plundering the northern coasts of New Laven?"

The prince shook his head. "How on earth did you have the time amidst all your cons, thievery, and rebellion?"

"Oh, this was long before then, when I was only a boy of eight."

"Eight years and already a terror," said Leston. "No wonder being a scoundrel comes so naturally to you."

"I'm not sure what His Highness is referring to," Red said loftily.

"I am referring to that damned shell game you were playing in the sitting room last night."

Red gave him a hurt look. "Really, Your Highness, it's the oldest con there is. I thought surely they had all heard of it."

Leston shook his head, still smiling. "I don't mind friendly wagers of a few coins among gentlemen. But did you have to let them bet their shoes?"

Red stretched out his feet, admiring his new soft, black leather boots. "You have to admit, Archlord Tramasta's boots suit me far better than him."

"You're impossible, Rixidenteron," said Leston. "I hope you realize that."

"Not nearly as impossible as you, Leston, my wag. How long have you been ignoring those two sotted mollies over there?" Red nodded his head toward the two women who stood at a respectful distance. Their orange-powdered skin and iridescent gowns sparkled in the early afternoon sun.

"I assume you are referring to Archlady Bashim and Lady Hempist?" Leston asked without much interest.

"How long have they been standing there waiting for you to come talk to them?"

"Half an hour, perhaps?" Leston didn't look too sure, which probably meant it was longer.

Of all the bizarre lacy rules of palace life, Red found the ones for mollies hardest to understand. Near as he could tell, unmarried ladies weren't allowed to just walk up to any tom they fancied. Unless they had been formally introduced by an older male family member, they had to wait for the tom to make the first move. As far as Red was concerned, this meant the people at the palace were missing out on about half the tossing they could have had. It made no sense.

"You let those poor lovely mollies stand over there in hopeful expectation that long?" asked Red. They *were* lovely, in that twittering, fragile way all the lacy mollies had. And standing in those pointy shoes and tight gowns for the better part of an hour, they had to be near passing out.

"You're going to drag me over to talk to them, aren't you?" asked Leston.

"Of course I am. Firstly, it's common human decency. And second, all those lordly gafs are pissed and peppered because you have shown little interest in chasing mollies, and they want an heir to keep your God-chosen line going. In other words, imperial babies, my wag." He nudged Leston in the side with his elbow and was rewarded with a blush. Whenever Red started talking about bending cocks and stretching cunts, Leston fell all askew.

"Must you talk about me like I am a breeding stud?"

"Listen, old pot. The job's got to be done. But if the trouble is that you fancy the toms instead, I'm sure we can find—"

"That's not it," the prince said quickly.

"No?" Red had noticed that at the palace, there was some objection to toms tossing toms and mollies tossing mollies. He'd tried to ask people why, but they all got red-faced and quiet.

"I am attracted to women," Leston said firmly. "But the ones at the palace are all so *dull*. Nothing to talk about except fashion, palace gossip, and the weather. I want to talk to *exciting* women. Like the ones you've told me about."

"And I promise you will meet them, somehow, someday. But for right now, I think you're missing the point here, Your Highness. The talking is only the first step toward *other* entertainments. The kind that could lead to producing that heir. It's a remarkably simple process, really. Alls you do is—"

"If I agree to meet these ladies, will you stop talking about sex?"

"It's just that the idea you've never tossed in your life fills my heart with sorrow. It's a splendid thing, being naked and leaky."

Leston stood up abruptly. "I'm going over to them."

"I still remember my first time, crystal as anything. I've told you about Nettles, right? Well, she would do this thing with her hips…"

The prince was now hurrying toward the ladies.

They watched him approach with a mixture of delight and panic. Red followed casually behind the prince, ready to divert whichever one the prince seemed less interested in. Filler had done it for him all those years, but he'd never fully appreciated it until he began helping Leston.

"Archlady Bashim, I trust you are enjoying this remarkable view of our fair city." Leston gestured out to the thick mass of buildings far below.

Red hadn't figured out if it was conscious or ingrained, but Leston always went for the higher rank. Frankly, Red found Archlady Bashim to be a bit of a sourface, so he was only too happy to keep Lady Hempist entertained instead.

"Your Highness is so kind to grace us with his presence," said Archlady Bashim in that careful way everyone at the palace (except Red) spoke to him. "Your company makes the view even more remarkable."

"You are too kind, my lady," said Leston, already beginning to look bored.

"Your Highness," said Red. "I'd imagine the ladies don't get into the city too often. It might amuse them to hear about our recent adventure on Artisan Way."

"Oh, would you favor us with the story, Your Highness?" asked Archlady Bashim, flashing Red a grateful look.

"Are you fond of the arts, my lady?" asked Leston.

"I adore them!" she said with so much sincerity that Red almost believed her.

"Really?" Leston began to warm up a little as he pointed down at the city in the general direction of Artisan Way. "Have you perused some of the fine works our citizens are creating down there?"

"Sadly, it is just as Lord Pastinas says. We so rarely get the opportunity to venture into the city. So

I would be most appreciative if you could describe some of them to me."

"I am always pleased to talk of fine art," said Leston. As he began to tell her of some of the pieces they'd seen and how they'd discovered the odd genius craftsman in the furniture shop, Archlady Bashim slowly, gently maneuvered him away from Red and Lady Hempist. She was good, Red had to admit. Although he was fairly certain that even her skills were no match for the prince's indifference.

"She hasn't the slightest interest in the arts, of course," said Lady Hempist quietly.

"Naturally," agreed Red.

Lady Hempist walked slowly over to the waist-high stone barrier at the edge of the cliff gardens. She gazed out, not down at the city, but up at the bright blue sky. "His Highness's passion for the arts is a somewhat new development, and has all the ladies scrambling in an attempt to educate themselves. At least, to the point where they would not appear completely at a loss, should they be lucky enough to speak to him."

"Very industrious of them," said Red, joining her at the stone wall.

"People say that *you* speak to him quite frequently."

Red leaned forward so that his elbows rested on the top of the wall. "He finds me amusing."

"So does the entire palace."

Red grinned. "Do they?"

"Don't act like you don't know, my lord."

It was such a bold statement from a lacy molly that Red looked at her with new appreciation. Lady Hempist had an inviting lushness to her. Her thick black curls were piled up on her head, showing off the graceful curve of her neck and bare shoulders. Her orange-powdered bosom made him think of ripe citrus fruit. She was also one of the few mollies who seemed confident enough to meet his gaze directly. Most of them pretended to look at him, but actually seemed to be looking at a spot just below his chin. He hadn't realized until that moment just how much it bothered him. He wondered if he might find another friend in Lady Hempist.

"They'll all tire of me soon enough, my lady."

She gave him a speculative look. "Not soon, I think, my lord. After all, you are His Majesty's first and only real friend."

"The prince is twenty-four years old. Surely he's had a wag or two before me."

"Not so, my lord. His Highness has never spent as much time with another soul. Not by half, even. I don't see that changing anytime soon. This puts you in a very attractive position." She laid her hand on his arm. "One which many ladies of the court are already pondering."

"Well"—Red gently lifted her hand and placed it next to him on the wall—"I'm afraid all their pondering and scheming is pointless, because my heart belongs to another. Even though we're hundreds of miles apart, she's the only one who will ever be for me."

Lady Hempist laughed, a light, tinkling sound. "But my Lord Pastinas, clearly you do not know the tastes of the ladies of this court. Tragically separated love only adds to your allure. When I spread this bit of gossip around, every unwed bosom, and a few others besides, will be burning for a glimpse of your rakish smile."

Red hoped she was joking, but there was something about the steely glint in her eyes that suggested she wasn't.

"Have no fear, my lord." She put her hand firmly back on his arm. "I will protect you."

Life at the palace wasn't all just chatting up princes and fending off the amorous advances of buxom ladies, of course. Each day, Red was required to spend a few hours with one of the biomancers from the council. That was the agreement which allowed him to roam freely through the palace and Hope to roam freely on the sea.

That afternoon, he was to meet Progul Bon in the palace library. The biomancers made a point of keeping their connection to Red quiet—which he was just fine with. So it surprised him the first time Bon told him to meet at the library. After all, the library was theoretically open to anyone in the empire of noble birth. But he quickly realized it might as well have been a secret chamber, because no one else ever came. It baffled him. Here was an entire group of people who all knew how to read, and had the largest library in the empire at their disposal. Yet none of them showed any interest. For Red, who had spent his childhood stealing whatever books he could get his hands on, it was incomprehensible.

The library was a large, open chamber that stretched up three levels, books lining the walls on all four sides, all the way to the ceiling. At each level was a narrow walkway with an ornately carved railing accessible by ladder from the level beneath. In the center of the chamber were large, thick tables, all of them gathering dust except the one Progul Bon favored in the back. That was where Red found him when he entered the library.

"Another day of fighting through the crowds to gain the knowledge of the empire, eh, Bon?" Red asked. Of the three biomancers who trained him, Red minded Progul Bon the least. Mostly because at least the gaf had a sense of humor, even if it was a very bookish one.

Progul Bon's fleshy lips curled up into a smile beneath his hood. The rest of his face was mostly hidden. Red still hadn't gotten a good, clear look at it yet. At first, he thought the biomancers were trying to hide their identities. But when he'd gotten a look at Ammon Set, he realized that it was more to conceal the strange deformities brought on by their biomancery. Each one seemed different. From what he could see of Bon's face, for instance, it was strangely droopy. Not like old wrink skin, but more like melted wax.

"It is to our advantage that the masses remain complacent in their ignorance, Rixidenteron." Progul Bon's voice matched his looks, sounding low and oozing, like thick oil.

"Still makes me a bit sad," said Red as he sat across the table from the biomancer.

"That is because you retain some fondness for the idiots. I am confident that time and knowledge will cure you of that." Bon always said things like that. Red didn't even bother to respond anymore.

"What's on the lesson plan for today, then?" he asked.

"The strategies of Emperor Bastelinus."

"*Still?*" asked Red. "We've been reading about that gaf for weeks now. Why can't we get to something more tasty? Like the reign of the Dark Mage. I bet that's a tale worth learning."

"We are not here for your entertainment," said Progul Bon. "We are here for your education, which, until I took a hand in it, seems to have been comprised almost exclusively of espionage fiction and folktales. Bastelinus was instrumental in shaping the empire as we know it today, second only to Emperor Cremalton himself. It is essential that you understand both his political and economic strategies."

"But why?" asked Red.

"When you are in the field, circumstances may arise that the Council of Biomancery had not predicted. When those situations present themselves, you must make independent decisions, and you cannot do that without an understanding of the larger picture and how that decision could potentially affect the empire."

"You still haven't told me what I'm supposed to *do* in the field."

"Protect the interests of the empire."

"By killing people."

"Mostly," conceded Progul Bon.

"I'm not an assassin."

"We are what we believe ourselves to be."

"You know what Ammon Set told me? He said that when you gafs are through with me, I won't even be a person anymore. I'll be a shadow of death, whatever that pissing means."

Progul Bon was silent for a moment. "Ammon Set talks too much."

———

That evening, Red attempted to teach Leston how to play stones. They sat at a table in the prince's apartments, which took up the entire forty-ninth floor. The fiftieth floor, the top floor, was of course the apartments for the emperor himself. Red hadn't seen those yet, but Leston said the emperor also had an outdoor parlor for entertaining guests. Leston said that wine had a stronger effect that high up, something Red really wanted to test out.

Right now, though, his focus was on making a decent stones player of the prince. It wasn't going well.

"No, Your Highness." Red's patient tone was starting to sink toward despair. "You can't put forty-three there because seven times six is forty-*two*."

"Oh, right." Leston frowned thoughtfully. "I knew it was something like that. And we can't just say that's close enough? I mean, what's the difference, really?"

Red restrained himself from leaning across the table and strangling the future ruler of the empire. The prince's grand indifference to precision in general and numbers in particular was one of the few things Red truly disliked about him. "Because, *Your Highness*"—He wished he could use some other words instead—"when it comes to math, there's no such thing as close enough."

"All right, all right. Calm down." The prince held up his hands placatingly. "I'm afraid fire is about to shoot from your eyes. I've never known anyone who cared for arithmetic as passionately as you do."

"It's gotten me out of more than a few scrapes," said Red.

"Tell me about one." Leston set down his stones and leaned forward.

Red gave him a wry smile. "You're not interested in learning this game, are you?"

"I tried, Rixidenteron. I really did. But all those numbers make my head ache. I have a man for that sort of thing. I'd rather just hear one of your stories."

Red sighed. "Well, thanks for trying, at least. Now, let's see which time I should tell you about . . ."

While Red considered which high-risk stones encounter to dramatize for the prince, there was a knock at the door.

"Come in," said Leston.

The door opened slowly and Hume stepped into the room.

"Forgive the intrusion, Your Highness, but there is a commoner who delivered a parcel for you earlier today. He said you were expecting something from him."

"Oh? Did he give a name?" asked Leston.

"A Mr. Blagely, I believe," said Hume.

"The gaf who owns that furniture shop you commissioned," said Red.

"The falcon!" Leston eagerly held out his hand. "Let's see it!"

But Hume only held out a small bag of coins and a folded sheet of paper.

"This doesn't look promising." Leston took the paper and opened it. He quickly scanned the short, crimped handwriting and his expression grew increasingly disappointed.

"What is it, Your Highness?" asked Red.

"That poor young artist has been murdered."

"Does it say how?"

"Apparently, last night he and five other men were meeting in a cellar beneath a tavern and they were all stabbed to death." He frowned at the note. "What a strange place for them to be meeting. I wonder if he was mixed up in something nasty. Perhaps a criminal element. What do you think?"

Red gave him a skeptical look. "As someone who spent most of his life among the 'criminal element,' he didn't seem the type."

"I suppose not," said Leston. "Poor boy. He was odd, but quite talented. What a shame."

It was clear that Leston was ready to leave the matter at that, but it didn't quite sit with Red somehow. What *was* that artist doing, hiding out in a cellar with a bunch of other gafs?

"Maybe it was some kind of seditionist movement," he suggested.

"Political dissidents?" Leston frowned thoughtfully.

"I have heard some rumors about small groups around the city. But they seem harmless, mostly just distributing pamphlets and manifestos. Frankly, I quite agree with them on one point, at least. My father *has* let the biomancers run roughshod over all other concerned parties in the empire. I've even heard complaints from the nobility."

"Really? Biomancers are a bunch of cockdribbles?" Red gave him a look of mock surprise.

"Yes, all right. I suppose this isn't exactly surprising information. Listen, I find them just as annoying as anyone else."

"*Annoying*? That's it?" Red leaned forward and looked intently at his friend. "Do you really not know how bad it is out there?"

"Well, I…" Leston looked uncomfortable.

"My wag, they are out there *slaughtering* your people on a regular basis!"

Leston held up his hands placatingly. "I know that their experimentation at times puts a life at risk, but really, I think you might be exaggerating when you say they are 'slaughtering' my subjects."

Red leaned back in his chair and stared at the prince. For the first time in a very long time, he was completely at a loss for words. The idea that Leston was this out of touch with the empire he lived in and would someday rule was almost too slippy for him to grasp. No wonder the world was such a mess.

He had the sudden impulse to lean across the table and slap some sense into the prince like Sadie had done to him any number of times. But instead, he took a deep breath and forced himself to calm down. Sure, he would someday turn the biomancers' training against them, and that was sunny for a long-term strategy. But this was something he could do right now. Red could be the voice of the people for Leston, so that when the prince ascended the throne one day, he might be the first emperor to actually understand something about the people he ruled over.

"Alright, my wag." He kept his voice gentle. Compassionate. This wasn't the time to point fingers or get Leston on the defensive. "Can I be completely crystal with you?"

"You know that you can," said Leston. "There are few people whose opinion I care more about."

"You don't get out of Stonepeak much, do you?"

Leston looked a little embarrassed. "Honestly, before I met you, I didn't even get out of the *palace* much. It's not that I don't want to. It's just..." He looked at Red helplessly.

"Listen, old pot. There's no need to fall askew on me. I think I keen. We all assume someone with as much power and privilege as you can do anything you want. But you have your own set of rules to follow."

Leston's face lit up. "Yes, that's it exactly!"

Red smiled. "But here's where you can be better than any emperor before you. Because I'll wager none of *them* ever had a proper wag of Paradise Circle as a friend who could tell them how things really are. Now, listen and I will tell you the story of Bleak Hope. And *then* you can tell me if I'm exaggerating about the biomancers."

5

$\mathcal{B}$leak Hope stood at the helm of the *Kraken Hunter*. The ship was near its top speed and the surge of the ocean thrummed up from the rudder, through the wheel, and into her one good hand. The wind blew strong out of the southwest, carrying with it a hint of the frozen bite of her homelands as it brought her closer to her quarry. It also brought swirling gray clouds, which hung overhead, steely and aloof. She could see faint flickers of lightning to the south, where the clouds were darker.

Missing Finn turned to look at the storm brewing in the distance. "Do you think we'll catch this biomancer before that storm catches us?"

"They had a two-day start, but the wind wasn't so favorable then," said Hope. "And the way the smith described the ship, it sounded like a cargo transport ship rather than a military vessel. With that many bodies and enough food and water to keep them alive, they'll be sitting low in the water. I think we'll overtake them by midday tomorrow."

"I reckon the storm will hit us early tomorrow morning. Southern storms move slow, but they're big and they're cold. Sometimes they'll even bring sleet as far north as Vance Post."

"Won't that be fun, then." Hope patted his arm.

"The helm is yours, Mr. Finn. I need to talk to Alash."

She moved swiftly across the main deck and down below to the gun deck. Alash and Filler were preparing the cannons. Brigga Lin watched them from a nearby barrel, her long-fingered hands wrapped around a steaming mug. She drank enormous quantities of tea. It was a trait she shared with Alash, so Hope assumed it was more of a lacy custom than a biomancer custom.

"Sorry we couldn't get your covers yet," Hope said as she picked up a long stick with a sponge on the end and began working powder residue loose in one of the iron bores.

"At the risk of cursing myself," said Alash, "one more time should still keep the probability of blowing my face off fairly low."

"It's a nice face, so let's try not to lose it." Hope rinsed her blackened sponge in a tub of seawater. "This really will be the last time, though. If we bring that smith's daughter back to him, he swore to give us the run of his shop as often as we like."

"The shop is quality," said Filler as he checked the breech ropes and ringbolts that kept the cannons from flying across the gun deck every time they fired.

"We could do a lot with a dependable resource like that," said Alash.

"Of course the intention is to rescue *all* the girls," said Hope as she moved on to the next cannon. "Twenty or so, according to Grenly. And that's assuming they hadn't picked up others on a different island first. Any ideas how to go about it?"

"With all those kids aboard, we'll need to be careful how we use the cannons," said Filler.

"Let's load them with chain and aim for the sails," said Hope.

"Got it," said Alash, opening a wooden crate filled with short lengths of thick iron chain.

"We can't use my ghost ship or water mirage," said Brigga Lin. "If there's a biomancer on board, he'll be able to see through such deceptions."

Hope nodded. "Grenly didn't see any cannon ports on the sides of the ship, so we don't need to worry about broadsides. And there's a storm coming up on our heels that should hit around the time we intercept. That might give us some cover."

"It'll also give them cover," said Filler. "If the storm is bad enough, we might sail right past without seeing them."

Brigga Lin sipped thoughtfully at her tea. "I should be able to track them."

"How?" asked Alash.

"Biomancery is based on the manipulation of living matter. In order to perform it at a distance, I must be able to sense its activity. With so many living beings crammed into such a tight space on the surface of the ocean, where most living things are *beneath* the surface, I should be able to take a general bearing on the ship."

"Wouldn't the biomancer on their ship be able to do the same thing to us?" asked Filler.

"I doubt it," she said. "Male biomancers practice the craft through touch, so he would not have developed the skill."

"Captain…," Alash asked Hope in that hesitant way he had whenever he was about to broach a request for one of his outlandish experiments. "You said a storm. Do you mean a thunderstorm?"

Brigga Lin looked sharply at him. "You don't mean to try *that* idea."

"What idea?" asked Hope.

"To harness lightning as a weapon," Brigga Lin said dismissively. "But it's purely theoretical. Far too dangerous and unpredictable for any practical application. Even if we could reliably capture lightning, there is no substance known that could store so much raw power. I assure you, it has been tried several times, always with disastrous results."

"The original idea of storing the power, yes," said Alash. "But what about a combat situation *during* an electrical storm. Then we simply need to redirect it. If we fixed an iron rod to the top of the foremast, and ran a chain from that rod to the enemy ship's mast, the lightning would be drawn to our iron rod, and travel down the length of the chain. When it hit the wood of the enemy mast, it would combust into flames, most likely splitting the mast and taking a goodly portion of the ship with it." He smiled expectantly at Hope.

She gazed levelly back at him. "And you want to try this on a ship with twenty innocent little girls on board?"

"Oh, right." Alash's face fell. "Good point."

Brigga Lin stifled a laugh.

"I promise you, Alash," Hope said gently. "Someday we will attempt this mad experiment of yours. But not today." She looked at them all. "Now is the time to eat and get some rest. Tomorrow will be a very long day."

Alash and Filler nodded and headed for the galley.

Brigga Lin handed her mug to Alash on his way out, then turned to Hope. "You, too, Captain."

"I will." Hope climbed the narrow steps to the deck. "I want to check in with Nettles and Sadie first."

"I'll come along." Brigga Lin followed behind her.

Hope looked back over her shoulder. "Don't you trust me?"

"To look after yourself right before a battle? No, I don't."

They found Nettles on deck near the stern with

Jilly. They were facing each other, each holding a knife.

"It's sunny that Red taught you how to *throw* a knife," Nettles was saying, "but what happens if you miss? You need to know how to use a knife in close quarters."

"I never miss," Jilly said airily.

"Everyone misses sometimes," said Hope as she walked over to them.

Jilly's attitude deflated when she saw Hope and Brigga Lin. In a slightly meeker tone, she asked, "Did Red ever miss?"

Hope and Nettles exchanged a glance. Then Nettles said, "Red had some...other advantages that the rest of us don't have."

"What advantages?" asked Jilly.

"I don't think we need to go into it all right now," said Hope.

"Why not?" asked Brigga Lin. "There's no point in keeping the child ignorant." She turned to Jilly. "Red is the result of one of the grandest biomancery experiments in the history of the empire."

"I wouldn't call it 'grand' exactly." Nettles's voice had an ominous tone.

"I only mean that the sheer scale and ambition of it was breathtaking," said Brigga Lin. "Nothing of that scope has ever been attempted, before or since. And the fact that it was a success further suggests—"

"Hold on, did you say *success*?" Nettles's eyes narrowed down to slits.

"Obviously there are variables that need to be addressed so that the results can be reliably replicated. Only then could it be considered a practical solution. But Red is living proof that the theory is sound. People can be enhanced dramatically while they are still developing in the womb."

"I don't give a cup of piss about your theories,"

said Nettles. "Do you know how many people died because of that *grand* experiment? It spread through downtown New Laven like a plague."

"But it wasn't like a plague at all," said Brigga Lin. "The council *could* have chosen to distribute it that way, but Progul Bon insisted that there be some element of choice. No one was forced to take that drug."

"It's so easy for you to say that." Nettles stepped in close. Her head didn't even reach Brigga Lin's shoulder, but she glared up at her, undaunted. "You've never been starved and beaten and alone on the streets with no hope of it ever getting better. People are desperate for any little comfort they can get their hands on. Anything that will keep the black despair at bay a little longer. But you rich lacy types wouldn't know a thing about that, would you?"

"I don't mean to diminish the losses," said Brigga Lin. "They *were* excessive. Grotesquely so. But you must understand what is at stake here. The empire has strong enemies who are only kept at bay by the ever-growing power of the biomancers. In order to maintain that growth, some level of sacrifice is necessary. Experimentation must take place in order to learn. And some degree of failure is inescapable. The art of biomancery—everything I know—is built on that."

Nettles spit out the words, "Then your art is built on a mountain of the dead."

Brigga Lin looked pleadingly at Hope. "Surely you understand what I'm trying to say."

"I understand your explanation," Hope said coolly. "But remember that my entire village was sacrificed in one of those experiments. I will never accept that such a loss was necessary."

"Of course not," Brigga Lin said quickly. "But—"

"You are more like Alash than perhaps you care

to admit," said Hope. "In your quest for knowledge, you lose sight of the most important thing. People." It wasn't so long ago that she had been just as caught up in her own ideology. Her obsession with vengeance had cost the lives of many that might otherwise have been spared. It had also cost her hand and had gotten Red captured. But she knew Brigga Lin would have to discover it on her own, as Hope did. So she only said, "As your friend, I hope that in time, you come to understand what Nettles and *I* are saying."

She turned to Jilly, whose eyes were wide as she looked up at her. Was it confusion? Fear? Hope couldn't quite tell. "As I said, I don't think we need to go into it right now. You all need to eat and get some rest. We expect to intercept the biomancer tomorrow."

Nettles nodded tersely and guided Jilly by the shoulders toward the galley.

Brigga Lin lingered, but her posture was uncharacteristically hesitant. "Hope…"

"I still need to talk with Sadie. You go ahead and rest up. Someone will wake you when it's time for you to start tracking our quarry."

Brigga Lin nodded, then turned to go.

"Don't think I don't see it," Hope said after her. "The contradiction of utilizing your knowledge, which was purchased at so great a cost."

"How do you make peace with it?"

"It's too late to save those already lost. So all we can do is make sure that whatever was gained is put toward the greatest good. Although it seems impossible, perhaps someday it will balance out."

Brigga Lin smiled sadly. "I hope we will see that day together." Then she turned and went to join the others in the galley.

Hope made her way to the quarterdeck where

Sadie lounged against a barrel, a fishing line held negligently in one hand, the other end trailing off the stern. She rarely caught anything, but when she did, she gloated for days and insisted everyone on board share it, even if it was something so boney there was barely a mouthful for each person.

Sadie's eyes were closed, so Hope thought she might be dozing. Rather than wake her, Hope stared out at the horizon. The sea was grim and stormy and beautiful. She listened to the howl of the wind, the roar and hiss of the waves that crashed against the ship—*her* ship. She closed her eyes and felt the fine cold spray on her face, smelled the salt brine mixed with the scent of the oncoming storm. She loved it all. Sure, she wanted to save Red and make the biomancers answer for their crimes. But she would be lying to herself if she didn't acknowledge that in these past months under the name Dire Bane, a hunger for excitement and the thrill of battle had slowly grown within her. Feelings no true Vinchen would ever indulge.

"What's on your mind, Captain?" asked Sadie, her eyes still closed.

"Do you know what I was thinking as I got dressed in my cabin this morning?"

"Hmm, let's see...," said Sadie. "You were thinking that it's been far too long since you bent a cock, so maybe at the next port of call, you'll get yourself a whore like a proper sailor."

Hope smiled. She had gotten used to Sadie introducing the topic of sex into every conversation. She had thought it would be less frequent when she gave Sadie and Missing Finn their own cabin. But she had discovered that the opposite was true.

"I asked myself why I still wear this armor." She tapped her chest. The black leather armor was scarred in a dozen places and stitched up with leather thongs here and there. But any proper Vinchen armor bore the mark of battles, and she polished it regularly, so it was still strong, supple, and a deep, unfaded black.

"Because it makes your ass look good for the toms?" asked Sadie.

"It's a practical choice, of course," continued Hope, ignoring Sadie's response. "It's lightweight, and offers some protection without hindering my movements."

"I promise you, Red noticed the ass first," said Sadie. "Or maybe the legs. Your armor shows those off, too. Doesn't do much for the tits, but then, you don't have much to work with anyway."

"And there is some sentimental value," said Hope, resolute in keeping the conversation on track. "It was made by Hurlo the Cunning, the man who took me in and taught me so much."

She allowed herself to get lost in the memories of her youthful training. It had seemed so arduous at the time. Now she looked back on it with a strange fondness, particularly when she thought of her teacher's kind old face. She had hated him sometimes, and loved him at least as often.

"But I wonder," she said at last. "If it still suits me."

Sadie sighed and opened her eyes for the first time. "Are we talking grave, then?"

"Yes."

"Of course it still suits you. It's Vinchen armor, and you're Vinchen. Easy."

"But I'm not a Vinchen. Not really."

"Yeah, yeah, the muggy gafs can't handle a molly good as them so they won't let you join the crew. You and I both know that's all just so much balls and pricks."

Hope shook her head. "It's more than that now. I swore vengeance on Teltho Kan. The Vinchen code says that the only true vengeance is the death of the offender. If the warrior fails in this, better that he die than live in such dishonor. When I chose to spare Teltho Kan's life, and didn't take my own life after, I turned away from one of the most important tenets of the code."

"But Red killed him a few minutes later, didn't he?"

"That doesn't matter, Sadie. The choice had already been made. And I feel as though every choice I've made since then leads me even farther away from that path."

Hope stared down at the frothy, white wake of their ship. She watched it grow wider as it receded toward the horizon. One ship, like one choice, leaving a trail that rippled ever outward. Who could tell how far it would go?

"Does it feel bad?" asked Sadie.

"Does what feel bad?"

"Whatever it is you're becoming."

Hope paused. "These past months have been hard. But they've also been some of the most wonderful I have ever known. As much as I miss Red, I feel like I have finally found a family of sorts. More than I did on Galemoor, and even more than when Carmichael captained this ship. What we are doing feels more right than anything I have ever done before."

"The life of a pirate agrees with you more than any of us could have guessed," said Sadie. "Maybe you should stop fighting it so much."

"Am I fighting it?" Hope mused. "I suppose I am to some degree. I find myself getting...excited for conflict. But that's something I was taught is bad to feel."

"No feelings are bad," said Sadie. "They're just feelings. And if you feel something that makes you more alive, why in all hells wouldn't you run with it?" She squinted up at Hope. "Maybe you *should* put that armor aside for a spell if it keeps shaming you. Ain't no room for poncey stuff like that in the life of Dire Bane, champion of the people."

"Maybe you're right," said Hope. "Perhaps I've been clinging to something from the past that's holding me back."

"Get yourself a captain's hat and coat to make you feel like a proper pirate." Sadie tapped her nose and winked. "It might distract a bit from your flat-chestedness, too."

———

Hope would have to wait on getting a hat and coat until the next time they made port. In the meantime, she decided to replace the top half of her armor with the loose, white linen shirt favored by many sailors. It wasn't the most practical decision, since they would most likely be engaging in close combat the next day. But she felt that a gesture of some kind was in order.

She was astonished at what a difference such a simple change made. As she walked the decks the next morning, the wind ruffled her sleeves and braced against her skin in a way that made her blood surge. She felt an almost childlike freedom, and for the first time, she allowed herself to revel in it.

"Captain?"

Jilly stood at a respectful distance, her back straight and arms at her sides. No doubt two years in the navy had drilled that stance into her.

Hope smiled, trying to put her at ease. "What is it, Jilly?"

"Finn says the storm is nearly on us, sir. He wants to know, should we batten down or press ahead?"

Hope decided to let the *sir* go. Like the posture and salute, it would fade in time. "Tell him we'll press ahead. Then go wake Brigga Lin and send her to assist Finn. She'll be our bearing in the storm."

"Yes, sir." Jilly saluted and turned smartly on her heel. But then she stopped and looked back at Hope.

"Was there something else?" asked Hope.

"Oh," said Jilly. "Uh...well...I don't understand how you can call her a friend." She bit her lip. "Brigga Lin, I mean. Sir."

"I knew who you meant. And I understand why it seems strange to you. Brigga Lin is not like the rest of us. Raised in wealth, trained as a biomancer. Both things we've learned to hate, or at least distrust. And she certainly doesn't make it easy to like her. But as aloof as she might seem, she cares a great deal about the welfare of those she considers companions. Watch her carefully, and you might be surprised to discover she's more like us than you first thought."

"Do you think *we're* alike?" asked Jilly. "I mean, you and me?"

Hope smiled again as she thought back to when she was that age, looking with awe at Hurlo, desperate to gain whatever it was that made him so magnificent. He had seemed larger than life back then. Did Jilly see her the same way?

"In some ways we are a lot alike," she told the girl. "Now, run along. I'm sure Finn is anxious to hear back."

Jilly saluted again, then left.

Hope turned to the south and saw the thick bank of seething, purplish clouds bearing down on them. She watched the lightning fork through the sky and counted the seconds until the rumble of thunder. Not long now.

The storm overtook them before they had the
biomancer's ship in sight. The sky grew as dark
as twilight and the wind came strong and capricious. The storm also brought a steady cold rain.
Not the fat, heavy drops that came farther north.
Southern storms brought thin sheets that hissed
spitefully as they drenched everything in a biting
chill.

Under normal circumstances, Hope would have
struck as much as half the canvas in a storm like
this. But if they did that now, they might lose all
the headway they'd gained, and along with it, any
chance of catching their quarry before it reached
Vance Post, their most likely destination. As the
third-largest island in the empire, Vance Post had
anywhere from three to five imperial war frigates
docked and ready to deploy. The *Kraken Hunter*
couldn't take on three frigates at once, even with
all their tricks and tactics. They would have to
catch this ship before it reached Vance Post. So
they stayed at full sail and Hope watched the rigging, and listened attentively to the creak of the
masts. Either they would catch their quarry, or the
storm would tear them apart.

After her inspection, Hope made her way across
the rain-swept deck to the helm. Missing Finn
held the wheel with white-knuckled hands, his
weathered face pinched as rain dripped from the
tip of his nose. Nearby, Brigga Lin held an umbrella
made from white waxed canvas stretched over a
wooden frame.

"I offered to share," said Brigga Lin, inclining her
head to her umbrella.

"A little rain never hurt no one," said Finn.

"Not rain itself," said Brigga Lin. "But one can

develop a range of illnesses from prolonged exposure to cold, wet environments."

"That's what the grog is for," said Finn.

"Not before a battle, though," said Hope. "I need your wits sharp."

"Of course not, Captain," said Finn, perhaps a little too quickly. "I'm dry as a dream. Well…" He wiped at his streaming face with his thick hand. "You know, on the *inside*."

Hope decided not to press the issue. Even with a weakness for grog, Finn was still the best sailor on the ship.

"Aren't you cold?" asked Brigga Lin. "You're not even wearing your armor."

Hope grinned. "I was raised in the Southern Isles. I don't get cold."

Brigga Lin sniffed. "Well, *I'll* continue to enjoy some nominal dryness, if you two salty sea dogs don't mind."

"Are you able to track the ship in this storm?" asked Hope.

She nodded. "They seem to be slowing down."

"It's the safe thing to do," said Finn. "If the ship is as big as that smith said, you don't want to lose control of it in a storm this fussy."

"Can you get a sense of exactly how far ahead they are?" asked Hope.

"I'll try." Brigga Lin closed her eyes, unconsciously spinning her umbrella so that droplets spun out in a pinwheel. A slight frown creased her face. "Approximately eight miles." Her frown deepened. "Wait, no, ten." Her frown fell into a pout. "Or maybe it is eight." She opened her eyes. "Sorry, I've never tried something like this before. It seems to be shifting between two distances, but I probably just need more practice."

"It's alright," said Hope. "At least we have a general idea."

"If it's eight miles, we should overtake her within the hour," said Finn. "Assuming we don't drown first."

"I'll let the others know," said Hope.

"Can *I* do it, Captain?"

Hope looked up and saw Jilly sitting on the main yard above them, her bare feet dangling.

"What are you doing up there in this weather?" asked Brigga Lin disapprovingly.

"Sat up in the crow's nest in worse storms than this when I sailed with the *Guardian*." A certain nonchalantly boastful tone crept into Jilly's voice that reminded Hope of Red. "A bit of rain was no excuse to leave your post." She winked at Finn. "Anyway, that's what the grog is for."

She dropped down to the deck. "You want me to tell everyone to beat to quarters, Captain?"

Hope looked inquiringly at Finn.

"I think it's one of them imperial navy terms."

"On a large ship with a big crew," said Jilly, "they pound this *huge* drum to let everybody know it's time to get to battle stations."

"I'm afraid we don't have a drum, and the rest of the crew wouldn't know the significance anyway," said Hope. "So just tell them to get ready."

"Aye, aye, Captain." Jilly gave her a sharp salute and hurried off, her bare feet slapping on the wet wood of the deck.

"The next time we're in port, remind me to get some shoes for that girl." Hope pursed her lips. "And maybe a drum."

"Do you really think we need one?" asked Finn.

"No, but I think it would make her happy to beat on it."

Finn grinned. "Aye, Captain."

A half hour later, the cargo ship came into view over
the starboard bow, heading east-northeast. She was
easy enough to spot, with lanterns lit at her bow and
stern. The endless curtain of rain made it difficult to
make out details, but from what Hope could tell, the
smith's description was dead-on.

As Filler, Nettles, Sadie, and Jilly trimmed the
sails to slow down the *Kraken Hunter*, Finn turned
to Hope and Brigga Lin.

"Why's she all lit up, I wonder."

"To see where they're going?" asked Brigga Lin.

Finn shook his head. "Those lanterns won't do
more than let other people see you."

"Maybe they're afraid another ship will run into
them?"

"Not likely out here," said Finn.

Hope was only half listening to the conversation
as she trained her spyglass on the cargo ship's deck.
She wanted to size up their crew. Once the ship's
sails and rigging were disabled with chain shot, the
battle would be decided by close combat. She wanted
to know exactly what they would be up against. Her
heart gave a lurch of excitement when she saw a
white-hooded form yelling animatedly at the helmsman. Of course, no true Vinchen would allow themselves such emotional indulgence. But she found
herself less and less concerned by that, and promised
herself that there would be one less biomancer in the
world by the end of the day.

She watched the crew of the cargo ship begin to
scurry around the deck in a panic.

"They've spotted us," she told Finn. "No point
being coy now. Take us north-northwest, and bring
us around her port side."

The storm was getting stronger. Thunder boomed

close and loud. The lightning lit up the ash-colored sky above in flickering bursts.

"Filler and Nettles, to the grapple guns," called Hope. "If we disable them on the first pass, maybe we can take them before the full strength of the storm is on us."

Finn eyed the swaying masts anxiously. "That would be good."

Hope slapped his sodden back and grinned. "I'd hate for you to get bored, Mr. Finn."

Finn eyed her speculatively. "I wonder if Sadie the Pirate Queen has been rubbing off on you."

Hope laughed, a spontaneous burst that surprised her as much as it surprised her crew. "You may have something there, Mr. Finn. Now, hard to starboard, if you please."

"Aye, aye, Captain."

There was a small flash on the cargo ship, and a streak of sooty orange light cut up into the stormy sky.

"Distress flare," said Finn as he brought the *Kraken Hunter* around. They were running parallel to the cargo ship, a quarter of a mile between them, but closing rapidly.

"Why would they do that?" mused Hope. "For any chance passersby?" She frowned. "Or else..."

"Hope, the life force is split," said Brigga Lin.

"What do you mean, *split*?"

Brigga Lin pointed off the starboard bow to the cargo ship. "It's there. But it's also there." She pointed off the port side. "I couldn't tell before because they were in line, but that's why I was getting conflicting distances. There's a second ship."

Hope turned her glass to the port side and saw it through the murky rain: an imperial war frigate bearing down on them at top speed.

"Piss'ell, I should have realized!" said Finn.

"*That's* why they're all lit up. So they wouldn't get separated from their escort in this storm."

"I need solutions, not blame," said Hope tersely.

"Is it bigger than the *Guardian*?" asked Jilly from her perch on the main yard.

"No," said Hope. "A little smaller, actually. But we could never have survived a head-on attack. The ghost ship, the mirage cloaking. We needed those elements. Those all take time—something we don't have."

Lightning stabbed across the sky, followed almost immediately by a hard clap of thunder.

"We could run," said Finn, just loud enough for Hope to hear him over the rain. "We could lose them in this storm easy."

"Abandon those girls to the experiments of biomancers?" she asked quietly.

"I don't like it either, but what other options do we have? You and I both know those guns could turn us to driftwood before ours even get in range."

Hope continued to watch the frigate. It would reach them well before they reached the cargo ship. There was a small flash from the bow, and a cannonball splashed less than fifty yards from their port side. A warning shot.

"It may be smaller than the *Guardian*, but I reckon it's at least as well armed," said Finn. "Looks to be twelve-pounders for bow-chasers. Likely twenty-four-pounders on the broadside, then. They'll be in range in another couple of minutes."

Hope collapsed her glass and nodded. Her body buzzed with the thrill of danger, but she felt calm. "Nettles and Filler, strike the remaining sails. Sadie, strike our colors and run up the white flag."

"Captain?" Finn looked astonished, rain still streaming down his face. The rest of the crew stared at her as well.

Hope turned to Jilly. "Go tell Alash to close all the gun ports."

Jilly saluted, but without her usual sharpness.

"Then," continued Hope, "tell him that he gets to try his lightning experiment after all."

6

$\mathcal{T}$he narrow room was filled with six thunderous gunshots in rapid succession, each flaring up
for a moment and followed by the acrid smell of
gunpowder.

Too noisy, too bright, and too pissing stinky,
thought Red as he placed the now-empty revolver on
the small table in front of him.

He was several levels underground beneath the
palace. People mistakenly thought the important
things—things that changed the empire—happened
at the top of the palace. But Red knew the real stuff
happened down here. This was where the biomancers conducted many of their experiments, and where
they housed most of their weapons and creatures.

"An excellent grouping," said Chiffet Mek, the
biomancer responsible for Red's weapons training.
He inspected the target and pointed to the small
cluster of holes in the center of the head. "I expect
that once you adjust to the particulars of using firearms, the spread will be so small, it will only appear
as one hole."

"I don't *like* firearms," said Red. "What's wrong
with my throwing blades?"

"Nothing is wrong with them." Chiffet Mek's
voice sounded like pieces of rusty metal rubbed
together. "Every weapon has its use. In close range,

with a limited number of targets and a need for stealth, your throwing blades are an ideal choice. But there will be times when you have a large number of targets at longer range and without a need for stealth. That is when firearms are the ideal choice."

"You still haven't told me who these targets are going to be." Red began to reload the revolver.

"Enemies of the empire," said Mek.

"Whoever you decide needs to die."

"Naturally. Now go again. This time, make sure you don't pull to the left when you squeeze the trigger. You may need to counter slightly with your other hand. But don't overdo it."

Red reloaded the revolver and fired another six shots, taking a little more time between each one. This time, only the last one strayed from the center slightly, so that it looked like one large hole and one small hole.

"Better. But you lost your focus on the last shot," said Mek.

Red affected a disinterested tone as he began to reload again. "Say, you didn't let one of the little beasts you keep down here into the city, did you?"

After learning about that woodworker's fate, he'd asked around. Servants, imps, anyone who ever left the palace on a regular basis and liked to gossip. Apparently, it was not the first incident where small groups of local wags had recently turned up dead. It had been happening for weeks now. It got him thinking that maybe the biomancers were behind it. Such underhandedness in the shadows was exactly their style.

"Beasts?" asked Chiffet Mek. "Not that I am aware of. Why do you ask?"

"Seems there's been a string of murders in the city. Nasty work, I hear. Always with a small blade of some kind, but nothing's ever been recovered at the

scene. So maybe it's claws? And nothing is ever stolen from the victims. The imps can't seem to figure it
out, although that could be because it's been exclusively regular folk getting killed, and we know imps
can't be bothered to make much effort on account of
that lot."

Chiffet Mek's lips quirked to one side beneath
the shadow of his hood. "And you believe one of our
experiments is responsible?"

Red shrugged dramatically. "The prince is getting
a bit concerned, is all. Near as I can tell, he doesn't
know much about what you do here in these basements. If these deaths keep up, he might come down
to investigate and find things you'd rather he didn't."

Red knew it was a bit of a gamble to bait Mek
like this. But he felt deep in his bilge that it had to
be something the biomancers let loose in the city.
He knew it would be difficult to prove, but maybe if
he threatened an imperial inspection of their more
secret activities, they'd call their beastie back home
and nobody else would die.

Chiffet Mek didn't take the bait, however, and
instead changed the subject. "You seem to have
developed quite a bond with His Highness."

"Say, I hope it doesn't make you nervous." Red
fired off all six rounds with a jaunty flourish, leaving
one hole in the target. "Me having my own friends in
high places, that is."

"On the contrary," said Mek. "Progul Bon is quite
pleased."

That shook Red's confidence slightly. Anytime
he pleased a biomancer, it never seemed like a good
thing. Especially not a schemer like Progul Bon.

"You better not do any of your biomancery on
Leston," he said ominously.

"Save your empty threats," said Chiffet Mek, with
the closest thing to a smile Red had ever seen. "Rest

assured we will not *do biomancery* on the prince. When he was born, the emperor had us swear not to alter him in any way with our arts."

Red knew that biomancers couldn't lie, or they would lose their powers. He didn't know why that was true, but it was one of the few things he had on them. And while he may not have pinned the murders on the biomancers, the news that Leston was safe from them was a bigger relief than he expected.

———

The following day, he was back in the secret basement levels of the palace, this time with Ammon Set, the head of the Council of Biomancery. They stood in a room without any light. Even with his enhanced sight, Red couldn't see. But just to make absolutely certain, Ammon Set had blindfolded him as well.

"We enhanced more than just your sight, Rixidenteron," Ammon Set said, his dry, dusty voice echoing in the pitch-black chamber. "Your other senses have been heightened as well. But you rely so much on your sight that your hearing, smell, and touch have not had a chance to develop as strongly. We will begin to correct that now."

"What about taste?" asked Red. "Is that enhanced, too?"

"Yes. Although there are few practical applications for that."

"Identifying poisons, maybe?"

Ammon Set gave a weary sigh. "I suppose..."

"If I'm kissing a molly, would I be able to tell what she had for dinner?"

"Probably, but—"

"What if I kissed her cunt? Could I tell if—"

"Let us continue with the exercise at hand."

"Sure, Ammon, old pot. Sure." Red smiled broadly

enough that Set could hear it in his voice. "What are we doing here in the dark?"

"Your task is to reach me on the other side of the room."

"Simple as sideways," said Red. "I can hear which direction you're in." He began walking quickly toward Ammon Set's voice. But then something hard slammed into his shin.

"Piss'ell!" he yelped.

"Something wrong?" Now it was Ammon Set's turn to have a smile in his voice.

"There's something in my way. Felt like a pissing table edge with its legs cut short."

"Yes," agreed Set. "In fact, there are *many* different things in your way. You must use your sense of hearing to avoid them. If you touch any of them, you must return to the other side of the room and try again."

"How am I supposed to *hear* a pissing table?" asked Red.

"Bats use a process called echolocation. By listening to the sound of their voice echo back from objects in the space, they can discern where those objects are located."

"Sounds like balls and pricks to me."

"Then you are in for a very long and painful afternoon."

Ammon Set was right. Red was in there for hours. He ran into things, stepped on things, and even banged his head on a few things hanging from the ceiling. He tried listening to his footsteps, his voice, and even hand claps. None of it seemed to work. Then, by accident, he discovered that if he clicked his tongue on the roof of his mouth, it was just loud enough and sharp enough that he *could* tell a difference if something was directly in front of him. He wasn't seeing the whole room, but by moving slowly, it was just enough warning to get him through the obstacle course.

"Well done," said Ammon Set.

Around the edges of his blindfold, Red could see that the room suddenly flared up with light. He closed his eyes as he took off the blindfold, and didn't open them until he had his smoked glasses on.

"I think that will be all for today," said Ammon Set. He was the only biomancer who didn't bother to hide his face under his hood. Patches of his skin looked like they were made of the same beige stone of the palace, and he was completely bald. He fixed his dull, colorless eyes on Red. "I trust you will be at the Annual Lord's Ball this evening?"

"The prince told me it was important."

"It is. You should go."

"Why?" Red had lost count of how many balls he'd been to, and they were all so dull that roping foolish lords into shell games was about the only way he could entertain himself. And they'd finally grown wise to that particular scheme. "How is this ball different from all the others?"

"Did you know," said Ammon Set, "that the Dark Mage could see the future?"

Red had learned that biomancers took an almost childlike delight in not directly answering questions that were put to them. He'd given up trying to fight it, so instead he sighed and said, "That's balls and pricks. Nobody can really predict the future. And anyway, didn't he go slippy?"

"It's true that his visions drove him mad," admitted Set. "But he wrote down many of his predictions while he was still capable of coherent thought. So far, all of them have come true."

"Like what?"

"He predicted his own death at the hands of Manay the True."

"He knew when and how he was going to die? That would make *anyone* slippy."

"The Dark Mage also predicted the uprising of the Jackal Lords that happened thirty years ago, as well as the withdrawal of the Vinchen order to the remote southern island of Galemoor."

"Not bad," admitted Red.

"He also predicted the invasion of Aukbontar as well."

Red's eyes narrowed. "Yeah, you gafs are real worried about that, aren't you? That's why you think you need me. Why you created coral spice to make people like me."

"It's why we have urgently explored every weaponized possibility of biomancery we can conceive of for the last twenty years," said Ammon Set. "In a desperate attempt to be ready to defend the empire when Aukbontar begins their invasion."

"I met someone from Aukbontar. Palla's a quality wag. If that's what most of them are like, it doesn't seem like anything to get worried about."

Ammon Set leaned in close. His breath smelled like old stone and dust.

"If you took every island in the empire and pressed them together into one great big land, it would still be only a third of the size of Aukbontar. Their armies are endless, highly trained, and ferocious. Their advancements in the mechanical sciences are beyond your comprehension. So yes, we are worried. You should be, too, Lord Pastinas, unless you want to see your precious New Laven crushed beneath their cold, merciless steel might."

"Why are you telling me all this?" asked Red.

Ammon Set turned his back on Red. As he walked toward the door, he said over his shoulder, "Go to the ball tonight, Lord Pastinas."

"Announcing Lord Pastinas of Hollow Falls!" boomed the head steward of the palace, a terminally serious old wrink who made Hume look like a merry prankster. It was his job to sit at the entrance to the ballroom and announce the name and title of each person as they entered.

One thing Red liked about all the lacy pomp was that the person arriving stood behind a velvet curtain until they were announced. Most people didn't take advantage of such potential for a dramatic entrance. But after Red's name was called, he swept out from behind the curtain with a gallant flourish.

"Thanks for that." He winked at the steward.

The steward replied with a withering look.

"Fancy a rematch on stones sometime?"

The head steward's jowls trembled. "Never again, my lord."

"Can't say I blame you."

The ballroom was one of the largest rooms in the palace, taking up most of the thirtieth floor. Tables were set with food along the perimeter, with chairs both at the tables and facing the center of the room, where a few of the braver lords and ladies were dancing to the tinkly strains of a string orchestra tucked away in one corner. Most of the guests stood in small clumps around the periphery, chatting and drinking wine.

Red made his way toward the wine table, but didn't get far before he heard a warm, lush voice say, "Quite a splendid ball, wouldn't you say, my Lord Pastinas?"

Red turned to see Lady Hempist in a silver gown cut so low, she was in danger of showing more than just her impressive cleavage.

He bowed slightly to her. "My lady, you look as delicious as ever."

She smiled, showing her pearl-white teeth. Red was always amazed at how lacies could keep their teeth as white as children's. He knew there were tiny brushes and powder involved. He had dim memories of doing it himself when his mother was still alive. But the streets of Silverback and Paradise Circle hadn't allowed him to maintain habits like that.

"And you look nearly respectable, my lord," said Lady Hempist lightly. "A clever deception."

Red plucked at his charcoal-gray frock coat. "Prince Leston pleaded with me to put on a jacket and cravat. Claimed it was the *ball of the season* or something like that. You know I can't stand to see my best wag fretful, so I did as His Highness commanded."

"Even ran a comb through your hair." She reached her hand up and brushed his bangs out of his eyes. She had a ring on every finger, and painted nails long enough to make it clear she was not someone who did work with her hands.

"More like the rake they use for the rock gardens."

"You've still got those tinted glasses of yours, though."

"So many lamps in the room," Red said truthfully. "Hurts my delicate eyes."

"I don't mind, my lord. Makes you seem aloof and mysterious. Almost unattainable."

He flashed a grin. "That's because I *am* unattainable, my lady."

"So you keep saying." She patted his cheek condescendingly. "It's quite adorable."

Red sighed. "You are impossible."

"I know it." Her eyes swept the ballroom, which was more crowded than Red had ever seen it. Apparently, even the minor lords and ladies from the outer islands trekked in for this particular ball. Red had no idea why, because it still seemed like every other ball he'd been to since arriving at Stonepeak.

"So what do you think of this *ball of the season*, my lord?" asked Lady Hempist, mimicking his mocking tone from earlier.

Red shrugged. "Not enough drugs, violence, or sex for my tastes." He wouldn't normally say something like that to one of the ladies of the palace, but Lady Hempist seemed determined to prove she could take anything he could dish out, so he'd see just how far he could push it. A part of him hoped she might storm off in a huff. It wasn't that he disliked her. In fact, he found her rather charming. And that was the problem. It was her appeal that made him uneasy. Like *he* was the one getting conned.

Instead of looking shocked, she gave him another pearl-studded smile and hooked her arm in his so that they stood side by side, looking at the gathering.

"You do us a disservice, my lord," she said. "Look more closely. There is Archlord Tramasta off in the corner, sniffing a fine white powder called cloud glass that he claims is medicinal, but I know from personal experience to be quite...invigorating."

Red examined the tall, gaunt archlord that he'd won a pair of boots from a few nights before and noticed an odd glaze to his eyes, with pupils that were unnaturally large. "Hmm, I see what you mean."

"And over there by the entree table," continued Lady Hempist, "Lord Weatherwight of Wake Landing seems to be doing some violence to that steamed lobster."

It was true that the portly, bearded man didn't seem to know how to get to the meat, and was making a mess of it with a mallet and knife. But Red shook his head. "I think you may be stretching the word to call that violence, my lady. Especially since the poor thing's already dead."

"Fine," she said, undaunted. "Perhaps there's less *physical* violence being done here than you're accustomed to, but what about violence of the heart?" She nodded over to where Leston stood in a dark blue frock coat, looking utterly bored as he sipped at his drink. "Observe Archlady Bashim, hovering nearby."

She stood near the prince in a high-buttoned, conservative pink gown. She kept turning suddenly, and Red realized she was trying to catch the prince's eye. Finally she gave up on subtlety, and walked over to him. Now that they'd been formally introduced, she could at least start a conversation with him. He nodded politely to her greeting, but then another lord came and spoke to him, and he turned away from her.

"Dear me, but that's cutting," sighed Lady Hempist dramatically. "It's as if she's back on the cliff gardens, but this time, her heart has been flung over the edge to splatter on the uncaring rooftops below."

"Okay," admitted Red. "I reckon that's a bit closer to violence."

"And as for the lack of sex…" Lady Hempist leaned in so close that her breasts pressed against his arm as she purred into his ear, "I'm certain you and I could correct that."

Clearly she was teasing him, and Red knew he needed to respond in some way. Either to retaliate in kind, which could escalate dangerously, or flee, which she might enjoy nearly as much. But just then, he was saved by perhaps the last person he ever expected to be saved by.

The orchestra went quiet and all heads turned expectantly to the ballroom entrance. The high steward's voice boomed in the sudden silence.

"Announcing, the Shining Light between the Dawn and the Dusk, the one chosen by God as the defender of the people of the Storm, His Imperial Majesty, Emperor Martarkis."

The orchestra burst into a processional march, and every head bowed low. Red followed suit a moment later, after Lady Hempist jabbed her elbow into his ribs.

This was why it was the ball of the season. Everyone came for a rare glimpse of the emperor. But why did Ammon Set think it was so important for him to be here? It certainly wasn't to be astonished by the power and majesty of the emperor. The old wrink moved painfully slow, as if he had to will each leg to rise and fall. His hair looked like strands of white silk. His skin was paper-thin, showing veins and sharp-angled bone beneath. His thick gold robes, embroidered with the imperial crest of a lightning bolt meeting a wave, seemed far too heavy for him to support. When he finally reached the golden chair at the far end of the ballroom, he collapsed into it with an exhausted wheeze.

Maybe that was what Set wanted him to see. If Aukbontar *did* invade, the empire wasn't exactly under the strongest leadership.

Once everyone stood straight again, and conversation resumed, Red murmured to Lady Hempist, "Piss'ell, but he looks like Death in his cups."

"Do you ever run out of those quaint little folk sayings?" asked Lady Hempist.

"Haven't yet." The moment he said that, he was reminded of a similar conversation he'd had with Nettles a long time ago. The combined discomfort and homesickness was more than he could take. He bowed to Lady Hempist and said, "Now, if you'll excuse me, I think the prince needs me for something."

She inclined her head, her eyes flashing. "Of course, my lord. I hope we can continue our plans for shoring up the missing components you feel make a successful ball at a later time."

Red forced a smile and hurried across the room to Leston, who hadn't signaled to him, but watched him approach with wry amusement.

"Has the dangerous outlaw Rixidenteron finally met his match?"

Red scowled as he bowed perfunctorily to the prince. "I don't know what her game is, but I think I'm losing."

"An astute observation," said Leston. "Lady Merivale Hempist is known to be a woman who is very good at getting what she wants. And at present, that seems to be you."

"Well, she will have to become a woman who is good at accepting that now and then, she *doesn't* get what she wants."

"Would it be so bad? She's clever, quite handsome, and her estates on Lesser Basheta are small but impeccably managed. By all accounts, she's an excellent match for you."

"There's only one match for me," said Red, unable to keep the sharpness from his voice.

Leston's expression softened. "Right. Your Bleak Hope."

"If I don't speak of her often, it's not because I don't care, or that I'm not thinking of her constantly. It's because it already hurts to be separated from her, and talking about her only makes it worse."

"I'm sorry, my friend," said Leston. "From everything you have described, she must be a remarkable woman."

Red's grin suddenly bloomed. "She is, quite possibly, the deadliest person in the world."

Leston laughed. "I hope someday to meet her."

"Preferably under friendly circumstances," said Red. "She's not overly fond of imperial authority."

"That seems a common theme among your friends," said the prince.

"Nothing personal, Your Highness. Poor people tend to hate the rich and powerful."

Leston's face brightened. "But with your help, perhaps that can change. What I have already learned from you about the plight of the common people has touched me deeply."

"I'm glad to hear it, Your Highness."

"That reminds me, apparently there was *another* murder last night."

"What does that make, five? Have you talked to your dad about it? Maybe he could push the imps harder to actually look into it?"

Leston's eyes strayed over to his father on the far side of the room. "I tried, but..."

They were silent for a moment.

"I think I understand the problem better, now that I've seen him," said Red. "How old is he?"

"Nearly a hundred and fifty."

"I thought that was just palace gossip. People exaggerating."

Leston shook his head. "He was one hundred and twenty-eight when I was born."

"How'd he manage that? Your mom must be quite a beauty to make a cock that old take notice."

Leston smiled sadly. "I suppose she is."

"How come I never see her around the palace? Think she'll come tonight?"

"Palace life was too strenuous for her. She retired to a small estate on Sunset Point when I was a boy. I visit her now and then, but she never comes here."

"I reckon there's a story there," said Red.

"You're probably right. But I doubt she'll ever tell it."

"We should go visit her. I'll bet I could wheedle it out of her."

Leston attempted a smile that didn't quite make it to his eyes. "Perhaps you could, my friend."

The general buzz of conversation suddenly dipped, and the orchestra ground to a halt, not with the clean precision of before, but as if every one of them suddenly forgot how to play. At the same time, heads turned toward the high steward again. His normally stoic features looked strained, and there was a sheen of sweat on his brow.

"Announcing..." He hesitated, and glanced behind the curtain, as if seeking confirmation of something. Then he swallowed and continued. "Citizen Nea Omnipora, ambassador of Aukbontar."

It sounded like a gust of wind blowing through the ballroom from all the shocked whispers that floated around.

"Ambassador of *Aukbontar*?" Leston looked unbelieving.

Then a woman stepped from behind the curtain. She was thin and graceful, with dark skin that contrasted strikingly with her brightly colored clothing. She didn't wear a gown, however. Instead, she wore a fitted lavender jacket with wide, pointed shoulders, and light blue loose-fitting pants that tapered down to a tight fit around her slender ankles. On her feet were flat-bottomed silk slippers that matched the jacket. Her long, jet-black hair was twisted into thick braids that ran down her back. Her calm demeanor looked neither cold *nor* merciless. Maybe Ammon Set was wrong about the Aukbontarens.

She glided placidly across the room, as if she didn't notice or care that everyone in the room stared at her. The only one who didn't look shocked to see her was the emperor. Instead, he just looked confused. When Ambassador Omnipora reached him, she bowed with one foot forward, like she was beginning a dance.

"Your Imperial Majesty," she said in a clear, loud voice, made liquid and musical with her accent. "I come at the behest of the Great Congress of Aukbontar as an ambassador of peace, so that our two peoples might find mutual benefit."

The emperor only stared at her. She might as well have been speaking in her native tongue for all the sense she seemed to make to him.

She paused a moment. If she was surprised or alarmed at his reception, she didn't show it. "I have traveled far, Your Majesty, and hope I can count upon your hospitality during my stay in your fair country."

"This molly is pat as paws," Red murmured to Leston. Then he realized Leston wasn't standing next to him anymore. Instead the prince was hurrying over to the ambassador.

"We are of course *delighted* to welcome the ambassador of Aukbontar." Leston bowed lower than Red had ever seen him bow. "I am Prince Leston, heir to the imperial throne. I'm sure that after such a long and arduous journey, you must be weary. It would be both an honor and a pleasure if you would allow me to see to your accommodations personally."

Despite her pat confidence, there was a flash of relief in the ambassador's eyes. "You are most kind, Prince Leston. It is *I* who am honored."

The prince held out his arm and she accepted it. Red thought it was interesting that this woman from another country was well versed in such minor lacy customs, when the common folk of this empire were unfamiliar with them. He remembered when Alash had done the same thing for Hope and she had been completely baffled.

Leston gave Red a meaningful look. "Lord Pastinas, would you be so kind as to accompany us?"

"Of course, Your Highness."

The crowds parted wordlessly as Leston led the ambassador out of the ballroom, with Red trailing a little behind them. As they left the ballroom, he heard the orchestra cautiously begin playing again.

"I must apologize for my father's rude reception," Leston said once they were out in the empty hallway. "He is old and unaccustomed to surprises."

Ambassador Omnipora frowned slightly. "Surprise? So neither of my messengers reached you?"

"Messengers? When did you send them?"

"I sent one before leaving Aukbontar, and another when my team and I arrived at Stonepeak early this morning."

"Strange. I heard nothing about it." Then he gave her a quizzical look. "What do you mean by 'team'? Like a team of horses?"

"Perhaps I use the wrong word...'Retinue'?"

"Ah, yes. Of course. And where are they now?"

"They stay at an inn named the Call to Arms, awaiting my return for further instructions. When we arrived, the innkeeper mentioned there was an important ball this evening, so I left my team in charge of transferring our cargo from the ship to the inn and hurried over here."

"They shall all be accommodated at the palace, of course. I will see to it while Lord Pastinas fetches them and your cargo."

"I am quite capable of fetching them myself," said the ambassador. "After all, I have just come from there."

"Yes, but that was before you so grandly announced your identity. Now, I'm sorry to say, you're in quite a bit of danger."

"From whom?"

Leston looked pained. "Aukbontar is greatly feared by my people. Hated, even, by some."

"But we have done nothing to you."

"There is... an elite group here that holds a great deal of sway over my father and therefore over the empire. They see the might of Aukbontar as a threat, and believe you are determined to invade and conquer us."

Red was surprised the prince knew about the biomancers' fears. How could he know that, but not have known about the countless people who had died so horribly because of those fears?

"What nonsense! I am here to *prevent* hostilities." The ambassador looked alarmed, but only for a moment. Then her calm demeanor reasserted itself. "If we set up mutually beneficial trade treaties, I am confident that tensions between our people will greatly diminish."

"I hope you're right," said the prince. "And in the meantime, we must keep you alive. You and your retinue will be safest in the palace. They would not dare to make an attempt on your life here. But out there in the city, they could lay the blame on thieves or dissidents. Even now they could be setting traps for you. Leaving the palace, particularly at night, would be extremely dangerous for you."

"My people will not be fetched by some stranger. They will only come at my direct order."

Leston sighed. "Then at least let Lord Pastinas accompany you."

"If what you say is true, I'm not sure one man will make much difference," said the ambassador.

"Trust me, Ambassador." Red stuck his head between them. "I'm better than a squad of imps."

"Imps?" she asked.

"Imperial soldiers," said Leston. "You will find

that Lord Pastinas is...rather eccentric. But there is no one in the palace I trust more."

"Your Highness!" said Red. "You'll ruin my reputation!"

Leston clasped his hand. "Please take care of her, my friend."

"I'll treat her like she was you, old pot."

"Except perhaps not the jokes," Leston said with a concerned frown. "Your manner with ladies can be somewhat...coarse at times."

"Why, princey, what a thing to say!" Red looked at him with mock horror, then patted him reassuringly on the back. He'd never seen the prince this concerned about someone before, or frankly this interested in politics. "You go and make the beds. I promise I will get her back to you as lovely as you found her, all international incidents avoided."

"Er, yes, thank you, Lord Pastinas. Good luck, then."

"Luck is never a thing I need, Your Highness." Red bowed to him.

Leston turned back to the ambassador. "Until we meet again, Ambassador Omnipora." Then he hurried down a side passage.

Red offered the ambassador his arm. "Shall we be off to defy politics and death on the hard streets of Stonepeak, my lady?"

"I'm not nobility, Lord Pastinas," she said as she slipped her arm through his and they continued down the hall. "My father was a machinist."

"Not sure what that is, but it sounds fancy."

She smiled, showing him the same bright white teeth as the lacies. "It's not. He worked with his hands. Honest labor."

"How'd you end up in politics, then?"

"We have no nobility in Aukbontar," she said. "No rigid class system. Each person is judged on their individual worth. My skills in language and diplomacy made me a natural choice for this position."

"No nobility? Everybody just does what they're good at? Sounds sunny to me."

Her smooth brow furrowed. "I thought I was adept in the language of the Empire of Storms, but you use words in a way that confuses me. 'Sunny' describes a day in which the sun shines brightly, does it not?"

"Words can have many meanings. You only learned what the common folk call lacy speak. In Paradise Circle, we have our own way of talking. The talk of *real* people."

"I have not heard of this Paradise Circle, but it sounds lovely."

"It is, in its way." Red's eyes grew distant as images of the Drowned Rat and Gunpowder Hall came to mind. Then he shook his head and grinned. "If you're real lucky, I'll take you there sometime. I know a few wags from Aukbontar down there. Maybe you know them."

"Aukbontar is a very big place, my lord."

"That's what I hear. One great big land, like a hundred islands, all mashed together. Not sure how you get from place to place with no waterways. But listen, since you don't go in for all that lacy balls and pricks, let's drop the 'my lords.' They're newly acquired and frankly, I don't think they suit me."

"Very well, what shall I call you?"

"My friends call me Red."

"And am I a friend?" she asked archly.

"Everyone's a friend," he replied. "Until they're not."

"An admirable stance, friend Red."

"Oh, I think you'll find that I'm all sorts of admirable."

When they reached the moonlit cobblestone

courtyard, Red took off his smoked glasses with relief and pocketed them in his jacket. He still hadn't found a way to keep his nose and ears from getting sore after wearing them for any length of time. Now that they were out of the stabbing lamplight of the palace, he was able to truly open his eyes and look around. The night sky was like day to him, the countless points of starlight as bright as tiny suns. He saw the guards by the tall front gate and guided the ambassador over to them.

"Evening, my wags," he said cheerfully. "This here's an important visitor and personal guest of Prince Leston. She and I are going to fetch the rest of her crew. When we get back with a whole group of unfamiliar-looking foreigners, I'd appreciate it if you'd let us in all chum and larder and not go shooting us. Keen?"

"Yes, my lord," they all said, loud and clear. These imps had seen Red escort the prince several times now into the city, and they were used to him. Red had to admit, they weren't bad toms either. Mostly local boys, with mollies and kids of their own.

Red pulled the guard captain aside and said quietly to him, "Say, old pot, not that I'm pining for trouble, but do you think I could borrow your revolver while I'm out? Give it back to you soon as we're through, I promise."

"My lord," the captain said gravely, "you spared my life when you had no just cause to do so."

"Did I?" Red squinted at the man's face, trying to remember.

"When those two...women attacked the palace. You followed after. Before I realized who you were, I tried to take a shot at you."

"Oh, yeah!" said Red. "But you missed by a lot, if I remember right."

"Even so, my lord, you could have killed me

right then, but you spared my life and made sure my daughter still has a father. So as far as I'm concerned, you can borrow my revolver anytime you like." He drew his gun and held it handle first to Red.

"Much obliged, Captain...What's your name?"

"Murkton, my lord."

"Captain Murkton, this is real sunny of you, and I won't forget it. Now, let's hope I don't need to use it."

"Indeed, my lord." Murkton signaled to the guards to open the thick iron gates.

Red tucked the gun into the back of his trousers so it was hidden beneath his jacket. He wished he had his longcoat and throwing blades, but this would have to do. Besides, as nice as it was to see the prince interested in someone or something for once, the wag was probably overreacting. How likely was it that someone would try to kill the ambassador already, not an hour after she'd been announced?

7

*I*t was all up to Jilly.

Well, okay, it was all up to Jilly, Alash's experiment, and a fair bit of luck.

Jilly moved cautiously up the rigging of the mainmast. Not because the height made her nervous. She'd conquered that fear well over a year ago. And sure, rain was pouring down so hard, it felt like God was pumping it straight from the ocean. But that wasn't the reason either. No, it was because Captain Bane had made it clear that if any of the soldiers saw so much as a shaky ratline, it would be over for all of them. The whole crew had put their trust in her, and she'd be damned to the wettest hells imaginable if she let this go leeward. So she made her way up the mainmast slow and steady, keeping as much canvas and mast between herself and the soldiers below as she could.

She had an iron rod tied to her back, a long, thin chain coiled crosswise around her middle, and a thick roll of parchment tucked into the chain. All the weight around her middle made it hard to breathe, but with so much water streaming from the sky, there wasn't much air to be had anyway. It was a bit noisy, too. But there was so much racket from the crashing waves, the booming thunder, and the shouting soldiers that the rattling sound of the chain was lost.

Far below, Captain Bane stood and watched impassively as soldiers swarmed her deck. Beside her stood Brigga Lin, Missing Finn, Filler, Nettles, Sadie, and even Alash. Just before the frigate came alongside them, he'd hurriedly explained to Jilly what needed to be done. Now it was up to her to do it.

As she climbed, she faintly heard their voices below.

"Which one of you is the captain?" said one of the lieutenants warily.

"I am." Bane's voice was calm and steady.

The lieutenant walked over to her, his revolver held stupidly in one hand. The younger officers liked to swagger around like they could fire off a gun single-handedly, which even Jilly knew wasn't possible with any sort of accuracy.

"A woman?" The lieutenant cocked his head to one side, as if that would somehow change what he was seeing.

"Very observant of you, lieutenant," Bane said without a trace of humor.

He scowled at her. "Where's the rest of your crew?"

"This is everyone."

"Damned if it is."

"Search the ship if you like."

"I think I will." He motioned to a few of the soldiers. "You, and you, take the officers' quarters. You and you, take the bow. And you three, take the holds." He watched them go for a moment, then added, "And beware of ambushes around corners!"

Just as the search began on deck, Jilly reached the top of the mast. She wrapped the tip in parchment. Alash had explained that this would help insulate the *Kraken Hunter* from the bulk of the electrical charge. Then she fastened the iron rod to the mast with one end of the chain.

The other end of the chain had a small grappling hook. All she needed to do was throw the grappling hook so that it attached to the naval frigate's mast. It seemed so simple when he'd explained it. But as she straddled the main-royal yard, she saw that both the *Kraken Hunter*'s mast and the frigate's mast swayed in a wind so strong that the rain fell on a diagonal. She'd have to time it to when they were leaning in toward each other. But the lightning that flickered hungrily above reminded her that she couldn't take too long. Alash had said that if the rod drew lightning while she was still holding the chain, *she* would be the one to explode.

Calm yourself, Little Bee, she commanded herself. Funny how, in moments of worry, that's still how she thought of herself. What Red called her, 'cause she was always so busy. She pictured him. His sparkling eyes. His firm grip on her wrist as he showed her the way she needed to follow through when throwing a knife. He'd remind her to take a breath and look at her target. *Don't look at it like you're trying to throw something at it,* he'd say. *Look at it like you're already there. Feel yourself there, touching it, connected to it, one unbroken line between you and the target.*

She saw it. That unbroken line. She was already there.

She threw.

The grappling hook sailed up in an arc, straight and true. Then a gust of wind pushed it off course and it caught the frigate's mizzen topgallant yard.

Was the yard close enough? She didn't know. Alash had said the mast...

"No one else on board, sir," she faintly heard one of the soldiers report to the lieutenant.

"All right. Get these people in irons and down into the hold, then make ready to raise the sails."

As Captain Bane had predicted, they planned to

claim the ship as a prize. It was why they boarded her instead of just blowing her out of the water. A sailor didn't earn much pay, but everyone on board was entitled to a share when a captured ship was sold.

Before the sailors could follow their orders, Bane spoke up.

"Wait, Lieutenant. I request that I may be permitted to present my sword to your captain. That is the custom, isn't it?"

The lieutenant didn't look pleased, but turned to one of his soldiers. "Fetch the captain to accept the formal surrender."

The soldier saluted, then hurried back across the gangplank to the frigate.

"Where would we be without our customs?" asked Bane. "Isn't that right, Lieutenant?"

Jilly knew this was her chance to fix things. The lightning seemed to be groping blindly toward the iron rod above her, but she ignored that and grabbed on to the chain with both hands. She slowly made her way, hand over hand, across the gap to the frigate. Her calluses were thick from her time at sea, but even so, the chain dug into her palms. Her feet dangled high above the churning water between the ships. The wind buffeted at her, sending her swaying side to side. One gust blew so hard, she could feel a small movement along the chain as the grappling hook gave a little. She froze for a moment. She hadn't considered whether it would hold her weight. But she was already halfway across, so it was too late now. And, she reminded herself, if she was still holding the chain when the lightning struck, falling would be the least of her troubles. That got her moving again.

Finally she reached the frigate's mizzen topgallant yard. She hooked her legs around the mast, her butt resting on the yard. Then she took the knife from her belt and pried off the grappling hook. There was a moment when she felt the full weight of the long chain, and it nearly pulled her down. But she quickly slammed the hook into the thick wood of the mast.

Now all she needed to do was get off this ship before the lightning struck.

She slid down the mast to the topsail yard. Below on the deck of the frigate, all eyes were on the *Kraken Hunter*, where Bane was formally presenting her sword to their captain.

Jilly's eyes scanned the rigging around her until they fell upon a nice stout sheet nearby.

She'd always wanted to try that...

———

Hope held the sheathed Song of Sorrows out to the frigate's captain, a squat, sweaty man with the florid complexion of someone who drank too much. Every muscle in her body cried out to fight. But while she and her crew could take the men on her ship, there were at least four times as many on the frigate, ready to spill across the gangplank at the first sign of trouble. And then of course there were the cannons that would tear her hull to pieces in a matter of minutes. So she had to have faith in Jilly and Alash, stall for time, and suffer this baboon of a captain for a little bit longer.

"I present to you the Song of Sorrows," she intoned.

"Very nice," the captain said impatiently. He tried to take it from her, but she bowed, which moved the sword out of his reach.

"This sword was forged centuries ago," she continued, her voice almost singsong, "by the powerful biomancer Xunera Ray for the legendary Vinchen,

Manay the True, so that he might slay the dread Dark Mage and end his reign of terror on the empire."

"Uh-huh," said the captain. He rolled his eyes but seemed unwilling to suffer the indignity of bending over in front of his men so that he could take the sword from her.

"Its blade has no match in sharpness or elegance," droned Hope. "It is said that by some art lost to the mists of time, it remembers every victim it takes, as if the very steel itself is alive. Its song strikes fear into all who hear it, its—"

At last there was a hiss and crackle from above, then the frigate's mizzenmast exploded. Flaming splinters as big as spears flew in all directions, impaling imperial sailors, shredding sails, and setting fire to the ship. Men ran screaming, trying to beat out the flames or pull long skewers of wood from their bodies.

"What in God's name—" The captain turned to his ship. That was a mistake. A moment later, he stared down at the end of the Song of Sorrows, which protruded from his chest.

Hope gritted her teeth as the surge of the captain's death went up her arm. She had never stabbed someone in the back before.

Brigga Lin gestured to the gangplank, which crumbled as the wood rotted away. Sadie and Finn hacked at the lines that attached them to the burning frigate.

Out of the corner of her eye, Hope caught movement up near the top of the frigate's mizzenmast. Then Jilly swung across the widening gap between the ships on one of the lines.

"Filler!" Hope yelled and pointed.

Jilly slammed clumsily into the *Kraken Hunter*'s foremast and dropped, but Filler caught her before she hit the deck.

Hope, Nettles, and Brigga Lin quickly worked

through the remaining sailors on board. With each slash or thrust, Hope felt their shock, their confusion, and their fear. Most didn't even have the presence of mind to defend themselves. And with each death, she felt another hard surge up her arm. She didn't fight it, but let it course through her body. If it truly was the blade's grief she felt, what right did she have to wield it if she didn't share in its burden? By the time the sailors were all dead, tears coursed down her cheeks.

"Captain!" called Finn. "The cargo ship is making a run for it!"

"Set course to come along its port side." Hope wiped the blood from her sword, then wiped the tears from her eyes. "Sadie, strike the white and run up our true colors. I want that biomancer to know who's coming for him."

"Aye, Captain." Sadie grinned her toothless grin.

"Captain," Filler said quietly.

There was something in his tone that made Hope turn immediately. He had Jilly cradled in his arms. A splinter of wood, as thick as a knife and soaked red with blood, protruded from her thigh. There was blood all over Filler now, and it was beginning to pool on the deck, thinning and spreading out in the rain.

"Stupid girl!" Brigga Lin hurried over to them. She looked furious. "Look at that. It must have punctured a major artery. Pull out the splinter so I can seal the wound."

Filler nodded and carefully eased out the wood while Jilly whimpered. Then Brigga Lin closed her eyes and placed her hands on Jilly's blood-drenched thigh. After a moment, Jilly's expression softened and her body began to relax.

"She's lost a lot of blood, but she'll be fine," said Brigga Lin, looking no less furious.

"Thank you," said Hope. Then she pulled out her glass and strode quickly to the gunwale. The cargo ship was moving slowly and things seemed even more chaotic than before on deck. The biomancer and captain were shouting at each other.

"Cannons at the ready!" Hope called.

She could hear them slam into place. The gun ports popped open as the cannon muzzles protruded from the sides of the *Kraken Hunter*.

"Port-side cannons at forty-five degrees!"

The *Kraken Hunter* slid alongside the cargo ship.

"FIRE!"

Clusters of thick chain exploded from the side of the *Kraken Hunter*, whistling through the air and tearing apart the sails and rigging of the cargo ship.

"Heave to!" called Hope. "Ready the grapples!"

Finn, Sadie, and Brigga Lin scrambled to stop the ship while Nettles and Filler prepared the spring-loaded grappling cannons at the bow and stern.

"Fire grapples!"

The grappling hooks shot out and latched on to the hull of the cargo ship. Then Filler and Nettles cranked the hand winches to reel the *Kraken Hunter* in close to the heavier vessel.

When Hope stepped up onto the gunwale, she saw only a small cluster of soldiers, nervous and unsure, their rifles clutched tightly in their hands. In front of them stood the biomancer, his face hidden by his deep white hood.

"Release the girls into our care, and I will spare your men," said Hope. "If you do it quickly and I find none of the girls harmed, I *might* even spare you."

"Miserable pirate," said the biomancer. "Do you have any idea whom you're dealing with?" Most biomancers' voices were altered or damaged in some way. Hope had learned from Brigga Lin that this was a result of practicing their arts for many years. But this biomancer's voice sounded surprisingly normal. Even a little young. When he lifted his head, his unblemished face confirmed it. His expression was set with an almost comical level of self-importance. "Prepare to suffer the wrath of biomancer Dulcay Mun."

Hope wondered if he had just graduated from his novitiate. "Don't you recognize this blade? Or that flag?" She pointed up to the crossed biomancer emblem.

The biomancer scoffed. "I have no need to concern myself with weapons or flags. If you doubt it, come and face me. I have told my men to stand down. You need fear nothing from them. Only from me."

Hope sighed wearily and stepped forward, half thinking she would beat him senseless with her clamp and leave him.

"No."

Hope stopped and turned to see Brigga Lin, her hands still stained red from Jilly's blood. "Please. Allow me."

Hope nodded and stepped aside. This would be the first time they had confronted a biomancer since their attack on the palace. Brigga Lin had become slightly less bloodthirsty since then. Hope wondered if she might spare this novice.

Dulcay Mun looked at Brigga Lin suspiciously. "What are you, woman, dressed as a biomancer?"

"I have been many things, Dulcay Mun. But starting today, I am the atonement for our kind. Now I have a question for *you*, errand boy. How many little girls do you have in the hold there to bring to the masters for their work?"

Dulcay Mun shrugged. "I don't know exactly. Some of them died already, and I haven't taken the time to count them."

"Funny how life is," she said musingly. "It tries desperately to persist, no matter the cost. Even at the cost of other life. Some must prevail, others must perish. It is the way of all things."

"Woman, cease your babbling or I will turn you into a hideous and painful shape before I kill you."

Brigga Lin smiled coldly. "You must be a powerful and knowledgeable biomancer indeed."

"The strongest of my year!" he said triumphantly.

"Since you are so learned, then no doubt you are aware that even within our own bodies, life competes. Creatures live in our guts that are so tiny, we cannot see them without the aid of a microscope."

"Of course I know that," said Dulcay Mun, although his bluster was beginning to falter. "We learn such simple things in the first year of our training."

"Good," said Brigga Lin. "Then what happens next will not confuse you."

She made several fluid gestures with her blood-stained hands, then pointed to him. A moment later, he grunted and doubled over, clutching at his stomach. He straightened up partially and looked at Brigga Lin with wide eyes. "What did you..." He winced and curled over again. "How did you—" His words were cut off by a hoarse groan that changed slowly into a whimper as he dropped to his hands and knees. He writhed for a moment, his breath only a harsh, constricted whistle. Then he reached out his hand to Brigga Lin. "Please..."

Her cold smile twisted into fury. "Is that how the little girls begged when you took them from their homes? When you stuffed them in the hold with no food or water or light or hope?" The soldiers moved quickly out of her path as she began to circle the biomancer, her hands on her hips. "Please! Please! *Please!*" she mocked.

Dulcay Mun fell onto his side, his arms and legs thrashing wildly. His stomach swelled until it looked like he was pregnant. The normally loose robes stretched tight across his abdomen.

"Do you know what's happening to you, Dulcay Mun, strongest of your year?" asked Brigga Lin. "All those tiny bacteria in your gut are multiplying at a previously impossible rate. Thousands become millions become trillions, all of them eating and multiplying, faster and faster, until there is simply no more room inside."

Dulcay Mun began to choke, and a strange wriggling cream-colored paste spilled from his lips. A dark wet patch began to form around his backside as well. He shuddered for a few moments as he tried to take in air through a throat filled with the paste. Finally, he grew still.

During the entire ordeal, the crew of the *Kraken Hunter* and the crew of the cargo ship watched, motionless and silent.

Brigga Lin turned to the captain, a thin man with a weak chin. "Well?"

"W-w-we surrender," he said meekly, taking off his hat to reveal thinning hair clumped with sweat.

The soldiers quickly placed their rifles on the ground and put their hands behind their heads.

"The first orderly action I've seen them perform on this ship," Hope muttered to Nettles.

They locked all the sailors and soldiers in their own brig. Then Hope turned to the captain and asked, "Where are the girls?"

"I'll take you to them directly," said the captain.

He led them to the cargo hold. A foul smell escaped when he unlatched the door. A combination of excrement and death that reminded Hope of the basements of Gunpowder Hall, where the people of Paradise Circle took their dying loved ones. She peered into the darkness and saw shapes shrink back from the opening.

"It's all right, girls," she said. "It's safe. You can come out now."

There were whispers and rustling movement, but none of them came forward.

Hope turned to Nettles. "I thought they'd be desperate to come out of there."

"Well, you and I maybe don't look like the friendliest mollies in the world. We are supposed to be pirates after all. Maybe they're afraid of getting out of the rain and into the flood."

"How do we convince traumatized little girls that we mean them no harm?" asked Brigga Lin.

"Get Sadie," said Nettles. "She looks all grandmotherly."

"Sadie?" asked Hope.

Nettles shrugged. "They don't know her like we do."

Filler volunteered to go get Sadie. When he brought her to the cargo hold entrance, she did not look pleased.

"Grandmotherly?" she asked Nettles.

"You got all them materny instincts from raising Red," said Nettles, a slight grin tugging on the corner of her mouth.

"I'll show *you* my materny instincts in a minute, you uppity slice," growled Sadie.

But she went into the cargo hold. Hope could hear her scratchy voice faintly, although she couldn't make out most of what she was saying. After a while, Sadie's head popped out of the hold.

"Best step back and give 'em space. They're still a bit wobbly."

Hope, Nettles, Brigga Lin, and Filler all moved away from the hatch as Sadie motioned to the girls in the hold, saying, "Come on, little mollies. Don't mind the scary pirates. Old Sadie'll keep 'em at bay."

They filed out behind her like ducklings, some no more than three years old. They were all thin and dirty and shivering.

The worst of the storm had passed by then, and the rain was only a drizzle. The sky was a dull gray, but the girls squinted like it was a sunny day. They clung to Sadie and called her grandma as she led them across the gangplank to the *Kraken Hunter*.

Hope turned to the captain. "Where were you bound? Vance Post?"

The captain shook his head. "We were stopping there for supplies, but the cargo—uh, I mean, those poor girls—were bound for Dawn's Light."

"Dawn's Light?" Brigga Lin's eyes went wide.

"I've been there," said Hope. "It's only an isolated military outpost, isn't it?"

"No," said Brigga Lin. "It's where the most desperate experiments are conducted. Those deemed so dangerous that if they were to be done on a closer island, it would be a risk to the entire empire."

"I don't know none of the details," said the captain, "but I hear from the men that there's something terrible happening on Dawn's Light."

"I see." Hope gave Brigga Lin a meaningful look. This sounded like something they shouldn't ignore. Then she turned back to the captain. "We'll relieve you of any money and supplies we need. But before we leave, I'll return the key to your brig so you can release your crew. It shouldn't take too long for them to repair the sails and rigging. We'll leave enough food so you don't starve in the meantime."

The captain looked surprised and cautiously hopeful. "You're...not going to kill us?"

Hope turned to the bloated corpse of Dulcay Mun. "I think we made our point. And if anyone asks what happened here today, you tell them it was

Dire Bane, come again to cast judgment on the biomancers and any who would side with them."

"Whatever you say," agreed the captain. "I'm
grateful for your mercy, Captain, both to me and
my men."

Hope looked down at the hat he'd been turning
nervously in his hands. It was black, with three corners. A long red feather protruded from it. "I will
take your hat, though, Captain."

The man practically shoved it at her. "Take it with
my compliments, Captain. I think it suits you."

Hope placed it on top of her head, liking the feel
of it more than she expected. "I think so, too."

———

Instead of sneaking ashore in a rowboat like last time,
Hope sailed the *Kraken Hunter* boldly into the harbor
of High Guster. A ship like hers was a rare sight on
that island and word traveled fast. By the time they'd
tied up at the dock, many townspeople already lurked
in doorways and peered through windows, eyeing the
new arrivals warily.

But when Sadie led the girls single file down
the gangplank, they all came out at once. Parents
scooped up their children, some crying, some laughing, some even singing and dancing.

Several embraced Sadie. Some tried to give her
money or jewelry. She shook her head and pointed
to Hope, who remained on the ship, watching from
afar. She took off her newly acquired captain's hat
and inclined her head to them.

"Filler, will you take Kapany to her father?"
she asked. "Then make sure he keeps his end of
the agreement. I'd like those cannon parts done as
quickly as possible."

"Sure thing, Captain," said Filler.

"Thought I might go ashore, too," said Nettles. "Haven't been on dry land in weeks."

"Good idea," said Hope. "You should all take some time to relax. You've earned it."

She watched them go down into the small town, which now seemed to be rallying for an impromptu celebration. So often her crew did hard, thankless work. She was glad they would have some enthusiastic recognition for a change.

"Not going yourself, Captain?" Alash asked as he joined her at the gunwale.

"Someone has to mind the ship. What about you?"

"Crowds make me uncomfortable."

"I know what you mean."

They watched the growing celebration for a while. People were bringing tables and chairs from their homes and setting them up in the middle of the dirt road. Others were bringing out food and casks of wine.

"I'm glad your idea worked, Alash," said Hope. "But it shouldn't have had to come to that. It was an act of desperation."

"What else could we have done?"

"I'm not sure. And that's what troubles me. I feel as though we are reaching the limits of what we can do with one small ship and a skeleton crew."

"That may be."

"Is it enough?" asked Hope. "Are we making any real difference?"

"We made a difference for these people."

"You're right. Of course this matters. It's just…" She trailed off, her eyes straining to see past the island of High Guster, past the many islands beyond it, still trying to catch a glimpse of Stonepeak across the miles.

"I know you want Red back," said Alash. "But aren't you the one who said it didn't matter how long it took?"

She smiled ruefully. "I did."

"I think you were right. We've taken some ships, but still have a ways to go before we pose a credible threat to the biomancers and can free my cousin. And in the meantime, we need to savor these little victories when we can. It's the only way we'll be able to sustain ourselves until we finally bring him home."

Hope watched a cluster of musicians begin to gather near the tables and food. When she heard the first strains of melody drift toward her, she turned to Alash.

"You're absolutely right." She held out her arm and gave him a playful smile. "Come, Mr. Havolon. Let us join the party after all."

"Oh, well, I don't know ...," said Alash.

But Hope grabbed his hand and pulled him down the gangplank with her.

"Doesn't someone have to mind the ship?" he asked.

"I think of all the times and places, this one I will chance it."

The sky was beginning to darken as they reached the gathering. People brought out lanterns and placed them on tables, casting a warm, flickering glow on everyone there. Hope saw Filler arrive from the smithy, his face still red from the forge. He accepted a cup of wine from one of the villagers and drank it down gratefully. Sadie and Finn had already had quite a lot of wine it seemed, and were now off to one side, sitting at a table, leaning peacefully into each other. Some of the village girls they had rescued were teaching Nettles and Jilly a local dance. Alash and Brigga Lin sat by the food, whispering to each other with uneasy looks, as if they didn't recognize some of the rustic dishes and were not entirely convinced they were edible.

There were moments in life, Hope decided, that

seemed too perfect to be real. She wished there was a way to capture a night like this—bottle it up and save it for the dark times ahead. But perhaps it was just as well that they remained only in memory, growing more beautiful and poignant with time. It was not a very Vinchen idea, but then again, she wasn't very Vinchen herself anymore. She was the dread pirate Dire Bane, champion of the people.

"Good to see you relaxing for a change."

Nettles handed Hope a cup of wine and grinned. Her face was flushed from dancing and there was a thin line of sweat at her temples.

Hope smiled back. "Trying something new, I guess."

Nettles took a large gulp of wine. "That's how you survive. Stay flexible. Adapt."

They watched as Jilly began teaching the girls of the village how to hold a knife properly.

"I think those girls have learned something about survival," said Hope.

"What do you think that biomancer wanted with them anyway?"

"I'm not sure. But the captain said something terrible is going on at Dawn's Light."

Nettles grunted. "I wonder what 'terrible' looks like to a gaf who's willing to steal twenty little girls and shove them into a ship's hold without food or water."

"Perhaps," said Hope, "we should find out."

8

*R*ed hadn't expected it to feel quite so *good* to walk through the dark city streets with the potential for danger behind every corner. His eyes took in every detail of the wide thoroughfare. The uniform beige walls of neat buildings glowed faintly luminous in the moonlight. He could hear the skitter of rats across cobblestones, and the distant creak of doors and shutters opening or closing. He could smell the salt tang of the sea on the cool evening breeze.

It was still well before midnight, but the streets were nearly empty. A few merchants hurried home from their shops, and a young couple kissed in a doorway. At this hour, Paradise Circle would have been at its rowdiest. The whorehouses would be filled to capacity. The previous few hours of post-labor drinking would have made even the honest gafs dangerous. And the truly dangerous ones would have been plying their trades of robbery and murder. Of course Red and his wags had been right in the middle of it all. He felt a sudden pang of longing for those simpler times and he wondered if they were now lost to him forever.

It occurred to him then, that among other things, the biomancers were trying to domesticate him. They allowed him his little eccentricities, such as dressing how he wished, and making friends with whomever

he wished. All the while, they were making him comfortable and tame. His stomach churned as he considered the full scope of his prison, truly seeing the
bars for the first time.

He glanced at Nea, who walked at his side.
Despite the prince's warnings of danger, she moved
with confidence, her head held high. If all the government gafs of Aukbontar were this pat, no wonder
the biomancers were practically pissing their robes
yellow. Maybe that was the real reason Ammon Set
had told him to go to the ball. To get a gander at
the person who was supposed to be his enemy. And
wouldn't they be upset to learn that he was actually
helping her?

"Why are you smiling at me?" asked Nea suspiciously.

"What's not to smile about? Beautiful night, beautiful molly, freedom, and the chance of a little scuffle
to warm the blood."

"You really think someone has been sent to assassinate me so soon?"

"Seems unlikely," said Red. "But they *did* manage
to intercept both of your messengers. They might
have already known you were here even before you
announced yourself at the palace."

"Who are *they* exactly?" asked Nea. "These influ-
ential people who want me dead?"

Red paused for a moment. Leston had been careful not to give specifics, so maybe he shouldn't either.
As nice as Nea seemed, she was still the ambassador
of a foreign country. It was probably wise to keep her
in the dark on the inner workings of palace politics.
*Knowledge only grants power when it is withheld from
others,* Progul Bon had said. Well, piss on that. Red
was no tame politician and he wasn't about to start
following the advice of the people who were actively
trying to ruin his life.

"You ever hear of biomancers?" he asked.

She raised an eyebrow. "Sorcerers with the ability to bend the laws of nature to their will? Yes, I have heard of them, but assumed it to be merely superstitious lore."

"I'm afraid it ain't all lore, old pot." He pulled her directly under a street lamp, even though the brightness pained him a little. "Take a good look at my eyes in this light."

He heard a sharp intake of breath, and a look of discomfort crossed her face. But a moment later she regained her composure.

"The reddish color is certainly unusual," she admitted. "And the shape of the pupils are slitted almost like a cat's. A curious birth defect, to be sure. But—"

"They *made* me like this," said Red. And for the first time in his life, he felt angry about it. Back when he thought it was just something that happened because his mom made some bad choices, he'd accepted it. Thought it made him special, even. But now that he knew it was part of some biomancer scheme, it didn't make him feel special at all. It just made him feel used.

The glare of the streetlight was getting too uncomfortable, so he stepped back into the shadows and started walking in the direction of the inn again.

"Why would they do that?" she asked, following him.

"Because they wanted to see if they could make someone able to see in the dark. They see regular people as nothing more than lab experiments. I've seen one turn a gaf's whole body to ice. I've seen other men crumble to dust. They took my best wag, Hope..." He felt a momentary pang of longing. "They massacred her whole village for one of their experiments. They do all this to develop weapons against *you*."

"Me?" asked Nea.

"Well, your country, anyway. They are so sure you're going to invade, they have been developing… bio-weapons, I guess you'd call them, for about twenty years now."

"What are these *bio-weapons*?"

"No idea." It was true that Red didn't know a whole lot about the biomancer weapons, but even he wasn't rash enough to give the few details he knew to the ambassador of Aukbontar. Thankfully, she had the grace not to press him on it.

"So these biomancers of yours," she said instead. "Do they hold any real political power?"

"Not officially. But they seem to have the emperor in their pocket."

"If he's as feeble as he appeared, that probably wasn't difficult," said Nea. "So it sounds like the best thing for the Empire of Storms would be if Prince Leston succeeded his father as soon as possible."

"I suppose."

"Can't you just declare the current emperor incompetent and have him deposed?"

"Is that something that happens in Aukbontar?" asked Red.

"Only in very rare cases," said Nea. "But yes, if a member of the Great Congress is deemed compromised, usually due to illness or old age, they are asked to step down. Most of the time, they do so gracefully. But every once in a while, one refuses, and there must be a trial to determine if they are truly fit to represent their city-state."

"Aukbontar sounds like a complicated place."

"A certain amount of bureaucracy is inevitable for any large country. Mavokadia is much the same in that respect, although of course they are a nationalist republic, not a social democracy like Aukbontar."

"Mavokadia?" asked Red.

"The country to the north of Aukbontar, of course." Nea squinted at him, like she was trying to determine if he was testing her.

"Oh, yeah," he said quickly. "That place." He'd never heard of Mavokadia. He'd never even considered that there might be another country to the north of Aukbontar. He wondered if even Progul Bon knew about it. "Well, we don't do anything like that. I think it would be like saying God made a mistake. Now, personally, I am ready to believe that if there is a God, he is making all kinds of mistakes. But most gafs feel that God not only exists, but is completely quality."

Nea winced. "Right. Divine rule. Sorry, I forgot about that."

"Don't be too hard on yourself, Nea, my wag. For a complete stranger, you know this place better than many who've lived here their whole lives."

"Thank you, Red." She smiled her lacy smile. "I pride myself on my thorough research. And it hasn't been easy. So little about your empire comes to us, I cannot help but think it is by design."

They continued through the quiet streets of Stonepeak. Red's eyes were everywhere. Down passageways, in doorways, on rooftops. He kept waiting for a few rough-handed gafs to jump out. Maybe they were lurking in the alleys, hoping Red was stupid enough to take the ambassador through a more secluded area. If that was true, they'd get more desperate the closer Red and Nea got to the inn.

When they were a couple of blocks from the inn, Red drew the gun he'd borrowed from Captain Murkton. If there were people lurking in the shadows, now would be the time they'd get bold enough to attack.

"Strange," said Nea, glancing at his gun.

"What's that?" Red asked distractedly as he scanned the nearby alleys.

"Your gun. It looks exactly like the ones our law enforcement officers carry in Aukbontar."

"A gun's a gun, right? How much difference could there be from one to the next?"

She looked at it more carefully for a moment, then smiled and shrugged. "You are right, of course. Let us continue on."

She quickened her pace, forcing Red to move faster to keep up. Soon they were across the street from the Call to Arms.

"Well, it appears Prince Leston's fears were groundless," Nea said with a mixture of relief and satisfaction. "There is my inn, and we have not encountered any assassins. I am sorry you had to waste your time escorting me, when you would probably much rather have been in your bed."

"I wouldn't rest easy just yet." Red pointed to the inn. It was a two-story building, not fancy but well kept. "Front door is wide open."

"Someone probably just forgot to close it."

"At an inn?" asked Red. "That lets in the ghosts."

"More superstitious nonsense."

Red shrugged. "Don't mean people don't believe it. No self-respecting innkeeper would let his door flap open like that. I reckon there's something going on inside. Stay behind me, just in case."

Nea reluctantly let Red take the lead as they cautiously crossed the street. Red had been learning from Ammon Set how to momentarily see at an even greater distance than usual. He squinted his eyes, and his vision gave a funny lurch and he saw at least part of the scene through the door.

"Piss'ell," he whispered, cocking his gun.

"What is it?" asked Nea, stepping impatiently to his side.

"Really. Stay behind me. Or better yet, stay out here."

"If my team is in danger, I need to go in," she said in a tone that made it clear this was not open to discussion.

"Fine. But *behind* me."

Nea again let Red go first. When they stepped through the door, Red got his first full view of the chaos inside.

Unlike the inns of New Laven, the layout of most Stonepeak inns had the dining and common area right in front, so that ideally, the first thing a potential customer saw when they walked through the door was a bunch of friendly-looking people relaxing and enjoying themselves. Now this innkeeper could see why none of the inns in Paradise Circle used this layout. Or he could have, if he'd still been alive.

It looked like a crew of boots had just walked in and opened fire on the place right at dinnertime. Bodies were on the floor or sprawled across tables. One boot was riffling through the pockets of the dead. On either side of this dining area was a staircase that led to an open second level lined with doors. There was a boot on either staircase, gun pointing toward a specific door. The last two boots were at the door. One had an ax, the other a sledgehammer. They were slowly tearing the door apart.

"What is—" began Nea, her eyes wide in horror as she again stepped to Red's side.

Red put his hand over her mouth and moved her back. So far, none of the boots had noticed them. They were too focused on whoever was behind that door.

"Citizen Omnipora!" A frightened face appeared in the widening gap in the door. *"Run!"*

Of course all five boots turned to see who he was yelling at. And of course Nea didn't run.

"Thanks, *team*," muttered Red. He took a deep breath and, much as he hated to do it, summoned all the instruction Chiffet Mek had given him. He took five shots and five boots fell dead.

There was a moment of silence after the gunshots faded and the smoke cleared. Then Nea cleared her throat. "It seems you were not exaggerating about your skill, friend Red."

Red nodded and stared down at his gun. There was no doubt about it. The biomancers had made him a better killer. He felt a little sick. He'd killed plenty before. But the ease with which he'd snuffed out five lives...it was on a different level.

"Well, look who it is. The biomancers' little pet."

Red looked up and saw a familiar face grinning at him across the dining tables.

"Brackson? What in all hells are you doing this far from Paradise Circle?"

Deadface Drem's old lieutenant sighed dramatically. He still had thin scars on his cheeks where Nettles had sliced him at the Rag and Boards. "Thanks to you, I wasn't so popular back in the Circle anymore. Thought I'd try my luck here at the capital. Seems to be working out so far."

"You think so?" Red pointed his gun at him. "I've still got one bullet, just for you."

"I wish we could do this proper. I really do." Brackson made a big show of regret. "But the biomancers were very specific in telling me to keep my hands off their favorite pet."

"I'm nobody's pet."

"Keep telling yourself that. Now, if you'll excuse me..."

"You ain't going nowhere." Red pulled back the hammer. The last thing he felt like doing was killing another person. But it looked like Brackson wasn't giving him a choice.

Brackson laughed and held up a tiny silver whistle. "You know what this is? A dog whistle, dog."

He blew on the whistle and it suddenly felt like the ground moved beneath Red's feet. He reached for a table to keep from falling, but the table seemed to move out of his reach, and the ground flew up to meet him. At the last second, he felt hands grab around his middle and stop his fall.

"I reckon we'll have to do this another time, Ambassador," he heard Brackson say. Then he heard footsteps rapidly retreat. He wanted to chase after him, but all he could do was lie there in Nea's grasp until the world stopped spinning.

"You're very heavy," she said, her voice strained.

"I'm okay now," he said, getting his feet back underneath him.

"What happened to you?" she asked.

"You didn't get dizzy when he blew that whistle?" asked Red.

She shook her head. "I did not even hear it. But when he blew it, you suddenly began to stumble around, like you were drunk. Then you pitched forward."

"Thanks for catching me," said Red.

"So you really do not know how that happened?" she asked, her face creased with concern.

"Not how. But I have a pretty good idea *who*."

The biomancers had done something to him. A fail-safe measure, in case he ever got out of hand. Here he'd been daydreaming about turning their own training against them. But he should have expected something like this. It was exactly the sort of thing they would do.

"I worried he was going to attack me while you were disoriented, but he just ran away," said Nea.

"Maybe he was worried it would wear off too quickly." Or maybe Brackson hadn't been willing to chance a shot at her while she was holding Red. Apparently keeping him alive was more important than killing her. Good to know.

"Let's go get your people and head back to the palace," he said at last.

As they made their way through the scattered dead bodies to the stairs, Red noticed that Nea looked ill.

"You alright?" he asked.

"I, uh...now that the danger is past, I am truly taking it all in for the first time."

"Don't see a lot of dead bodies in Aukbontar?"

"I have never seen one before in my life," she said quietly.

"Never?"

She shook her head.

"Wow," was all Red could say. What kind of place was Aukbontar that someone who wasn't even nobility could go their whole life without seeing a single dead body?

As they climbed the staircase, Red said, "I reckon you regret coming here now."

"No," she said firmly, her face now full of purpose as she climbed the stairs. "We are doing important work here. There has not been diplomatic communication with the Empire of Storms in over three hundred years. I will not fail the Great Congress."

Once they made it to the second-floor landing, she called, "Citizens! Come out. It's safe now."

"Citizen Omnipora?" a frail male voice called.

"Yes, Etcher. Please come out. All of you. We must move to the safety of the palace as quickly as possible."

Red heard furniture scrape across the floor inside the room. Red guessed they must have barricaded themselves inside. At least someone in there was smart. The half-broken door began to open, but then came loose from its hinges. Red pulled Nea aside as the door fell forward and landed with a hard smack.

Three people stepped awkwardly over the door. All of them had the same dark skin as Nea. They also wore the same broad-shouldered jackets and loose-fitting pants, although in different colors.

"This is Catim Miffety." Nea indicated a large man in a red jacket and tan pants. His hair was so short, it was little more than black stubble. "He is here to assure the safety of the team."

"I should have gone with you to the palace," Catim said in a deep, soft voice that reminded Red a little of Filler.

"Nonsense," said Nea. "As you can see, I am perfectly safe. And had you not been here, something terrible might have happened to Etcher and Drissa. Then where would we be?"

Catim grunted, then narrowed his eyes suspiciously at Red. "Who is this?"

"This"—Nea put her hand protectively on Red's shoulder—"is Lord Pastinas, a close friend of Prince Leston and the reason that I *am* safe."

Catim nodded. "My thanks, Lord Pastinas."

"Don't mention it, old pot," said Red.

"Old pot?" he asked.

"And this," continued Nea smoothly, "is Etcher Kinto, our expert in natural philosophy." She pointed to a small, thin man wearing a green jacket and yellow pants. "He is here primarily to witness and catalogue the astonishing plants and animals we have heard exist in your fair country."

"Is it true you have mole rats as big as lions?" Etcher asked eagerly, wringing his hands.

"What's a lion?" asked Red.

"There will be plenty of time for that later, I am sure," said Nea. "The last member of my team is Drissa, our master machinist." She indicated a short, stout woman in a dark blue jacket and dark green pants. She also had a dark green cloth that covered her hair. She said nothing, but nodded shyly.

"A machinist?" Red asked Nea. "Like your dad?"

"Similar, but much more advanced. Isn't that right, Drissa?"

Drissa smiled and looked down at her feet.

"Drissa can understand your language well enough, but speaking it does not come easily to her. Her skill lies in other areas."

"Well, it's sunny to meet you all, toms and molly alike, but we better slide before any more boots show, keen?"

All four of them looked at him in bewilderment.

He laughed. "Let's go before anyone else starts shooting at us."

———

Nea's "team" had a wagon made of steel. Even though it wasn't large, it was so heavy, they had four horses to pull it. Most of the wagon was taken up with crates. Catim and Drissa sat among them. Nea took the reins up front, with Etcher and Red sitting next to her. The crates were stacked so high that Red couldn't see the two passengers in the back. But he figured they weren't really in that much danger. If Brackson was the one in charge, it would take him a while to run back to the biomancers and tell them everything that happened, and longer for him to get another crew together.

It was a good thing, too, because the wagon moved extremely slow as it made its way back to the palace.

During the drive, Etcher battered Red with questions about animals and plants that were apparently unusual in Aukbontar. Mole rats, oarfish, seals, and goblin sharks seemed particularly interesting to him. He even asked about krakens, although Nea laughed and told him to be serious. Having grown up in New Laven, Red hadn't encountered any of those animals personally, but he'd heard a few things from Finn and others, so he did his best to answer.

They finally arrived at the palace gates just before sunrise. The predawn light tinted the white outer walls of the palace a faint red as Red stood up on the wagon and waved to the guards above the gate.

"Hello, my wags! I've returned home with the prince's very special guests! Would you mind letting us back in?"

The iron gates slowly opened and the wagon trundled through. Once they were past the threshold, though, an imp stepped in front of the horses and held up his hands for them to stop.

"Sorry, my lord," he said apologetically to Red. "All cargo must be inspected for security risks. Orders from the commander."

"Alright. I guess we're safe enough now that we're through the gates," said Red. "And I *suppose* the prince can wait a bit longer for his guests."

The imp flinched when Red mentioned the prince. "We'll have you through just as soon as we can, my lord."

"Thanks. Is Captain Murkton still on duty?"

"His shift ended a couple hours ago, my lord."

"Tell Captain Murkton his revolver might well have kept peace in the empire. At least for tonight." He handed the gun down to the imp.

"I'll pass that along, my lord."

Red had assumed the inspection would take only a few minutes. But the sun slowly rose while he and

Nea still waited. He put his tinted glasses on and turned to Nea. "I'll go see what the trouble is."

He hopped down and walked to the back of the wagon. Two imps were looking suspiciously at an open crate. Inside was a metal contraption like something Alash would put together, but much larger. Ammon Set's words came back to him: *Their advancements in the mechanical sciences are beyond your comprehension.* But Red wasn't about to let biomancer paranoia get the best of him.

"Something gone leeward, my wags?" he asked the imps. "Maybe I can help move things along."

"It's this...thing, my lord." One of the imps pointed at the contraption. "They won't tell us what it is or what it's for."

Catim was looking impatient, bordering on angry, and Drissa was saying something nervously over and over again in her language.

"I *did* tell you," Catim growled at the imps. "It is a machine."

"But what *is* that?" retorted the imp.

"Oh, a machine." Red pointed to Drissa. "She's a *machin*ist, so I reckon she knows all about it."

"Yes, my lord," said the other imp. "But she can't speak a word of the empire's tongue. Just jabbers on in some foreign nonsense every time we touch it."

Red looked hopefully at Catim. "You got nothing for me here, old pot?"

"It is a machine," he said helplessly. "An engine. It makes things go."

"Okay, now we're getting somewhere," said Red. "Makes *what* go?"

"Anything you like. A ship, a train—"

"What is a *train*?" one of the imps demanded.

"It is a..." Catim stretched his hands wide, then scowled and made fists. "I do not know the words for it!"

"Alright, calm down, Catim, my wag," Red said soothingly. "Let's go get Nea. She can probably sort this out, simple as sideways."

But just as Red got back to the front of the wagon, he heard Prince Leston's voice crack across the courtyard, sounding angrier than Red had ever heard him. He looked like he hadn't slept that night either.

"What is the meaning of this? Why are you detaining my honored guests?"

"S-s-sorry, Your Highness," said the imp in the front. "The commander said—"

"Tell the commander I will speak with him at great length later today. Now, release my guests."

"Yes, Your Highness." The imp hurried to the back of the wagon and a minute later, all three guards moved quickly back to their posts at the wall.

Prince Leston moved to stand next to the wagon. He looked up at Nea, his face pained. "Ambassador Omnipora. I must apologize for the rudeness of my men."

"No apology necessary," she said. "I now understand why safety is such a concern for you and your subjects."

Leston's expression creased with worry. "So my fears were founded?" The prince's sudden, passionate interest in politics still seemed very odd to Red.

"I'm afraid so, Your Highness. My people are unharmed, but a great many of yours were killed. We would likely have shared their fate if not for Lord Pastinas."

Leston grabbed Red's upper arms and held them tightly. "Thank you, my friend. I may never be able to repay you for what you have done tonight."

"Oh, it's nothing any upstanding lord raised in the slums of New Laven couldn't handle."

Leston held out his hand to Nea. "My men will

bring your things up to your chambers. Will you do me the honor of allowing me to escort you there?"

"That would be wonderful, Your Highness," she said. "It has been a very long night."

Red watched the prince help her down from the wagon and a suspicion began to grow in his mind. Maybe it wasn't about politics after all. Was the prince such a salthead that he let himself get sotted with a molly at first sight? And one who happened to be the ambassador of a foreign country? Red hoped not.

"I want you to know, Ambassador," Leston said, once Nea was on the ground, "that I am at your beck and call. I dearly wish to make up for this terrible night and hope that from now on, your stay here is as pleasant and productive as possible."

"I am grateful, Your Highness," said Nea. "The open and friendly communication between our two peoples is the most important thing in the world to me."

"Then it is to me, as well," said the prince.

Yep, thought Red. *Completely sotted.*

9

*H*ope allowed the crew a slow start the morning after the celebration. Then they loaded the new cannon plates Filler had made onto the ship. It was nearly noon when they finally set sail, heading east-southeast. It wasn't the most direct route to Dawn's Light, but with the sizable imperial presence at Vance Post, Hope felt it was worth taking a more circuitous passage to avoid that island.

They sailed for several days without incident. But once they were getting close to the Breaks, Hope put everyone on guard.

"We'll cross the north end, but I want you to give it a wide berth," she told Missing Finn. "The current is so strong, this ship barely made it past the last time."

"You've made this crossing before?"

"Once, when I first joined the crew of the *Lady's Gambit*. Which reminds me…Jilly, I want you up in the royals. Be on the lookout for pirates. Possibly a small party in a sloop."

"I don't reckon they've got much of a chance against us," Jilly said confidently.

"Probably true, but we've proven a lesser ship can overcome a larger one with enough surprise. So let's not give it to them."

Jilly gave her a smart salute. "Aye, Captain."

"Didn't Brigga Lin get you a pair of shoes in High Guster?" asked Hope as she watched the barefoot girl clamber up the ratlines.

"She did, Captain. And much obliged. But shoes aren't good for climbing in the rigging." She hooked her legs over the main yard and hung upside down so her head was near Hope's. More quietly, she said, "And to speak crystal, the shoes she picked are a bit too lacy for me. All pointy and smooth."

Hope nodded gravely. "And that's not pat, is it?"

Jilly gave her an upside-down grin. "No, sir, it ain't!" Then she pulled herself up and continued her climb up the rigging.

"You ever seen a monkey, Captain?" asked Finn.

Hope shook her head. "I've read about them."

"I seen one once. A wag from Aukbontar had it as a pet. Our Jilly climbs just like one of them, natural as you please. I bet she'd put her hammock up there if you let her."

"I don't think Brigga Lin would approve."

"Well, I certainly wouldn't want to displease *that* one." He shuddered. "What she did to that bio-mancer...I never seen a thing like that before."

"Sometimes it's easy for us to forget that she was raised most of her life as one of them."

Finn looked at her. "Does a person ever really come back from that?"

"I'd like to think we can all come back from whatever darkness we've encountered," said Hope. "With time. And perhaps some help."

———

When the *Kraken Hunter* reached the Breaks, Hope found them just as impressive as she remembered. A line of reefs that ran north to south, jutting thirty feet or more up into the sky. They stood against the prevailing current that ran east to west, so the water seemed to boil at their base. The last time she'd seen the sight, it had been with Sankack, Ticks, and Ranking—all crew members of the *Lady's Gambit*, now dead.

As Missing Finn took a wide arc around the northern tip of the reefs, Hope called up to Jilly. "Any sign of pirates, Jilly?"

"No, Captain!" the girl yelled down from her perch.

"You look almost disappointed," said Finn. "Craving a bit of action, were you?"

"There's something about it that makes me uneasy," said Hope. "This has always been a popular area for pirates. One ship gets sunk, another comes to fill the void. So if there aren't pirates anymore, is something worse here now?"

Once they'd crossed the northern tip of the Breaks, Hope saw the strange collection of shipwrecks piled up on the eastern side of the reefs. After a moment, she walked over to the hatch and stuck her head down the steps to the lower deck.

"Alash, you'll want to see this."

Hope returned to the quarterdeck, and a few minutes later, Alash joined her.

"You wanted to show me something?"

Hope handed him her glass and pointed to the shipwrecks along the reef.

Alash turned the glass to the reef. "Ah, ships pulled on the prevailing westerly into the reefs. Yes, I would think—wait, is that..." His mouth opened wide. "Is that an *iron* ship?"

"There are a couple of them, if you look close," said Hope. "I remembered seeing them a few years ago and wondered how such a thing could stay afloat. I thought perhaps you might have some ideas."

"Well, the theory is sound, and of course there

have been small working prototypes made. But this...The *scale* of these ships...It's a feat of engineering that borders on the miraculous!" He was smiling broadly now, and pressing the glass to his eye. "I'm not sure I would have believed it possible if I hadn't seen it myself. Thank you for showing me this!"

"Where do you think they come from?" asked Hope.

"Most likely they drifted from the east."

"From across the Dawn Sea?"

"I suppose some could have come from the north, or wrecked right here coming too close to the reefs. But considering we've seen nothing like these iron ships, I'd say it's possible they came from a civilization on the other side of the Dawn Sea that is even more advanced than our own!" He turned his glass to the empty horizon, as if he could somehow see across the leagues to mysterious, fantastical lands. "Can you imagine? The world never disappoints, does it!"

This was the side of Alash that Hope liked best. The earnest, wide-eyed, wondering scientist who had nearly run her over with one of his strange contraptions the first time they'd met.

"What's he going on about now?" asked Brigga Lin as she walked over to them.

"Miss Lin, come share this with us!" Alash beamed at her, a red ring around his eye from where he'd pressed the glass so hard it left a mark. "The world proves once again that no matter how much we *think* we know, there is still so much more to discover! Isn't it marvelous!" He grabbed her hands and pressed them to his chest. It was such a simple and impulsive gesture, but Brigga Lin's eyes went wide and her entire body stiffened.

Alash saw he had crossed a line and hastily

released her hands. His eyes fixed on the deck as he stammered out, "I am so sorry, Miss Lin, to let my enthusiasm get the better of me. Please forgive my rudeness."

Hope watched Brigga Lin's expression carefully, but she gave nothing away. After a pause, Brigga Lin reached out and took Alash's hands again.

Alash looked at her, his expression cautious, but hopeful.

"It is a gift," Brigga Lin said quietly, "to have friends for whom the world still holds so much wonder." Then she let go of his hands, turned, and walked away.

Alash stared wistfully after her.

Hope patted his shoulder. "That could have gone worse."

Alash gave her a sheepish smile. "I'm not much good with women, am I?"

"Not much," she agreed.

———

Dawn's Light was only a dot on the horizon when Hope gave the order to strike sails and drop anchor.

"We've still got a fair bit of daylight left, Captain," said Finn.

"I know," said Hope. "Let's have an early meal and make our plans now. It's going to be a busy night."

The crew of the *Kraken Hunter* met over a simple meal of hardtack and salted pork a short time later.

"I want to approach Dawn's Light with caution," said Hope. "Under cover of darkness as far as we can safely get without being seen. Then take a small group ashore the rest of the way in the boat. This will be observation only."

"Sneaking around, maybe cutting a throat or

two if necessary?" asked Nettles. "That plays much more to my quality than a boarding party. Count me in."

"Good," said Hope.

"You'll need me, too," said Brigga Lin. "If the idea is to assess the biomancers, their strengths and possible plans."

Hope nodded.

"You want me, too?" asked Filler.

Hope gave him an apologetic look. "Your leg would be too loud for something like this."

Filler sighed. "Never been too good at sneaking anyway. Red always said so."

"We really need to see what enhancements we can make on that brace," said Alash, tapping his chin thoughtfully. "We threw it together in a rush ages ago and haven't reexamined it since."

"Good idea," said Hope. "That will give you two a project while I'm gone."

"What about me, Captain?" asked Jilly. "*I* can sneak."

"This is a serious thing for grown-ups to do," said Nettles dismissively.

"It's much too dangerous for you," agreed Brigga Lin.

Jilly looked crestfallen and Hope felt a pang of guilt. She agreed with Nettles and Brigga Lin. But she remembered what she'd been like at that age, always eager to show Hurlo what she could do. And he had never coddled her. If anything, he'd pushed her to the brink of what she was capable. But then again, he had the right to do that, because he'd trained her. And that's when an improbable idea occurred to her that seemed so dangerous, and yet so right, she felt a quiet rush of pleasure.

"It's true that you're not ready for something like this," she told Jilly. Then she turned to Nettles and

Brigga Lin. "But perhaps that's our fault. How can she become ready, if we don't teach her?"

"I could do a bit more," admitted Nettles.

Hope turned to Brigga Lin.

"Surely you don't mean *me*?" asked Brigga Lin.

"Jilly is a bright, motivated, and independent girl," said Hope.

"She does show some promise," conceded Brigga Lin.

"And she risked her life for all of us with Alash's slippy lightning device," said Nettles. "So you know she's not some poncey coward."

"True," admitted Brigga Lin.

"Here is what I propose," said Hope. "I will take her on as a student and train her in the Vinchen arts, if you train her as a biomancer."

Brigga Lin stared, her mouth slightly open. She tried to speak several times, but nothing came out. At last, she managed, "It would take *years*."

"Yes," said Hope. "It will. But what you and I started shouldn't end with us. Don't you agree?"

Brigga Lin frowned thoughtfully, but said nothing.

"I'm a real good reader, Miss Lin," said Jilly. "Red taught me a long time ago. I read all kinds of things. Just 'cause I don't speak all lacy, don't mean I'm not smart. I can learn anything you teach. I swear."

For some reason, Brigga Lin looked at Alash then. He had stopped paying attention to the conversation by then and was busy examining Filler's leg brace, making notes to himself on a scrap of parchment.

Brigga Lin watched him for a few moments, then without turning said absently, "Don't use double negatives."

"What?" asked Jilly.

Brigga Lin turned to her. "If I am to teach you, it will begin with grammar. Biomancery requires precise thoughts. Precise thoughts require precise language. Do you understand?"

Jilly's eyes went wide. "Yes, Miss Lin."

"Sorry," said Missing Finn. "But do I understand right that you and Hope plan to make Jilly here into a *Vinchen biomancer*?"

"Progress is inevitable, Mr. Finn," Brigga Lin said primly. "Do try to keep up."

———

They waited until the sun had dropped behind the horizon before they weighed anchor and sailed the rest of the way to Dawn's Light. It was a tiny island only a few miles across, with one small, empty dock, a squat military barracks, and no town or village. It looked exactly as Hope remembered it.

Except for the tents. When she saw them, old dread began to stir deep within her. Feelings of darkness she thought she'd left behind.

"You okay?" asked Nettles as she rowed their dingy quietly toward shore.

Hope nodded. "Those tents bring back unpleasant childhood memories."

"Biomancers frequently use them as temporary labs when there are no permanent structures suitable," said Brigga Lin.

"So it might not be the same experiment I saw before?" asked Hope.

"It would be highly unlikely."

"Good," said Hope.

"But keep in mind that this island is used for experiments deemed too dangerous even to be conducted on a remote island in the Southern Isles."

"So you mean it'll be something worse?" asked Nettles.

"Not necessarily *worse*," said Brigga Lin. "But

with a higher chance of either contamination or uncontrollable escalation. The reason this island is so barren is because they've already had to strip it clean of life more than once."

"And here I am, rowing toward it," said Nettles grimly. "Sunny."

"Stop rowing." Hope squinted her eyes out across the dark water, straining to see whatever had made the faint splash she'd just heard.

"I was joking," said Nettles.

"Shhh!" It was a new moon and there wasn't much light. So once Nettles put down the oars, Hope closed her eyes and listened. She heard Nettles and Brigga Lin breathing. Beyond that, she heard the water lapping against the side of the boat. And beyond that... she heard something cut across the surface of the water, then disappear.

"There's something out there," she murmured as she slowly fastened her clamp to her sword.

"I thought it was strange that there was no naval escort at the dock," said Brigga Lin. "They must have put some other security measures in place."

"Like what?" asked Nettles.

Something bumped against the small rowboat hard enough to send it drifting sideways.

"Piss'ell, I really hope it's not seals." Nettles squinted into the darkness.

"Seals would have tipped the boat by now," said Brigga Lin.

The water around the boat grew still again as the three waited. Then a shape burst out of the water. Hope's sword was in the air but the cramped conditions prevented her from getting a good swing while seated. Instead she held it up, the flat side facing out, her hand pressed against it near the tip. A pair of powerful jaws with rows of sharp teeth closed around the blade.

"Goblin shark!" said Brigga Lin.

The goblin shark was over fifteen feet long, dark purple in color, with a long pointed snout and jaws that could not only extend beyond the snout when attacking, but also rotate a full ninety degrees in either direction. This last detail was one of the biomancers' enhancements, along with the ability to swim comfortably in shallow waters, increased strength, and aggressiveness.

Its dark eye fixed on Hope as it bit down on the blade. Its jaw twisted hard one way, then the other, trying to wrench it from her grip. The force was so strong, if she'd been holding the sword with her hand, it would have worked. The Song of Sorrows might have been lost forever, along with her life.

The clamp held strong and the sword stayed where it was. Even so, she could feel the tension wires strain. If she didn't do something quickly, they would rip her tendons.

Nettles's chainblade snapped out and stabbed the eye. The goblin shark shuddered and began to pull back. But the Song of Sorrows had embedded itself so deeply in its jaw that it couldn't get away. It yanked desperately on the sword and on Hope's straining prosthesis. She grunted as bolts of pain shot up her arm.

"Release the sword!" said Brigga Lin.

Hope gritted her teeth and shook her head.

"Drown it all," muttered Brigga Lin as she wove her hands in an intricate pattern, then gestured to the goblin shark.

The shark shuddered as its teeth and jaw began to decay and crumble until it finally disintegrated. Blood poured from the gaping hole in its face as it fell back into the water.

"We should move quickly," said Brigga Lin, sliding over to sit next to Nettles and taking one of the oars. "They've been modified to become pack animals, so there's more close by. And once they smell the blood, they'll start to swarm."

Brigga Lin and Nettles rowed rapidly toward the shore. A few minutes later, Hope could hear the water churning as newly arrived goblin sharks fought over the wounded shark.

———

Once they reached shore, they dragged the boat up the beach until they reached an area with enough scrub brush to partly conceal it.

"It's not much," said Hope. "But we should be gone by daybreak anyway."

Most of the island was a flat expanse dotted with rocks and low shrubs. Now Hope was thankful that there was hardly any moon. Even so, she felt their exposure keenly as they crept across the wide, open area until they reached the cluster of tents.

In the center was a large rectangular tent, perhaps fifty yards across. Smaller tents formed a rough circle around the larger one. Hope couldn't see anyone around, but there were lanterns lit at regular intervals.

"I'd hoped they would all be asleep," whispered Hope as they crouched behind a stack of crates that smelled strangely of swamp mud. "But obviously, they wouldn't leave lanterns lit while they slept, so they must still be working."

"Some experiments are photosensitive and must be conducted at night," said Brigga Lin.

Hope pointed to the closest small tent, which was unlit. "Let's check that one first."

There was a small gap between flaps in the tent's entrance. Hope peeked in and saw a body on the ground, feet pointed toward her. The ankles were wrapped in chains and staked securely to the ground, but there was no movement. The faint light prevented her from making out any more details, but she caught the unmistakable stench of death.

She motioned to Nettles and Brigga Lin to follow, then slipped into the tent for a better look.

"Piss'ell," whispered Nettles when she entered the tent.

It was the body of what appeared to have been a little girl, filthy and naked. She was chained at the arms, wrists, knees, and ankles, all staked to the ground. The head had been removed.

"Why's it *chained*?" asked Nettles.

Hope turned to Brigga Lin. "Any idea?"

Brigga Lin's face was tense, but she shook her head. "Let's look in another tent."

Hope hated to leave the body there, exposed and desecrated as it was. But they needed to leave no trace of this visit. There would be time later, when they returned, to bury the dead.

The next tent was much the same. Small and dimly lit. Inside was another dead, naked girl chained and staked to the ground. This one still had her head, but her heart had been torn out.

Hope and Nettles turned questioningly to Brigga Lin.

"I have a suspicion. But it's..." She bit her lip. "I need to be certain. Let's look at another."

They moved to the next tent. As they crept silently along, Hope could feel the dark rage beginning to coil itself around her. The girls of High Guster had been bound for this fate. How many more had there been before? How many more to come if she didn't put a stop to it?

They found another girl in the next tent, naked and in chains, seven years old, perhaps a little younger. She still had her head and her heart, but she had been cut completely in half across the abdomen. Her entrails spilled across the ground, splayed out to reveal the severed backbone beneath. The girl's face still had a frown fixed on it, as if in the middle of an unpleasant dream.

"This...," said Nettles. "It's too much." She reached for one of the stakes, but Brigga Lin grabbed her hand and yanked it back. She looked ill, and her eyes showed something Hope had never seen in her before. Fear.

"What is it?" asked Hope. "You know what they've done?"

Brigga Lin only stared at the corpse. Hope looked back down at it as well. That's when she saw the eyelids flutter.

"Did it just—" began Nettles.

The eyes snapped open. They were yellowed and shot through with red veins beneath a milky film. They rolled around in their sockets as her head moved side to side, making unsettling cracking and popping noises. Her mouth opened and closed, the teeth making faint clicking sounds as they came together hard over and over again. Her arms pulled against her chains and her torso writhed, her entrails dragging through the dirt.

Then she noticed them, and strained harder at her chains. Her mouth opened and a guttural hiss escaped from the back of her throat.

Fear, horror, and revulsion all welled up inside Hope. But none of those emotions could compete with the dark rage for what had been done to this child. Before she even had the thought, the Song of Sorrows was out of its sheath. The clamp locked on and she grabbed it with her other hand as well. With as much force as she could muster, she stabbed the thing that had once been a girl between the eyes. It shuddered a moment, then grew still.

As her rage began to recede, and reason returned, Hope realized that instead of the usual pang of grief from the blade, she felt a prickly line of cold up her arm, as if ice had flown up through her veins.

"Necromancy," said Brigga Lin tonelessly. "I never imagined they would go so far."

"Necromancy?" asked Nettles, still staring at the corpse. "Like summoning ghosts and the like? I thought that was just balls and pricks. A con for the grieving and desperate."

"Ghosts, yes. But that isn't what the art of necromancy truly is. As biomancery is the manipulation of life, so necromancy is the manipulation of things that were once alive."

"They bring back the dead?" asked Hope.

"They don't bring the people themselves back. They animate dead bodies. These things are near-mindless creatures who lack any will of their own and obey the necromancer completely."

"Where does this art come from?" asked Hope.

"I thought you knew," said Brigga Lin. "Did your grandteacher never tell you? Necromancy comes from *your* people."

"*My* people?"

"From the self-proclaimed Jackal Lords of the Southern Isles."

Hope's throat felt tight. She had to force herself to speak. "I...knew of the Jackal Lords. My teacher was the one who stopped them from assassinating the emperor. But he never told me they were from the Southern Isles."

"Perhaps," said Brigga Lin, "he meant to spare your feelings."

"I thought the biomancers and Jackal Lords hated each other," said Nettles. "So why would they be working together now?"

"It's possible they've simply stolen the technique

from them. It appears these experiments are being conducted to see what injuries the reanimated corpses can and cannot survive. That suggests their knowledge may be incomplete."

"But why are they doing it?" asked Nettles.

"Perhaps it's time we looked in the central tent," said Brigga Lin. "The answer may be there."

"Not through the main entrance," said Hope. "We haven't seen any of the biomancers yet. They may all be gathered in that one large tent."

"Leave it to me." Nettles pulled a knife from her boot and gestured for them to follow her out of the tent. They circled around to the side of the large tent that was most shielded from the faint moonlight. Then she dropped down to her hands and knees and cut a small slit in the tent at her eye level. She held the knife handle out to them. Hope knelt next to her, took the knife, and cut a slit for herself, then handed it to Brigga Lin.

Hope had to steel herself before looking through the slit. She had never looked away from the horrors of the world. This time would be no different, but she felt a strange foreboding as she peeked through.

At one end of the tent, by the entrance, rows of small bodies lay on the ground, lined up head to foot. There were about fifty of them, with just enough space between each row to leave a narrow aisle. Biomancers moved among the naked corpses, stopping at each one to paint the skin with a thick, milky liquid.

At the other end of the tent were more naked corpses. But these were on their feet, like statues, lined up row after row, numbering in the hundreds. Perhaps more than a thousand all told.

A biomancer inspected the foremost row carefully. Beside him stood a man in the ragged brown robes that Hope knew were worn by the Jackal

Lords. The hood was thrown back, so she could see that he had chin-length blond hair and skin as pale as hers.

It wasn't that she'd disbelieved what Brigga Lin said. But to actually see someone who could have easily come from her home village, and watch him coldly examine one of the rigid, naked girls, brought a welter of questions and fears into her mind. Perhaps Brigga Lin was right, that Hurlo had been trying to shield her from the truth. But now it made her question her entire heritage. Had her parents known about the Jackal Lords? Had there even been one among the people of her village? She didn't remember seeing anyone in a brown robe when she was a girl, but her memory of those early years was patchy at best. What if her people hadn't simply settled in that inhospitable land out of a desire to find peace and simplicity? What if, centuries ago, they had been exiled there? Maybe when Northerners spoke of the savagery of the Southern Isles, this is what they'd meant.

The necromancer turned to one of the biomancers. His voice was a whisper, yet somehow it carried through the tent, like an invisible but inescapable stench.

"That's the last of the raw material we had on hand. When does this month's shipment arrive?"

"Any day now," said the biomancer.

Hope suspected that the "shipment" they were referring to was the group of girls she had just rescued. She allowed herself a grim smile that they would be disappointed when it didn't arrive.

"I hope your people are more careful about keeping them alive than they were with the last shipment," said the necromancer. "There are several days of predeath steps to the process that are required if you want them controllable."

"We must have complete dominance over them. Any who die during transit should simply be discarded."

"Waste of material," said the necromancer.

"Gathering the subjects is none of your concern," the biomancer said tersely. "You will be furnished with as many as you need."

The necromancer gazed at him with his pale eyes. "And how many is that, exactly? You still haven't told me."

"Until the council tells us to stop."

The necromancer shrugged. "I suppose that guarantees my continued usefulness for the foreseeable future." He went back to inspecting the stacks of corpses.

Nettles whispered in Hope's ear, "Am I right in thinking they're making a pissing army of the dead?"

"It ends now." Hope's hand shook as she pinched the slit in the tent shut and turned to Nettles and Brigga Lin. "There are only ten biomancers and one Jackal Lord. We can take them."

"What if they can wake that army whenever they want?" asked Brigga Lin. "Clearly, the ones lying down are still being prepared. But the much larger group on their feet look as though they are merely waiting for the command to move. If we charge in there, we may find ourselves facing that army of the dead all on our own."

Hope stared at her for a moment, then looked back through the slit in the tent at the rows of girls. How many more islands like High Guster?

"Hope..." Nettles's voice was uncharacteristically soft. "You know we're wags and I trust you with my life. And seeing those poor dead girls, all naked and stacked up like wooden soldiers, makes me sick. But I don't think even you two can handle this on your own."

"I'm not sure what effect my biomancery would even have on the dead," admitted Brigga Lin. "One reason biomancers have always distrusted necromancers in the past is because we have no power over their creatures."

Hope closed her eyes. For as long as she could remember, the image of her dead village in that tent had haunted her. She had not realized it before, but she had drawn strength from that image. It was the source of that darkness that had driven her onward for the last ten years.

But now when she closed her eyes, she saw *this* tent instead. She saw row upon row of dead girls treated like objects. And looming over it all was someone who might well have been a neighbor. She found she could draw no strength from that. Only grief.

"Okay," she said at last, her voice sounding strained in her own ears. "We'll go back to the ship and talk to the rest of the crew. Maybe together we can come up with a better plan."

Brigga Lin and Nettles looked at each other.

"Hope...," said Brigga Lin. "When I said 'your people,' I didn't mean—"

"It doesn't matter," said Hope. "Let's go."

―――

When they returned to the *Kraken Hunter* in the predawn light, the rest of the crew was waiting for them.

"Didn't any of you sleep through the night?" asked Hope as they climbed aboard.

"Piss on that," said Sadie, her eyes eager. "Judging by your grave looks, you've got things to say."

Hope took a slow breath. "It appears that the biomancers have enlisted the aid of a Jackal Lord to raise an army of the dead."

"Little girls," said Nettles flatly. "Made into little monsters."

Alash's eyes widened. "That's what the girls on that cargo ship were meant to be?"

"Aye," said Hope. "Obviously that wasn't the first ship. And from what we overheard, monthly shipments are coming in with no end in sight from all over the empire."

"What could they want with such a thing?" asked Finn.

"There is only one reason they would be driven to such desperate methods," said Brigga Lin. "They must believe an invasion from Aukbontar is imminent."

"How would Aukbontar invade from across the Dark Sea?" asked Jilly. "And *why*?"

Brigga Lin shrugged. "I don't know. But the Dark Mage predicted it would happen."

"Didn't the Dark Mage die centuries ago?" asked Alash.

"Old men cling to their prophecies," said Brigga Lin. "I used to believe it, too."

"And now?" asked Hope.

"To massacre thousands of the empire's children in order to protect that empire is utter madness," Brigga Lin said calmly.

"Maybe you're coming around to my way of seeing things." Nettles turned to Hope. "So what are we going to do about it?"

"What *can* we do?" Hope asked. "Even mortars would be out of range of the main tent, so we can't simply raze the island. And we don't have enough people for a frontal assault. What's worse, we've already lost the element of surprise. If they don't already know we were there, they soon will."

"Don't blame yourself for putting that one out of its misery," said Nettles. "I'd been just about to do the same thing myself."

"Hope has a point, though," said Brigga Lin. "Once they realize they've been discovered, they'll bring down imperial frigates from Vance Post. They'll probably fortify the shores as well. It won't be easy to get even this close again."

"So, what're we going to do?" asked Jilly, her eyes showing both eagerness and dread.

They all looked expectantly at Hope, but she had nothing to offer them except the sickness and grief in her heart.

"You know, I been thinking lately," said Nettles finally. "Seems like we keep taking imp ships, and it don't make much difference."

"These things take time," Alash said quickly.

"But I don't think it needs to," said Nettles. "See, that's where the original Dire Bane went wrong. He always wanted to go it alone. But he didn't have to. And we don't either."

Sadie's eyes narrowed. "I think I see where you're going with this." She turned to Hope. "If we had more ships and people, could we take the island?"

"Probably," said Hope. "But where would we get them?"

"Paradise Circle, of course," said Nettles. "Biggest shipyard outside of Stonepeak."

"We were able to recruit people to defend their own neighborhood," said Hope. "You think those people will follow us halfway across the empire?"

"Once I explain how they don't want an army of dead girls showing up at their doorstep."

"We don't even know who's controlling the neighborhood now," said Hope.

Nettles shrugged. "Whoever they are, I'm sure they'll be willing to negotiate with enough coin. We got all that money we been taking from the imp ships. We hardly use any of it."

"It makes a certain amount of sense," said Sadie.

"You agree with this, then?" asked Hope.

"Seems to me," said Sadie, "that this is a perfect opportunity."

"For what?" asked Hope.

Sadie turned to Brigga Lin. "Them biomancers got a lot riding on this project, right?"

"To fall in with a necromancer? I should say so."

"So if we take this down, not only do we stop them from killing a bunch of girls, but we kick them biomancers right in the balls so's they feel it. Maybe then they'll finally be ready to talk about freeing Red. This could be the chance we've been waiting for."

"But even assuming we could get enough people here," said Hope, "*should* we? Is it *right* for us to put them in this much danger?"

"Look," said Nettles. "You promised me a year ago that you were taking up the name of Dire Bane, champion of the people?"

"Yes, I—"

"Then you better start putting some faith in the people. It's a pissing insult to treat them all like a load of frightened babies. They face danger every day in Paradise Circle, and for a lot less than we're offering. This is their empire, too, and if you ask me, it's about pissing time they stepped up and did their part."

"A whole armada under the flag of Dire Bane...," Finn said quietly.

Sadie laughed delightedly. "It would scare them biomancers right out of their robes!"

"It's about time *they* were the scared ones for once," Jilly said.

Hope had never felt such doubt before. They were all looking at her with such enthusiasm now. And what they said made sense. But she was reluctant to spearhead such a massive undertaking, even if it was for a good cause.

She turned to Filler. "What do you think?"

"Is it so different from what we did to Drem?" he asked. "Bigger scale, maybe. But we inspired people to be more than they usually were. And they did it. They stood up for what was right and they won. What if we could do the same thing, but for the whole empire?"

"But do we have the right?" Hope asked.

"Are you seeking *permission*?" Brigga Lin said, her expression scathing. Perhaps even disappointed. "Why do I suddenly feel like we're back at that tavern in Stonepeak? Remember when you tried to tell me it was *our* fault for being women who wanted to do more within a patriarchal society? When you said *we* were the ones to blame for stepping outside an oppressive system?"

"It's not the same thing," objected Hope.

"Isn't it? You think it's a coincidence they're using *girls* for this experiment? They've been taking the boys into conscript to fill out their ranks for the war they believe is coming against Aukbontar. But not the girls, because girls don't belong in ships or in regular armies. Apparently they think the only way girls can serve any useful function in war is if they're turned into mindless, murdering corpses. So you tell me if it's the same thing."

Hope looked at her helplessly. Everything they said made sense. And yet something held her back.

Alash tentatively touched Hope's arm. "I think I understand your hesitation. Difficult though it is for me to believe, perhaps even you lose confidence in yourself in the face of a daunting task."

Was that it? Were her own fear and ego getting in the way? Perhaps even her shame at learning about her heritage? A leader should try to look at the larger picture. This was bigger than her, or even freeing Red. It was bigger than any one person. There was a passage in *The Book of Storms* that spoke of the people like drops of water. Individually, they might make little impact. But when they rose up together as a wave, nothing could stand against them. The biomancers knew this. It was why they purposefully instilled such fear. Perhaps there needed to be a symbol to combat that. Bleak Hope could never be that. But perhaps Dire Bane, champion of the people, could.

She looked around at them all again. This family she had collected over the last year. She might doubt herself, but judging by the look in their eyes, they did not doubt her. She had asked them to trust her many times in the past. Perhaps it was time for her to trust them.

"If we are all agreed, then that's what we'll do." With each word she spoke, her voice grew stronger. More certain. "Then what we have done up till now was only to prepare us for this. If the biomancers are so eager for a war, Aukbontar may not oblige, but we will."

PART TWO

For most people, the darkness descends unexpected and cruel. It is a torment they would rather be rid of. But for some of us, it is as impossible to escape the darkness as it is to escape from ourselves.

—from the secret writings of
the Dark Mage

10

*C*aptain Vaderton clung to the wheel of the *Guardian* because there was a very real risk he might fall over if he let go. He had not slept for any substantial length of time in days. He would allow himself to doze against the wheel for short periods, but the risk of anything longer was too great. In sleep, he might miss sighting land. Or he might run aground somewhere. Or he might encounter more pirates. With a dead crew and no cannons, even a tiny sloop of the lowliest cutthroats could take his ship as a prize.

He had chartered a course for Kelvacka, which was the island they'd disembarked from before encountering the *Kraken Hunter.* Kelvacka had a small but well-maintained imperial station. Better still, he knew the officers there would remember him from his recent visit, and he hoped that would give him some credibility. He would need it, if he wanted them to believe the fantastical news he had to impart.

But they *must* believe him. Days earlier, he had watched the *Kraken Hunter* sail away, leaving him bereft of ammunition, crew, and honor. He had sworn that he would survive long enough to reach an imperial outpost and warn them of this terrible new threat to the empire. He'd been able to get the *Guardian* moving, although not at any great pace. It should have been only three or four days to Kelvacka, but

with only a few sails set on this hulking mass of a
ship, it would take a week or more. And that was if
the weather and wind held. A ship like the *Guardian*
was not meant to be sailed by one man.

The only thing he didn't need to worry about was
supplies. There was enough food and drink to last
two hundred men a month. It would go bad before
he could eat it all. But that didn't mean there was no
urgency in his task. After all, he had to warn everyone
about Dire Bane as soon as possible. He feared this
had been merely her opening gambit in a much larger
and more ferocious campaign to terrorize the seas.
His superiors needed to know about her unconventional methods of attack before she took another ship
as big as the *Guardian*. Before any more men died.

He had debated for some time on what to do with
his own crew of dead men. Naval law dictated that
in times of conflict, burial at sea was acceptable. But
he could not bring himself to simply throw two hundred men over the side of the ship. Besides, what if
the officers at Kelvacka wanted proof of what had
happened? If they didn't believe that Dire Bane had
a woman capable of biomancery among her crew,
the grotesque corpses she had left behind would
quell their doubts. So he had dragged all those on
deck down to join their fellows on the gun deck to
await inspection and proper burial. Unfortunately,
the smell permeated everything below, including
the captain's cabin. He had to remain topside at all
times. And even then, as he stood hour after hour,
day after day at the wheel, he thought he caught the
stench of death seeping up through the deck now
and then. But perhaps that was his imagination.

Once the decks were clear, there was little else to
do but keep the ship pointed in the correct direction
for as long as it took. All he had to do was stay awake
and stay sane.

The second task was at times even more challenging than the first. He'd seen prisoners interrogated with any number of methods, including sleep deprival, so he knew what lack of sleep could do to a man. But foreknowledge didn't make it any easier. There would be moments he would find himself disoriented, unable to remember where he was and what he was trying to do. Eventually, in one of his more lucid moments, he found a small bucket of tar and painted the direction and purpose on the deck next to him:

> **Head 38° north-northeast to Kelvacka to warn them about Dire Bane!**

As the days and nights bled into one another, that black scrawl at his feet became a lifeline. He read it aloud frequently. In general, he found talking out loud a great comfort. He decided to rehearse what he would say to the officers on Kelvacka. After all, he would need to be careful he didn't come across as a lunatic. Even if they recalled the calm sobriety with which he had conducted himself during his last inspection, the things he needed to tell them— about decoy phantoms and invisible ships, about sword-handed Vinchen warrior women and lady biomancers who could cast from afar...if he did not deliver this information with a calm equanimity, they might think he had gone mad. They might even accuse him of murdering his own crew, as preposterous as that seemed. He had to convince them of the urgency of his news without resorting to hysterics. Captain Vaderton had never been hysterical in his life. But he had never been given to sudden fits of laughter either, and he'd caught himself doing that several times now. It was oddly like a sneezing fit. Something he seemed unable to predict or control. He needed to be more vigilant against such outbursts.

Day after day, he held it in and stayed the course and reminded himself why he must. Then, finally, on a pleasant, sunny afternoon, he spotted land.

"Land ho!" he cried. To celebrate, he allowed himself the hysterical laughter he had been holding back for a while. But the trouble was, once he started, he couldn't stop. It felt like a geyser bubbling up from deep within. He laughed so hard, his insides ached. He laughed so long that rather than find a dock, he simply ran the ship aground on an empty stretch of beach about as far from the imperial station as one could get. It wasn't until he heard the thunderous crack of timbers in the hull of his great warship that his laughter subsided.

He gathered as much food and water as he could. It was somewhat difficult, what with the ship leaning at an angle from its broken keel, but he delighted in the newness of this challenge, even making a bit of a game of it.

Finally, he was ready to disembark. He had on his captain's coat and hat, plus food and water strapped diagonally across his chest with a sash.

He climbed carefully down the side of the hull. Once he stood on the sand, he allowed himself one last look at his precious warship. The *Guardian*'s sails were in tatters, its hull pockmarked with cannon shot. It leaned awkwardly on its side, like a beached whale. As he gazed at it, he began to laugh again.

Still laughing, he trudged up the beach and into the dense forest that separated him from his goal.

As he walked, he continued to laugh. Sometimes it was only a giggle. Other times, it grew so strident he would have to pause for a moment until it lessened again. There were even a few times he thought someone else was laughing instead of him. In those moments, he would grow suddenly silent, his wide eyes rolling around in their sockets as he tried to look everywhere at once. But then he would realize that, no, it was still just him, and he would burst out again with renewed laughter.

By the time he reached the edge of the forest and saw the small, bustling town, his uniform was splattered with mud and torn in several places. He'd lost his hat somewhere along the way, and his hair was matted with twigs and leaves. He had cuts on his face from lashing tree branches, and his teeth were bared in a tight grimace, his jaw clenched in case another onslaught of laughter erupted.

When he staggered into the station house, he did his utmost to sound calm and reasonable as he explained the grave new threat to the empire. The young officers in their pristine white uniforms listened to everything he had to say with wide eyes, not interrupting once.

Then they clapped him in irons.

———

Vaderton decided that the best thing about being thrown in the brig was finally being able to sleep. And with sleep, he regained at least some sense of self-awareness. But sadly, that led to a fuller understanding of his situation.

When he woke, he found himself in a neat, tidy eight-by-ten cell with a bunk built into the wall. There was a tray of bread with a bowl of water. The view through his bars only showed an empty wall, and there were no windows. He didn't see or hear another person. That was just as well. He was still exhausted, and doubted he'd be able to present his case much better than he had before. So he ate and drank, relieved himself in the chamber pot in the corner, and went back to sleep.

"Time to wake up, sir."

Vaderton clawed his way back to consciousness once again and sat up in his bunk. A young officer in crisp white stood on the other side of the bars. Vaderton had been relieved of his own ruined uniform and now wore a simple cotton shirt and loose trousers belted at the waist with a bit of rope.

He moved slowly, gingerly over to the bars, aware he now looked more like a common crewman than an officer. He tried to give the young officer on the other side of the cell a companionable smile.

"I feel greatly recovered after a good rest, and believe I can now better communicate the urgent intelligence I uncovered at the edge of the Dusk Sea."

"With respect, sir, there will be time for that when we arrive at Keystown."

"Keystown?" Perhaps they were taking his warning more seriously than he'd feared. Keystown was the military barracks on New Laven, second only to Stonepeak in authority, and charged with protecting the entire southern half of the empire. Since his clash with Dire Bane occurred within their jurisdiction, it only made sense they would want to hear his report first. They might even take the report to Stonepeak themselves. The admiralty was reluctant to allow a mere ship's captain to go directly before the emperor.

"Let's be on our way, then," Vaderton said. "Time is of the essence."

"Yes, sir," agreed the young officer. "If you would put your hands through the slot, sir."

There was a horizontal slot in the bars just big enough to fit a pair of hands. That way, the prisoner could be manacled safely before the cell door was opened.

"I see." Vaderton looked gravely at the officer as he put his hands through.

"Apologies, sir," said the officer as he secured the cold iron manacles. "Orders, you know."

"Of course," said Vaderton, displaying a confidence he didn't quite feel. "This will all get sorted out once I get to Keystown."

"I'm sure it will, sir," said the officer.

They were accompanied from the station by two other officers down to a small imperial messenger sloop docked in the harbor. Off to one side, Vaderton saw villagers going about their morning routine, occasionally glancing curiously at Vaderton and his uniformed escorts. He couldn't help but wonder if they thought him some terrible criminal. Maybe even a pirate. He was surprised to find a small urge to laugh again. Perhaps he had not completely recovered from his trauma yet.

It was only a couple of days to New Laven. There was no brig on such a small ship, so they kept him confined to a cabin. They were courteous, but distant. He suspected that even if his story were believed, he would still have to face a court-martial. He'd lost the greatest warship in the empire and its entire crew on his first tour. He'd probably have to spend a few months in the officers' brig, coupled with a hefty fine. Perhaps even a public lashing, if they thought it would set an example for the other officers. And after he'd endured all that, it seemed unlikely they would ever let him captain an imperial ship again. They might even discharge him. And then what? He would have to resort to captaining a merchant ship, or worse, a pleasure yacht for the rich and idle.

But still, he must do his duty and deliver his intelligence, no matter the cost.

He watched through his tiny portal as they sailed into the bay. He couldn't see Silverback to the south, but he could see Keystown to the north. He'd always liked the look of it. Unlike most of New Laven, it was pragmatically designed and clean.

Once the sloop had been secured to the docks, the

officers from Kelvacka put him back in manacles and led him up to the deck. There they were met by a squad of six fully armed imperial soldiers.

"We'll take him from here, sirs," the lieutenant said bluntly.

The officers from Kelvacka looked nervously at one another and nodded. While they technically out-ranked the lieutenant, officers on smaller islands like Kelvacka were unaccustomed to such forceful military bearing. They watched from the deck of their sloop as Vaderton was led into Keystown with far less courtesy than they had showed him.

The soldiers led him through the civilian area of Keystown, which looked much like Stonepeak, with its white-walled, neatly spaced buildings. The few people they passed acted as if they didn't even see the small procession. Vaderton had a sudden urge to wave and shout to them. Further evidence that he still had not recovered from his ordeal, no doubt. Or, he reflected, perhaps it was the quiet anxiety building in him about a possible further traumatic experience to come. Because if he could glean any information from his dour, silent escorts, it was that he was not going anywhere good.

Of course not, he reminded himself. He had failed in his duties as captain, after all, and deserved to be disciplined. But it would be a fair and impartial pun-ishment. The navy was strict, but there were rules in place concerning self-governance that would prevent gross abuse toward the officer class, even if they were suspected of misconduct.

He clung to that thought as the soldiers led him into the area of Keystown restricted to military per-sonnel only. They led him past rows of barracks and soldiers training in firearms.

They took him into the admiralty building, a stately building with tall archways. He thought that was an encouraging sign. At least they were taking his warnings seriously enough to warrant an audience with command.

But rather than take him to the main audience room, they took him down a side hallway, past several closed doors, and what little encouragement he'd felt evaporated. They opened the last door on the right and pushed him roughly inside.

It was clearly an interrogation room, windowless and bare except two chairs and a table with a large latch in the middle that could be secured to manacles. That didn't bode well.

But then the lieutenant removed his manacles. So Vaderton didn't know what to think. He watched uneasily as the soldiers left the room, locking the door on their way out.

"Captain Brice Vaderton, I presume," came a voice directly behind him. He could have sworn the room had been empty a moment before, but when he turned back to the table, he saw a biomancer seated across from him. His deep white hood hid most of his features, but Vaderton could see some deformity in his lower jaw, as if his face were melted wax.

"Please sit, Captain." The biomancer gestured to the empty chair across the table from him.

"Yes, sir." Vaderton sat.

The biomancer smiled. "Fitmol Bet said you always knew your place. I'm glad to see that's still true."

"I live to serve the empire, sir."

"As do I, Captain. Now . . ." The biomancer leaned in a little and steepled his hands in front of him. "Tell me everything you remember about this one-handed female Vinchen calling herself Dire Bane, and the supposed female biomancer she had with her."

11

$\mathcal{A}$s Nettles walked with Filler down old familiar streets, she decided that it felt good to be back in Paradise Circle. Like an old lover you knew from back when, it was easier to reconnect than she expected.

There were places that everybody gathered, and she still recognized most of the faces. And there were her favorite little nooks and crannies only she knew about, still waiting for her. Even the filthy streets held a strange comfort in their stubborn refusal to ever change. She took in a deep breath of air flavored with bodies, food, spilled ale, mud, piss, and a hundred other things, and she sighed.

"Well, Filler. We're back."

Filler nodded. "Hasn't changed a bit."

"I reckon we have, though."

"Seen a lot this year."

"I suppose so," said Nettles. "Now, let's see if we can still talk ourselves into a free place to sleep at the Slice of Heaven."

Hope had given Nettles all the money she'd asked for. The imperial ships they'd raided always had healthy strongboxes, and while some of that had gone toward regular repair of the ship and supplies for the crew, there was still a lot left over. More, in fact, than Nettles had ever held in her hand at once. It was tempting to put up in the nicest inn Paradise Circle had to offer, but the more money she could keep for bribes, the better. And it couldn't hurt to call in a few favors from her old crew. Besides, Nettles needed to find out what had been happening around here in the last year. And as any proper wag of the Circle knew, whores always had the best gossip.

It was a short walk from the docks to the Slice of Heaven. From the outside, the building was indistinguishable from its neighbors. A plain, unadorned three-story structure with no sign and all the curtains drawn. It was late afternoon, so business hours had begun. Nettles knocked three times slow, then three times fast on the dull pink door. A moment later, a girl Nettles didn't recognize peeked out. She wore a thin slip that covered a great deal but still managed to show just about everything.

"Welcome to Slice of—"

"Skip it, molly," Nettles said. "I used to work here."

The girl halted and nodded awkwardly, then shuffled out of the way. *Poor girl,* thought Nettles. Still getting her feet. The new ones always had door duty. Mo usually didn't have them start taking clients until after the first month.

The parlor was filled with old velvet and silk-covered furniture. Half-naked toms and mollies lounged idly around, waiting for the evening rush to begin. When Nettles stepped into the room, she was met by exclamations of "Nettles!" and "She's back!" Some even jumped up to give her a hug. She graciously allowed it. She couldn't deny it felt nice to be missed. Near as she could remember, this was the first time she'd ever had the experience. But she did have a reputation to uphold. One she'd most likely be needing quite a bit in the weeks to come. So after a few moments, she cut it off.

"Yeah, alright. Enough of that. I'm not staying for good, so don't get your hopes up. Is Mo around?"

"I'll take you, Nettles!" shouted Misandry. He popped up from his spot on one of the couches, sending two other toms sprawling to the floor.

Misandry was one of the most popular toms at the Slice of Heaven. He was tall and slender, with long hair and a finely pointed face. His birth name was Andrew, but when he began whoring he decided to call himself Miss Andy. A short time later—this was back when Red and Nettles were tossing—Red started to call him Misandry. Since it was a bit easier to say, everyone else picked up on it and soon it was the only name people knew. Months later, Nettles and Misandry learned that it was one of Red's little book-smart jokes. *Misandry* was a real word that meant "hatred of men." But by then it was too late. The name had stuck.

Nettles had been angry, worried it would turn away male clients for him. But Misandry thought it was just as funny as Red did. Nettles reckoned it was whore humor that Red had picked up from his dad. The name never caused problems with the clients anyway. Probably because none of them knew what it meant either.

Misandry came up to her now. He was bare-chested, his lean torso hairless and tightly muscled. He wore loose pants that hung low enough on his hips to hint that he was hairless all over.

"Thanks, Misandry," said Nettles as she eyed him up appreciatively. "Got someone else to keep you neat, I see."

His lip turned down in a pout. "She's not as good as you. Nicked my balls the other day. Thought I'd never stop bleeding." He led them across the parlor to a set of unmarked doors in the back.

"Is it worth it?" asked Nettles. "Seems like a lot of trouble to me."

"The toms love it." He slipped over to stand next to Filler. "Ain't that right, Filler?"

Filler shrugged. "Not really. Just didn't want to hurt your feelings."

Misandry scowled at him. "What do *you* know?" He threw open the doors, his head high as he moved in front of them. "*Most* toms love it."

He led them down a dim hallway, past the rooms where the whores actually slept, past the baths, and the kitchen, to the last set of doors.

He knocked respectfully. "Mo, got an old friend visiting."

"I don't have old friends," came a smooth, calm voice from inside. "Only enemies and ex-employees."

"The second, then," Misandry said impatiently.

"You may come in, then."

When Misandry pushed open the door, Nettles saw that Mo hadn't changed a bit. Chin-length hair, fine, elegant features, a perfectly tied cravat and impeccably tailored jacket. Mo sat behind a dark wood desk scattered with books, papers, a pipe, and a box of tobacco. The lingering scent of pipe smoke still hung in the air, mixing with the scented candles that flickered on the shelf edges of an already overstuffed bookcase. A glass of neat whiskey sat just within reach on the desk.

No one knew if Mo was male or female. Mo had been running the Slice of Heaven since as far back as anyone who worked there remembered, even old Betty Pits, the cook. It was easy to think Mo was fairly young by the smooth face, and a certain undefinable allure that both men and women of all preferences felt. But it was impossible to say for sure. No one knew where Mo came from, or even if Mo ever left the Slice of Heaven. Despite the lack of knowledge, or more likely because of it, speculating about Mo's origin was one of the favorite pastimes for the employees at the Slice of Heaven. Everything from disgraced royalty to escaped biomancer experiment. It all seemed equally likely.

Whatever Mo's background, the one thing everyone knew for certain was that the whores at the Slice of Heaven had the best quality of living of any brothel in Paradise Circle, which brought the most attractive whores and in turn, the best-paying customers. Mo was also famously loyal to her employees, past and present. Nettles was counting on that.

"Well, well," said Mo laconically. "Our Briar Rose come back to us? Only for a visit, I think."

"Just for a little while, Mo," said Nettles. "If you can spare the room."

Mo's head tilted curiously to the side. "Have you actually taken a tom?"

Nettles glanced back at Filler. "Him? Nah. He's just a wag and doesn't run that way anyhow."

"You're asking for both of you, though?"

"I'll vouch for him, too, Mo," said Misandry, putting his arm protectively through Filler's. "He has terrible taste in grooming style, but otherwise, he's a sugar lump."

"I suppose for a little while is fine," said Mo. "But more than a week, I'll expect at least one of you to start taking clients." Mo smiled faintly at Nettles. "Your old position has been filled."

Misandry made a sour face. "Cabbage is about as fun to talk to as he sounds."

"He keeps my employees safe, and that is what I require of him," said Mo.

"If all goes according to plan, we won't be here long anyway," said Nettles.

Mo looked carefully at Nettles. "Whatever your *plan* is, it stays out of this establishment. Understood?"

"I keen," said Nettles.

"Very well. Welcome home, Briar Rose."

"Thanks, Mo. You're a true wag of the Circle. You know if Tosh is around?"

"I believe she is just finishing up with a client."

"Alright. I'll go say hi."

"I can keep this one entertained, if you want," Misandry said, still holding Filler's arm. "Even give you a discount, since he wishes I was all *hairy*."

Filler gave her a hopeful look. She sighed and dug a coin out of her bag. "This will not be a daily occurrence." She tossed the coin to Filler, then looked at Misandry. "And mind his leg. I need him no more damaged than you found him."

"What happened there?" asked Misandry as he led Filler back down the hall. "I don't remember you having that brace the last time you were here."

"Got shot during the raid on the Three Cups."

Misandry's eyes widened. "Really? I had to *work* that day." He threw a quick scowl back at Mo, then continued to pull Filler down the hall, leaning into him conspiratorially. "So I missed all the excitement. You'll have to tell me *everything*."

Once they were gone, Mo asked, "How is Red?"

Nettles turned back to Mo. It was those pissing eyes. Dark and open and completely free of judgment. She never could stand up to them all the years she worked here, and the same seemed to still hold true now. She tried to say something quick and dismissive. Or something clever, even. It all stuck in her throat, and her eyes stung with suppressed tears.

"That bad?" asked Mo patiently.

Finally she caved. A single tear rolled down her cheek. In a ragged and poncey voice as soft as any artist from Silverback, she said, "He's gotten himself into the worst fix you could imagine."

"I'm sorry to hear that."

"Yeah." Nettles swiped fiercely at the offending tear with her sleeve. "Well, we ain't giving up. We'll bring him home yet."

"I knew his father," said Mo.

"What?"

"Not well. But our paths crossed several times. He was a beautiful man, and always very kind to me during my...troubled period. So if there is anything I can do to help, as long as it does not endanger my employees, you may ask."

Nettles nodded. She wanted to find out more, but Mo hardly ever volunteered even this much about her past. So instead she just said, "Thanks, Mo. You're still the mom and dad I wish I'd had."

———

Nettles made her way up to the second floor to the room where Mo said she'd find Tosh.

"Come in." She heard Tosh's light, cheerful voice.

But when she opened the door, she saw Tosh on the bed with a naked man lying on top of her.

"I thought you were done," said Nettles.

Tosh sighed and rolled the unconscious man off her. "Apparently I am. Knew this was going to happen the moment he came in. Had that combination of nervous and drunk that frequently leads to a quick squirt and a long nap."

"For the chute, then?" asked Nettles. The Slice of Heaven had an understanding with many local captains. Customers who didn't pay, acted up, or were just plain annoying tended to get drugged and dropped down a chute that emptied out by the docks. They usually woke up the next day miles from shore, conscripted to a ship headed for somewhere unpleasant, like the Southern Isles.

"We're not really doing that anymore," said Tosh. "Cabbage can't really manage it like you could."

"Ah well. It was a nice little bit of money," said Nettles. The captains were supposed to leave a little bonus in a drop box for the brothel for each crew

member they gained. It was an honor system, and for
the most part they kept their end of the agreement.
Every once in a while, one would try to slip out without paying. But they'd return to New Laven eventually. And when they did, Nettles had been there to
explain to them how things were in the Circle. Usually with her chainblade.

"How you doing otherwise?" she asked as she sat
down on the edge of the bed.

Tosh stretched luxuriantly, arching her back to
give Nettles a nice look at her large bare breasts.
"Can't complain. Money's good. Not sure how many
more years of this I've got in me, you know. So I've
been saving up proper."

"You always were one of the smart ones." Nettles
took one of Tosh's feet and placed it on her lap. Then
she began to rub with slow, gentle pressure.

"Mmmm." Tosh closed her eyes. "What are you
back in town for? I thought you were off to *find a better you* or something."

"Got some things to take care of," said Nettles,
sliding her hands up to rub Tosh's ankle and calf.
"It would be nice if someone filled me in on what I
missed while I was away. How things are now in the
Circle."

"That so?" Tosh opened one eye and smirked. "I
suppose I could do that for you. How's about you finish me from where that gaf left off for old times' sake
while I catch you up."

"Yeah, alright." Nettles pushed the naked, unconscious man off the bed. He snorted and groaned
when he hit the thick rug, but didn't wake up. Nettles stretched out next to Tosh on the bed. She loved
being fully clothed next to someone naked. There
was power in that.

Her hand reached out and made its way from
Tosh's collarbone, down her breasts, lingering for a

moment at the nipple before then slipping down to dance on her rib cage. Eventually she made her way to Tosh's abdomen. She lingered there a bit before pressing her palm against the hair between Tosh's legs. She could feel the heat as Tosh pushed back against her.

"Finish you off?" asked Nettles. "You're barely started."

"It'll give you something to do while I talk," said Tosh. "A lot can happen in a year. I promise I'll be thorough."

"Then I suppose I should be thorough, too," said Nettles as she gently stroked between Tosh's smooth thighs. Then she settled in more comfortably and got to work.

———

Tosh didn't really have much to say that Nettles couldn't have guessed. But it was nice to reconnect with a molly she'd had many happy memories with. She also appreciated that Tosh was not one for sentiment or cuddling after.

Nettles washed her hands and face in the water basin on the table by the bed while Tosh squatted over the piss pot on the other side.

"So there's no one who's really taken the lead here, now that Drem's gone?" asked Nettles.

"Not really," said Tosh as she peed. "I suppose there's one gaf with a few more boots than the rest, which gives him a slight edge. Says he was born and raised in the Circle, but I'd never seen him before. Heard through a client that he got in trouble a long time ago with Jix the Lift. Ran off to Hammer Point, then spent a few years on the Empty Cliffs."

"Oh yeah?" A suspicion began to crawl through Nettles's gut. "This gaf got a name?"

"What was it…" Tosh frowned. "Oh yeah. Mick the Sick."

"Piss'ell," groaned Nettles. "Of all the cunt-droppings in the sea, it had to be him."

"You know him?"

"He's my pissing brother," said Nettles.

———

"I didn't even know you *had* a brother," said Filler as the two walked down Central Street. The sun had set and the imps in white and gold uniforms were lighting the street lamps.

"That's because I'd hoped I didn't have one anymore," said Nettles, her eyes darting constantly. The familiar cobblestones of Paradise Circle no longer held the same comfort, now that she knew her brother was in town. "I hear people fall off the Empty Cliffs all the time. Some get pushed, some just can't take it and jump."

"And you were counting on one of those two?"

"Nah, I figured it much more likely he'd get pushed. He's that kind of gaf."

Filler nodded and didn't push for more. Nettles could always count on him to know when to let things be. Red would have had a hundred different questions, the answers to which she likely didn't want to think about, much less talk about. He could be exhausting like that, because he never quite understood how it really was in the Circle. He *thought* he did. He had his own version of the Circle, filled with scoundrels and clever schemes. But unless you were born into it, you'd never be more than someone who skimmed across the top of the muck. The truth was, terrible things happened in Paradise Circle. Nettles understood that in a way Red never could.

She turned to Filler. "If Mick's making a play

for the neighborhood, Handsome Henny knows something about it. And we'll find Henny at the Drowned Rat."

The Drowned Rat had been around since before Nettles was born. It had changed hands a few times, and maybe it wasn't as popular as it had been in the legendary days of Bracers Madge. But it was still a place where true wags of Paradise Circle could get a tankard of ale and brag about the misdeeds they'd been getting up to lately.

When Nettles and Filler stepped into the dim, smoke-filled tavern, Prin the bartender waved to them.

"Well, look at you two blown in on the wind!"

"Hey, Prin," said Filler.

Nettles gave Prin a quick wave as she scanned the tables for Henny. She found him in the back at the same old table with the Twins. "Round of dark for the old crew, would you, Prin?"

"Coming up, Nettles," said Prin. "You and Filler are on me, though. Good to see your faces here."

"That's real sunny of you, Prinny!" said Filler, who was at least as fond of ale as he was of pretty boys.

Handsome Henny's back was to Nettles. The Twins saw her coming and their eyes went wide, but Nettles put her finger to her lips, and they eased back into their chairs, giving each other a quick smirk. Brimmer and Stin weren't actually twins, or even brothers. But their red hair was so unusual in the predominantly dark-haired population of New Laven that everyone assumed they must be related. By the time anyone realized the truth, the name had stuck. And like Misandry, when you got a name in Paradise Circle, it tended to stay.

Nettles snuck up behind Henny. He was complaining about something, as usual. She crouched down, got in close, then jammed her thumbs into his rib cage while shouting, *"You're under arrest!"*

Handsome Henny shot forward, diving across the table and landing in a heap between Brimmer and Stin, who were now laughing hysterically. He jumped to his feet, his face flushed with anger until he saw it was Nettles who had done it to him. Then his face softened. Which wasn't to say he looked any more pleasant. Handsome Henny got his nickname after a guard dog bit his nose off.

"Oh yes, very funny." He glared at the Twins. "And thanks for the warning, my wags."

"Sorry, Hen," said Brimmer.

"It's only Nettie and Fill," said Stin.

"Right," said Henny, still looking irritated. "What if I'd accidentally shot them instead? Wouldn't be so funny then, would it? Like to happen as not, times being what they are."

"Oh, come off it, Hen." Nettles sat down in his chair, still grinning. "We all know you're the type to bolt, not turn."

Filler pulled up a chair next to her.

"Things is different now, Nettie." Handsome Henny shoved a space open between Brimmer and Stin so he could sit down across from her. "You don't know."

"True." Nettles paused as Prin came over with a tray of foamy tankards. Once Prin was gone, Nettles shoved a tankard at each of them. "So why don't you tell me?"

Henny took the tankard suspiciously. "What's your game, Nettie? And where you been this whole time?"

"Fill and I been just about everywhere in this empire, and seen a great many things. I came back because bad things are happening for the whole empire and Hope needs help fixing them. I meant

to ask whoever might be running things here in the
Circle to help us out. This is about the only friendly
place she knows of and I figure a Hero of the Circle
deserves some consideration, at least."

"So you're here to—" began Brimmer.

"I said that's why I *came*. But I'm afraid that won't
be enough now. Tell me true, Henny. Is Mick the Sick
making a play for Paradise Circle?"

Henny's eyebrows rose. "He is. But how'd you—"

"And since you are a betting wag, would you say
his chances are good?"

Henny frowned. "I don't like to think it, and the
margin ain't wide, but I'd say that he has a better
chance than any of the other gafs that are making
moves."

"I figured." She drank down her tankard in one
go, then leaned back in her chair. "You know how
Mick the Sick got that name?"

Henny and the Twins exchanged glances.

"Didn't think so," said Nettles. "Back when we
were kids, my brother used to torture animals. Dogs
and cats mostly. Then after a while, that wasn't
enough. He started doing it to other kids in the
neighborhood. He'd cut on them, break fingers and
the like. But even that wasn't enough."

She let that sink in a moment as they looked at
each other uncomfortably.

"So one night I come home and he's got this boy,
maybe a little younger than us. The boy's dead and
Mick has slit his belly open. While the blood and
guts are leaking out, he's got his cock stuck inside
the wound, groaning and sighing like he's tossing."

Henny gaped at her. Stin put down his tankard
and pushed it away. Brimmer looked like he might
throw up in his.

"Once he realized I was there, he...went after
me." Nettles's throat started to tighten up, so she

took Stin's abandoned tankard and drank it down. "I managed to get away eventually, and told Jix the Lift. Now, Jix was a lot of bad things, but he couldn't abide cruelty to kids. Since Mick was still just a kid himself, though, Jix decided to let him live, as long as he never came back to Paradise Circle."

"And this...is your *brother*?" asked Handsome Henny.

"That's right. Now, let me ask you, is this someone you want in charge of the Circle?"

Mutely, they all shook their heads.

"Then we have to do everything we can to make sure it doesn't happen," said Nettles. "Even if that means *I* have to take Paradise Circle for myself instead."

12

*T*ry this one, Humey." Red handed Hume a small tin whistle.

Hume accepted the whistle, his expression as grave as ever. He waited until Red set his feet far apart and put his hands on the shop counter. Then he blew.

The sound gave a piercing, unpleasant shriek, but Red didn't feel the least bit dizzy. It was the fifth whistle they'd tried and he was starting to worry he'd never find the one that nearly knocked him out.

The night he'd escorted Nea to the inn, there had been so much going on that he hadn't fully comprehended the enormity of what the biomancers had done to him. They had given him a weakness that only *they* understood. What's more, they had somehow done it without him even being aware of it. It was a rude awakening that even the little rebelliousness he'd been quietly nursing meant nothing. They had him by the balls.

But they'd slipped up and shown their hand. Or Brackson had, anyway. And a secret weapon wasn't as effective once it wasn't secret anymore. Because if he could find the same kind of whistle, maybe he could figure out a way to counteract it.

He turned to the tinsmith, who had been anxiously watching the whistle sampling on the other side of the counter.

"You sure these work right, my wag? Maybe this is a bad batch?"

"A bad batch?" The tinsmith's face flushed.

"My lord," Hume said calmly. "Mr. Ifmish is known to be the foremost tinsmith in the empire."

"Oh, hey, no offense, old pot." Red patted the smith on the back.

"As I said before, my lord, these are *dog* whistles. The pitch is much too high for people to hear."

"Right, and..." Red paused, then looked at Hume. "And we can't hear these, can we?"

"That is correct, my lord," said Hume.

"Ah. No. Of course we can't." He turned back to Ifmish. "Right, so clearly these whistles are quality. But seeing as how you're such a *renowned* fellow, maybe you can answer something that's been on my mind."

"I will do my best, my lord," Ifmish said, clearly struggling to keep his temper. Red had noticed some of these artisans could be as rigid as lacies.

"That's real sunny of you," said Red. "Now, my question is, do you know of a different pitch like this that most people can't hear? Something other than this dog pitch?"

Ifmish pursed his lips and Red watched his arrogance and exasperation replaced with curiosity. That was the difference between lacies and artisans. In the end, most artisans still cared more about their art than their ego.

"There is no other whistle commonly made that is either above or below the pitch of human hearing, but that isn't to say one couldn't be made."

"Below human hearing?" asked Red. "That can happen, too?"

"In theory," said Ifmish. "But it would have to be a very large whistle."

Red shook his head. "This one was really small. Smaller than all of these."

"Generally speaking, the smaller the whistle, the higher the pitch."

"Could you make me one as high-pitched as possible?"

"Higher than these, I take it?" Ifmish gestured to the dog whistles.

"As high as you can and still call it a whistle," said Red.

"I suppose. But it will involve some trial and error. And tin isn't cheap."

"How's this to start?" Red slid a stack of gold on the counter and watched the tinsmith's eyes light up.

"I'll make it my top priority, my lord. I should have something for you in a few days."

"Sunny, Mr. Ifmish. It's hard to put into words, exactly, but trust that you're doing me a true service."

"I don't often get a real challenge that doesn't take away from putting food on the table for the family," said Ifmish. "This will be a rare pleasure."

"I understand that more than you might think, my wag, and I'm very glad I could give you both."

As Red and Hume left the tin shop and began walking down Artisan Way toward the palace, Red felt the first tiny prickle of hope he'd felt in weeks. He might not understand what the biomancers had done to him yet. But once he did, then *he'd* be the one with a secret weapon.

"Sorry for dragging you all over the city like this," Red said to Hume. "It's just that I needed someone to help me out with this, in case…things went leeward."

"I am pleased to be of service, my lord," said Hume.

"It's also a personal problem of a real…delicate nature, keen?"

"I will of course speak to no one about it," said Hume. "But might I suggest you discuss it with His

Highness? The two of you seem quite friendly, if you'll permit me saying so."

"I thought about it," admitted Red. "But this is a sort of…biomancer problem. I know he has to walk carefully with that lot, being prince and all. Don't want to put him in an awkward situation, you understand."

"I do indeed, my lord. And am I to assume this matter is also too delicate to discuss with Ambassador Omnipora?"

"I get on well with Nea. She's a fine molly and clever as claws. But my biomancer problem is the sort of complicated inner government stuff you don't want anyone outside the government knowing about, no matter their quality. So—"

"My Lord Pastinas! Is that you?" came a familiar voice from behind him.

Red whispered to Hume, "Is that Lady Hempist behind me?"

"It is, my lord," murmured Hume, his lips not moving.

"Can you cause a distraction so I can escape?"

"I would be happy to, my lord. Although if I may be so bold as to make a suggestion, I have noticed that Lady Hempist seems eager to please you, and within certain circles, she is well known for her… anti-biomancer sentiment. Perhaps she could be of some assistance to you with this…delicate problem of yours."

"Hume, you are a gem." Red squeezed his boney shoulder.

"You're kind to say so, my lord."

Red took a deep breath, put on his best smile, and turned to face his pursuer.

"Lady Merivale Hempist."

She wore an emerald-green gown that was slightly more modest than the one she'd worn to the ball.

Red appreciated that he wouldn't have to exert quite as much effort to keep from staring at her cleavage. She also wore cream-colored gloves that went past her elbows, and a small round hat that was set precariously on top of her hair. Red suspected this was her "going into town" look. She was flanked by serving men in gray, their arms filled with packages.

"How absolutely *slippy* to run into you like this," she said, sweeping toward him, her servants hurrying to keep up.

"What was that now?" asked Red.

"Slippy?" she asked, looking suddenly in doubt. "Isn't that one of your folk words? I feel quite sure I've heard you use it at some point. Doesn't it mean crazy?"

"It means crazy as in unreasonable or insane, not as in 'oh how wild.'"

"Oh dear." Her pink-painted lips curled into a pout as she flipped through a small book in her hand. "Oh, I see. Yes. My mistake."

"And what do we have here?" Red tried to peek at the book.

She snapped it shut and tucked it under her arm, then gave him a mischievous smile. "Nothing you need to concern yourself with at present."

Red refused to take the bait. Instead he nodded to the two burdened serving men behind her. "Bit of shopping, my lady?"

"You know how it is." She sighed dramatically. "I was just popping down to the bookshop, but a few items along the way caught my eye. Must keep the wardrobe fresh, you know."

"Of course, my lady."

"Don't think I don't know when you're patronizing me, my lord," she said sweetly.

"I always assume you catch all my cleverness, my lady. It's what makes you special."

"Oh, I think you'll find that I have any number of appealing qualities, my lord." She slipped her arm through his. "I have one more stop to make before I return to the palace. Will you be so kind as to keep me company? My servants are lovely people, but I'm afraid they lack your advanced conversation skills."

"It would be a pleasure, my lady."

Red had no illusion that if he wanted something from Lady Merivale Hempist, he would have to let her get close and think she had the upper hand. But as they walked, and he felt her soft warmth press against his arm, he wished it didn't feel quite so nice.

"If you'll permit me to say, you smell remarkably un-perfumed today, my lady," he said. "More like an actual woman and less like a bouquet of flowers."

"I have observed that strong smells, even pleasant ones, deter you, my lord."

He tapped his smoked glasses. "I'm afraid my vision is not the only sense that's delicate, my lady."

"I thought as much. So I entreated my perfumer to employ a quality she had never had occasion to use before."

"And what quality was that, my lady?"

"Restraint."

Red laughed. "You shouldn't go through so much trouble on my account."

"On the contrary, since I had every intention of getting close to you, it seemed only courteous to make certain it was as pleasant for you as possible."

"And is this mysterious book another of your ingenious plans to lull me into a false sense of security?"

"False?" She gave him a look of playful outrage. "I can assure you, Lord Pastinas, that you are completely safe in my presence." Then a glint of steel appeared in her eyes. "Certainly safer than you are with Ambassador Omnipora."

"Nea? She's safe as shores."

"She *is* a foreigner."

Red gave her a sincere look of disapproval. "Don't be like the rest of those close-minded lacies. You're better than that."

She paused for a moment. Then her pink bow mouth curved down into a pout. "You *have* been spending quite a lot of time with her."

"Wait. Are you *jealous*?"

She sighed. "Here I spend all this time and effort tangling you up in my webs and she comes along and unknowingly tears them all to tatters. It's quite vexing."

Red was fairly certain she was joking again. "Now, now, she's the prince's honored guest, and as his best wag, I need to make sure everything is sunny for her. Besides, you might not know this, but there are people who want her dead."

"That's just palace gossip, I'm sure. Who would ever harm such a lovely creature?"

"I'm afraid it's not gossip."

"Oh? And how have *you* come by this intelligence?" she asked teasingly.

"There were five of them who came to kill her the night she arrived," Red said quietly. "And I stopped them."

She seemed to consider that for a moment, but she was so hard to read, Red couldn't tell what she made of it.

Finally, she asked, "Did you kill them?"

"I did."

"Pity."

"Why's that?"

"You could have questioned them and found out who hired them."

Red hadn't expected such a pragmatic response. Lady Hempist continued to surprise him. Maybe Hume was right, and Merivale could be an ally against the biomancers. But he didn't want to risk it with his own problem without testing her first. And Nea's assassination attempt could be the perfect opportunity to find out where Merivale's sympathies really lay.

"I'm pretty sure I know who it was," he said at last.

"Oh?"

"Biomancers."

"Really," she said noncommittally, which itself was something of a comment.

"But I gather you wouldn't be overly surprised to find out that the biomancers sometimes meddle in politics."

Merivale's well-shaped eyebrow arched, and she turned back to Hume, who walked behind them with her serving men. "Have you been telling stories about me, Hume?"

Hume's expression didn't show the slightest trace of embarrassment. "I hope you will forgive me, my lady, but I did give Lord Pastinas to understand that you were not overly fond of biomancers."

"I see."

They continued on down the street for a little while in silence. Red wondered if he had overstepped. Maybe Hume had been wrong. Or maybe Merivale thought Red was trying to lure her into a trap. And yet, she didn't draw away from him, and her face remained calm, as if they were out on an innocent stroll through the city. He decided it would be best not to push. She knew where he stood. If she wanted to continue that line of conversation, she could. If not, he would let it drop and try to figure something else out.

Just ahead, Red noticed a wagon in front of a tavern called the Wheelhouse. It was hitched to a horse with gold and white imperial livery. One imp sat at the driver's seat, looking bored. As they walked past, two imps came out roughly carrying a corpse between them. It was of an older man, clearly a commoner. His throat had been cut and his chest was covered in dried blood. The imps tossed him unceremoniously into the wagon, then went back into the tavern.

"Oh my," said Merivale. "It appears there was a bit of trouble here."

Red had a sinking feeling he knew what the trouble was. Between Nea's arrival and the discovery that the biomancers had given him a secret weakness, he hadn't given much attention to the murderer who still stalked the streets of Stonepeak.

"Would you mind waiting a moment?" he asked Merivale.

She pressed herself into his arm and smiled. "I have no urgent business elsewhere at the moment."

"Thanks," he said distractedly as he watched the entrance to the tavern. A minute later, the two imps came out again. This time they were carrying a young woman. There was a big, bloody wound in her side and there was dried blood on her lips. It looked like someone had slid a knife through her ribs to puncture her lung, then let her drown in her own blood.

"How grisly," remarked Merivale.

"It is," agreed Red as he watched the imps throw her into the wagon on top of the old man. "If you'd like to continue on to your errand, I understand. I need to watch this a bit longer."

"If you can stomach it, so can I," said Merivale, with an oddly wry tone to her voice.

When the imps returned with a third body, this time a young man who looked like he had been stabbed in the heart, and dropped him just as disrespectfully as the others, Red decided he was done playing well-behaved lacy.

"What happened here?" he demanded, walking up to the imp on the wagon.

The imp looked at him and Merivale apprehensively. "Begging your pardon, my lord and lady. Nothing you need to concern yourself with."

"How many people were killed here?" pressed Red.

The imp frowned thoughtfully. "Six?"

"Seven," called one of the other imps as he and his partner headed back into the tavern. His tone was surly, as if it was the dead people's fault he was being made to do so much work.

"Seven, then," said the imp on the wagon indifferently.

"It's another killing, then," said Red. "I've heard there's been a string of them over the last few months."

The imp shrugged. "Folk have been calling him the Shadow Demon, because he comes and goes like a shadow, and kills without mercy or honor." He seemed mildly amused by that for some reason. But then he looked anxiously at Red and Merivale again. "Nothing for you to worry about, though, my lord and lady. This Shadow Demon, whoever or whatever it is, never goes after the nobility."

"What a relief," said Merivale, although Red was surprised to hear a measure of acid in her tone. "Yet, aren't the common folk subjects of the emperor?"

"Of course they are, my lady."

"Then as the emperor's enforcers of the peace, shouldn't you be more concerned with catching this murderer?"

"Oh…well…" The imp looked mildly panicked. Red guessed he'd never been directly admonished by a noble before. "It's just, we don't have any leads at present, my lady. We'll keep looking, of course. But you know, if it really is a *demon*, well, I don't know how much we can do about it."

"Demon or no, we cannot allow a killer to run loose on the streets of the imperial capital," said Merivale, the steel returning to her eyes.

"Y-yes, my lady." The imp couldn't even look her in the eye. "We'll redouble our efforts."

"See that you do." She turned to Red. "Shall we continue on, my lord?"

"Yeah. I think we're finished here."

Red looked at Merivale in a new light as they walked down the street, leaving behind the imp and his wagon of the dead.

"Perhaps you will do me the honor of taking lunch in my apartment?" asked Merivale. "Where we may discuss your... biomancer problem in a more intimate setting?"

———

The apartments of Lady Hempist on the thirty-second floor were as surprising as their resident. The furniture, rugs, drapes, and decor were finely made, but there was a simplicity to her home that bordered on austere. The few paintings and sculptures on display were geometric shapes in bright colors that popped out immediately in the predominantly beige setting, yet gave nothing away about their owner, except perhaps a very mathematical mind. He couldn't help but wonder what kind of stones player she would make.

As they sat down at her spotless glass dining table, he noticed there was something different about his host since they'd arrived at her apartments. No, not different, but rather something *additional*. She was still the cheerful and flirty lady as she discussed with her cook what to serve for lunch, but the occasional hints of steel he'd seen before were now fully present.

"Now, then, Lord Pastinas," she said as the cook hurried off. She looked as though she was about to declare a shocking revelation of some kind, her eyes clear, her face calm. But then she smiled and said, "Care for some wine while we wait?"

"Sure," said Red. "Ale is more my preference, but wine seems to be what the lacies drink, so I'm learning to like it."

"How adaptable of you." She nodded to another servant, who had been standing by with a carafe of wine. Red wondered if all her servants were men. It seemed appropriate, somehow.

As the servant began to pour, she asked as lightly as she had about the wine, "So you think the biomancers mean to assassinate the ambassador?"

Red glanced at the servant.

She nodded. "Your caution does you credit, my lord, but rest assured that everyone in my employ has been carefully vetted."

"I'm taking a chance on you, Merivale," he said quietly.

"But you need an alliance. Someone with more extensive connections in the palace. Someone you know who isn't frightened by the biomancers."

"Well, someone who won't buckle to them, anyway," said Red. "You'd have to be bludgeon not to be scared of what they can do, once you've seen it."

"Trust me, my lord. I am far from stupid, and unfortunately, I am intimately familiar with what they are capable of. So I am an ideal choice. Also, you're terribly charmed by me."

Red grinned. "Am I?"

"Naturally. Most intelligent men are."

"It seems that you may have fallen victim to my rakish charms as well."

"It's possible," she conceded.

"How do I know that you're serious about

this, and it isn't an elaborate plan to trick me into marriage?"

Her eyes twinkled with amusement. "I fail to see how that would conflict in any way with our alliance against the biomancers."

"Well…" Red had been expecting her to at least make some effort to deny it.

"Besides," she continued, "you're so clever, I'm sure you'll be able to use my affections to your advantage and still slip the noose of matrimony well before I pull it tight."

Red was beginning to suspect that he was not actually the most skilled con artist at the palace. "You flatter me, my lady."

"Are we done dancing around, then?" she asked.

"I suppose," said Red. "So, here's the length of it. The biomancers have used the fear of invasion from Aukbontar as justification for their cruel experiments on common folk for decades now. If Nea is able to convince the emperor that Aukbontar doesn't want conquest, the biomancers lose a great deal of their power. Naturally they'd want to stop this." And of course, if there was a way for Red to reduce the biomancers' power, it might help him escape their grasp.

"It's a sound theory," said Merivale. "But where's your proof?"

"It's true I killed the five boots who were after Nea and her people, but they were being led by a gaf named Brackson, who I knew back in New Laven as someone helping kidnap people for the biomancer experiments. Brackson escaped, but not before he made it crystal he was still working for the biomancers."

"That may confirm your suspicions. But if you want to bring a legitimate claim to the emperor, you'll need the testimony of this man."

"My testimony isn't good enough?" asked Red.

"All testimony needs corroboration."

"What about Nea? She was there."

"Ah, but she has a vested interest in discrediting the biomancers. Also, she's not a citizen of the empire, so I'm not sure she would even be allowed to testify."

"That might be a problem." Even if Red did manage to get ahold of Brackson, and somehow force him to testify, there was the risk that Brackson might reveal Red's own connection to the biomancers. On the other hand, maybe Red didn't need to actually get him to confess. Maybe he could simply threaten it, which might give him enough leverage against the biomancers to bargain for his freedom. Once he had that, it would change the entire game.

"A problem?" prompted Merivale.

"I'm...not sure how I would track him down."

"Then perhaps you could draw him out of hiding," suggested Merivale.

"I don't follow."

"If the biomancers assassinated Nea while she's here at the palace, that would draw down the wrath of Aukbontar. If they fear it as much as you say, they will avoid that at all costs. But if Nea were to leave the palace—better yet leave the city entirely—that might prove a tempting enough target for this Brackson of yours to make another attempt on her life."

"Use Nea as bait, you mean?"

"You'll be there to protect her again, won't you? And this time, make sure he doesn't get away."

"Right..." Red would need to figure out how to protect himself from that whistle before he confronted Brackson again. He hoped Ifmish didn't let him down.

Merivale tapped one dimpled cheek thoughtfully. "You know, I believe the ambassador has yet to meet Her Imperial Majesty."

"That's true," said Red. "And she lives in seclusion way over on the northwest coast somewhere, doesn't she?"

"She does indeed. Palace life was too much for the poor dear."

"So I hear."

"But she certainly couldn't turn away the ambassador from Aukbontar. And I can't imagine Nea being less than thrilled to meet the mother of the empire." She gave Red a shrewd look. "That is, if you were to suggest this little outing to her."

"It's not a bad idea," admitted Red.

Merivale smiled winsomely. "Luckily for you, courtly intrigue is one of my specialities."

"Oh, I'm sure the advice comes at a price, my lady."

"Naturally." She leaned over the table, giving him ample view of her cleavage. "But I promise it won't be unpleasant."

Red forced himself to look at her eyes. "Well, uh, if I'm going to confront Brackson again, I'm going to need a few days to prepare."

"It will take at least that long to organize an official visit to the empress," said Merivale. "But I strongly recommend you put forth the suggestion as soon as possible."

"Why, do you think the biomancers will make some kind of move soon?"

She smiled. "Actually, I was thinking that this is the ideal season to visit the west coast of Stonepeak. The sunsets at this time of year are quite romantic, you know."

"Merivale, this alliance of ours...You know it doesn't actually change anything between us."

Her smile turned almost predatory. "I admire your fortitude, my lord. But change of some kind is inevitable."

Red was mostly able to squelch the vague feelings of dread that statement produced. He was beginning to wonder if Lady Hempist might be an even more formidable opponent than Brackson or the biomancers.

———

That evening, Red and Leston were invited to Nea's apartments to experience some traditional Aukbontaren cuisine. He knocked on the ambassador's door and a moment later, Catim opened it. The big man looked down at Red, his eyes hidden in the dim hallway by a furrowed brow.

"You're late," he said.

Red grinned impudently. "Didn't you know, old pot? Makes a wag seem pat to be a little late."

"You almost missed the ambassador's performance."

"Performance?" asked Red. "She never said anything about a performance."

"A traditional Aukbontaren meal is always begun with music," said Catim, as if it was common knowledge. Which, Red supposed, in Aukbontar, it probably was. "An ambassador must represent the culture of Aukbontar as well as the government, because the two are linked."

Red patted the large man on the shoulder as he walked past. "Well, thankfully for me, I made it in time."

Prince Leston sat on a small sofa with a glass of clear liquid in his hand. Drissa and Etcher sat in chairs on either side of him. All three faced Nea, who sat on a stool with an instrument on her lap that reminded Red of an oversize fiddle.

"There you are, Lord Pastinas. Late as usual." The prince turned back to Nea. "I told you he would be along. I think he's only ever on time when he's planning to do something disreputable."

"That should set your mind at ease, then, Ambassador," said Red as he dropped down on the sofa next to Leston. "My apologies, though. I didn't know we were to be graced with music."

"I would have been sad if you'd missed it, Red. But I suppose you could have prevailed upon me to play for you another time." Nea held up her instrument. "As I was explaining to His Highness, this is a traditional Aukbontaren instrument called a guitar. It has evolved a great deal over the centuries. Originally, it was made from a dried gourd, but as you can see, the modern guitar has a hollow wooden body, which gives it a much richer resonance."

"It's a lovely instrument," said Leston as he leaned forward.

"I'm glad you think so, Your Highness. Let's hope you like the sound as well."

"I'm sure I will, Ambassador," said Leston immediately.

Nea smiled and set the instrument back on her lap. Red was fairly certain she knew the prince was sotted with her, but he still hadn't figured out how she felt about it. She walked a fine line of never discouraging it, but also never actively encouraging it. It made sense. If she alienated the prince, she ran the risk of losing her one true ally in the palace. And yet if she encouraged his affection, that opened a whole new set of political complications. The prince had unintentionally put her in a very awkward situation. Red was impressed with how well she'd been handling it so far.

"Many generations ago," she said as she strummed lightly on her instrument, "the Aukbontaren people were nomadic. We do not have the wide-open seas that you do. Instead we have miles and miles of grassland. Our people moved constantly with their herds. They were great lovers of music, but they needed an instrument that would travel easily. The guitar evolved so that it was small enough to be played anywhere, even on horseback, and yet still loud enough to reach from the back of the caravan to the front."

Red wondered what it would be like to see all that open land in front of you. Miles and miles of it. He found the idea both thrilling and a little frightening. A wag would feel awfully small in such a place.

"There are two types of traditional guitar songs," Nea continued. "The first were travel songs, which were lively and repetitive songs with an element of call-and-response. These songs were played to keep spirits up as they rode over many hours. The second type of songs were fire songs. These songs were played at night as the caravan rested around a large open fire. These were softer songs that lulled the children to sleep and told folk stories of that caravan. Since it is night, I will play a fire song for you." She smiled. "You will have to imagine the fire."

She began to play a slow, delicate, rippling melody on the guitar. There was a solemnity to its beauty that was only enhanced when she began to sing. Her voice was simple and unadorned by the warbling and stylistic flourishes that Red had grown used to hearing at the palace. In fact, it reminded him of some of the songs of his childhood. Gentle, mournful airs Old Yammy would sing while cleaning up the ramshackle apartment that his dad had neglected since his mother's death. Songs mostly about loves separated by war and death.

Red didn't know what Nea's song was about, since she was singing it in her own language, but there was a catch in her voice—an ache that made him wonder if she might be more like him than he realized. Was she separated from a love as well? Forced by duty to come to this strange and unwelcoming land? If that was true, it only made the prince's affections all the more trying on her. He was just another in a long line of obstacles between her and her love.

There were so many obstacles between him and Hope. Biomancers and old enemies, princes and foreign countries and seditious nobility. He'd thought that as time went on, he'd get closer to seeing Hope. But it had been a year since he'd traded his freedom for her life, and he'd never felt farther away from her. What was she doing out there? Still beheading biomancers and insisting on being the one of honor in a den of thieves? Was she grateful Red had saved her, or resentful that he'd put that on her shoulders? Was she still with Sadie, Filler, and the rest, or was she alone again? She would never admit it, but she was terrible alone. That was the only time Red truly worried about her. She needed someone to make sure she didn't run herself through when she messed up. The image still haunted him of seeing her in Silverback when she thought she'd lost Teltho Kan. Her sword pointed at her chest, her expression one of absolute despair.

If Filler were there, he'd make sure she didn't do anything so bludgeon. God, he hoped Filler was with her. That wag needed someone to look after anyway, now that he couldn't look after Red. He could see them both in his mind, so far away. At least they were still together, supporting each other. They better pissing be, anyway. And Sadie and Nettles. The lot of them better be together and making up for Red, who felt so alone, so abandoned even though it had been his choice. He hadn't felt this weak and miserable since he'd been a poncey little art boy from Silverback newly arrived in Paradise Circle.

Then he realized that the song was over.

"Red," Nea said quietly, her eyes wide. "Are you okay?"

"Sunny." He took off his smoked glasses and wiped calmly at his red eyes with his sleeve. "Good song. Reminds me of home."

———

One nice thing about polite society, Red decided, was that nobody made a fuss if a wag shed a tear or two. They just glossed over it and kept moving.

After the song, Nea guided them to the dinner table. Everyone ate at the table, which Red approved of. When he was invited to eat at any of the lacy apartments, only the nobility ate at the table. Everyone else ate in the kitchen. But Nea never treated her people like servants. She was in charge, and she held that authority as easily as Red held a throwing blade. But she never threatened any of her people with it or tried to put them in a lower place. Red still had a hard time imagining an entire society without nobility, but after watching Nea these past few weeks, he was beginning to believe it was possible.

Nea sat at the head of the table, and Prince Leston at the foot. Red and Etcher sat on one side, while Drissa and Catim sat on the other. In the middle of the table were five bowls of food with large wooden spoons. There was also a platter with a stack of soft flat circular bread.

"This is a traditional Aukbontaren meal," said Nea. "It is a meal reserved for special occasions."

"Is this a special occasion?" asked Red.

She smiled warmly. "Certainly, to have such honored guests." She pointed to the platter of flat bread. "This particular bread is made partly from corn, which is not grown in your empire."

"Is corn a type of grain?" asked Leston.

"A vegetable, actually," she said. "Fortunately, I knew you did not have corn, so I brought some with us. I did have to make one important substitution, though." She pointed to one of the bowls, which contained a brown gravy with chunks of meat. "You do not have cattle, so I made it with pork instead." She flashed a smile at Catim, who looked a little uneasy. "I am certain it will be fine."

"So, how do we..." Leston seemed a little lost as he looked around the table. "I see no forks..."

"This particular meal originates from our nomadic ancestors, who did not use utensils. In honor of that time, we traditionally leave them aside and eat as our ancestors did." She peeled off the top piece of flat bread and held it up. Then she laid it on one side of her plate. On the other side she spooned small amounts from each bowl. Then she tore a piece of bread off and used it to scoop up some of the food and pop it into her mouth. She smiled at the prince with closed lips as she chewed.

"I see," said Leston, looking amazed.

Nea gave him a sympathetic look. "If you are uncomfortable with it, we can certainly bring you a fork. I assure you, we would not be offended."

Leston shook his head. "No, of course not. I want to have the authentic experience."

Nea inclined her head. "Very good, Your Highness." Then she turned to Red.

"Oh, I'm just fine eating without forks," said Red, already spooning dollops of food onto his plate. "Back in Paradise Circle, we did it all the time. Not out of a tradition, mind you, but just because we didn't have any."

"You were too poor?" asked Catim.

"Catim!" said Nea.

"Actually, he's got the length of it," said Red. "In fact, often as not, we didn't even have a plate."

"Where would you put the food, then?" asked Etcher.

"Well, if it was bread and fish and some vegetables, they'd just roast it on a stick, then hand you the stick. Or if it was stew, what they'd do is take a round loaf of bread, hollow it out, and put the stew into the loaf as a bowl. Then you'd use the bit they cut out to scoop up the stew. And when you were done, you'd eat the bowl."

"Very efficient," said Catim approvingly.

Prince Leston was tentative at first in eating with his hands, but as the meal continued, he grew more confident. Etcher filled in a lot of the conversation with his observations on the limited amount of wildlife and plants available to him at the palace. He also went on at length about his discovery of oranges and how he must get his hands on more of them.

"For study, of course," he said quickly, giving Nea a guilty look.

While Catim interjected into Etcher's rambling monologue occasionally, Drissa still seemed content to remain silent. Red wondered if even her understanding of the language was limited. She frequently had a faraway look in her eyes, as if she wasn't paying attention to the conversation.

"I hate to ask, Your Highness," said Nea near the end of the meal, "but has there been any progress on getting me an audience with the emperor?"

Leston winced. "I have been trying, Ambassador, but it's slow going." After a moment of uncomfortable silence, he added, "He's very busy, of course."

Nea smiled just as calmly as ever, but Red thought she had to be screaming on the inside. She had been waiting for weeks now with no progress. This presentation on Aukbontar culture tonight was no doubt meant for the emperor. But what could she do if the emperor continued to ignore her?

And that's when Red saw his opening. For a moment, he was reluctant to take it. He liked Nea. Was it right to put her in danger? No, he corrected himself. She was already in danger. But rather than wait for it to come to them, he would be drawing it out on his terms. And once he figured out the whistle problem, he would have the clear advantage this time.

So he said lightly, "Who gives a piss about that old emperor anyway. The one *I'm* dying to meet is the empress."

"That is right!" Nea's face brightened and she smiled warmly at the prince. "I have not had the pleasure of meeting Her Imperial Majesty yet."

"Oh...well...," said Leston. "She doesn't live at the palace anymore. She's retired to Sunset Point on the northwest coast of Stonepeak."

"Is it far from here?" asked Nea.

"A half day's carriage ride," said Leston. "Perhaps a little longer. It's quite rural out there, so the roads aren't as good."

"A small excursion like that would be most welcome," said Nea. "I could use some fresh air and sunshine, couldn't you?"

"Certainly," said Leston, not looking certain at all.

"Of course, Her Imperial Majesty may not want visitors." Red held the prince's gaze as he said it. This was Leston's opportunity to stop this from happening. "Perhaps she prefers solitude."

Leston's face set firmly. "No, don't be silly. I know for a fact she would love to meet the ambassador. It's a splendid idea." He turned back to Nea. "I would be honored to introduce you to the mother of the empire."

"Wonderful," said Nea.

"Can I come along?" asked Etcher. "I've gotten

to see so little of the native flora and fauna. I hardly have anything to bring back in my report."

"I suppose you should," said Nea. She watched Drissa gaze off into a corner of the room for a moment, then said, "Catim, I will need you to stay behind with Drissa."

"But what about you, Ambassador?" said Catim. "There has already been one attempt on your life. There may be more once you are outside the safety of the palace."

"I believe Lord Pastinas has proven he can protect me." Then she gave him a meaningful look. "And we both know that Drissa is vitally important to what we wish to accomplish here."

Catim looked like he wanted to object, but then took a deep breath and sighed. "Yes, of course you're right. You can count on me to keep her safe."

Nea smiled. "Thank you, Catim."

"Rixidenteron." Leston's tone was unusually firm.

"Yes, Your Highness?" Red asked lightly.

"If I allow you to meet my mother, I expect you to be on your very best behavior."

Red beamed at him. "I swear on my father's purple prick."

13

Silverback was just as Bleak Hope remembered it. Loud, chaotic, colorful, and marginally cleaner than Paradise Circle. Performers stood at nearly every corner, sometimes even competing for space. They were musicians, jugglers, acrobats, magicians, or things Hope didn't even know the name for—all with far more talent than one might normally expect a street performer to possess.

The narrow sidewalks were packed with tradesmen, merchants, laborers, and artists, as well as imperial police from Keystown and wealthy landowners from Hollow Falls. As the buffer neighborhood between the poor downtown and the rich uptown, it blended the two groups into a strange mix that somehow not only worked, but made Hope feel like true communication between them was possible. That's what the arts were for, after all, she reflected. Connection at a level that transcended class and culture. A way to bridge gaps in humanity.

"It certainly is lively." Alash walked beside Hope, his eyes wide as he took in the boldly dressed people and garishly decorated storefronts.

"Have you never been here before?" asked Hope.

"Before you and my cousin arrived, I'd never even left Hollow Falls."

"Never?"

"It's not all that strange," said Jilly at her other side. "People keep to their own kind mostly. I never been up here either, and I probably wouldn't have even gone as far as Hammer Point if I didn't have to go live with my aunt. In New Laven, your neighborhood is your world."

Hope remembered how uncomfortable Filler, Nettles, and even Red had been when they went to Hammer Point to meet Big Sig. It hadn't seemed all that much different to her, but they'd acted like they were going to a foreign land.

"But I see a lot of people here from Hollow Falls." Hope pointed to a group of young, well-dressed, orange-powdered lacies in spotless coats and gowns. "You never ventured down here for a play or concert? Did you know that your aunt's artwork was recently on display at one of the most renowned galleries in the empire?"

"I confess I've never really had much appreciation for the arts," Alash said sheepishly.

"As similar as you look, it's amazing how different you and Red are," said Hope.

"Both in artistic talent and charm, I fear," Alash said gloomily.

Jilly ducked behind Hope and punched Alash playfully on the shoulder, then quickly moved back to her own side. "Come on now, you salthead. You're not bad on the gander. You just lack confidence. Mollies like a tom who's pat, that's all."

"What would *you* know about such things?" asked Hope.

"Oh, I know all about toms and mollies. I'm nearly a woman myself, after all."

Hope smiled. "Is that so?"

"Sure. Sadie says I'm due for my first bleed anytime now."

"And that's what you believe makes a woman?" asked Hope.

"Well, what else?" demanded Jilly.

"You're a bit short," Alash said.

"Nettles is short," said Jilly. "Nearly as short as me when you put us side by side."

"I suppose that's true," said Alash. "She *seems* taller, due to her...eh...personality. And anyway, she has other womanly attributes."

"So you're saying I either need to be taller or have big tits to be a woman?"

"Not exactly..." Alash's face was beginning to redden.

"See, *this*," said Jilly, "is the point where you should stop talking and just look pretty."

"And now I'm getting advice from little girls," muttered Alash.

"If the shoe's already on, lace it." Jilly skipped over and gave him another punch.

"What does that even *mean*?" Alash rubbed his shoulder.

Hope found it interesting how Jilly had begun to change during her time aboard the *Kraken Hunter*. Much of her military manner had faded away to reveal a clever, talkative girl who reminded Hope pleasantly of Red.

"Becoming a woman has little to do with your body," she told Jilly. "It is a state of confidence and strength you reach over the course of many years of both success and failure."

"When did you become a woman?" Jilly asked, then added, "Teacher." Since Hope had begun the initial stages of Jilly's Vinchen training, Hope had decided she should use the traditional form of address.

"I think that the process is still ongoing," Hope said. "But perhaps it began when I chose to step away from the path of the true Vinchen and make my own way. We are all faced with choices that, for better or worse, define our lives."

"Like how I chose to join your crew?" asked Jilly.

"What was the other option?" asked Hope. "To remain behind on a ship of the dead and one lone survivor who hated you for being a girl?" Hope shook her head. "Not much of a choice, was it?"

"I guess not." Jilly looked disappointed.

"Don't be in such a hurry to grow up," said Hope. "Learn from me and Brigga Lin. I'm sure even Alash here has things he could teach you."

"Me?" Alash looked surprised.

"Of course. Imagine a Vinchen biomancer who embraced your mechanical sciences."

"That would be a nice change," Alash admitted.

Hope turned back to Jilly. "Learn all you can from anyone who will teach you. Then, when the time comes for you to truly take command of your destiny, you will be ready."

Jilly nodded, her face serious.

"You know," continued Hope, "the woman we're going to see now probably has a few things she could teach you."

"Really?"

"Old Yammy taught Red a great many things, including his uncanny ability to talk himself into and out of trouble."

"Are we almost there?" Jilly's eyes were suddenly eager.

"Nearly," said Hope.

But when they arrived at Madame Destiny's House of All, it was boarded up.

"Strange." Hope frowned as she stared up at the darkened spot on the lintel where the sign once hung.

"Perhaps she moved?" said Alash.

"I suppose. But it doesn't seem likely. This has been her shop for a very long time."

"Maybe something happened to her," said Jilly.

"That's what I'm worried about," said Hope.

"Let's ask around," said Alash. "Perhaps one of her neighbors knows what happened."

Before Hope could stop him, Alash walked over to an old man sitting on a nearby stoop. The man was grimy and bleary-eyed, and didn't look to Hope like the sort of person who noticed things.

"I say, fronzie!" said Alash.

The man flinched and seemed to withdraw into himself. "Begging your pardon, your lordship. I ain't done nothing wrong."

"Drown all that," Alash said impatiently. "We want to know what happened to the woman who owned this shop."

"I ain't got nothing to do with it," he said quickly.

Hope approached more slowly, so as not to alarm him any further. "Do you know Old Yammy? I'm a friend of hers."

The man looked at her suspiciously. "Maybe I know her. Maybe I don't."

Hope held up a coin between two fingers with a slight flourish, just as she'd seen Red do it. "Does this help you remember?"

His old face curled up on either side, one big wrinkly smile. "Now that you press on the matter, I do remember a kind, neighborly sort who sometimes went by that name. Used to give me a bite to eat on a bad winter day."

"Do you know what happened to her, then?"

"A couple of imps came one night. Made such a noise it woke me up. They put her in a wagon and took her off."

"Do you know why? Or where they took her?"

"Not sure, but I might remember a little more to help you along your way." He looked meaningfully at the coin. "If pressed a bit further."

Hope pulled out another coin, not bothering with the flourish this time.

The man's face lit up again. "Ah yes, well, I don't rightly know the whys or the ways, but I reckon her friends across the way might."

He pointed to a small theater on the other side of the street. The building looked shabby, with peeling paint and a dingy sign that read:

Honey Street Players present:
New shows nightly!
Poetical perils! Tragic terrors! Rollicking romance!
Featuring that shining star of Silverback, the
Luscious Lymestria!

"Her friends live...there?" asked Alash.

"Or work there." Hope tossed the coins to the old man. "Thanks, old wrink. Don't drink yourself to death with it."

As they crossed the street, Jilly asked, "Why do you use words like a proper wag sometimes, teacher?"

"A good question," said Hope. "I'm not really sure. It just seems the right word to use at that moment. Maybe I've heard it spoken around me so much that it's become a part of my language as well."

"I reckon it's the spirit of the original Dire Bane coming into you more every day," said Jilly.

Hope smiled. "Perhaps."

It was only midafternoon, well before most theaters opened. Hope knocked on the door with her clamp. They stood silently for a moment, but there was no response, so Hope knocked again, this time much louder.

Finally the door opened to reveal a tall, shirtless man with a vast, hairy belly and a long full beard. He wore an odd hat that looked like the top of a seal head, so it seemed like two sets of eyes glared down at her.

"House don't open for three hours," he said

roughly. "Come back then." He began to close the door.

"I'm looking for my friend, Old Yammy," Hope said quickly.

The door paused.

"Do you know what happened to her?" asked Hope.

The door slowly opened again. "Old Yammy never mentioned having a Southie friend," said the hairy man.

"I don't know her very well," admitted Hope. "But she helped raise a good friend of mine."

The man's bushy eyebrows rose. "Raised him, huh? What's the name of this good friend of yours?"

"His full name is Rixidenteron, but he usually goes by—"

"Red!" The man's whole demeanor changed. He stood straighter, his voice no longer harsh but clear and booming. He put his thick, hairy hands on her shoulders and looked pointedly at her. "You know Little Rix?"

Hope sighed. "If he owes you money, I'm sure we can work something out."

The man chuckled and patted her shoulders, then released her. "You know him, alright. Wonderful! Come in! Come in!" He herded them into the dim lobby and closed the door behind them.

"This is Alash, from Hollow Falls," Hope said. "Alash is Red's cousin."

The man grabbed a lit candle that guttered on the ledge of the box office window and held it up to Alash.

"Damn it to all the hells, but they could be brothers! I can't believe I didn't see it right away! But where are my manners? I am the Great and Mysterious Broomefedies!" He bowed low, spilling wax onto the floor from the lit candle he still held. "But most people call me Broom."

"This is Jilly from Paradise Circle," said Hope. "You may call me Captain Dire Bane."

Broom's eyes narrowed. "Dire Bane, is it? A bold moniker." He continued to gaze at her for a moment, then suddenly smiled. "Come! We must drink together to the health of Old Yammy and Little Rix!"

He turned to a set of large double doors and shoved them open dramatically. If Red spent part of his childhood with this man, she was beginning to see where he got his flair for showmanship.

"Well," she said to Alash and Jilly. "I think we've made a new friend." Then she followed Broom into the theater.

It was a modest space of about two hundred seats with wooden backs and threadbare cushions. A gaslit chandelier hung overhead, festooned with strips of blue and green fabric. The stage was on a steep rake and scattered with rocks that had been painted to look like coral. One person was painting with old sponges to make the textured look of coral, and two others were hanging additional strips of fabric around the stage. All three wore seal-head hats like Broom's.

Broom gestured to the stage, his round belly bouncing slightly. "A new design we're trying for our current production."

"It's very pretty," said Jilly, looking impressed.

"What's the play called?" asked Alash.

"Ah! It's called *The Rape and Ignominious Death of Lady Porsepine*. What do you think?"

"I suppose the title gives us everything we need to know," said Hope.

Broom's high spirits suddenly plunged. "Yes, a tawdry affair hardly worthy of being called a play." He scratched at his gut, his expression gloomy.

"Times being what they are, it's the only sort of thing that brings 'em in. I tell you, there's no appreciation for true artistry on the stage anymore." Then he slapped his belly, the sound reverberating through the theater, and his grin returned. "But that's the way of things. My old theater master said the same to me, and whichever poor bastard I pass my legacy on to will say it as well. Now, how's to a drink!"

He picked up a large, flat plank of wood and dropped it on top of the seat backs. Then he placed an earthenware jug on the plank and gave them a wink. "I always say that a table is wherever I put my drink!" Then he sat down in one of the theater seats.

Hope and the others awkwardly positioned themselves around the plank as well.

Broom hefted the jug. "To bad luck and better days!" He took a swallow and passed it to Hope.

"It seems as though you know Red very well." Hope placed her captain's hat on the table, then took a sip from the jug and winced. She had no idea what was in the jug, but she thought perhaps it might be a solvent or cleaning solution of some kind. She handed the jug to Alash with a look she hoped communicated caution.

"Know him?" asked Broom. "There were times we couldn't get rid of him! When he was very young, maybe about three or four, his father would sometimes appear in our plays. He was not a great actor, but you can never have too many pretty people onstage, and he was about the most handsome man I ever saw." He sighed, his eyes growing distant. "And that Gulia...she knew how to throw a proper party..."

Alash began coughing and gasping. He stared down at the jug as if afraid he'd just ingested poison and might die at any moment. He held the jug out to Broom.

"Hey, what about me?" asked Jilly.

"I'm not sure you would enjoy it," said Hope.

Jilly grabbed the jug from Alash. "Two years in the imperial navy. I could drink more than both of you put together." She tipped the jug back and took a large gulp. She let out a wheeze and wiped at her watering eyes. "That's some quality drop, my wag. Where'd you get it?"

Broom beamed. "We make it ourselves down in the cellar." He took another swallow and wiped at his own eyes. "An artistic mind needs trimming now and then," he said to Hope with a hint of defensiveness. "Otherwise it grows heavy with adornments and affectations."

Hope smiled. "I am not overly artistic myself, so I will trust to your good judgment on the matter."

Broom returned her smile. He scratched at his shaggy beard. "Now where was I..."

"My aunt Gulia gave great parties?" asked Alash.

"Ah yes. And so, with them in the community, so to speak, Little Rix was always underfoot. Practically the company pet for a while. You wouldn't believe how the cast would dote on him. Then of course Gulia started to have some troubles. I told her to lay off the coral spice. That stuff will eat the brains right out of your skull, I said. But you know how it is." He shrugged helplessly. Hope didn't really know how it was. It was the thing about Red's childhood she struggled with the most. His mother didn't sound like a stupid woman. She had seen what the drug had done to her child. Why did she continue to take it? But Hope had never struggled with addiction or had the mixed blessing of an artistic mind. Perhaps it was something she would never understand.

"Anyway," said Broom, "she took offense to what I said, stormed out, took her family with her,

and that was the last I saw of them. Heard from Old
Yammy that his parents passed on and that Little
Rix had disappeared. Years later he came back, as
handsome as his dad and as feisty as his mom. Paradise Circle was a little too hot for him right then, so
he decided to lay low with Yammy awhile. He stayed
with her, learning whatever strange things she had
to teach during the day. But at night he'd come over
here and help out."

"He acted in plays?" asked Hope.

"He surely did!" said Broom. "Natural talent for
stagecraft. I even tried to get him to stay on as my
apprentice, become the theater master when I'm
too old and fat and drunk to do it anymore. But of
course he had more...dangerous aspirations." He
took another drink and belched loudly. "What can I
say? Thievery pays better than theater."

"Broom, you goat-pricked ass-tosser!" A penetrat-
ing female voice rang through the theater. A moment
later, a woman with long flowing hair swept onto
the stage. She wore a red-and-black-checkered gown
that covered almost none of her large bosom.

"Ah, Lymestria!" said Broom. "You look lovely!"

"Don't *lovely* me, you aging, has-been cock-dribble."
Lymestria walked to the foot of the stage and glared at
him, her fists on her hips. "You are ruining my career!"

"Oh, piss," muttered Broom. Then louder, "Whatever do you mean, oh treasure of New Laven theater?"

"I'm talking about this new play in which my character is raped to death onstage by a pack of seals! It's
an outrage! I won't do it!"

Broom gave Hope an apologetic smile. "Won't
you excuse me a moment?" Then he stood up and
sidled out into the aisle. He pulled the seal hat off,
revealing a shiny bald dome with a fringe of long
curly hair. "My darling Lymestria, I promise you,
this play will *save* your career."

She folded her arms across her chest in a way that pushed her large breasts even further out. It seemed to Hope that they were almost like a defensive weapon of some kind.

"I should be playing Archlady Ramfist! Or the Madwoman of Walta! *Real* roles in *real* plays!"

Broom reached the foot of the stage, but instead of climbing up to stand next to her, he remained below and reverently took the hem of her gown in his hands. "I couldn't agree more, brightest light in Silverback. You are without a doubt the greatest actress of our age and it is a privilege to work with you."

He tenderly kissed the hem of her skirts and her expression softened somewhat. But then she took a deep breath, her bosom rising to new heights. "Well, then, shouldn't I have the roles that befit my talent?"

"You *should*!" he said vehemently. "It is an outrage that you do not have the opportunity to truly spread your wings as you were meant to do. But…" He sighed heavily. "The times being what they are…" He sighed again. Hope wondered if he felt dizzy from all the sighing. "People don't appreciate the classics anymore. Nobody will pay to see a masterpiece like *The Madwoman of Walta* these days." He held up his seal hat and glared at it. "This, oh jewel of the empire, is what they want to see. And what *I* want, more than anything else in the world, is to have a theater full of your fans every night. Isn't that what *you* want?"

"My fans…" Her voice faltered and she placed her hands over her bosom. "I must…give them what they want. Mustn't I?"

"It is your choice entirely, my darling."

"As a thank-you," she continued, her voice growing stronger, her expression growing firmer, "for the years of faithful patronage."

"Not only are you the greatest actress of our age, but the most generous as well!" said Broom.

"Fine," she said, her fists back on her hips, a haughty expression on her face. "I will perform this piece of garbage, but *only* for a limited run. Do you understand? Then I want some *real* theater. A role I can sink my teeth into."

"Absolutely, my dear! After this show, they will follow you anywhere!"

She pointed down at him. "You better be right about that." Then she spun around, her gown swirling, and stalked off the stage.

Broom clapped his seal hat back on his head and returned to the makeshift table, a satisfied look on his face.

"Is it always like this around here?" asked Hope.

"Usually," said Broom. "I may have overdone it with the sighing, but sometimes with Lymestria you have to paint in broad strokes."

"Is she really the greatest actress of the age?" asked Alash.

"She's not bad."

"Does she really have all those fans?" asked Jilly.

"Her breasts do, at least," said Broom. "Now, I should probably begin preparing for tonight's show soon. What was it you came here for again? Probably not to hear old stories about Little Rix."

"I would like to know what happened to Old Yammy," said Hope.

"Ah," said Broom. "I'm afraid she's been taken to the Empty Cliffs again. But this time, I'm not sure she'll be coming back."

"The Empty Cliffs?" Jilly looked pained.

"How awful," said Alash.

"What are the Empty Cliffs?" asked Hope. "I've heard mention of them before."

"It's a prison," said Broom. "A small bit of land

maybe a mile across that juts out of the water off the northeast coast of New Laven. It's perhaps a half-mile high, sheer cliffs on all sides. The top is flat and prisoners are simply left up there, with daily provisions delivered somehow. I never learned."

"No need for bars or doors in a place like that, I suppose," said Hope.

Broom nodded. "People used to come back. They would stay out there perhaps six months to a year, depending on the severity of their crimes. But about five years ago, we began to notice that no one was coming back anymore."

"How many people do you think get sent there every year?" asked Hope.

Broom took a long drink from his jug. "It's hard to say. They get sent from all over New Laven. And even from other islands. Hundreds, maybe?"

"If no one has left for over five years...," said Alash. "Wouldn't it be extremely crowded by now?"

"You'd think," said Broom.

"Unless something was being done with them," said Hope.

"Biomancers?" asked Jilly.

Hope took another drink from the jug, and this time the burning sensation felt appropriate somehow. She turned to Broom. "Do you know anyone who's actually been on the Empty Cliffs?"

"I think Lymestria was sent there about seven or eight years ago. Back when she was first making a name for herself. An admirer got a little too familiar at the door. Wanted to actually *feel* the famously luscious bosom. She keeps a pistol strapped to her thigh for situations like that. Gave a warning shot. In his foot. Sadly, he turned out to be Lord something or other and had her arrested. She spent a year on the Empty Cliffs, and you can be sure that she learned her lesson."

"What lesson was that?" asked Alash.

Broom winked. "Now her warning shots are through the head."

"I would like to talk to Lymestria and see how much she remembers about the place," said Hope. "Layout, personnel, that sort of thing. Would that be possible?"

"I don't see why not. She'll want something in return, but her demands are usually reasonable."

Alash gave Hope a worried look. "I think I can guess what you're planning, Captain."

"Old Yammy helped me out of a desperate situation not once, but twice," said Hope. "I owe her."

"But, teacher," said Jilly. "Nobody's ever been rescued from the Empty Cliffs before."

"Then it's long overdue, wouldn't you say?" asked Hope.

I still don't like it here," Filler said quietly as he and Nettles walked through the broken streets of Hammer Point.

Nettles gave him a sideways glance. "After all the places we've been to, you still hold on to that old rivalry?"

"Other places is other places," said Filler. "This is still this place."

Nettles sighed and let it alone. She used to feel the same way. A deep distrust that bordered on loathing for anything or anyone who came out of Hammer Point. As she looked around, it was easy to see how it started. Paradise Circle was no prize painting, but it had a certain seedy charm. The Hammer was a bleak and foreboding thing, scarred with endless gang wars.

The Circle had the advantage of the docks, it was true, but its truest advantage was its unity. A long succession of powerful ganglords who allowed no competition. They didn't just rule by force, though. The wags of Paradise Circle were a headstrong lot, and they wouldn't stand for simple bullying, no matter how nasty. The recent fall of Deadface Drem was a perfect example of that. People of the Circle had to believe that whoever was in charge was a true wag of the Circle. Someone who would stand for the freedom of the Circle and all its people against the imps and anyone who would take that freedom away.

Each ganglord brought something different to the Circle. Yorey Satin was before Nettles's time, but she'd heard from old wrinks that his was a golden age of dance halls and fat, rich lacies to roll on nearly every corner. After him came Jix the Lift. Jix didn't see much value in dance halls, and turned them into gambling houses and brothels. The lacies got scarce, but there was new money to be made at the tables and on your back, particularly from the sailors who came and went as often as the tides.

Jix had been a hard man, it was true, and not gentle. But he had been a true wag. Nettles's parents worked for him, and when they'd been killed in his service, he made sure Nettles and her brother Mick had a place to sleep and a way to make money. At that time, they were too young to be thieves, boots, or whores, so they would "make mayhem" for him. That meant they would start a commotion in a public place to distract people from whatever crime was being committed around the corner by Jix and his boots. Often, Mick and Nettles (or Rose, as she was called back then) would act like they were getting into a fight in the middle of the market or in front of an imp squad, and by the time people pulled them apart, Jix was long gone with the prize. Nettles loved it. After all, not only did she get to punch her big brother without fear of reprisal, but she got paid for it.

But Mick grew tired of punching his little sister. Even when he punched his hardest, she would often grin and just punch him back, like it was a challenge. Mick wasn't looking for a challenge. After a while, he started pulling other kids—innocent bystanders—into the fight. He would wail on them mercilessly until they screamed and begged him to stop. He didn't even stop when Jix's boots gave the all clear and it was time for them to slip away into the crowd. That was when Nettles understood that Mick just liked hurting people.

One time he beat a little girl so badly, right there in the market, that not even the imps could ignore it. They took him down to the Hole and questioned him. He didn't give up Jix, which saved his life. But that didn't mean Jix was happy with him for stepping outside the plan. So Jix took him off mayhem duties and put him on cleaning duties.

Jix let Nettles keep working, though. That's how she met Tosh, before she was a whore, and Henny, when he still had his nose. The three of them together had been true artists of mayhem. Once they got their routine down, they could stir up a proper bit of controlled chaos in under five minutes, then melt away in seconds. They became one of Jix's favorite crews. On one occasion, they nearly started a riot right on the front steps of the Hole, all over a made-up rumor about an ale tax. Every imp in the station had been out there trying to calm the crowds. It got so ridiculous that Henny started to laugh and Nettles had to kick him in the balls to keep him from breaking character.

But while Nettles was getting known in the neighborhood, Mick was slowly becoming a monster. Maybe it was jealousy of his sister's popularity. Or maybe it was a seed that had been planted since watching their parents get beaten to death during the dock riots. Or maybe he'd just always had a monster inside. That's what happened when you were born in the Circle. The darkness got to you so early, it was hard to say what you would have been like otherwise.

"You sure this is the right thing to do, Nettie?" asked Filler, cutting into Nettles's thoughts.

"You mean forming an alliance with someone in Hammer Point?" asked Nettles.

"I mean making a play for Paradise Circle. I get he's your brother and he's done terrible things to you. I get you don't want to see him in charge of the Circle. But can't we just help someone else do it?"

"Who?" asked Nettles. "Bertie Bull? Gander Shane?" She shook her head. "Those are the other two gafs making a play, and neither of them have been able to stand up to Mick. They've already lost too much face. If I want to make sure Mick doesn't take over the Circle, I've got to do it myself."

"But...I mean..." It was strange to see Filler arguing. Clearly, it felt strange for him, too. He struggled to put the words together. "It's not what we came here for. We took Hope's money and we said we'd come back with ships and wags to sail them. We said we'd help all them little girls."

Nettles patted him on his broad back. "And we *will*, my wag. Once I'm in charge of the Circle, we'll be able to give her as many ships and stouthearted wags as she needs."

"Promise? When this is all done, we'll do what we said for Hope?"

Filler looked like he really wanted to be convinced. Maybe he was just used to Red making all his decisions for him. Red, and then Hope. And now her. He always looked for confirmation from someone. So she gave it to him.

"I promise, Filler. After I take Paradise Circle, we won't forget about Hope, or Dawn's Light, or them little girls."

Even as she said it, she felt the tiniest prickle of doubt. But she wasn't accustomed to doubt, and shoved it down as hard as she could on general principle.

Palla's base was a weaving mill in the northeastern part of Hammer Point. It was well after dark by the time they arrived. The mill was closed and all the workers appeared to be gone. But Nettles could see light coming from a room on the top floor.

"How do we get up there?" asked Filler as they approached the thick, closed double doors of the entrance.

"You don't," said a voice. "So piss on home before I shoot your big, ugly, easy-to-target head."

Nettles squinted in the darkness, trying to see where the voice was coming from. "I'm a friend of Palla's. I need to talk to him."

"I know all Palla's friends." The voice was high-enough-pitched that it was either a molly or a young boy. "I never seen you around."

"You weren't at the storming of the Three Cups, then," said Nettles. The voice sounded close, but a little high, maybe a sniper in one of the windows. But which one? It was a three-story building. Leaving out the top floor, which was all lit up, the first and second floors had five windows each. A good shot with a long barrel rifle could hit them from the centermost three on each floor, making for a total of six possible sniper positions. "Why weren't you there?"

"Some of us had to stay behind to guard the mill."

"In other words, you got left behind," said Nettles. "Did you have to do the washing, too? Rinse out the bedpans, maybe?"

"I could just shoot you right now, right between the eyes." The voice sounded petulant.

"In this light? I doubt it," said Nettles. "Besides, even if you managed to shoot me, the powder flare would give away your position, and my wag here don't take kindly to his friends getting shot."

"Then maybe I'll shoot him first." The voice was starting to sound a little nervous.

Nettles smiled. "That would be a real mistake. Because I'm nowhere near as nice as he is."

There was no response.

"Sounds like we might have a bit of a stalemate," said Nettles. "So instead of a bunch of people dying, including yourself, why don't you just go ask Palla if he knows a molly named Nettles? We'll wait right here, patient and true."

There was another pause. Then the voice said sullenly, "Door's locked anyway. It's not like you could get in while I'm gone." There was a flicker of movement in one of the first-floor windows, and the sniper was gone.

After a moment, Filler said, "What if he was on the second floor? If he'd shot at you, I wouldn't have been able to reach him."

"Glad he wasn't, then," said Nettles.

"Pretty good bluff."

Nettles grinned. "Thanks. Red ain't the only tricky one, you know."

A few minutes went by before they heard the locks shift and the door swung open. On the other side stood a boy of about fourteen. The long barrel rifle slung over his shoulder was almost as tall as he was.

"Well, look at you, tiny tom," Nettles said teasingly. "Glad I didn't have to kill such a precious little thing."

The boy glared at her. "Piss off. Palla wants to see you." He pointed at a staircase next to the door.

Nettles patted him on the head as she walked past. He looked like he was thinking of lashing out, but then glanced warily at Filler, who towered over him, and just bit his lip. Nettles smiled to herself. Some mollies didn't like it when toms underestimated them. Nettles didn't mind because the look of surprise on their face as she slipped a knife in their bilge was so sweet. That was the trouble with being known, though. In the Circle, nobody mistook her for harmless anymore. So she savored it in Hammer Point while she could.

Filler's leg brace made climbing steps difficult, so they ascended slowly. As they moved, Nettles looked down at the vast open floor of the mill with rows of looms lined up neatly.

"You ever think what life would have been like if you did something normal, like work in a mill?" she asked.

"Not really," said Filler as he patiently shifted his weight and swung his metal leg around to the next step. "What would be the point?"

"It's not something I ever felt a need to try myself, mind you," said Nettles. "But looking down there makes me wonder what kind of person could do it, sitting there day after day, without going completely slippy."

They had finally reached the top step by then. Filler stopped for a moment to catch his breath. Then he said, "The sort that can't take what they need, I suppose."

"That's probably true," said Nettles. "I couldn't see Alash fighting for his meals on the streets of Paradise Circle. Thank God he was born a lacy."

Filler grinned and nodded. There was something wistful in his eyes that made Nettles a little curious.

"You ever think about what it would be like to toss a lacy like Alash?"

Filler's smile widened and he looked down at his boots. "Maybe." Then he looked back at Nettles. "Don't tell me you haven't."

"Of course I have. It's been ages since I bent a cock, and seeing his pretty face every day, a molly gets certain thoughts regular enough." She made a face. "But he reeks of the marrying type, and you know how I feel about *that* foolishness. Besides, I'd probably break his poncey cock off at the root before I'd had my fun."

They walked down the dim hallway toward the doorway with light spilling out of it. Nettles unhooked her chainblade, just in case the greeting wasn't as friendly as she anticipated, then peeked into the room.

It was a large square space. Off in one corner, a few gafs sat playing at stones. In another corner, a few more were folding sections of woven fabric and packing them into crates. Palla sat in the center of the room at a big table, a ledger book open in front of him, a quill in his hand. Although he had the dark skin of someone from Aukbontar, he had lived in Hammer Point for over ten years now and dressed in a jacket and trousers like any other wag in downtown New Laven.

There was a moment in which Nettles was able to take it all in. But then Filler's leg brace squeaked, and suddenly there were six guns pointed at her.

"Your boots have nice reflexes," she told Palla.

He smiled and made a calming gesture with one hand. "They're okay. You can relax."

The gafs abruptly went back to what they'd been doing, as if they'd suddenly forgotten that Nettles and Filler were there.

Nettles nodded a thank-you to Palla and walked slowly toward his table. She still held her chainblade loose in one hand, just in case.

"How you been, Palla?"

He raised his hands in a shrug. "Some good, some bad. That is life." He still had a trace of an accent, which Nettles found very pleasant to hear. She thought back on her earlier comment about the tragic lack of cocks in her life and decided that maybe once she'd gotten everything else she wanted from Palla, she'd get that, too.

"To what do I owe the pleasure of a visit from the Briar Rose of Paradise Circle?" he asked.

Nettles tilted her head slightly, her eyes hard. "Not many know that particular nickname."

"I know some people," he admitted. "And of all the names I heard connected with you, that one struck me as the most fitting."

"It's a name you have to earn to use."

Palla steepled his hands together. "Perhaps you have come with a way for me to earn it?"

"As a matter of fact, I have." She glanced around at his boots. "We alright to talk here?"

"These are my best and most loyal wags," said Palla.

"So, I'm making a play to take Paradise Circle."

Palla's forehead crinkled. "Are you? How interesting. And you were hoping...what? That it would be like last time? My wags and I would come marching boldly over to help you take power? If so, I must say—"

"No, of course not," Nettles said, a touch of impatience creeping into her voice. "That would be ridiculous. First, the moment you all left here, Sharn or Big Sig would come sweeping in and you'd return to nothing. So it don't make sense for you. And if I'm going to take the Circle, what kind of loyalty would I inspire if I did it with a bunch of gafs from the Hammer? None at all. So it don't make sense for me either."

Palla looked impressed. "Perhaps deadliness and beauty are not your only attributes."

Nettles turned to Filler. "I like how he's always slipping in compliments."

"It's nice," agreed Filler.

"So, no," continued Nettles, "I don't want to

borrow your boots. What I want are guns for my own wags."

"Ah." Palla's expression looked slightly pained.

"That a problem? I'm not looking for handouts. I can pay."

"No, it's just..." He paused for a moment, then sighed. "We are a bit low on guns and ammunition. At the moment."

"Oh?"

"Yes."

"So who has the most guns in Hammer Point?"

"Sharn," Palla said in a flat voice.

"Yeah..." Nettles pressed her finger to her cheek and acted like a thought was just coming to her. "She didn't help us out with Drem and that biomancer problem, did she?"

"No. She did not."

"I wonder if she got something out of that..."

Palla's eyes narrowed. "You already knew about that, I take it?"

"I know some people," she admitted. "But it's good to have confirmation. What I've heard is that Sharn has been getting a lot of guns over the past year. And that's good for her, since so many of her people have been mysteriously disappearing. I hear she's a bit shorthanded these days."

"The extra guns help with that," said Palla. "You don't need as many skilled fighters if you just put a gun in every hand."

"That's what I was thinking," said Nettles. "See, my rival has the numbers, so I need the fire-power."

"Are you proposing that we join together, take Sharn, then split her weapon cache?"

"Things haven't been easy for you, Palla," said Nettles. "Sig got Thorn Billy's gang. Sharn has her imperial rat agreement. What do you got?"

"If I take Sharn's gang and resources, that puts me on equal footing with Big Sig."

"I thought it might," said Nettles.

"With so many armed opponents and so few of our own, we won't be able to go charging into Sharn's territory."

"Charging in ain't my style, anyway," said Nettles. "I was thinking more along the lines of what you, me, and Hope did at the Three Cups. But on a much bigger scale."

"Infiltrate quietly," said Palla.

"Take them down singly or in small groups. With a bit of luck, we'll cut her numbers in half before she even knows we're there."

"I like this idea," admitted Palla. "You think we have enough people skilled that way?"

"I know just about every thief in Paradise Circle by name. And nearly all of them have been known to cut a throat or two when the need arises."

Palla was silent for a moment. Then he looked at Nettles, his eyes suddenly hard.

"We will do it. On one condition."

"What's that?" asked Nettles.

Palla's hand trailed over to his spear, which rested against his desk. "*I* kill Sharn."

———

The next night, Nettles called her first meeting. She chose Apple Grove Manor as her base of operations for several reasons. It was the oldest structure in the neighborhood, built back when there were more trees than buildings in lower New Laven, so it had a certain weight all its own. It had also been the base of Jix the Lift when he ran Paradise Circle. For all his faults, Jix had been a true wag of the Circle. It was a way to remind people that her brother was no true wag of the Circle. And because of its associations with Jix, Nettles knew Apple Grove Manor was the one place Mick might avoid.

There was one more reason she chose Apple Grove Manor, although it was something she found difficult to articulate, even to herself. The strange pond in the basement, with its blind, luminous fish, gave Nettles a sense of calm she hadn't experienced anywhere else. Of all the "special" places Red had shown her back when they were tossing, it was the only one she had truly liked. There was a stillness to that pond which made her feel as though she had stepped out of time, and all the pressure that went along with its inexorable movement toward some dark future disappeared. If she was really going to make a go at taking all of Paradise Circle in her hands, she knew that beating her brother would not be the only hard thing she would have to do. Difficult times and difficult choices always came with leadership. She could already see it beginning to weigh on Hope. If Nettles was to stand up under the pressure of running the neighborhood, she wanted to know that the still, dark waters of the pond were beneath her feet, and she could visit them as often as she liked.

The rest of Apple Grove Manor had a tarnished and crumbling beauty to it. The floors were a dark stained wood, scuffed and scraped by centuries of boots. Wallpaper in faded and peeling sheets showed calm pastoral scenes unrecognizable and (to Nettles, at least) a little unbelievable. The three-story building had a distinct lean to it, and not a single doorway was plumb.

On the ground floor, in what had once been a grand parlor, Nettles sat beside a great roaring fireplace and polished her chain as wags from all over the Circle began to trickle in.

Filler was already there, of course, standing

behind Nettles, his arms crossed, his face half-hidden in the flickering firelight. Handsome Henny and the Twins were the first to arrive. Next came some wags she knew from the docks, like Gavish Gray and his best wag Fisty. Some drinking wags from the Drowned Rat slid in soon after, like Snakefeet and Built Slim. Filler and Red's old pickpocket wags came slinking in a bit later. She didn't know them as well, but she knew a few names, like Moxy Poxy, Ladyarch, and Mister Hatbox. Mo had even given Misandry and Tosh the night off, which was about as close as Mo would ever get to giving an official endorsement of Nettles's play for the neighborhood.

All in all, it was a solid crew of wags. A wave of relief came as she watched them gather close. It's one thing to know you're quality enough to be a gang-lord. It's another when you start seeing people agree with you. She didn't let it show, however, except a little self-satisfied smile. But to the wags there who knew her well, that might as well have been a shout of hysterical joy.

"Well now," she said to them. "Some of you I know well, others I know by reputation, and all told, I'm pleased to see you."

"Where you been, Nettles?" Gavish Gray was one of the best smugglers in this part of the empire. A true pirate, not the pretend types that Sadie and Hope were. He had prematurely gray hair and wasn't too bad on the gander. Not for tossing, though, on account of his clingy nature. But that made him about as loyal a wag as Nettles had ever known.

"You all remember Bleak Hope, Hero of the Circle, who killed the biomancer at the Three Cups, and gave her freedom in exchange for everyone else's at Gunpowder Hall," said Nettles. "Filler and I been sailing all over the empire on her ship. Every-where we gone, we saw the same thing as here—imps closing in on the poor common folk, taking what little they got and turning them into playthings for the biomancers. It's like they've declared war on all of us, and it's sure as piss not a time for the Circle to be struggling like it is. When I came back and found that the only real contender to lead the Circle is my cunt-dropping of a brother—who is not fit to even live here, much less run it—I could not abide it. So I'm making a play for it myself."

She'd had Henny and the Twins spreading rumors about her taking the neighborhood since they'd spoken at the Drowned Rat, so this was not news to anyone. But she gave it a moment to set all the same.

"Now, Mick may have the numbers," she continued, "but we're going to have guns. Lots and lots of guns."

"Guns ain't easy to come by these days," said Gray. "Where we going to get 'em?"

"It just so happens," said Nettles, "there's a slice over in Hammer Point with a whole lot of guns who won't be needing them soon. On account of her about to be dead. And that, my wags, is where you all come in."

———

The idea of sneaking into Hammer Point and stealing a bunch of guns from a gaf who cut a deal with biomancers went over well enough, but hackles started to rise when Nettles talked about working with Palla's wags. Thankfully, Nettles had enough money to smooth that over, and everyone left happy.

Apple Grove Manor set the right tone for someone gunning to be ganglord, but it wasn't as comfortable as the Slice of Heaven, and was sorely lacking in amusements. Filler, Henny, and the Twins seemed content to get drunk by the fire, but Nettles was too wound up to sit still.

"Think I'll go walk the Circle a bit," she said to the wags.

"You want me to come?" Filler asked.

"What, you think I need a pissing bodyguard or something?"

He shrugged and went back to drinking with Henny and the Twins.

Nettles stepped out into the dark, chilly streets. She regretted snapping at him. She didn't blame Filler for his protective instincts. He was used to taking care of Red, then Hope. Good old dependable Filler, always there. She'd even leaned on him a few times. Even so, she didn't want to make a habit of it. Not if she was going to be running the Circle. She had to stand on her own.

She'd forgotten how much she liked walking the Circle at night. The yellow streetlights cast shadows that made everything look mysterious and heavy with meaning. Red always accused her of not being romantic, but that wasn't it. She just had her own tastes—a preference for the dark and moody. It felt more honest to her. Because if these streets did have secrets, they were grave ones.

"Hello, Rose."

Nettles froze. The hairs on the back of her neck stood up and her gut twisted into rope.

"Mickey." It came out of her mouth like a curse word. Had he been following her? She doubted the meeting was accidental.

He stepped out of the dark alley and into the streetlight. He'd been a boy the last time she saw him. A lot had changed. He was quite a bit taller than her now, taking after their father in that respect. He was big, too—chubby, even—with a round face and a thick neck. But that look in his eye was the same.

Or maybe worse. The look of desperate hunger that could never be filled.

"Looking good, little sis," he said.

"What do you want?" she asked quietly, her hand resting lightly on her chainblade.

He smiled. "I've been hearing some distressing talk. About you challenging my play for the Circle. And making all kinds of accusations about my character."

"Not accusations. Reminders."

"I wish you'd let the past go. We could do so much, you and me. We could run this neighborhood together, side by side. We could make it the family business. Think how proud Mom would have been."

"It's been a long time since you did anything Mom would have been proud of," said Nettles.

His smile faltered. "It's so easy for you to judge me. I didn't have your looks. I couldn't get in with Jix like you could. He just wanted a taste of that pretty little slice of yours."

"Balls and pricks. You couldn't get in with Jix because you were a twisted cock-dribble, and I'll wager you still are."

His cheeks started to redden, but then he took a slow breath and returned to his smile. "I spent a total of three years on the Empty Cliffs. I'm a changed man, Rose. Rehabilitated."

"Like hells you are." There was a part of her that wanted to just end it now. Put her blade right in his fleshy throat. But even though she hated this man, he was still her brother, and outright killing your own blood was wrong as wrong could be. You didn't come back from something like that.

"I'm asking, as your brother, to either join me or step aside. Because otherwise, even though it won't give me any pleasure, I will have to hurt you. And remember that I know how to hurt you better than anyone."

"Actually, I think that claim went to Dad."

"Better than anyone else *living*," he amended.

Nettles's voice got low and quiet. Almost a growl. "You been gone a long time, Mickey. So let me explain to you how it is in the Circle now. We don't stand for sickboys like you. There is no hell in which you get to run this place."

"Actually, *you've* been the one gone lately, so let *me* explain. That may have been true a year ago, when Drem was running a tight ship. But things have changed since then. Times have grown hard and mean. This neighborhood has welcomed me back with open arms, and they don't give a piss how I get things done as long as they have food in their bilge and a place to sleep at night. Your problem—or one of them, anyway—is that you have lines you don't cross. Things you won't do. The wags of Paradise Circle are too desperate right now to afford someone with that many morals weighing them down."

"They might think so right now, but once they see what you're truly capable of, they'll turn on you, true as trouble."

His lip curled up into a sneer. "You're even worse than Mom with all her 'people united' ideals. When did you get so *poncey*?"

"That's right, Mickey," said Nettles. "I want you to keep thinking that. I'm just your delicate, poncey Rose. You won't get no trouble from me. You're safe as shores."

He glared at her for a long moment. "Just remember, I tried to warn you. I tried to keep you out of it." Then he turned and began to walk away.

"Hey, Mickey," she called.

He turned his head just in time to get the weighted

end of her chain in his mouth. He cursed and spat out a broken tooth.

"There." She coiled her chain back up. "That's *your* warning. Sorry I'm not as good with words as you."

He spat more blood, his hands reaching out like meaty claws. "You pissing slice, I will—"

"You'll what?" She fingered the bladed end of her chain, letting it glint in the streetlight. "Come on, big brother. Let's see what three years on the Empty Cliffs really taught you."

His hands clenched into fists. "You'll see, sweet Rose. You'll see soon enough." Then he walked off, much more quickly than before.

15

*H*ow is the ambassador?" asked Progul Bon in his dark, oily voice. He and Red sat at their usual table in the back of the imperial library. Most days they spent in quiet study of history, but every once in a while, Bon brought up current events before they began the session.

Red wished he could see the biomancer's eyes beneath the deep hood. He didn't like not being able to read him. "Don't pretend to care about Nea. I know you and the rest of the council want her dead."

"On the contrary," said Bon. "As long as she remains in the palace, we wish her the best of health."

"Meaning, if Aukbontar suspects you've killed her, they will come down with a fleet and tear this place right off the side of the mountain," said Red.

"It is a possibility." Progul Bon paused for a moment, as if considering an idea. "Of course, if something were to happen to her outside the palace, perhaps on a short trip to some less populated part of Stonepeak... well, we can't be blamed for such foolhardy actions on the part of the ambassador. All manner of things can happen out there amongst the criminals and seditionists."

"Go ahead and send Brackson," said Red. "I'll be ready for him this time."

"Yes," said Bon. "Unfortunate that he used the whistle so soon. He has been punished appropriately."

Red's stomach dropped. The plan had been to lure Brackson out into the open and use him. But if Bon's idea of "punishment" was anything like biomancers he'd seen before, Brackson wouldn't be useful to anyone now.

"But don't worry," continued Progul Bon. He sounded almost cheerful, which was very out of character for him. "We've chosen someone much more skilled this time. Someone who's apparently becoming a bit of a local legend."

"That Shadow Demon? I'm not worried," said Red, showing a confidence he didn't quite feel. "Thanks to what you gafs have taught me, I think I can handle just about anybody."

Progul Bon's cheerful air dropped away. "You have learned nothing from me if you still don't understand how dangerous the ambassador is to the empire. They come with promises of friendship and mutual benefit, but they will twist that treaty into a hook that will drag us down into a world so terrible, it will make any hell you can imagine look idyllic in comparison. The Dark Mage saw this."

"The Dark Mage was slippy."

"That doesn't make him wrong." Progul Bon's hand shot out and gripped Red's wrist. It felt cold and clammy. He leaned in and lifted his face so that Red got his wish and looked directly into the biomancer's eyes. He wanted to take that back. Beneath a sagging brow like melted candle wax, the biomancer's eyes swirled like a putrid black sludge that seemed to transfer directly into Red's chest, sending a creeping chill down his back.

"Nea Omnipora is a grave threat to the empire and must die," he intoned.

Red shook off the slimy grip and stood up. "Not while I'm alive."

Even though he'd just arrived for his lesson, Red turned and left the library. Progul Bon did not try to stop him.

———

Apparently the prince couldn't just pop over to his mom's house whenever he wanted. First, a messenger was sent to inquire with the empress if a visit was convenient. The messenger returned the following day to say that yes a visit from her son was quite convenient. After that a small army of servants were assigned to prepare supplies, gifts, horses, and carriages. Red had also assumed it would just be him, Leston, Nea, and Etcher going on the visit. But it appeared half the nobility of the palace would be coming with them.

This was why Merivale had said it would take several days at least to organize the trip.

"I had no idea this would be so…complicated, Your Highness," he told the prince as they stood in the courtyard the morning of their departure. Around them were enough carriages, horses, and wagons to make a traveling circus.

Leston gave him a forlorn smile. "The worst part is, my mother despises all the pomp and ceremony. But the lords and ladies so rarely get to pay their respects to the mother of the empire, I fear it would appear unkind of me to deny them."

Red was actually grateful for the lengthy preparations, however, because Ifmish had run into some problems making his whistle. Red had only received the message the night before that it was finally ready. He'd have to stop at the shop on his way out of the city. Then he'd have to find a secluded spot to test it, and verify that the cotton swabs he had in his pocket would mute the sound enough to protect him from its effects. Even if Brackson wasn't the assassin hired to kill Nea this time, the biomancers had most likely given his replacement a whistle as well. He had to be ready for it.

"Your Highness! My Lord Pastinas!" came the light and easy voice of Lady Merivale Hempist. "Splendid day for a trip to the country, wouldn't you say?"

Red had no idea how she was always able to sneak up on him like this. He turned and saw her beaming from the window of a green and gold carriage. "My lady, a delight as ever."

"The sight of you two handsome gentlemen makes the day even more splendid," she replied. "I hear we're nearly under way, if only Lord Weatherwight can squeeze himself and his wife into their borrowed carriage."

"Excellent," said the prince. "With this many carriages, it will be slow going, so the sooner we start, the better."

Hume walked over from where he had been hitching the horses to the prince's massive white and gold carriage. "My lord, that…item you requested will require a slight deviation from the route to the Rain Gate."

"Thanks, Hume," said Red. "It sounds like this carriage train is going to move pretty slow. If I start out now, I can probably walk there and meet up with the prince's carriage before it's left the city."

"Nonsense, my lord!" said Merivale, a twinkle in her eyes. "I would be happy to take you in my carriage."

Leston coughed, holding his hand over his mouth to hide his smile.

Red couldn't think of a way to refuse the offer

that didn't seem suspicious, so he gave her a florid bow and said, "You are most kind, my lady."

"Marvelous." Her eyes gleamed as she opened her carriage door. "Let's away, then."

As Red climbed into the narrow carriage and sat down next to Merivale, he heard the prince call out, "My lady, I do expect to see my friend safely delivered to me. Please don't whisk him off to Lesser Basheta and marriage quite yet."

"I promise I will return him to you as soon as possible in the same condition I found him. Or nearly."

The prince's laughter was drowned out by the crack of the whip and the clatter of wheels on flagstones as the carriage lurched forward.

"So, my lord," said Merivale when they had passed through the palace gate. "Where can I take you?"

"Ifmish's tin shop."

It was an odd coincidence that Hume should bring up going to the tinsmith while Merivale was in earshot with her carriage ready to go. Or more likely, it wasn't a coincidence at all. Had the two of them engineered some "private time" for Red and Merivale?

It was just as well, because Red needed to tell her about the change in plan.

"Look, I appreciate the ride, but we've got a problem," he said.

"Oh? What problem is that, my lord?"

"My...sources tell me that Brackson is out of the picture."

"Really?" asked Merivale.

"I think instead they're sending that Shadow Demon who's been killing people for them in the city."

"But this is marvelous news!" she said.

"Is it?" asked Red.

"Of course. If you can capture this 'Shadow

Demon' and force him to confess, you would be able to not only charge the biomancers with an assassination attempt, but also with wantonly slaughtering subjects who spoke out against them. It sounds like your plan is working out even better than I'd thought."

"But how can I protect Nea from this...monster if I'm trapped inside *your* carriage?"

Merivale leaned into him, her hands wrapping around his upper arm. "'Trapped' has a rather interesting ring. It sounds as though you are at my mercy."

"Merivale," he said levelly. "Can we be serious for just a minute here?"

She sighed dramatically. "I *suppose* I could contrive some way to get you back to the prince's carriage once we get your...what are we getting?"

"A whistle."

"That's all?" asked Merivale. "I'm driving you to the tinsmith all the way out by Coral Lane for a *whistle*?"

"It's a *special* whistle," he said defensively.

"In what way is it special?"

"It's nothing you need to worry about," said Red.

She rested her chin on his shoulder and gave him a sly look. "You know, they say there is a specific pitch that makes a woman uncontrollably aroused."

"You just made that up," he said, trying to ignore the heat of her skin so close to his.

"Perhaps," she said. "You have to admit, it would be interesting."

"As long as you didn't find the male equivalent."

She leaned in so close, her breath tickled his ear. "Who's to say I haven't?"

Red decided that the carriage was far too small. Unless he jumped out the window, there was no escaping the advances of Lady Hempist. And Red had to admit, if it weren't for Hope, he wouldn't want to. The more he got to know Merivale, the more he liked her. He didn't trust her, of course. But if things had been different, he could have found a way to work around that.

Fortunately, a moment later the carriage slowed to a halt and the driver said, "We've arrived, my lady."

"Thank you, Lurum," she said, then turned to Red and gave him an arch look. "Well, my lord. Shall we? Or was there something you wanted to attend to first?"

"Let's go." He quickly climbed out of the carriage and took a moment to breathe in the air of freedom before helping Lady Hempist down from the carriage. He had hoped she wouldn't come into the shop, but again couldn't think of a way to refuse that didn't draw more attention.

As soon as they walked into the shop, Ifmish hurried over to them. "Ah, there you are, my lord." He held out the tiny whistle. "I'm so sorry for the delays. It took a few different attempts, and quite a bit of wasted tin, but I think I can say with confidence that you won't find a higher-pitched whistle anywhere in the empire."

Red hoped that wasn't true, and that this one matched the one Brackson used. "Thanks, old pot."

"Did you want to try it out?" Ifmish asked eagerly.

Red glanced at Merivale. She was examining a decorative piece hung on the wall and didn't look particularly interested. But Red had watched her feign both interest and disinterest enough to know her expression meant almost nothing. What if the whistle worked? How would he explain suddenly losing all sense of balance?

"Sorry, we're in a bit of a rush." He slipped it into his jacket pocket.

"Yes, of course, my lord," Ifmish said, looking a little disappointed.

Red patted the tinsmith on the shoulder. "I'll be sure to let you know how it works when I have a chance."

"Thank you, my lord. You know I do get invested in the more challenging work. I can't help myself."

"It's an admirable quality, my wag," said Red as he led Merivale out of the shop.

She waited until they were back in the carriage before saying, "I will not pry into this whistle business that you seem so intent on keeping to yourself."

"Thank you, my lady. A tom's got to have a few secrets, after all, or he loses his mysterious allure."

She moved in so close, their cheeks were nearly touching, and her soft breast pressed against his arm. "I'm afraid there's little mystery in your allure, my dear Lord Pastinas. You've got the ear of the future emperor, you're uncommonly handsome, remarkably intelligent—given your background—and you have an adorably naive idea that you have some say in your future romantic involvements."

Maybe it was being once again confined to the small carriage, or maybe he was just tired of playing the coy flirtation game when there were so many more important things to worry about. But his patience for the whole thing suddenly evaporated. "Even though the majority of that was a compliment, I have to tell you, I'm insulted."

Merivale turned her lips down into a pout. "Is it the comment about your background? Should I have said, 'remarkably knowledgeable' instead?"

"No, I'm proud of where I came from. It's the last one that bothers me."

"Oh?" She smiled mischievously.

He didn't return her smile. "Since you and I can speak crystal on politics, let's talk true on this as well. I am dead serious that my heart is for one woman and there will be no other. Every time you make light of that, it is an insult to her and what she has done for me. And to insult her is to insult me."

She gazed at him for several moments, her eyes clear but expressionless. "I see," she said at last. "Forgive me for the misunderstanding, my lord. In the society I was raised, love and marriage have little to do with each other. Marriage is primarily a political and economic arrangement. I did not fully comprehend that your love for this distant woman precluded the possibility of us entering into a matrimonial alliance that would have been both pleasant and advantageous for both of us."

"I'm sorry," said Red. "I agree that it would have been fun. But I can't do it. And I *will* see her again. Someday. I have to believe that."

Merivale nodded and moved almost imperceptibly so that they were no longer touching. Red felt the loss of her warmth more keenly than he would have liked to admit.

They rode in silence for a little while, the clatter of horse hooves and carriage wheels suddenly loud in Red's ears.

"If I may inquire, Lord Pastinas," said Merivale, her eyes fixed out the window at the passing buildings. "Since you love this woman so much, why don't you simply go to her?"

It must have been a hard thing to ask. Red didn't like hurting what had become one of his favorite people on Stonepeak, and he was afraid he was losing the friendship. So when she asked the question, he couldn't bring himself to directly lie to her.

"Not all prisons have bars, Lady Hempist."

———

It was an uncomfortably quiet ride to the front of the carriage train, which had only made it halfway through the city by then. But Red did have an honest excuse for transferring back to the prince's carriage. When they pulled up next to the still-moving white and gold carriage, Red stuck his head out and waved. Nea was closest to the window on that side and waved back.

"Permission to come aboard, Ambassador!" he shouted over the noise of the carriages.

"Should I ask them to stop?" she shouted back.

"Don't bother. Just open the door."

Nea gave him an uncertain look but opened the door. Red turned back to Lady Hempist. "Merivale, I'm…"

"Don't worry about me, my lord. As I said, this was more in the nature of an intriguing business proposition than an affair of the heart for me, so I won't be crying into my handkerchief the moment you depart." She gave him a small smile. "And rest assured, this isn't any sort of good-bye. You and I still have a great deal to accomplish together."

He was tempted to ask what those other things might be, but decided to leave it alone for now. Instead, he jumped across the gap to the prince's carriage, tumbling into a forward roll at their feet. He lay there for a moment, grinning up at them. Nea laughed delightedly. Then the prince helped him to his feet.

"Escaped the clutches of Lady Hempist without a wedding ring, I see," said Leston.

Red winced. "I'm afraid I won't have to worry about that anymore."

"Did you do something to offend her?" he asked.

"Near enough. I told her I would only marry the woman I loved. Apparently that was a new idea for her."

"Ah," Leston said quietly.

"She said marriages are merely alliances for nobles."

"Not just nobles," said Nea. "Even though we do not have nobility in Aukbontar, marriages are often more for political or financial gain. I myself will probably be expected to marry for a political alliance, rather than love."

"Perhaps it could be for both," Leston said quietly.

Red internally cringed. The prince's sot talk was getting clumsier and more overt by the day. But as usual, Nea handled it perfectly. She smiled with what Red had come to understand was her practiced diplomatic smile, and said, "That would be a rare and wonderful gift." Not a yes, not a no. Aukbontar really had sent their best diplomat.

Red glanced out the window as they rode through the city streets. The prince's carriage was second in the carriage line behind the imperial vanguard wagon, which was armed to the neck with soldiers. It really set the mood, and the crowds were quiet as they watched the long train of lacy carriages go past. It bothered Red even more than usual that people might see him and put him in the lacy category. He was tempted to do something outlandish, just to let them know he was on their side. But often as not, those sorts of things backfired. And besides, his main goal was to keep Nea safe, and drawing attention to himself would not help.

A short time later they reached the Rain Gate. The city was enclosed on the west and east sides by twenty-foot-high walls made of the same black rock as the mountain. The only way through those walls was the Rain Gate in the western wall and the Wind Gate in the eastern wall. There had once been a gate at the southern end called the Thunder Gate that separated the city from the large system of docks and warehouses, but it had been torn down hundreds of years ago by order of Emperor Bastelinus, who saw any impediment to trade and commerce as something to be removed. The gate at the north end of the city was officially called the Lightning Gate, although most people simply referred to it as the palace gate, since that's what was on the other side.

The Rain Gate itself was wide enough to allow two wagons side by side. It was usually shut with a wrought iron barrier that was raised and lowered on a pulley system. It had not been successfully breached since the Dark Mage's army took the city centuries ago. Of course, Red was pretty sure there hadn't been any serious attempts to breach it since then. The iron didn't look particularly well maintained. It was spotted with rust, and when it was slowly raised, the shriek of corroded metal was so sharp, Red had to make a conscious effort not to cover his ears.

"Red, are you okay?" asked Nea. "You look pained."

"Perhaps he regrets breaking Lady Hempist's heart." Leston grinned.

"I doubt her heart," said Red. "Her plans for political conquest, maybe. But even then, I reckon she has at least one or two fallback plans, so I'm not worried about her too much."

The carriage crossed through the gate and out into the wide-open countryside. Rolling grass meadows stretched as far as Red could see. It was more empty land than Red had ever seen and it gave him an unexpected feeling of peace. It also made him feel a bit small, but with all the pressure he'd been under lately, a little perspective wasn't a bad thing.

"Is this what Aukbontar looks like?" he asked Nea.

"In places." Her eyes grew distant, as if picturing it in her mind. "Aukbontar is very large, with a wide variety of terrain. Some places are more sand and rock than this. Very dry and desolate, but lovely in their own way. Other places contain nothing but jagged mountains as far as the eye can see. And still others contain forests so dense that you cannot see the sun as you walk through them."

"And you've seen all these places?" asked Leston.

She smiled. "How could I represent a country if I did not know all of what I was representing?"

"Very well said." Leston's eyes shone with something very close to adoration.

Red had a sudden urge to smack his friend. He knew for a fact that the prince hadn't seen the majority of the country he would eventually be representing.

Perhaps Red should talk to the prince. Try to explain to him that he was putting Nea in an awkward position and making an ass of himself in the process. But he knew his friend well enough to know that no matter how much sense he made, the reaction would not be positive. Princes, he suspected, were not generally used to being told what to do.

The line of carriages crawled slowly west across the meadows until they reached the coast in the early afternoon. The sea sparkled in the sunlight, stippled with the strong sea breeze. The shoreline was composed of a coarse sand dotted with seagulls and bits of shells and seaweed.

Nea sighed audibly. "I find ocean views very soothing."

"Do you?" asked Leston, looking a little surprised.

"You do not?" she asked.

"It's just the sea," he said. "There's nothing remarkable about it."

"Ah, Your Highness!" said Etcher, looking pained. "I do not like to disagree, but the ocean is one of the most astonishing marvels in the world. Did you know that more of the world is covered in water than dry land?"

"I assumed that was the case," said Leston.

"Yes, well…" Etcher looked slightly deflated, but he continued. "Did you know that the ocean is in places so deep that we have yet to reach the bottom?"

"In *The Book of Storms*, it is said there are places in the sea that have no bottom," said Leston.

"Impossible," said Etcher, then flinched when Nea gave him an ominous look. "That is, uh, I am unaware of what physical properties might make that possible."

Leston laughed. "I have noticed that the people of Aukbontar seem to put a great deal of faith in their physical sciences."

"Of course," said Etcher. "It's far more reliable than ritual and superstition."

"Etcher has spoken out of turn, Your Highness," Nea said coldly.

If it were possible for Etcher to climb inside himself, Red thought he would have done it. He looked downright terrified of Nea in that moment.

"It's all right," Leston said. "I generally don't seek the company of biomancers, but I would be greatly amused to witness a conversation between one of them and Etcher. Each of them is so convinced of his superiority, but it seems to me the best choice is a union of the two philosophies." He looked fixedly at Nea. "Wouldn't you agree, Ambassador?"

"Of course, Your Highness. I always favor a cooperative solution."

Leston seemed not to notice the tension that ran beneath the statement. Red decided that, regardless of how his advice was received, the next time the two of them were alone, he'd tell the prince to ease off all the romantic innuendo. If it continued like this, he'd eventually put her in a corner and then there would be no outcome that was happy for both of them.

The carriage train turned north and followed the coast for a few hours. Not even Red could keep a conversation going that long among four people who already saw one another daily, so the carriage had lapsed into a comfortable silence, when Red saw a large building slowly begin to rise behind the rolling sand dunes.

"Is that Sunset Point?" he asked.

The prince followed his gaze, then nodded.

Red gave his friend a wry smile. "When you said your mother had gone into seclusion, this wasn't exactly what I imagined."

"Really?" Leston looked genuinely surprised.

Sometimes Red forgot just how sheltered the prince was. He supposed that compared to the palace, Sunset Point might seem small. But as Red took in the slowly growing view, it became apparent that it was not only larger than the humble cottage he'd pictured, but was big enough to put stately Pastinas Manor to shame. Sunset Point sat at the end of a narrow peninsula. It was only one story, but the grounds covered most of the peninsula, and the house itself was massive. It was bordered on three sides by a wide deck that stretched out over the water, making it almost appear to float on the sea.

"Look!" Etcher suddenly shouted in the small carriage. He pointed excitedly out the window. "An albatross!" He pulled out his sketchbook and began to draw.

"Are those uncommon in Aukbontar?" asked Red.

"Very," said Nea. "Once a year they appear on the southern coast."

"And that's it?" asked Leston.

"Long ago, it was how we knew of the existence of the Empire of Storms, although we didn't know it by name. We just knew that if a bird came from the south, it must mean that there was land of some kind to the south that could sustain life." She smiled sadly. "Of course, we didn't realize just how far an albatross could fly, so we did not understand just how far away you were. For nearly a century, expeditions ventured into the Great Southern Sea, what you call the Dark Sea. Some came back, half-dead with nothing to show for it. Others didn't come back at all."

"What changed?" asked Red. "I mean, you can reach us now."

"There were improvements to our ships and advancements in food and water preservation. We now have the ability to store food and water in a way that allows it to keep for over a year."

"Really?" Red turned to Leston. "Can we do that?"

He shook his head.

"Have we ever even *tried* to get to Aukbontar?" asked Red.

"Not that I know of," said Leston. "Certainly not since my father took the throne. He accepts what the biomancers tell him. That Aukbontar is dangerous and should be avoided." He smiled apologetically at Nea.

"I hope we will correct that misconception in the near future," said Nea.

"And of course," continued Leston, "there is the Guardian, who roams the northern border of the empire. I believe it exists to keep us here as much as it does to keep Aukbontar out."

"So the Guardian is real?" asked Nea. Her tone was casual, but Red sensed there was something much stronger underneath.

"Come now, Ambassador," said Etcher. "A real kraken? It's—"

Nea said something to him in their language. Red had no idea what it meant, but the tone was harsh and Etcher again sank back into his seat.

"My apologies, Your Highness," Nea said in a

milder tone. "As you can see, I am still working on Etcher's sensitivity toward other cultures."

"It's quite all right," said Leston. "Even our own citizens have a difficult time believing the Guardian is real until they see it with their own eyes."

"Have you seen it?" she asked.

"Several times," he said quietly, his eyes gazing out the window. "I have never seen it out of the water, so I can't speak to its exact size, but it is a monstrous thing, bigger than the largest whale. It is fiendishly clever, too. It understands at least enough to know that the people are *inside* the ship, so it tears the hull apart like cracking a nutshell, then reaches in with one of its long tentacles and scoops out the hapless victims and stuffs them into its gaping maw."

Red shuddered. "You're not too bad at telling stories, Your Highness."

"I wish that were all it was," said Leston. "To tell the truth, I am uncomfortable with its presence in our waters. We pretend that the imperial navy is the greatest power in the sea. But it is nothing in the face of that biomancer abomination."

16

$\mathcal{A}$re we sure about this?" Alash asked nervously.

Hope had been about to knock on Luscious Lymestria's dressing room. She paused, her knuckles only an inch from the grimy, scratched wooden door.

"Are you nervous?" she asked, unable to keep the amusement out of her voice. "After all we've encountered?"

"Yes, well, typically *you* do the encountering, while I stay behind to fire the cannons and such." He smiled weakly.

"He *is* nervous," said Jilly, more contemptuous than amused. "Sometimes I can't believe you and Red are even related."

Hope gave Jilly a long look. "A Vinchen strives to maintain empathy for the weak, not scorn."

Jilly looked down at the boots Hope had bought her. "Sorry, teacher."

Hope turned back to Alash. "It's going to be fine. As far as I can tell, Lymestria has one formidable weapon in her arsenal, and breasts can't actually hurt you."

"Miss Hope!" Alash's face reddened.

Hope laughed, then knocked on the door. "Ms. Lymestria? We're friends of Broomefedies. Can we speak with you a moment?"

The door opened to reveal Lymestria, now in a

dressing gown only loosely tied at the front. She did not appear to be wearing anything underneath. She gave Hope and Jilly haughty looks, but when she saw Alash, her expression warmed.

"I suppose I could spare a few minutes of my time," she said at last.

"Thank you, we'll be brief, then," said Hope as she took off her hat and followed Lymestria into the small dressing room. "Do you know Old Yammy?"

"Doesn't everyone?" Lymestria's eyes remained riveted on Alash.

"We hear she's been taken to the Empty Cliffs," said Hope. "We intend to rescue her."

"How marvelous for her," said Lymestria without enthusiasm. "It's a dreadful place."

"Yes...," said Hope as she watched Lymestria examine Alash's jacket and cravat. "We, uh, understand you spent a year there and we were hoping you could give us some insight on the security and defenses."

Lymestria finally turned to Hope. "I'll tell you all I know about the place, *if* you let me borrow this one tonight." She pinched Alash's cheek.

Alash was too shocked to respond, so Hope asked, *"Borrow?"*

"I have a party tonight and a handsome-looking lacy like this on my arm will do wonders for my reputation."

"A party?" Alash looked terrified. "I'm not... terribly good at parties, you see. I may not—that is, perhaps I'm not an ideal escort for you, Miss Lymestria."

"Nonsense. You're adorable. A little fine-tuning, perhaps..." She put a hand on each of his shoulders and pushed him out of his habitual slouch. Then she took his chin between her thumb and forefinger and tilted it up slightly. Finally she brushed a few stray hairs at his temples back behind his ears. "But they'll all think I've got a rich benefactor who's utterly smitten with my charms."

"He doesn't actually have any money anymore," said Hope. "In case that was part of your plan."

"The truth is irrelevant. If I show up with him, I won't even need to say anything about it. The gossipmongers will do all the work for me."

"Alash is an extremely valuable member of my crew," said Hope. "I can't simply hand him over to you."

"Yes, thank you, Captain!" Alash looked greatly relieved.

"If you are to take him," Hope continued, "I will need to come as well. I'll keep my distance in order to maintain your deception, but I insist on being able to see him at all times."

Lymestria sighed heavily, her body slouching forward. "Fine. You can go with Broom."

"What about me?" Jilly asked eagerly.

"You are going back to the ship," said Hope. "I believe you have some reading assignments from Brigga Lin."

Jilly sighed as heavily as Lymestria. "Yes, teacher."

———

Hope was surrounded by clothing. *Costumes*, actually, although she wondered if there was really all that much difference. After all, wasn't most clothing an attempt to portray a certain identity or allegiance? Whether it was a white robe, or black armor, what did it mean, really?

She stood in a windowless room beneath the theater. All around her were rows of costumes on long, sturdy racks. It smelled a little musty, and all sound was absorbed by the walls of fabric, making everything muted and unnaturally quiet. She looked around at the costumes with a strange sort of wonder. She'd never actually seen a play. Theater was Red's world, not hers. There had been a time, not so long ago, when she would have been tempted to dismiss theater as frivolous—a distraction, even, from the important things in life. But as she looked around now at the lush gowns, stately uniforms, and fool's motley, she felt as if she was being absorbed into the old tales her mother had whispered to her as a girl, and she wondered how she had ever been so hardhearted. So unsentimental.

Something was changing inside her. She understood that, even if she didn't know what the change was, or where it was going. It was like she had spent ten years of her life with her fists clenched tight, and now her grip was slowly loosening. It was frightening in some ways. But she was so tired of clinging to old darkness, old anger. Surely there had to be something better.

"Here we are!"

Broom thrust his way through a rack of costumes, looking very pleased with himself. He held out a red captain's coat.

"It's fortunate you have such a boyish figure!" he said. "This should fit nicely."

Hope let that comment go as she looked dubiously at the bright red coat.

"I would have preferred black."

"Hell's waters, my girl! Dire Bane doesn't wear dour black! If you plan to use the name, you must look the part! Besides, this will match the red feather in your hat."

She reluctantly pulled on the coat. "Well?" she asked Broom.

He waved his hands at her impatiently. "Button it up properly!"

She did as she was told, then looked at him.

"See for yourself!" He seemed giddy as he shoved aside some more costumes and wheeled over a tall mirror.

Hope had to admit that it fit nicely, loose in the shoulders for easy movement, tight around the midsection, and flared out slightly below the waist. She had never been a vain person, and preening in front of a mirror seemed a little foolish to her. But as she looked at herself, she couldn't help but smile a little.

"I do cut a dashing figure," she admitted.

"*Now* you look like Dire Bane!" declared Broom. "Let me find something suitably complementary for myself, and we'll be ready for the party."

A short time later, with twilight just beginning to fall, Hope, Broom, Alash, and Lymestria set off from the theater. Hope and Broom let Lymestria walk arm in arm with Alash a block or so ahead so they wouldn't spoil her little act. It made it easy for Hope to keep an eye on Alash anyway. Although as they made their way down Honey Street, her eyes were constantly drawn to Broom, who walked at her side.

Broom's idea of "suitably complementary" was a large purple hat and trousers, and a black leather vest that he'd claimed was exactly the sort of thing a first mate on a pirate ship would wear. He wore nothing underneath his vest, and his vast hairy belly was proudly on display as they strolled beneath the street lamps.

"Clearly this isn't a formal event," said Hope, indicating his costume.

Broom chuckled. "I take it you've never been to a proper Silverback party?"

"I'm afraid not."

"Restraint and decorum are not prized very highly. Best parties in the empire. Just keep an eye on your drink. Not everyone around here understands or respects a drug-free lifestyle."

"I won't be drinking," said Hope.

"That's a shame. The wag hosting this party brews the best ale on Honey Street. I keep telling him he should stop trying to sell those rubbish poems of his and start selling his drink."

"You appreciate finely crafted ale, then?" asked Hope.

"For a fat old man, there are few things better."

"I grew up among the finest brewers in the empire."

He gave her a curious look. "Who would that be?"

"The Vinchen monks of Galemoor."

Broom scratched his gut. "Ah, the famed ale of Galemoor. I had a taste of that once. It was after I'd won the Boardmaster, which is a sort of prize for the best theatrical performance of the year. My theater master spent God knows how much money on that little jug, but as I recall, it tasted like liquid gold." He shook his head sadly. "It'd be even more expensive now, I suppose."

"Why's that?" asked Hope.

"Well, there's no brewery on Galemoor now."

"I think you must be mistaken," Hope said sharply. "That brewery has been in operation for centuries. Since the days of Manay the True."

"All I know is that not a single barrel has come out of there in the last two—maybe even three—years. I heard that any merchant who makes the trek down there is turned away at the gate."

The idea that the Vinchen monks no longer made ale was not an idea that Hope could accept easily. They had always taken great pride and simple pleasure in the crafting of fine ale. It had become as much a part of the order as combat. With Hurlo dead, Hope assumed Racklock had become grandteacher.

But she doubted even his twisted soul could spurn something so integral to the Vinchen order.

Ahead of them, Lymestria and Alash turned a corner and were out of sight.

"Is that the right way to go?" Hope asked.

Broom nodded. "We're nearly there. Don't worry about your tom. Lymestria will make sure he doesn't get into too much trouble."

"He's not my tom. Just a friend."

"Oh? My mistake. You do have one, though? A tom of your own?"

Hope's thoughts went immediately to Red. But maybe that was foolish. A man she hadn't seen in a year. A man who, as Brigga Lin had cautioned, might be very different from the one taken from her. It wasn't that she had given up on him, exactly. But when she thought about it, she'd known him for only a short time. She'd spent far longer with her crew, so it was possible she actually knew Alash better than Red at this point. And even if Red had been who she thought he was, and even if he was *still* that man, perhaps he no longer felt as deeply about her. Unless the biomancers were keeping him completely isolated, he'd probably met many other women at the palace. Glamorous, elegant women. Undamaged women. She had to prepare herself for the possibility that when she did finally rescue him, he saw her as nothing more than a fellow wag. It would be grotesque of her to harbor any resentment if that was how he felt. And yet...

She smiled sheepishly at Broom. "It's...complicated."

He laughed. "I have a few of those myself."

They rounded the corner in time to see Lymestria and Alash enter a large building. The entrance was lit with torches. A man wearing an apple-green cape and nothing but his undergarments pounded on a small drum.

"What's the drum for?" asked Hope.

"It's to make sure everyone knows where the party is tonight."

"Is it the only party in Silverback tonight?" asked Hope.

"Of course not." Broom gave her a broad grin. "But it's the only one that matters."

The drum reminded Hope of Jilly's "beat to quarters," which, she realized, was oddly appropriate. The people of Silverback seemed as dedicated to celebration as the navy was to battle. Presumably with fewer casualties.

They walked past the semi-naked drummer to the front doors. Two large men stood just inside, not looking nearly as festive. When they glared at Hope suspiciously, her clamp went automatically to her sword.

"The bouncers," Broom said quietly. "Not to worry." He waved and smiled. "She's with me, boys."

"Ain't seen you out in a while, Broom," one of them said, suddenly smiling.

"Got to make sure people don't forget me," said Broom.

"Have fun in there. Sorry about the fiddler."

"Sorry about the fiddler?" Hope asked Broom quietly as they walked through the foyer. Then she heard him. He sounded like he was attacking his fiddle with a piece of metal. And when they reached the main room, she saw that her guess was not far off. He had wild, shaggy hair and a beard like a beast. He sat in a corner and scraped a sliver of rusted iron across the strings of his fiddle, making a sound that was so unpleasant, Hope could almost taste it on her back teeth.

"Modern composers," said Broom sourly. "No respect for the classics. But what do you think of the party?" He gestured broadly to the rest of the room.

Hope was more prepared for the spectacle than she'd expected. The room was packed with people, but no one was fighting. The air was hot and stifling, but perfumed with incense and fragrant pastries. People were drinking excessively and probably doing drugs of some kind, but no one appeared to have overdosed and there was no vomit on the floor. While many people had stripped off the majority of their clothes, and some were kissing, no one was completely naked or having intercourse. In other words, compared to Gunpowder Hall in Paradise Circle, it was quite tame.

"Very pleasant," she told Broom. "Now, where is Alash?"

"He's over there." Broom waved vaguely to one side. "He's fine."

Hope would not have said he was "fine," but perhaps that's because she knew him better than Broom did. He was currently surrounded by a small group of people all vying for his attention, while Lymestria kept her arm possessively around his waist, a gloating smile on her lips. Hope knew Alash didn't like being the center of attention, but she had to admit that while he might be uncomfortable, he didn't seem to be in any danger. Perhaps the experience would even be instructive for him.

"Well?" asked Broom. "What should we do?"

"As long as I can keep an eye on Alash, I don't much care," said Hope. "You be the guide."

"Then it will be my pleasure to introduce you to some of the greatest theatrical talents in the world!"

As the evening wore on, Hope sympathized more and more with Alash. Broom took her from one small group to the next, showing her off like she was a rare curiosity.

Hope had assumed practitioners of the creative arts to be worldly. Perhaps because she saw a connection between the craft they practiced and the meditation that was central to a Vinchen's growth and enlightenment. But for enlightened artistic individuals, this group certainly seemed provincial. It was as if the world outside Silverback was irrelevant to them. When she asked how things were in Paradise Circle, most hadn't even realized there had been riots. When she asked if there was any news from Stonepeak, most of them looked at her incredulously and laughed. As if the very idea they might know or care about anything going on at Stonepeak was a joke.

Finally Broom introduced her to one old man who said, "I might have heard a thing or two that way." The man had clearly been handsome once, but years and unhealthy choices had stripped most of that away, leaving a pale shadow behind. His face was gaunt and sallow, and he had a painful-looking open sore on his lip.

"Allow me to introduce Avery Birdhouse, who has trod the boards more years than you or I have been alive," said Broom.

"Honored to meet you," Hope said gravely. "And eager to know what you've heard from the capital."

"I know a few wags up there working with a group called the Godly Naturalists," said Avery.

"Sounds like a religious cult," said Broom.

"More like an anti-biomancer cult," said Avery. "They believe that biomancers always messing with nature is the whole problem with the empire. They reckon that the biomancers have grown too powerful. That they're even more powerful than the emperor."

"How can anyone be more powerful than the emperor?" asked Broom. "That doesn't make a drop of sense."

Hope thought back to her brief time at the palace.

She hadn't seen anyone from the imperial court. Almost as if their existence was irrelevant and the Council of Biomancery acted on its own with impunity.

"What are these Godly Naturalists doing about the biomancers?" Hope wondered if they might be allies at some point. "Have they taken any action?"

"I think they have some, but they're scared to do too much lately. The biomancers have some new creature. Folks call it the Shadow Demon, and it hunts down the biomancers' enemies at night."

"Shadow Demon?" Broom gave him a skeptical look. "Has anybody ever seen it?"

"Nobody's seen nothing that I heard, on account of it does all its killing in the dark. Like it don't even need light to see. As I hear it, the victims are always sliced open, but no knife has ever been found at the scene. Chilling, ain't it?"

"Very," said Hope. It could all be coincidence, of course. A "creature" controlled by biomancers that could see in the dark and favored blades. But what if it wasn't? What if they had turned Red into some kind of killing machine? It would be even worse than Brigga Lin had warned.

"Where's Lymestria and that lacy of yours got to?" asked Broom.

Hope's focus snapped back to her surroundings. She scanned the dense crowd for signs of either of them. Her shoulders slowly tightened with each moment she didn't see them. It had gotten more crowded since they'd arrived, and the buzz of conversation was closer to a roar as people competed with the grating shrieks of the fiddle player.

"Captain, I *must* tell you something!" Alash's voice was directly behind her.

She spun to see him looking at her with wide, glazed eyes, his pupils so dilated she could hardly see his irises. Lymestria still held on to his waist, although now it looked more out of necessity than possessiveness.

"Alash, have you been taking drugs?" she asked.

"Drugs? Me?" He turned to Lymestria, who giggled and nodded. "Apparently I have. I do feel a bit strange. Not bad, though. I feel marvelous, in fact."

Hope glared at Lymestria. "What did you give him?"

"Just a drop of black rose, my darling." Her voice was muffled because her face was pressed into Alash's side. "He was terribly anxious, you see. Apparently it's the crowds. I felt dreadful, of course. So I thought I'd give him a little something for his nerves."

"And how much did you give yourself?" asked Broom, looking weary.

"Don't give me that look, Broomie. I can handle myself," Lymestria told Alash's jacket. She seemed to be slowly sliding down his body as her grip on him loosened.

"None of that is *important* though." Alash gave Hope an intensely earnest look.

"Oh?" she asked. "What *is* important?"

"I'm so glad you asked!" He beamed at her for a moment, then put his hands on her shoulders. "*You* are what's important. You are *amazing*! You must know that!"

"Uh-huh..." Hope gave Broom a sideways glance. He shrugged apologetically.

Alash leaned in closer, looking at her adoringly with eyes that were not quite focused. "Your keen insight. Your bold leadership. Your drive and commitment to your beliefs. Your generosity and unexpected kindness. And of course, I hardly need to mention your beauty."

Hope couldn't quite decide if she found his

inebriated fawning sweet or irritating, but she summoned all the patience she could. "Alash, I think it's time to go."

"Already?" he asked.

Then Lymestria lost her battle with gravity and fell to the floor.

Broom picked her up and threw her over his shoulder. He smacked her butt and grinned at Hope. "I've got mine. Collect yours and let's be off."

Hope gently removed Alash's hands from her shoulders, then guided him toward the door after Broom.

Alash seemed to perk up a little once they were out in the chill night air. "I hope I wasn't being too forward."

"It's okay."

"But you know, I so rarely express my full feelings toward a person. Why is it usually so difficult?"

"I find it hard as well," said Hope.

"What if there was someone, let's say, a person we had strong romantic feelings for. You would think we could just tell them and it would be easy. It's only words, after all. Only *talking*. It's not so scary."

"I suppose not," said Hope.

"Then *why*?" He lifted his arms up to the starry night sky, as if expecting it to answer. Then he dropped his arms and groaned. "I think I may be in love with Miss Lin."

"I was fairly certain you were," said Hope.

"She thinks I'm bumbling, weak, and naive."

"You don't know that."

"I do, actually. She told me so."

He said it so matter-of-factly that Hope couldn't help herself. She laughed. Under normal circumstances, Alash probably would have been mortified, and rightfully so. But with the black rose still coursing through his veins, he joined her with his own light, merry laugh.

They walked for a while down Honey Street, which still surged with music and life. Slowly their laughter faded away to silence.

Finally, Alash said, "That won't be nearly as funny tomorrow, will it?"

"No," Hope agreed. "Probably not."

17

Seeing her brother the night before gave Nettles an extra bit of edge that she knew would come in handy taking down Sharn. However, it also made her a little less gentle with others. And she was never particularly gentle to begin with.

"You sure you want me to stay behind?" asked Filler as he sat and watched Nettles work a nick out of her chainblade with a pumice stone.

"Don't be bludgeon, Fill. You can't go creeping around with that thing." She tapped his leg brace with the toe of her boot.

"Yeah, alright."

The others were all getting ready. The room was filled with a quiet, eager tension as knives were sharpened, strangle wires were coiled, and darts were dipped in poison. Filler's shoulders sagged as he watched them. Nettles felt a tiny prickle of guilt for leaving him behind.

"Sorry, Filler, that's just how it is."

"I know."

"Look." She placed her chainblade on her lap and put her hand on his big shoulder. "I need you here anyway."

He eyed her warily. "You're just saying that."

"No, I'm talking true. I need someone to keep an eye on Mick. He's got some plan or other. He might try to make a move while I'm gone tonight, so I need someone I can trust to tell me what's what the minute I get back." She actually had Tosh and Misandry on that task, but she couldn't let poor old Filler sit around with nothing to do.

"I suppose that could happen, couldn't it?" he admitted.

"This is a big operation we're running here, my wag. I can't be everywhere at once and you're my number two, aren't you?"

"Sure, Nettie."

"So I'm counting on you to be in charge when I'm not here."

"I can do that."

"Thanks, Fill. I owe you." She squeezed his shoulder and went back to working on her blade. It was strange, getting people to do things. She'd seen Red do it countless times, sometimes even been on the receiving end. But she hadn't done it much herself. It was easier than she expected. That was good, because if she really was going to take the Circle, she needed to get used to it.

Once the sun had set, Nettles and her crew said good-bye to Filler and headed for Hammer Point. There were eleven of them in total. Nettles in front with Handsome Henny and the Twins, followed by Gavish Gray, Fisty, Moxy Poxy, Built Slim, Snakefeet, Ladyarch, and Mister Hatbox.

Along the way, they walked past the Three Cups. Its windows and door gaped open like the head of a corpse.

"Nobody's moved in there?" she asked Henny.

"Nah. A biomancer died there, you know."

"I know. I was there when our own Bleak Hope took off the top half of his head."

"Right. Well, folks reckon any place a biomancer gets killed must be haunted by the worst sort of ghosts."

"Load of balls and pricks."

"You want to move in there, then?" asked Henny.

"Not in Drem's place. Sets the wrong tone."

"There, see? Biomancer, Drem. Whatever name or reason you like, the place sits badly in everyone's mind."

After they'd walked past it, she said, "Still, it's where I first met Red, you know. So I guess it's not all bad memories."

"I been meaning to ask, Nettie." Henny glanced at the Twins, who gave him encouraging looks. Then he turned back to Nettles. "Filler said you and Hope are working on a way to get Red back from the biomancers. That true? I mean... do people ever come back from the biomancers?"

Nettles walked in silence for a little while. "Don't tell Filler, or anyone else for that matter. But honestly, I ain't so sure."

"Then why you been sailing around with her for the last year?" asked Stin.

"I didn't sail on the *Kraken Hunter* for him. I did it for her."

"Why?" asked Brimmer. "She ain't even in the Circle."

"She's better than the Circle. I thought I was, too."

"But you're back," pointed out Henny.

"Yeah. Reckon I was wrong."

"About which part?"

But Nettles didn't respond. The truth was, she wasn't sure. All she knew is how good she'd felt since she'd come back. How *right* she felt. In charge of her own crew, knowing every street like it was a part of her. Maybe it *was* a part of her. Like she'd told Tosh, she'd sailed all over the empire to find a "better" her. Wouldn't it be strange if it wasn't until she came home that she actually found it?

They met Palla and his crew at a place called Pit House. Nettles didn't know Hammer Point well, so she hadn't known what to expect. Pit House turned out to be the charred foundation of a building that looked like it had been blown up from the inside. Part of the front wall still stood, including the door frame, but the bricks and beams were blackened and cracked in places. The roof and the other walls were all gone. Most of the floor was missing as well, exposing the dirt basement level beneath, which Nettles guessed was where it got the name Pit House.

"Piss'ell," muttered Henny. "What kind of a bomb could do that much damage?"

"Not a bomb, but a drug-making laboratory." Palla and his crew emerged from the recesses of Pit House. "Someone trying to mix things to make their own coral spice. It didn't go well."

"I'd say," said Gavish Gray.

Both sides were tense with suspicion. Nettles could practically taste it in the air. To show everyone how it was, she walked over to Palla and pulled him in a rough embrace. "Good to see you, Palla."

"My, my," Palla murmured. "Does this mean I can call you—"

"Don't push it." She turned to her crew. "We got no time for bluster and grudges. I want Sharn and her crew taken down and half her guns and ammunition in our possession by sunrise. Keen?"

Everyone nodded.

"Sharn's territory is the far eastern portion of Hammer Point," said Palla. "She has sentries spread throughout, all of them well armed. Her headquarters is a mill set right on the water."

"You move your crew down from the north, I'll

move my crew up from the south. We'll take out the sentries as we go, picking their weapons. By the time we meet at the mill, we should be well armed enough to deal with whatever resistance we find there."

Palla nodded. "Remember your promise."

"Right." Nettles turned back to her crew. "You'll recognize Sharn as an older woman with white hair and an eye patch. Nobody takes a shot at her. She sold out Hammer Point to the biomancers, and we'll leave her to Hammer Point justice. All we want are the guns, keen?"

"One question," said Moxy Poxy, more growl than voice. Like always, she was dressed in tattered brown and green robes. Her thick matted hair hid her eyes from view. "Can we take trophies?"

Nettles sighed. "As long as it don't slow us down, I suppose that's fine."

"Trophies?" asked Palla.

"You probably don't want to know," said Nettles.

———

Nettles had her crew fan out into three groups. Henny took the Twins and Ladyarch. She knew Gavish Gray to be a solid wag, so she put him in charge of Fisty, Built Slim, and Snakefeet. She kept Moxy Poxy and Mister Hatbox with her. Not that she didn't trust them, but they were…special cases, and not the sort you wanted to just let loose on an unsuspecting neighborhood.

Nettles and her two wags came across their first sentry shortly after entering Sharn's territory. A woman standing on a street corner with a rifle in her hands and a revolver at her side. The thing about being so well armed, Nettles decided, was that it tended to make a person overconfident. The woman didn't even see Moxy until she had a razor at her throat. Moxy opened her from ear to ear with one smooth motion. Then, while the woman was still alive, thrashing and struggling and gushing blood, her eyes wide with terror, Moxy pulled out pruning shears and cut off one of her fingers.

"Piss'ell," muttered Nettles as she took the rifle and revolver. "You could have at least waited until she was dead."

Moxy Poxy grinned as she wiped the blood spatter from her face with her ragged cloak. "Just using my time wisely. You were the one who said don't let trophies slow us down."

"It does have a certain logic to it." Mister Hatbox wore a severe black coat, white shirt, and black cravat. His bland expression gave nothing away beneath his black top hat.

"Like you'd know," said Nettles.

Hatbox shrugged, looking unconcerned.

"Come on, let's keep moving," said Nettles.

They spotted the next sentry sitting in a second-floor window, his legs dangling over the sill, and his rifle in his lap.

"Mine," said Mister Hatbox.

He moved in a wide arc, then closed in at the peripheral until he was directly beneath the sentry. He used the sill of the first-floor window as a step and carefully inserted a pin into the gaf's ankle. He stepped back to the ground and watched, his expression still bland, as the sentry yelped and grabbed at his suddenly spasming leg. He fell from his perch and landed on the cobblestones and a moment later, Mister Hatbox darted in and inserted a pin into the sentry's shoulders and neck.

"Oh, I like it when he does this," Moxy whispered to Nettles as they watched from the cover of a nearby wagon.

The sentry seemed frozen in place, his entire body

quivering as he lay on the ground, his fearful eyes following Hatbox's every move.

"See, they can't move, but they can still see and feel everything," Moxy told Nettles.

Hatbox crouched down and gazed at the man, as if deciding what to do next.

"I used to think it was just the pins. You know, like he knew some special place to put them," said Moxy Poxy. "And I guess that's partly true. But to reliably get the effect he wants, he also coats his pins in a poison of his own making. Not deadly poison, mind you. Just to keep 'em still. Mister H, he don't like fuss."

Little noises escaped the man's throat, but he couldn't seem to cry out as Mister Hatbox stood back up, then slowly, deliberately pressed his foot down on the man's windpipe until he grew still.

Moxy Poxy tapped her nose and winked at Nettles. "Pleasure to see a true craftsman at work, ain't it?"

Nettles was beginning to question her choice of crew. It seemed they'd actually gotten worse in the year or so she'd been away. She was trying to stop her sadist brother from taking the Circle. Using other sadists to do so didn't seem the right way to go about it. She knew Hope wouldn't approve, and that bothered her more than she expected.

As they got closer to Sharn's headquarters, the sentries were placed more frequently and in twos or threes. For one pair, Mister Hatbox simply began walking toward them. The combination of his bland expression, his perfectly tailored suit, and the silent wraithlike quality of his movements gave the two sentries just enough pause to allow Moxy and Nettles to strike from the sides. One threesome was huddled so close together in an alley that Moxy Poxy was able to drop down from the roof and take them all out at once.

"These gafs are barely paying attention," Moxy said as she clipped a finger from each of them.

"The complacency of success, perhaps," said Mister Hatbox. "Let it be a lesson for us."

"You got that right, Mister H," said Moxy as she shoved the bloody fingers into a leather pouch at her waist.

"What do you *do* with those anyway?" asked Nettles.

"Well, first I dry 'em and cure 'em so they don't rot. Then I make stuff with 'em."

"Make stuff?"

"Sculptures and jewelry, mostly. I've got the soul of an artist, you know. Should've been born in Silverback."

"I've seen some of her pieces," said Mister Hatbox. "Quite exquisite."

"And they each hold their own special memories," said Moxy. "No two kills exactly alike, you know."

Nettles recalled telling Palla he didn't want to know about the trophies. She'd heard about the finger thing, but hadn't realized how involved it was. How...wrong it was. And she had a feeling that it only went deeper with these two. Bringing them along had definitely been a mistake. It was too late for tonight, but when they were all safely back in Paradise Circle with the cache of guns, she would tell those two their services were no longer needed. She hoped they didn't hold a grudge and went gracefully. As twisted as they might be, killing members of your crew just because you didn't like the way they do things was not looked on favorably in the Circle.

They continued to work their way to Sharn's headquarters, leaving a trail of grotesque and mutilated corpses in their wake. Nettles prided herself on her strong stomach, but by the time they reached the mill, she felt a little sick.

Palla and his crew were already waiting, as were Gavish Gray and his group. Henny and his group came soon after.

"No guards out front," Nettles observed.

"Why would she spread her crew out so thin and not even have someone at the door?" asked Henny. "It don't make sense."

"Neither does making an alliance with biomancers, but that's what she did," said Palla.

They distributed the rifles and revolvers that they'd picked up along the way.

"We just going to break down the door?" asked Gavish.

"I should be able to open it a bit more quietly," said Mister Hatbox.

Nettles was unnerved to learn that he was nearly as good at picking locks as Red. Something about a man like that being able to get past any locked door didn't sit right with her.

Once the door was open, they encountered little resistance inside. There were one or two gafs that they gunned down on sight. A few others managed to barricade themselves in the kitchen. Built Slim was preparing a small explosive device at the door to blow it up when Sharn came down the staircase, taking the steps two at a time.

"Enough!" she called.

Gavish instinctively turned his gun on her, but Nettles knocked it aside.

"Mind your manners," she growled. "We're guests here."

Palla gave Nettles a quick nod of thanks, then stepped forward, his spear held loosely in both hands.

"Sharn."

"Palla." She didn't look surprised. "I reckoned this is my judgment. Always hoped it'd be you. Sig can be insufferably smug. I trust you'll let the rest of my people go free if I cooperate?"

"I'll even offer them a place in my crew," said Palla.

"That's sunny of you, and I appreciate it. They ain't done nothing wrong. It was all me. Now, how do you want to do this?"

Palla held out his spear. "I intend to earn it. Single combat."

"Sporting of you. Coulda just gunned me down." She pulled two thin short swords from the sheaths on her back.

"But before we begin, I must know why."

She smiled sadly. "Why what?"

"Why did you work with the biomancers?"

"They offered guns to help me take the neighborhood if I stayed out of the thing with Drem. I said no. So then they took my sister. They said they wouldn't kill her if I stayed out of the thing with Drem. But I also had to give them a person each month for their experiments." A bitter grin stretched across her thin mouth.

"Did they keep their word?" asked Palla.

Her grin drained away. "I suppose they did. They still gave me the guns. And they did give my sister back. Alive, even." She shook her head and the grin returned. "But they'd somehow...removed all her bones and skin, see. She was just a bunch of innards held together with veins and nerves and stringy bits of muscle, floating in some kind of fluid inside a big glass case that they wheeled into the house. You could see her heart and lungs still working. Her eyes followed you as you moved. They told me how to make a solution I could put in the water that would act like food. They said she could live a full lifetime like that."

She stared down at her thin swords for a moment.

"I decided that wasn't any kind of life, so I stuck my sword right through her heart, and I told them we were through. They said they'd take people with or without my help."

"That's why you had so many sentries spread so thin," said Nettles. "You weren't using them to protect yourself. You were protecting your people."

Sharn looked at her for a moment, then back at Palla. "Joining with the Circle gafs again?"

"Times are changing," he said.

"There's bad things on the horizon, Sharn," said Nettles. "Things that make neighborhood rivalries look petty. Believe me when I tell you, the biomancers are just getting started."

"Like as not, I won't live to see it," said Sharn. "Come on, Palla. Let's get to it."

"I take no pleasure in this," Palla said quietly. "Especially after learning the details. But the justice of the Hammer must be served."

Sharn was quicker than Nettles expected from a wrink. She came in so quick with both swords overhead, Palla barely had time to block her. Despite what she'd said about not living, she seemed determined to fight. And she did get a respectable number of strikes past Palla's guard. But after a few minutes, it was clear she was no match for him. The wood of his spear was supple enough that he could snap it around like a switch, but it delivered enough force to break one of her arms and send one sword clattering to the ground. It was a real honor to watch the man work. A combination of elegance and power that was rare. He spun it. He pivoted his body around it. Sometimes he ducked under it. It was as if he and his spear were partners in a dance. The only person

Nettles had ever seen that connected to a weapon was Hope with that sword of hers.

When Palla delivered his final blow, it was a straight thrust that struck with enough force to send the spearhead cleanly through Sharn's body to emerge a foot out of her back. She clutched at the shaft in her chest and shuddered. Then she collapsed and slowly slid from the spear and onto the ground.

Every true wag in the room stood silent and respectful for a moment. There was strength in this death. Nobility. Nettles decided that when it was her time, she wanted it to be like this. Clean, brave, and at the hand of someone she respected.

The sun was just beginning to rise over the building tops as Nettles and her crew made their way back to Paradise Circle lugging sailcloth rolls packed with enough guns and ammunition for a battalion of imps.

"First victory, Nettie," said Henny. "How you feeling?"

"Sunny." She glanced over at Mister Hatbox and Moxy Poxy. "Probably a few adjustments to make before our next big step, but all in all, it went about like I figured."

"I think you're *it*, Nettie," said Brimmer. "A proper ganglord who looks after the Circle."

"Thanks, Brim."

"Me, too," Stin said. "I was already going to say that. Just hadn't got it out yet."

Nettles grinned. "I figured. Now, let's hurry on. I won't be able to really celebrate and count this as a win until these guns are safely stowed at the manor."

"You think Filler's going to be jealous?" asked Henny.

"I felt bad leaving him behind, but there was no help for it. That leg of his would have been heard before we even reached Hammer Point. Maybe if I give him first pick of guns, that'll make him feel a little better."

"I reckon it will," said Henny.

At night, Apple Grove Manor had a dark, brooding air. But in the gentle morning light of Paradise Circle, you could see hints of its past grandeur. Two columns framed the front entrance and supported the second-floor balcony. Either side of the building was fringed with a strip of mud and weeds that had once been a garden. Above the second floor, the manor stretched to a third floor that was only half the width of the lower two floors. A stone seal jutted from each corner of the roof, mouth pulled back in a snarl to reveal fearsome teeth. An argument could be made that despite its age, or perhaps because of it, Apple Grove Manor was the finest building in the Circle. At least, Nettles always thought so. But that morning, her image of the manor was marred forever.

Filler was stretched between the two front columns with a length of thick chain. He was covered in gashes, bruises, and dried blood. His metal leg was gone and his damaged leg was at a strange angle. Parts of his hair had been burned away, revealing spots of black, singed scalp. And there was a slice in his lower abdomen that was puckered, leaking blood and what was almost certainly semen.

Perhaps it was a blessing that he was dead.

"Oh God," said Henny in little more than a whisper. "Oh God, Filler..."

Nettles stared up at the naked, abused corpse of

one of her best wags in the world. She felt something within herself... give up.

She'd been fighting so hard and for so long, she'd almost forgotten why she'd taken the name Nettles. She'd been born with the name Rose. And as soon as her personality began to assert itself, nicknamed Briar Rose. Pretty, but don't touch. That's how her mother introduced her to Jix the Lift. When she got a little older, her father made the mistake of trying to touch her. He ended up with a fork in his thigh, mere inches from his cock. Thereafter, he confined himself to safer activities, like beating up her mother and collecting debts for Jix.

"Get him down," she said quietly.

Henny and the Twins hurried over to the columns and started working the chains loose. Nettles watched as they laid Filler's body gently on the front steps. It was stupid, really, them being careful like that. Like he could feel how they handled him. Filler couldn't feel anything anymore.

Nettles hadn't felt much when she'd watched her father get beaten to death at the dock riots. He'd been in the wrong, after all. He and the rest of Jix's boots had been trying to collect on an unfair "tax." The dockhands were already poor enough and they'd finally gotten tired of it. So they fought back. Perfectly reasonable. Then Nettles's mother had gotten caught up in it. She'd been trying to get everyone to calm down and work together, like always. But it had been too late for that. So instead, she had been swallowed up by the dark rage that every true wag of the Circle knew as a constant companion. As Nettles watched someone kick her mom's head in, she had wanted to cry. But to her surprise, she found she couldn't. She'd wondered if it was because she'd refused to cry for her father. Mick, on the other hand, had cried for hours.

She had taken the name Nettles years later, when she started working at the Slice of Heaven. It was the closest thing she'd ever had to a nurturing environment, and she never wanted to leave. So when Mo informed her that she would need to refine some of her sharpest barbs if she wanted to remain working there, she decided to reinvent herself. Nettles were still prickly, but not as painful as briars. And she'd really thought that if she took a new name and started acting differently, she would become a different person. Maybe not right away, but eventually. She'd even thought she *had* changed while she was sailing with Hope.

But the Circle had wasted no time in reminding her of who she truly was. And she was so tired of fighting against it. Of trying to be the person everyone wanted her to be. Hope, Red, Mo, all of them. But people couldn't really change. They always came back around, worse than before.

She knelt down next to Filler's body. She touched his bruised and lacerated face. He'd never been particularly handsome, but he had one of those faces you just felt you could depend on. Good old reliable Filler. Never made a fuss. Willing to come when you needed him, stayed behind when you didn't. Did he die because she'd left him behind?

No, of course not. She'd left him behind to *protect* him. If she held any of the blame for this, it was in not killing that cunt-dropping of a brother when she'd had the chance. A mistake that she fully planned to correct. Because there could be only one response to an injustice of this magnitude. And it was not something she could ever come back from. Nor did she want to. She was done running away from who she was.

"Bring him inside, clean him up, and put some clothes on him."

As her crew hurried to comply, she turned to Moxy Poxy and Mister Hatbox. "You two. With me."

Moxy Poxy and Mister Hatbox exchanged a grave look, then hurried after her as she walked past Filler's body and into the manor.

18

*E*ven with Sunset Point in view, it was hours before the carriage train reached the front gates of Empress Pysetcha's "secluded" home. By then, a proper princely welcome had been set. Leston's carriage took the lead and crossed under the tall, decorative wooden arch and into the courtyard. As they trundled slowly down the sandy path toward the house, Red gazed at the small army of servants that had been assembled on either side, all standing smartly at attention as the carriage passed. A small band stood off to one side, composed of a drummer, a trumpet player, and a small chorus. They performed a triumphant hymn as though the prince was a conquering hero returned home from battle.

"Quite a welcome, my wag," Red told Leston.

"It's a bit much, I suppose," he said sheepishly.

The path ended at the raised wooden deck that wrapped around the house. A woman in a pale lavender gown stood on the deck awaiting them. She was older, perhaps in her fifties, but with a regal beauty Red had never seen matched, even at the palace. Her long brown and gray hair was blown by the hard ocean winds as she watched them draw near.

"I take it that's your mom," Red said to Leston.

He just smiled and nodded, his eyes fixed on her.

"The radiance of Empress Pysetcha outstrips any at the palace," Nea said.

"I'm very much looking forward to you meeting her," said Leston.

"Hey, what about *me*?" asked Red, feigning hurt.

Leston gave him a wry smile. "I think 'deeply concerned' would be more accurate for you. My mother is a sweet and thoughtful woman, not accustomed to your often irreverent and lewd remarks."

Red grinned. "I swear I will talk to her as if she were my own mother."

"Wasn't your mother a counterculture bohemian painter and drug addict who married a whore?"

"So you're saying I shouldn't talk about sex, art, or drugs?" asked Red. "I'll try, but it doesn't leave much left for interesting conversation, does it?"

Leston sighed. "In all seriousness, please do try to behave yourself for once."

"Don't worry, Your Highness, *I* will make certain Lord Pastinas is well behaved," said Nea.

"Oh?" asked Red. "And how do you plan to do that?"

"Perhaps you did not know this, but the tips of my shoes are reinforced with steel. If you say something inappropriate, I will subtly kick you in your shin."

"But, Ambassador, that would hurt!" said Red.

She smiled impudently. "So behave, friend Red."

Once the prince's carriage reached the end of the path, the rattle of wheels slowly faded away as the entire train came to a stop.

"Best smiles, everyone," Leston said quietly as he climbed out of the carriage. Red had never seen him so tense. Was he so desperate to please his mother?

Red followed behind Leston and Nea as they walked toward the empress. She didn't look particularly hard to please, but there was no rushing into each other's arms when mother and son met either.

Once he reached the deck, Leston stopped, keeping a few feet of distance between them.

"Welcome, my son," she said in a rich, steady voice that carried easily over the wind. The other lords and ladies remained in their carriages, but Red was fairly sure most of them could still hear her.

"Your Majesty." Leston bowed deeply. "You remain the brightest jewel of the empire."

It was all a lot more formal and reserved than Red had expected. Was this a normal greeting between lacy parents and children, or something specific to Leston and his mom? Red glanced over at Nea, but as usual, her thoughts and emotions were hidden behind her mask of artful diplomacy. He found himself wishing that Merivale were there to explain this behavior to him.

"Your Majesty," continued Leston in his formal tone. "I have the honor to introduce you to Ambassador Nea Omnipora of Aukbontar."

Red could almost taste Leston's desperation that these two get along. But Red was confident that if anyone could handle such a situation, it was Nea.

"It is thrilling beyond measure to meet the jewel of the Empire of Storms in person," said Nea. "Your Majesty, I fear my poor grasp of your language leaves me unable to properly communicate the awe I feel in your presence."

"Oh, I don't know." Empress Pysetcha said, her eyes showing a tiny twinkle of mischief. "I think you're doing just fine."

"Thank you, Your Majesty."

The empress turned back to her son, her expression once again solemn. "I look forward to meeting your other companions and speaking with them all at dinner this evening. In the meantime, perhaps you would like to settle into your lodgings and rest from your journey while I greet the remainder of your company."

Leston gave her a pained look. "My apologies for such a large retinue, Your Majesty. I tried my best to keep it to a manageable number."

She smiled and shook her head. "It is both my duty and privilege to welcome so many lords and ladies to my humble home. Now, if you will excuse me, I must begin, or I fear I won't make it in time for dinner."

A man in a white suit stepped forward. "If Your Highness and his companions will come with me, please."

They followed the man into the house, while the empress remained behind to greet each and every lord and lady who made the pilgrimage to Sunset Point to see her.

The inside of the house reminded Red somewhat of Merivale's apartments in its openness and minimalist decor. But where Merivale's home was all hard angles and geometric shapes, the empress's home was all curves and smooth flowing lines that made the entire space feel connected from room to room. There were skylights in every room made of semitransparent glass, tinted periwinkle, mint, or lavender, which cast tones of mood as well.

The man in white took them down several twists and turns through the colored maze until they came to the far side of the house. The rooms at this end had windows that faced the sea and doors that opened out onto the wooden deck, which hung over the water.

"Here is your suite, Your Highness." The man indicated the largest of the three rooms.

"Thank you, Kurdem," said Leston.

"Gentlemen," Kurdem said to Red and Etcher.

"Your room is here on the left. And madam." He inclined his head to Nea. "Yours is on the right."

Nea peeked into the room. "I see it has two beds. Will I be sharing the room?"

"My sincerest apologies, Ambassador. With so many guests in our humble home, it may be necessary, in order to accommodate everyone."

"It is perfectly fine." Nea gave him her bright, diplomatic smile. "I was merely curious."

Leston leaned over to Kurdem and whispered something. With his enhanced hearing, Red could have heard it if he made the effort, but it seemed wrong somehow. He really was beginning to lose his edge if he was starting to think eavesdropping was a bad thing.

"As you wish, Your Highness. Now, if I may take my leave, I will make certain your luggage arrives with all haste."

"Thank you, Kurdem," said Leston.

"Oh, one more thing," said Kurdem. "I'm sure I don't need to remind His Highness, but the rest of you may want to make a point of stepping out onto the deck just at sunset so you can experience for yourselves why Her Majesty wisely gave this home its name."

"My thanks, Kurdem," said Nea. "We will be sure to do so."

Kurdem nodded and headed back toward the front of the house.

———

Red hoped he could find some excuse to sneak off somewhere and test out his whistle and cotton earplugs. The luggage arrived only a few minutes later. Red unpacked quickly, but before he could slip away, he got dragged into helping Etcher, who had quite a lot to unpack.

"What is all this stuff?" Red asked as he tried to fit a collection of small empty cages under his bed.

"I am hoping to encounter some authentic wildlife during our stay here," said Etcher as he tried to cram a few empty painting canvas frames in the wardrobe. "Do you think the seal statues on the cornices indicate that they are common in this area?"

"Probably not," said Red as he slid a large wooden trunk under Etcher's bed. "You see them on a lot of lacy houses for some reason. At least, I *hope* there aren't any seals around here. I heard they're nasty as goblin sharks, and more clever."

Etcher placed a three-foot-long sailcloth sack on the ground and began to pull curious little wooden contraptions out of it, examining each carefully. "You've never seen one yourself, then?"

"I'm more of a city wag, old pot. Nature and I tend to keep our distance from each other. I did meet a gaf once who sounded like a seal when he laughed, though." Red made some barking noises. "Maybe he was part seal?"

Etcher gave him a suspicious look, as if trying to determine if Red was joking. "I *have* heard that biomancers can blend animal and man."

Red's smile dropped away. "Yeah. I did see that once."

"Really?" Etcher abandoned his contraptions on the floor and pulled out a notebook. He sat on the edge of Red's bed, a stub of pencil poised eagerly. "You must tell me all about it."

"It was someone my best wag Hope used to sail with. Gaf by the name of Ranking. He killed their captain, so she cut off his arm."

Etcher's eyes grew wide. "A *friend* of yours did that?"

"She'd sworn to protect the captain. She's Vinchen, and they take their vows more seriously than most."

"Vinchen...I've heard of them. A religious order, correct?"

"Are they?" Red had only ever known them as warriors, but it made a certain sense. The way Hope stuck to her principles did have a bit of religious zeal to it. Plus, the whole celibacy thing. "I suppose they might be. Anyway, we were in a bit of a hurry after that so we didn't know what happened to Ranking. I assumed he just bled out on the tavern floor."

"You say that with such casualness," said Etcher. "Does that kind of thing happen often here?"

"Here? No. In Paradise Circle, often enough that you wouldn't think too long about it."

"But this Ranking. He did not bleed to death?"

"I'm sure he wished he had. Because when we saw him a few weeks later, after a biomancer got ahold of him, you wouldn't even call him human anymore."

Etcher tapped his pencil on his notebook. "Describe him in as much detail as you can."

"Why are you so interested in it?"

"Are you joking?" Etcher's eyes widened. "It defies everything we know about science. Things in your empire that seem commonplace to you go against what we have always believed to be the very laws of nature. Is there simply some aspect that has always eluded us? Or have we been completely wrong for centuries?" He shook his head, staring down at the blank page of his notebook. "I must know and then understand these anomalies to whatever extent I am able. I must bring back proof, if any can be obtained, so that I can convince the scientific community that everything we thought we knew must be reconsidered."

"So you're saying stuff like this doesn't happen in Aukbontar at all?" asked Red. "It only happens in our empire?"

"Well, no," admitted Etcher. "We have heard...

similarly troubling rumors from visitors to Haevanton. But I am skeptical of any intelligence that comes out of there."

"Haevanton? Where in all hells is that?"

"The Haevanton Triumvirate? You're not familiar with it?"

"Is it like...another country?" Red thought of Mavokadia, the country Nea said was located north of Aukbontar. Were there more?

"Technically, it is three countries united under one government. And it is to the east of both our countries, across the Tragic Sea."

"The Tragic Sea?" Red felt completely lost now.

"Sorry," said Etcher. "The official name for it is the Tranquil Sea, but everyone calls it the Tragic Sea because people who cross it almost never return. Although now that we know about the southern waterway, that will be less of a problem." He tapped his pencil on his chin. "Assuming, of course, that we get a treaty in place with the Empire of Storms."

Red knew he was only dimly grasping what Etcher was talking about, but that last part sounded like some sort of diplomatic goal of Nea's. One that she hadn't shared with Red or Leston yet.

"What does this Haevanton have to do with the empire?" he asked, keeping his tone casual. Almost disinterested.

"Oh." Etcher looked suddenly panicked.

"Oh?" asked Red.

"Maybe I should not be talking about that..."

"It's alright, my wag," Red said smoothly. "You and me are old pots. Last thing I'd want is for you to get in some sort of trouble with Nea."

"I find it all very challenging," Etcher said plaintively. "I am a scientist, not a diplomat. I believe *all* knowledge should be shared for the benefit of the entire human race, not just one country."

"I couldn't agree more, Etch. We're all in this rotten old world together, aren't we?"

"Exactly my point!"

"But you got to follow the boss, don't you? Frustrating as it is. So anytime you're burning to discuss some bit of knowledge but can't go telling the whole world, you just come to me and I'll keep it safe for you."

"Thank you, Red. That is very generous of you," Etcher said earnestly.

Red didn't know exactly why he was working his way into Etcher's confidence, but as much as he liked Nea, he suddenly felt like she was much more devious than he'd originally reckoned.

"No problem, my wag. Us underlings got to stick together. Let the bosses worry about the big stuff, right?"

"I wish I had been able to come here on a purely research-focused mission," admitted Etcher. "Politics makes my head hurt. But the expense of traveling this distance was too great to justify a simple exploratory expedition. The Great Congress likes a...multifaceted approach."

"So you hitched a ride on Nea's diplomatic mission instead," said Red. "Very clever."

"Let us hope so," said Etcher. "If things go poorly in negotiations, there may be..."

He froze, his eyes locked on the door behind Red that led to the deck.

Red turned and saw Nea smiling at them, the last light of the setting sun casting her in silhouette.

"Gentlemen, it is nearly time for the sunset. Kurdem made a point of mentioning it, so we should not miss it."

"Of course, Ambassador!" Etcher jumped to his feet, looking guilty. "I've been looking forward to it."

Red stood up with deliberate ease and smiled at

her. "I do love a good sunset." It was a lie, of course. Watching the sun directly hurt his eyes, even with his darkened lenses. But if Nea was keeping things from him, he would keep things from her.

Red followed Etcher out onto the deck, which connected all three rooms. He saw Leston leaning against the rail, gazing out at the fiery ball of red that hung just above the waterline. It sent streaks of crimson into the darkening sky while ripples of liquid ruby spread across the sea. It really was beautiful. Painful and terrible to his sensitive eyes, but gloriously savage.

He took a spot on the rail next to Leston and the two watched it for some time. Red knew he'd be seeing spots for a little while after, but it was worth it.

"I do hope you'll forgive the intrusion, Your Highness and your lordship," came a familiar voice. "But I was instructed by the ambassador to come and witness the sunset with all due haste."

Red turned toward the voice. The spots prevented him from seeing her face, but he didn't need to.

"Lady Hempist, your delightful company is never an intrusion," Red said dryly. "What brings you to this side of the house?"

"His Highness requested that I be Ambassador Omnipora's roommate," she said.

"Oh?" Red gave Leston a meaningful look, even though the spots would prevent him from seeing the reaction.

"Lady Hempist and Ambassador Omnipora have become great friends of late." There was a touch of defensiveness in the prince's voice.

"Really," said Red.

"As a matter of fact, we have," said Merivale.

The lingering spots still prevented Red from seeing her expression, but he detected something taunting in her tone.

"How delightful," he said evenly, wondering how authentic this new friendship was.

"Yes," said Leston. "So I thought that if the ambassador had to share a room with someone, it should be with a friend rather than a stranger. Wouldn't you say?"

"Makes perfect sense," said Merivale.

"And of course, she'll be accompanying us to dinner with my mother," said Leston.

"Naturally," said Red, forcing a cheerful tone.

"I'm looking forward to it immensely," said Merivale with a similar tone.

"I do hope," said the prince, "that the two of you can resolve whatever ill will has come between you."

"Is that an imperial command?" Merivale asked.

Leston thought about it a moment. "Yes, as a matter of fact, it is."

———

The formal dining room was in the center of the house. As far as Red could tell, it was the largest room in the house as well. It looked more like a banquet hall than a room, and held seven round tables. Six were spaced out evenly on the ground level. The seventh table was on a raised platform so that all the lords and ladies could look up and enjoy the radiant beauty of the jewel of the empire while they ate.

And she *was* radiant. As he sat down at the table, he was struck again by her presence, which was at once warm and generous, yet somehow still daunting. She certainly seemed more imperial than that broken-down old man in golden robes back at the palace. Empress Pysetcha inspired an almost reverent awe in everyone she spoke to. Even, he had to admit, in himself.

"And who is this man with the curiously lovely

eyes?" she asked as her gaze fell directly on Red for the first time.

"This is my dear friend, Lord Rixidenteron Pastinas," said the prince, who sat to her right.

"Indeed?" The empress sipped wine from a crystal goblet. "I recall the previous Lord Pastinas." She said it without any hint of what her opinions about him might have been.

"My late grandfather, Your Majesty." Red accepted a goblet of wine from a servant with a nod of thanks. "He passed away about nine months ago."

"I am sorry for your loss."

"Not much of a loss, Your Majesty." Red was taking a gamble being so honest, but if his instincts were right, it would pay off. "I hardly knew him, and what little I knew, I didn't like."

"I hope you'll excuse Lord Pastinas," Leston said quickly, putting down his wine. "His upbringing was...unconventional."

"Not at all," said Pysetcha. Red was relieved to see that twinkle returning to her eye. "A little candor is refreshing. And I'm pleased to see you making friends, Leston. Even unconventional ones."

"Thank you, Your Majesty." Leston's face flushed and he grabbed at his goblet like a man who needed to steady himself from a swoon. Red realized it was probably the most intimate thing she'd said to him since their arrival.

The empress nodded to Merivale. "Lady Hempist I know all too well. I trust you've been actively whittling away your family fortune on clothing and baubles, my lady?"

Merivale smiled graciously and lifted her glass as if toasting her. "Your Majesty does know me well. Although I have recently discovered something new to spend my family's money on."

"And what, pray tell, is that?"

"Books, Your Majesty. I recently picked up a very engaging biography of the famous proto-Passionist painter Lady Gulia Pastinas." She turned to Red. "Why, I do believe you are related to her, Lord Pastinas?"

"My mother." Red was unable to keep the tension out of his voice. Apparently, if Merivale couldn't flirt with him, she would spar with him instead. He wondered if this was the book she had been so coy about showing him when they met on the street a little while back.

"Ah. This must be the unconventional upbringing my son referred to," said Empress Pysetcha.

"In part, Your Majesty." Red had worn his background proudly his whole life, even at the palace. But under the royal gaze of the empress, he felt a tickle of shame for the first time. So rather than elaborate, or spin it into one of his grand tales, he decided to leave it at that.

Merivale apparently had other ideas. "It's a very moving narrative, Your Majesty," she said blithely, as if it were only a story and not part of Red's life. "Fraught with the pathos and tragedy one might expect from the life of a Silverback artist. And the author, a fellow by the name of Thoriston Baggelworthy, included the most amusing appendix about the folk slang of New Laven. Such charming little phrases like 'true as trouble' and 'simple as sideways.'"

"How droll," said Empress Pysetcha. "Lord Pastinas, are you familiar with this folk slang?"

"It is the language of my youth, Your Majesty." He took a large gulp of wine.

"You speak as someone who is no longer young, my lord. But unless my eyes deceive me, you can't be more than twenty."

"Youth and innocence are quickly lost where I

come from, Your Majesty." Red decided there was only one way to escape this needling from Merivale. To get out in front of it. "When one is raised in the slums of downtown New Laven."

There was a moment of total silence at the table. Red could not read the empress's expression at all, and he wondered if he had been just a bit too candid. He knew that on the whole, lacies didn't like to be reminded of the poor and suffering. As the servants brought out the first of several courses, platters heaped with more food than he would have seen in a week as a boy, he understood that perhaps it was their own shame that troubled them. Under ordinary circumstances, he would have been pleased to deliver that experience to a sheltered lacy. But he didn't want the empress to feel that way. Not just because it might cause problems for Leston or Nea. He found himself nearly as desperate for her approval as the prince. If he had upset the empress, he might well need to leave the table.

But then she smiled, and it was like the sun shining on him, only better because it didn't hurt his eyes.

"Then what a clever and resourceful man my son has chosen for a friend, to come from such humble beginnings, all the way to the empress's own dinner table."

He returned her smile with a grateful one of his own. "There may have been more than my fair share of luck involved as well, Your Majesty."

"Either way, you are welcome here," said Empress Pysetcha. Then she turned her gaze to Nea. "I find it troubling that in our empire the few have so much and the many have so little. Is it a problem that plagues your country as well, Ambassador?"

"To some extent, Your Majesty," said Nea. "Although we do not have such a rigid class system.

All citizens are given equal opportunity to show their worth."

"What a fascinating society it must be," said the empress. "I should like to hear more about it another time. But right now, I am far more curious about the reason we owe the rare pleasure of your visit."

"I come as a representative of the Great Congress of Aukbontar in hopes that after centuries of isolation, we might bridge the expanse of the Dark Sea with a mutually beneficial alliance between our peoples."

"Very interesting," said the empress. "And what is it, specifically, that you seek in this alliance?"

"Oh." Nea looked taken aback. "Well…"

Red was surprised by the empress's directness as well. He'd thought this dinner, and possibly the entire trip, would be nothing but charming pleasantries and idle small talk. But with that question, she had changed the entire tone of the conversation.

But Nea rallied quickly. "There are a great number of resources available to the empire that we in Aukbontar have little to no knowledge of."

"Such as?" asked the empress. "If you could ask for only one thing in this treaty, what would it be?"

Nea seemed to weigh several options in her mind. Finally, she said, "A thorough understanding of both the theory and application of biomancery."

Of all the things Red might have guessed, that had not been on the list. Red distinctly remembered Nea telling him that she believed biomancery to be superstitious lore. A quick look around the table told him he wasn't alone in his confusion.

The empress, however, seemed unsurprised. "I see. And in exchange for this highly complex and sensitive knowledge, what are you prepared to offer?"

Nea hesitated for a moment, then gave her an embarrassed smile. "I apologize, Your Majesty. I thought this to be a social visit rather than a treaty negotiation, so I did not bring my full team and presentation materials. I fear mere words alone may not do it justice."

The empress leaned across the table and patted Nea's hand. "My dear ambassador, your original assumption was quite correct. This *is* a social visit. I am merely a curious woman who delights in learning new things. Although I urge you to do your utmost to help me understand, in spite of your lack of…materials. After all, I do believe my opinion does hold some small sway at court still?"

"Indeed it does, Your Majesty." Merivale nodded to the six tables below them full of the finest lords and ladies of the land doing their best not to stare outright at the mother of the empire.

"It will be my pleasure, Your Majesty," said Nea. "While we have no understanding of biomancery, how or why it even works, we have made great strides in other sciences far beyond what your empire has discovered. In particular, the steam-powered engine is something we believe you could make great use of."

"Pray, what is this steam-powered engine?" asked the empress.

"It is a mechanical device with almost limitless application. It could power your wagons, your mills, your cannons, even your ships."

"That's how you crossed the Dark Sea," Red blurted out. "Your ship was powered by one of those engines instead of the wind."

Nea inclined her head to Red. "Yes, Lord Pastinas. The wind is unpredictable, particularly in the middle of that great ocean. Before the development of the steam engine, a trip across the Dark Sea was perilous, and ships were often lost. But now we can cross with confidence because we are no longer beholden to the elements."

"So you would give us one of these steam engines?" asked the empress.

"Better than that, Your Majesty," said Nea. "We are prepared to teach a team of your most capable subjects not only how to use a steam engine, but how to construct and repair them yourselves. As a show of good faith, I have brought one such engine with me, as well as a machinist to adapt, operate, and repair it as needed." She gave her embarrassed smile again. "Both of which, unfortunately, are back at the palace."

"Is that Drissa's role in all this?" asked Leston. "Given her limited language abilities, I wondered."

"She does struggle with learning your language," admitted Nea. "But she is one of the most talented young machinists in Aukbontar."

"You have an interesting proposal, Ambassador Omnipora," said Empress Pysetcha. "An exchange not of goods, but of knowledge."

Put that way, Red could understand why Nea was so reluctant to share other knowledge, such as the existence of the Haevanton Triumvirate, whatever that was. In this context, information was a high commodity. She could be withholding certain information not for some sinister plan, but merely as a smart business move. Perhaps she could use it to sweeten the pot later if the emperor was dragging his feet during negotiations.

"You put it perfectly, Your Majesty," said Nea.

"Thank you for sharing this with me, Ambassador. I wish you the best of luck presenting it to my husband and his…advisors." The empress took a sip of her wine, and for a moment there was a flicker of bitterness in her expression. It made Red suddenly curious about why the empress had chosen to remove herself from the palace. Perhaps she knew about the control that the biomancers had over her husband, and chose to give it a wide berth.

Another thing Red wondered about was why Nea's Great Congress wanted to learn about biomancery. The very idea made his skin crawl. Maybe they didn't really understand what they were asking for. If only he could show Nea the reality. That they weren't just mysterious wizards or holy men, but people who twisted nature for their own power and gain, and were themselves twisted in the process.

———

"Well, that could have gone worse," said Red later that night as he and Leston stood at the deck railing behind their apartments and gazed out at the starlit sea.

"True," said the prince. "I wonder about Merivale, though. It's as if she holds some animosity toward you for spurning her matrimonial advances."

"You think?" Red said dryly.

"I admit I'm a little disappointed in her. I thought she would be on better behavior for my mother."

"I'm not so sure. It almost seemed as though your mom expected her to behave like that." Red shrugged. "Either way, I handled it, and near as I can tell, everything is sunny between me and your mom."

"Thankfully, it seems things are friendly between her and Nea as well." A stupid grin slowly began to spread across his face. "Wasn't she marvelous, the way she handled that unexpected pressure?"

Red let him bask for a minute. Then he said, "You know, Nea is here to make a treaty."

"Of course."

"You getting sotted with her only makes a complicated thing more complicated."

"I don't know what you mean." The prince stood up from the rail, his face tense.

"Come on, Leston, don't make me 'Your Highness'

you into submission. We're wags, you and me, so let's speak crystal. It's plain as day you're sotted with her."

The prince stood for a moment, then sank back to the railing. "Do you think she feels the same?"

"I think right now she can't *afford* to," Red said as gently as he could. "Her country is counting on her to do this thing. Politics isn't so different from games, really, and I know right now she couldn't let herself feel for you even if she wanted to, because you're not on the same side. If she lets her feelings for you affect her, it could affect the treaty, too. What if she screwed it all up, gave us a better deal than she should have because she didn't want to say no to you? Would you want her to go back to Aukbontar and have her Great Congress punish her? Would you want that for Nea?"

"Of course not!"

"So then ease off, my wag. At least for now. Maybe when it's all settled, then you can start wooing her. Hells, I'll even help you."

"Will you?" Leston looked eager. "I've never felt this way about someone before, so I don't really know what I'm doing."

"You really don't," agreed Red.

"Hey!"

"Which is why I'm offering my own proven expertise in being a charming scoundrel. But *only* after the treaty is either signed or abandoned. Keen?"

Leston sighed. "You're right, of course." He put his hand on Red's shoulder. "Thank you. You're such a good friend to me. And to Nea."

———

Red was pleased with how he'd handled the various courtly intrigues that had come at him that day, thinking he was really learning how to play this game. But now that everyone else had gone to their rooms and Etcher was already snoring softly in the bed next to him, it was finally time to test out his whistle and plugs.

First, to see if the whistle had any effect on him. He sat on top of his bed and reached into his pocket.

His chest gave a lurch. The whistle was gone.

He tried to remain calm as he checked the pocket carefully. There was a small hole in the corner that he hadn't noticed before. The whistle must have fallen out somewhere. Maybe when he was helping Etcher put away all his research materials? He dropped to the floor and yanked out the cages. It hadn't fallen into any of them. He crawled under the bed, but it wasn't there either. He checked the wardrobe, shoving the canvases aside as panic began to coil up his spine.

"Lord Pastinas?" Etcher asked sleepily.

Red froze at the wardrobe.

"Is everything okay?"

Red forced himself to swallow. In as steady a voice as he could manage, he said, "Everything's chum and larder, old pot. Just about to settle in for the night."

Red reluctantly returned to his bed. He lay on his back, his eyes staring unseeingly up at the ceiling. The whistle could be anywhere, really. Merivale's carriage, the prince's carriage, somewhere along the way between his carriage and this room, or even in the dining room. It could have slipped out at any one of those places. Hells, it could have even fallen into the rolling tides while he'd been leaning over the rail, staring at the painful blaze of the setting sun. He certainly wouldn't have seen or heard it fall then.

He still had the cotton plugs. He'd just have to pray that they worked. He held them tightly in his hands as he lay in bed. He couldn't put them in yet, of course. He needed to be able to hear everything. Not even this "Shadow Demon" could be quiet enough to escape his attention. He allowed himself a brief, bitter smile as he thought about all those painful lessons with Ammon Set in honing his listening skills. The satisfaction of using the biomancers' own training against them soothed some of his panic.

He was still tense, but he considered that a good thing. It would keep him alert while he kept his vigil.

However, this was the first time he'd slept so close to the water in a while. He'd forgotten how soothing it was to listen through the open window to the slow hiss of the waves sliding over the sand. The hours ticked by, and sometime around midnight, he drifted off.

A voice rose up in his mind, as if coming up to the surface from the bottom of dark, oily water. It whispered urgently, *Nea Omnipora is a grave threat to the empire and must die!*

He sat up and looked around. He was somewhere unfamiliar, yet as was often the way of dreams, he knew where to go. He couldn't find his customary clothing, so he would have to go without. At least there were a few throwing blades in a small trunk. That was all he needed.

He slipped through a door into the chill night air. There were others around, he knew. But unless they interfered, he was not allowed to kill them yet. Just her.

He moved carefully, his bare feet making no noise on the smooth wooden deck. To his left was the ocean. To his right, the outer wall of a building of some kind. After a few strides, he came upon a door. There were no lights on inside, but he didn't need lights. He saw the one he had been told he would *never* be allowed to kill.

He continued along the wall until he came to the next door. He peeked through the window and saw her, sleeping on a bed, secure in the belief that she was safe. No one was ever truly safe from death.

He slowly eased the door open and slipped into the room. He watched her blankets gently rise and fall with her chest. Her face looked sweet and innocent, but such details held little interest for him.

As he lifted a throwing blade, the steel glinted in the faint moonlight that spilled in through the window. He allowed himself a moment to appreciate its cold, perfect beauty. One flick of his wrist and this person would cease to be a grave threat to the empire. One more life taken by death.

Then a screeching noise ripped through the air. It felt like a large needle inserted into his ear. The floor beneath him spun so that he could not tell which way was up. He tried to move back and found himself slamming into the hard ground.

The sound continued to weigh on him as he lay there, like it was trying to crush him. His vision flickered in and out. The last thing he saw before he lost consciousness was the woman in the other bed. She blew on a tiny silver whistle, and in her eyes was a cold, steely look as deadly as any blade.

19

*I*t's true, I tell you," said Brice Vaderton for probably the twentieth time. "Dire Bane has been reborn!"

"Right. As a *woman* no less," said Kismet Pete, a tall, lanky man without any hair. He'd had a sickness as a boy that had made all the hair on his body, including his eyebrows and eyelashes, fall out, and it had never grown back.

Vaderton didn't know why he even bothered to tell people anymore. No one ever believed him. Most of them didn't even believe that, until recently, he had been the youngest captain ever to command an imperial frigate. He certainly didn't look like an imperial captain anymore. His hair was shaggy and disheveled. His face was swollen and bruised from the beatings that small squad of imperial soldiers had given him during his lengthy interrogation. Vaderton had willingly told Progul Bon everything, but that hadn't seemed to satisfy him. After the beatings, he'd even used some sort of biomancery to force Vaderton to tell the truth. He'd told the biomancer his childhood fears, and about the girl he'd loved as a schoolboy and the child they'd accidentally conceived together. He'd even confessed his fear that his naval career was over. Progul Bon had laughed at that and told him it wasn't just his career that was over, but his life as a free man as well. Then the biomancer left, and soon after, the soldiers had brought Vaderton here, to the Empty Cliffs.

"Look, Vade," said Kismet Pete. "It's not that I don't *want* to believe you." He and Vaderton sat with several other prisoners on the lee side of a boulder, sheltered from the wind that endlessly raked the top of the Empty Cliffs. "Hells, if Dire Bane came back to us, I'd be first in line to join up. But if imp ships were being taken like you say, we would have *heard* about it. It would be the talk of half the empire."

"He's got a point," said another prisoner named Biscuit Bill. "I was sailing on an imp ship not two weeks ago. Dire Bane being back, there would have been long talk amongst the crew, but I heard nothing."

"Because they're covering it up!" said Vaderton. "That's why they put me here. So I couldn't tell anyone."

"Maybe they put you here as punishment for losing your whole crew, like you said." Bill looked to the others for support, and they nodded.

"No, that's not how the navy works," said Vaderton. "If I was being disciplined, they would have put me in an imperial prison, not here on this...*biomancer stockyard*."

That shut them all up. Nobody liked to be reminded that once a week or so, a biomancer came with a small squad of imperial soldiers and took someone away. On his first night, Vaderton watched an old woman get taken. She screamed and begged them to kill her on the spot. One of the soldiers knocked her unconscious with the butt of his rifle and they carried her to the lift. As far as Vaderton knew, there were two ways off the Empty Cliffs. Biomancers or death. Many nights he had stared over the edge to the waters far below and wondered if it might not be better to throw himself over the side and be done with it. He knew better than most that death was a mercy compared to becoming a bio-mancer experiment. But God help him, he wasn't quite ready to die yet.

Since bringing up biomancers was the quickest way to kill the mood of any conversation, the other prisoners started to drift off, muttering to themselves and making little gestures they foolishly believed would ward off biomancery. Vaderton stayed where he was, sheltered from the raw, cold wind that never died. That was the hardest part about living on the Empty Cliffs. It wasn't the chaos of criminals given free rein on the island, or the boredom, or the mea-ger, tasteless food. It was the wind. You practically had to shout to be heard over it. It dried your skin and your eyes and your throat, unless it was raining. Then it just chilled you to the bone. There were no shelters on the island either. Just boulders and the occasional stunted shrub. There was grass, thank-fully, which at least kept the dirt from flying up into your face. But that was it. Off in the distance, New Laven stretched out almost like a model replica or a map with topographical features on it. At times it seemed beautiful, and Vaderton would stare at it for hours. But at other times it seemed only there to remind him of the hopelessness of the Empty Cliffs.

"Don't worry about those gafs," said Old Yammy as she hunkered down next to Vaderton. "They'll know you speak true soon enough."

Vaderton gave her a wan smile. "You don't need to humor me, Ms. Yammy." He didn't know why she was so kind to him. From the day he arrived, she'd stuck up for him. She was a slight woman, always wrapped up in a thick woolen scarf. She looked to be about his age, although everyone called her *Old* Yammy for some reason. She was one of the most respected people on the Empty Cliffs. Even the true criminals—murderers, rapists, and sadists—were careful to the point of outright courtesy in her presence. Vaderton had no idea why, but he was grateful for it. She was, he realized, probably the second female who had saved his life.

"I'm not humoring you, Captain. I'm keeping your spirits up," said Yammy. "There is a big difference."

"I don't know why you bother, Ms. Yammy."

"Because, *I* have something you don't yet." She had a twinkle in her eye, as if daring him to ask further.

"Oh? And what is that?"

"Hope." Then she laughed like it was a joke. In addition to being the kindest person on the Empty Cliffs, she was also quite possibly the strangest. There were rumors among the prisoners that she could perform a magic of sorts. She did nothing to discourage those rumors, and in fact frequently hinted that she could see into the future. After everything Vaderton had seen, he knew better than to dismiss such things out of hand.

Still, her claims that someone would rescue them from this place strained his credulity to the limit. After all, there was nothing that could scale the sheer face of the Empty Cliffs, and there was only one other way on or off: the great iron lift in the center of the island. It traveled up and down a large hole drilled through the center of the island all the way to sea level. The lift was operated at the base, and heavily guarded at all times. It came up only once a day to deliver rations, and one night a week to claim someone for the biomancers. To access the lift at sea level, one needed to approach the island from the mainland in a small boat. The boat must be rowed, because the tunnel through the side of the cliff to the lift was too narrow for a mast. It was a long tunnel, well lit by some mysterious biomancery, with several soldiers armed with cannons at the other end. Should an unwelcome boat enter the tunnel, it would move so slowly that the people on board could be picked off by the soldiers at leisure and well before it was in danger of reaching the lift. They made a big show of pointing this setup out to every prisoner when they arrived, to illustrate just how little chance there was of rescue.

"Even if someone *did* rescue us," he said to Yammy, "and that would take nothing short of a miracle. Even then, what would I do? My naval career is over. Not that I would ever sail under such treacherous leadership again anyway. But what would I do instead? Who would I be, if not the captain of a ship?"

She patted his raw, windburned hand with her gloved hand. "You'll be a captain again, just under a different flag. I promise."

———

Time dragged on for Vaderton as days melted into one another. He lost count of just how many. Weeks, certainly. Months? Possibly. He found he cared about such things less and less. It was curious how a man who had lived his whole life by a pocket watch could let go of something so essential to who he was. Or *thought* he was. But if Vaderton was certain of anything at all these days, it was that a man might change any number of ways, given the right circumstances.

Or the wrong ones.

He stared down at the child who writhed on the ground. The boy had been on these cliffs when Vaderton arrived. He'd stood out in Vaderton's memory because he'd lost both his legs from cannon fire during the riot at the Three Cups in Paradise Circle the

year before. The word around the Cliffs had been
that after he'd lost his legs, he'd taken to bomb making and tried to blow himself up, along with the
Paradise Circle police station. He'd turned out to
be a terrible bomb maker, and no one was injured,
not even himself. But they threw him on the Empty
Cliffs anyway.

The week before this, Vaderton had watched the
biomancers take him away. Now he was back. Vaderton had never seen someone come back before, but
Biscuit Bill assured him they did return occasionally. And it was never pretty.

The boy had legs now, but judging by the smell
and the sagging, putrid flesh, they were the legs of a
dead man.

Sometimes Vaderton felt that his entire existence
on the Empty Cliffs was merely a training exercise in
letting go. Not just of time, or his pride, or hope. The
entire person he had been now seemed like only a distant memory to him. Who had that man been? The
one who imagined himself special because he had
gained the favor of a biomancer. Chosen by a man
of "true power." He'd still been terrified of them, of
course. But with that terror had come a strange sort
of pride. He'd hardly thought about the costs at all.

Now he could think of nothing else. He *wanted*
to think of nothing else. He forced himself to stare
down at the pain etched into the boy's face. To listen
to the harsh gasps of breath. To breathe in the smell
of rot. To understand what the power of biomancers
truly brought: cruelty and madness.

What possible reason could they have to graft the
legs of a corpse onto the boy? And then simply to
leave him back here? The boy seemed to be able to
move them, but they were far too rotted to support
his weight. He could really only feel them slowly dis-
integrate, as he lost his second pair of legs.

The boy's first night back, he'd begged people to kill him. But they had all been too afraid. As if biomancery was a sickness the boy had brought back with him. When no one had offered to put him out of his misery, he had begun to drag himself to the edge of the cliff. Vaderton could only stand to watch for a little while before his fear was finally drowned out by the misery of watching someone suffer so terribly.

"What're you going to do, Vade?" Kismet Pete asked quietly.

"What we should have done already," Vaderton said grimly. He knelt down and picked the boy up. He weighed almost nothing.

"Your soul goes to the hell for murderers," said Pete anxiously. "Even if you kill them 'cause they want it. That's what my old wrink used to say."

"I'm going to a worse hell than that already," said Vaderton. The special hell for those who helped biomancers.

He walked slowly toward the northern cliff. Others watched silently. No one stopped him. In fact, those in his direct path moved out of the way and bowed their heads respectfully as he walked past.

Once he reached the edge, he held the boy up. "This what you want?"

"Please...," the boy whispered. "Can...can you throw me? So's I don't get dashed on the rocks? I just...I just want the sea."

Vaderton nodded. He widened his stance. He wasn't sure how far out he could throw the boy. Whether it would be enough to avoid the rocks. Then he felt a hand on his shoulder. He turned to see Kismet Pete, his hairless face serious.

"Alright, if you're going to do it, let's do it proper, keen?"

Vaderton nodded.

They took the boy between them, and heaved him out into the open air.

Perhaps he imagined it, but in the split second before the boy dropped, he thought he heard a sigh of relief.

———

People treated Vaderton differently after the day he and Pete threw that boy off the cliff. Under other circumstances, such an act would have warranted hatred. But on the Empty Cliffs, among a group of criminals and murderers being preyed upon by government-sponsored sadists, such an act was both noble and kind. From that day, people began to listen to him. To respect him. Not with the loyalty he had commanded when he'd been the captain of a warship. But the man he had become wouldn't have accepted such unquestioning obedience anyway. Now he appreciated the rough-handed courtesy and coarse friendliness they gave him.

But more and more, Vaderton found there was one person in particular whose good opinion meant a great deal more to him than anyone else's.

"They think you're a witch," said Vaderton as he sat down next to Old Yammy on the lee side of her favorite boulder.

"Do they?" She sounded more amused than concerned. "And what do you think?"

"I think I've seen more strange things in this world than to ever dismiss something simply because it seems impossible."

"A very wise way to live."

They sat in silence for a little while. Not true silence of course, since the endless winds continued to howl. But a comfortable silence. They never ran out of things to say, but with all the time in the world to talk, there was little urgency in saying anything. It took Vaderton a while for the question in his mind to work its way to his lips.

"Why do they call you *Old* Yammy?"

"Because it's my name."

"But you're not old."

"Aren't I?"

He squinted at her, trying to see if she was being coy with him. "You don't look old."

"How old would you say I look?" She had a mischievous look in her eye, and he began to suspect she was either teasing him or flirting with him. Possibly both.

"That is an unfair question to ask a gentleman."

"All this time on the Empty Cliffs, that is the one thing you cling to?"

"Absolutely," said Vaderton. "My mother would spin in her grave if I did not give a lady the courtesy she deserves."

"I'm not a lady, and I'm not sure I deserve a great deal of courtesy."

"I hope you will forgive me if I disagree on both counts."

She smiled warmly at him then, and he thought perhaps he could live on these Empty Cliffs for a lifetime, as long as he had such a smile to look upon each day.

"Would you believe me if I said we were the same age?" she asked.

He considered it a moment. "Perhaps a bit younger than me."

She laughed, a light, yet earthy sound, like water over stones. "A very gallant, yet safe response."

He felt a blush rising to his cheeks, as though he had been chastised in some way. "I always seem to make the safe choice. The lawful choice, I suppose."

"It's funny, then, that you ended up in a prison."

"It is." He laughed suddenly. That crazy laughter had never completely left him, but since he'd accepted it as part of him, it didn't dominate him as it once had. Instead it left as quickly and easily as it came. "You know, I always imagined that sailing was a way to seek things out. But it took being forced to stay in one place for a time to help me realize that sailing had become an escape."

"From yourself?" she suggested.

"How does one escape from himself?"

"You don't," said Yammy. "But it is difficult for a good man to acknowledge that he has made bad choices. So you run away instead."

"What bad choice do you think I'm running from?" he asked carefully. He hadn't told anyone on the Empty Cliffs about his time serving the biomancer Fitmol Bet. But perhaps if Yammy truly had magical powers, she had divined it somehow.

She smiled again, but this time it was tinged with sadness. "I want to show you something." She stood up and brushed the dirt from her long cloak.

Vaderton followed wordlessly as she led him across the rocky ground until they reached the southern cliff. It used to give him an uncomfortable squirming feeling to look out at the empty space. But lately he couldn't help thinking about that quiet sigh of relief the boy with the dead legs had let out when they threw him over the edge.

"Do you know that ship?" she asked.

He looked out at the expanse of ocean below and the island of New Laven in the distance. Anchored off the coast was a trim little two-masted brig that he would never forget.

"The *Kraken Hunter*," he said. "But what is Dire Bane's purpose in coming here?"

"Why, to set us free, of course. That is always the purpose of the one who holds the title of Dire Bane."

"Why us?"

"It may be that she feels indebted to me in some way. Or that she needs me. Probably both. At least, that is the reason she *thinks* she is coming here. But it is also because, while she doesn't know it yet, she needs you as well."

"Me? I have a hard time believing that."

"She has a great conflict coming. One which even she cannot face alone. She will need capable captains who are loyal to her cause."

"And what cause is that?"

"To free the empire from the grip of the biomancers and what they are about to bring down upon us all."

She put her hand on his arm. He could feel its warmth through his thin woolen sleeve, despite the hard, endless winds. "I know you, Brice Vaderton. Better than you realize. You yearn for a way to pay off the life debt you owe her. You also long to redeem yourself for your part in aiding the biomancers. And when I tell you what is coming, I think you will not just willingly swear allegiance to Dire Bane, but you will do it with a passion and sincerity you have not felt in years."

20

The *Kraken Hunter* sat anchored off the coast of New Laven, bobbing gently up and down in the anxious seas. To the south was the rural fringe of the main island, dotted with tiny fishing villages. To the north rose the flat, sheer face of the Empty Cliffs. It was midday, and the sun shone down directly above, but its light was wan in the gray, cloudy skies and provided little warmth.

Hope and her small crew sat in the *Kraken Hunter*'s mess, eating the food Broom had pushed on Hope that morning when they left Silverback. It was the sort of rich and filling meal that didn't keep well on a ship, with rice, spring onions, squid, and shredded seaweed, so they relished the treat as they discussed plans for breaking into the Empty Cliffs based on Lymestria's information.

"There is an opening on the western side of the Cliffs at water level," Hope told Brigga Lin. "A tunnel that leads to the center of the island. At the end of the tunnel is a small cave with a lift that takes you up through the inside of the Cliffs to the top."

"So we just sail in?" asked Brigga Lin.

"The tunnel is too low for that," said Hope. "We would need to get a small vessel, like a yawl or a jolly, to row through the tunnel. But apparently there are several imperial police stationed in the cave with cannons and rifles to guard the lift."

"Would I be able to see them?" asked Brigga Lin.

"Probably not in enough time." Alash was the only one not enjoying the meal. He looked pale, and there were dark circles under his eyes. His hands shook slightly as he sipped the medicinal concoction that Brigga Lin had brewed for his hangover. He winced at the flavor, then said, "The tunnel is well lit with some sort of phosphorescent fungus or moss, but the guard station is only minimally lit. The idea being that the time it took you to row through the tunnel would give them ample opportunity to shoot you, even if they weren't very good shots."

"Where would we get a small craft like that anyway?" asked Finn.

"We could steal one from them little villages," said Sadie.

"Those poor people don't need any more hardships," said Hope. They reminded her far too much of her childhood village to even consider such a thing.

"What if we traveled through the tunnel beneath the surface of the water?" asked Brigga Lin. "Then they wouldn't see us coming."

"The tunnel is roughly a quarter of a mile long," said Hope. "I don't think any of us could hold our breath that long."

"What if we didn't need to?" pressed Brigga Lin.

"I have considered trying to devise some sort of long-range diving bell," said Alash. "But it would take weeks to build a prototype and test before I would feel confident enough to let you use it."

"That is time we don't have," said Hope. "There have been rumors circulating that prisoners on the Empty Cliffs are being given over to the biomancers. We have no way of knowing when they might take Old Yammy."

"So we don't even know if she's still there," said Sadie.

"True," admitted Hope. "But we must try. Not only for her sake, but for all those imprisoned and doomed to become material for the army of the dead being built at Dawn's Light."

Finn's eyes widened. "You mean to free them all?"

"Of course," said Hope. "We can't just leave them there."

"What'll we *do* with them all?" he asked.

"I suppose we'll drop them off on the coast nearby and they can do what they like," said Hope.

"Or we could invite them to join up," said Sadie.

"You mean go with us to Dawn's Light?" asked Hope.

"Why not?" asked Sadie. "Most will be so grateful for getting off that miserable rock, they'll be happy to do whatever you ask. Like as not, some will already know their way around a ship. The rest you and Finn can train in whatever time remains before Nettles contacts us."

"I suppose it makes sense...," said Hope.

"Hope, it's a good idea," said Alash. "We'll need every able body we can get, won't we?"

"It just seems like we're taking advantage of them," said Hope.

"It won't matter either way if we don't figure a way to break them out in the first place," said Finn.

"I've already sorted that out," said Brigga Lin.

"Oh?" asked Hope.

"It's quite simple. I will temporarily give us gills so that we can swim the length of the tunnel underwater without being seen."

"Gills?" Alash blanched.

The others glanced at one another uncomfortably.

"Don't be such a bunch of babies," said Brigga Lin. "I won't even be *adding* any animal aspects. The aquatic nature already lies dormant within us. It's such a simple process, I'm almost tempted to have Jilly do it."

"Me?" Jilly's eyes grew alarmed.

"Perhaps we should save Jilly's first trial for something with...slightly lower stakes for the rest of us," suggested Hope.

"That's why I said I was *almost* tempted. Putting that much pressure into even a simple transformation can be problematic for a beginner."

"So, you will give the two of us gills," said Hope. "We will swim through the tunnel beneath the surface where the soldiers can't see us. Then when we reach the end, you will get rid of the gills so we can catch the soldiers by surprise and take control of the lift."

"Exactly," said Brigga Lin.

"Can't I come, too?" asked Jilly. "Without Nettles and Filler here, you could use my help, I bet. I'm good in a fight. I've been practicing close fighting with my knife for *weeks* now."

Hope looked at Brigga Lin. "What do you think?"

"Did your master coddle you?"

"We call them teachers," said Hope. "But no, he didn't."

"Mine either. So why would we coddle her? If she wants to go, it's her choice to risk her life, and we should respect it."

Hope turned back to Jilly. "Can you swim?"

"Two years in the navy, of course I can swim," Jilly said with a lofty air.

"Can you swim *well*?" asked Brigga Lin.

"Better than you, I bet," said Jilly.

Brigga Lin smiled. "We shall see."

———

"Clothing will weigh you down in the water," said Alash when they reconvened a short time later on the deck. "You'll want to wear as little as possible while swimming."

"I'd rather not rescue Old Yammy in my undergarments," said Hope.

"Might help with the recruiting, though," said Sadie. "I know many a tom who'd follow a pair of legs like yours. Granted, you'd get even more people if you had bigger tits."

"Thank you, Sadie." Hope gave her a withering look. "I'm so grateful for the wisdom of your years. Your many, *many* years…"

"Oho!" Sadie nudged Finn with her elbow and grinned. "This one's finally growing fangs!"

"If I may continue," said Alash, "I think I've found a way for you to bring your clothes along and keep them more or less dry." He patted a small open barrel next to him. "We'll pack this with your clothes and seal it with pitch. I've weighted the bottom with ballast, which will hopefully offset the buoyancy of both the wood and the small amount of air trapped in the barrel. We'll tie a rope around it and you can tow it behind you as you swim. Once you reach the cave, just break it open."

"Very considerate of you, Alash," said Brigga Lin. "The salt water would probably ruin my gown."

"I *did* just get this coat." Hope looked down at the red captain's coat that Broom had insisted she take with her.

"That's the trouble with fancy clothes." Jilly plucked at her sailcloth breeches and rough cotton shirt. "I'll be just fine."

Hope slipped off her coat and shirt, then unbuckled her leather pants and boots. Finally she stood on the deck in a thin cotton halter top and men's under-breeches. The weak New Laven sun offered only minor warmth to counteract the chill of the sea breeze. Her pale skin stippled with goose bumps, but she didn't shiver. A woman of the Southern Isles did not tense against the cold, but allowed it to enliven and strengthen her.

She stuffed her clothes into the barrel as tightly as she could, then turned toward Brigga Lin. "Well, are you..."

Brigga Lin was naked. There was something about the way she stood there on the deck, completely unself-conscious, that was at once bizarre and admirable.

"Something the matter?" asked Brigga Lin.

"You took Alash's suggestion about wearing as little clothing as possible quite literally, I see." Hope turned to Alash. "Didn't she?"

Alash's face was bright red as he made little noises that Hope guessed was an attempt to speak.

"What's wrong with him?" Brigga Lin put her hands on her bare hips.

"I think this may be the first time our boy has seen a molly in her naturals," said Sadie with a smirk.

Brigga Lin looked offended. "It's not like there's anything wrong, is there?" She turned around, making sure to give Alash a view of every angle. "I think I did an excellent job."

"That you did, Ms. Lin." Missing Finn grinned wide.

"Alright, enough leering, you leaky wrink," said Sadie.

"Beauty unappreciated is a tragedy," said Finn, adopting a pious look. "Says so right in *The Book of Storms.*"

"How would you know? You can't even read," said Sadie.

"I'm sure it's in there somewhere."

"I think we were not quite expecting...full nudity," Hope told Brigga Lin.

"You Vinchen are so puritanical. It's just a body."

Brigga Lin squinted critically at Hope for a moment. "You know…maybe Sadie is right about your breasts. I could do something about that, if you like."

"They would just get in the way of fighting," Hope said curtly. "Now, can we get on with this?"

"Certainly." Brigga Lin folded her gown, then looked skeptically at the small barrel. "It's going to be so wrinkled. Maybe I should just leave it behind."

"Excellent recruiting strategy," said Sadie.

"Put it in," said Hope.

Brigga Lin sighed and shoved her gown into the barrel. Then she turned to Alash. "You can seal it now."

Alash's hands were trembling again as he tamped the lid down on the barrel and sealed it with thick black pitch. Hope was fairly sure that this time it wasn't from a hangover.

"Thank you, Alash," she said gently.

He nodded and stepped back.

"I can only do this one at a time, so who's first?" asked Brigga Lin.

"I'll go first," said Hope.

Brigga Lin placed her cold fingertips on Hope's neck. They stared into each other's eyes for a moment, then Brigga Lin stepped away with the detached air of someone examining their handiwork. A moment later, Hope felt a searing pain as gills split open on either side of her neck. There was also a strange wrenching feeling in her chest as her lungs began to transform.

Abruptly, she was suffocating. Her mouth opened wide as she gulped for air that gave no relief.

"Into the water!" said Brigga Lin.

Hope nodded and dove over the side of the ship, cutting cleanly into the sea. Every instinct in her body fought against trying to breathe under the water. She had to will herself to take the first gasp.

Seawater passed through her, cooling the hot panic in her chest.

She continued to focus on slow, steady breaths as she took in her surroundings. The seafloor was a hazy, uneven shadow beneath her, dotted with boulders and seaweed that waved gently in the currents. The longer she floated there, the calmer she became. There was a quiet beneath the sea that she had never known before, not even back at the monastery. That, combined with the sensation of near weightlessness, gave her a rare feeling of peace. She was like a jellyfish, content to let the current take her wherever it went.

Then there was a splash above and Jilly swam down next to her. She didn't seem to have the same instinctual reluctance to breathe underwater. She grinned excitedly at Hope and spoke in words too garbled for her to understand.

Hope pointed to her own ears and shrugged.

Jilly looked disappointed, but nodded.

Hope continued to float while Jilly swam down to the seafloor, then examined the underside of the ship.

Finally, Brigga Lin made her graceful entrance. Her long black hair trailed behind as her sleek form knifed down almost to the bottom.

The small barrel hit the water with a loud splash, sinking a few feet beneath the surface, then slowly rising back up until the top of the barrel just barely broke the surface.

Hope grabbed the rope tied to it and signaled to Brigga Lin and Jilly. Then the three began to swim toward the dark base of the Empty Cliffs that loomed in the distance.

Now that they swam toward the Cliffs, Hope no longer felt the quiet peace she'd enjoyed earlier. Instead, her focus shifted to combat preparedness, and her senses tuned in to possible sources of danger. Vision was limited. She could see details no more than twenty feet ahead. Beyond that, shapes were hazy and indistinct. Hearing was also hampered. While noise traveled quite a distance, the details were distorted.

But her sense of smell brought her quite a bit more information than she was used to. At first, it was such a deluge of textures that she had a hard time making sense of it. She closed her eyes and concentrated on it, much like Hurlo had taught her to do with sound. Slowly she was able to tease apart the various components. She could smell the wood of the ship. The metal tang of the sword belted to her side. The lush vegetative scent of seaweed. She could even smell Jilly and Brigga Lin as they swam a short distance in front of her.

Another scent slowly began to intrude. It was one she was not familiar with, but it reminded her of wet dog. It grew stronger the closer they got to the Empty Cliffs. There was something predatory about the scent that put Hope on guard. She called out to Jilly and Brigga Lin, but they were too far ahead to hear her. She was swimming slower than they were, since she had only one hand. But they had also been boasting about their skill at swimming and she wondered if they were competing to see who was faster.

They were close enough to the Empty Cliffs by then that Hope was able to make out some details of the dark, barnacle-encrusted rock. There were strange holes irregularly spaced across the surface that were large enough to fit a person. Or something even larger.

That's when she saw them—dark shapes moving swiftly from either side, bearing down on Jilly and Brigga Lin. Six of them, each twelve feet long and roughly half a ton. A pack of seals.

Hope had always thought of seals as fat, ungainly
things, but these appeared to have been modified
by biomancers to adapt to warmer climates. They
moved like bullets toward their unsuspecting prey.

She screamed again, as loud as she could, to warn
her friends, but neither slowed down or even turned
their head.

Then the smell of seal grew sharp in her nose.
She turned just in time to see that one had been
bearing down on her from behind. Her awkward,
one-handed swimming had obviously marked her
as the weakest and therefore the first to attack. The
seal's cold black eyes glittered as its mouth opened to
reveal sharp canines, each over an inch long. Hope
tried to slam her clamp into its snout, but she was
not used to close-quarters fighting underwater. The
seal easily dodged her clumsy blow and darted down
beneath her. Then it neatly summersaulted and
came up from below. Had she been wearing boots,
her feet would have been protected. She might have
even been able to kick it away. But her legs were bare
below the knee. The seal bit down on her ankle, and
didn't let go. Instead it shook its head back and forth.

Blood clouded the water with its metallic, bitter
scent. It was a smell that traveled quickly to Jilly and
Brigga Lin, and one they knew well and reacted to
instantly, which may have saved their lives.

Jilly unthinkingly drew her knife moments before
the closest seal struck. She had just enough time to
dodge to one side and plant the blade into the side of
its furry neck.

Brigga Lin had no weapons, of course. She used
the moment of warning before the seal struck to
modify her own body. She held up her forearm, and
the seal sank its teeth into her flesh. But then it shuddered as venomous spines grew from her skin. The
seal released her and began to convulse and writhe.

The rest of the pack gave her a wide berth when they saw that, which gave her enough time to heal the bite on her arm.

The seal's teeth scraped against Hope's anklebone as it continued to shake its head from side to side. She gritted her teeth against the pain, and instead of trying to rip herself free, she grabbed the end of the rope that was tied to the barrel and looped it around the seal's neck. She yanked hard, but the blubbery softness of its neck prevented her from crushing its windpipe. It did release her ankle, at least. It swam toward the protection of the rest of the pack, but the rope was still around its neck. Hope held on and let the seal drag her closer to her friends. A ribbon of blood trailed behind from her ankle. The other end of the rope was still tied to the barrel, which slowed the seal down and allowed Hope to inch her way up the rope with her knees and her one hand until she was close enough to thrust the point of her sword into the back of its neck.

The seal's death sent a surge of grief up the blade and into Hope's forearm. Even though the animal had been trying to kill her, the loss of an innocent creature pained her more than anything she'd felt before. It was like fire shooting all the way to her toes and into her brain.

She steeled herself for more as she turned to help her friends. But thankfully, that was unnecessary. Brigga Lin had given Jilly venomous spines as well and the seals were staying clear of them.

Brigga Lin swam over to Hope and pointed at her bloody, torn ankle. A moment later, Hope felt soothing relief as her wounds closed.

The three continued their swim toward the Empty Cliffs, this time staying close together. The remaining seals lurked nearby, but didn't come any closer.

Once they reached the tunnel entrance, Brigga

Lin removed Jilly's spines and then her own. They pulled in the barrel, which had a tendency to bob at the surface if given slack, and continued into the opening.

Lymestria had been right about the tunnel being illuminated. Hope couldn't make out much detail above the surface, but a faint phosphorescence filtered into the water from overhead. The bottom and sides of the tunnel were smooth, and appeared to have been carved out with tools.

It took them a quarter of an hour to reach the end of the tunnel. When they were about twenty feet away, Hope signaled to Jilly and Brigga Lin that she would take the center and they would come in on the flanks. But Brigga Lin shook her head and indicated that she wanted to go in the middle. Hope nodded. They had fought together too many times for her not to trust that her companion had some plan in mind.

Hope took the right side of the tunnel, and Jilly the left. The closer they got to the end, the murkier the water got. Hope wondered if something was making it dirtier. Perhaps gunpowder residue or oil from a swivel cannon. She still couldn't tell what they were up against, other than a series of dark shapes spaced evenly along the shore.

Finally they were close enough that even murky water might reveal them. Hope let the rope go and the barrel drifted to the surface about ten feet behind them. Once she heard shouts and gunshots above the surface, she signaled to the other two and they quickly swam the rest of the way to the steep bank of the shore.

When they reached the waterline, Brigga Lin tapped her mouth to signal it was time to close their gills. She sealed her own up first, then gestured first to Hope, then to Jilly.

Hope felt the gills in her neck close, then the

familiar pressure of holding her breath. She had to remind herself not to take another breath until she was out of the water.

Hope was surprised to see Brigga Lin already emerging from the water. She should have been last, since she was in the middle. Perhaps this was part of her plan, or perhaps she simply couldn't hold her breath any longer. Either way, Hope quickly pulled herself out of the water.

The transition from water to air forced her to take longer than usual to assess the situation.

Fortunately, Brigga Lin bought Hope the time she needed when she emerged in front of the soldiers, a naked beauty, her long black hair streaming water down her breasts and stomach.

"Hold your fire!" one of them screamed in an almost hysterical voice.

"Who in all hells is that?"

"A gift from Heaven!"

"Temptation from some hell!"

"Piss on you, then you don't get none!"

There were two swivel cannons, with a pair of soldiers manning each, and three snipers sitting in shallow trenches. Once Hope had her bearings, she moved swiftly, the air chill on her wet undergarments. She killed two of the snipers and one pair of cannoneers before they even knew they were under attack. As she moved, she relished the lack of resistance the air provided, feeling even faster than she ever had before, although she doubted it was actually true. She killed the two remaining cannoneers as they fumbled to draw their revolvers. Their lust-tinged panic shot up her arm as they died. The final sniper fell to Jilly's knife.

Hope turned to Brigga Lin, who still stood gloriously and unabashedly naked.

"*That* was your plan?"

Brigga Lin shrugged. "Men can be dumb animals."

They retrieved the barrel that contained Hope and Brigga Lin's clothing and cracked it open.

"Pitch stain," Brigga Lin said critically, holding up her white gown to show them the black spot on the shoulder. "And the wrinkles, as I expected."

"I wish I'd put *my* clothes in the barrel after all." Jilly fingered one of the many holes that now dotted her shirt and breeches left behind by the venomous spines.

"We'll get you new clothes," Hope assured her as she pulled on her coat.

"This must be the lift, teacher." Jilly pointed at a metal cage against the back wall of the cave. It was roughly eight feet tall and five feet wide, with a door that covered most of the front. A thick cable was attached to the top, and stretched up into the darkness above. The cable was made from thin strands of metal braided together. Hope walked over and examined it carefully.

"How is such a thing possible?"

"Not with biomancery," said Brigga Lin as she finished putting on her gown. "Imbuing living force within metal is nearly impossible. In fact, the method to do so has been lost for over a century. That's what makes your sword so special."

"So it's true that biomancers can only work with living things?" asked Hope. "Then how do you make guns explode?"

"Microscopic organisms can live on nearly anything, including gunpowder," said Brigga Lin. "I simply make those organisms combust."

"I thought you had to *see* them to do something to them, though," said Jilly. "How can you see something that small?"

Brigga Lin arched her thin black eyebrow.

"Haven't you read chapter five of the *Biomancery Praxis* yet?"

"Uh, well, I started," said Jilly. "But it's real hard to follow. My mind keeps slipping to other things."

"Did you think it would be *easy* to grasp the fundamental interconnectedness of the universe?"

"Well, no, master, but—"

"When we return to the ship, I want you to read that chapter from start to finish, and expect me to question you thoroughly on it."

Jilly looked crestfallen, but bowed her head respectfully. "Yes, master."

Hope didn't like that biomancers used the title of "master." It reminded her of the cruel Vinchen novice Crunta, who had tormented her as a girl. She always appreciated that Hurlo called himself a teacher instead. Still, she had invited Brigga Lin to participate in the radical idea of training Jilly in both traditions, and she couldn't just pick and choose which parts Brigga Lin would impart.

She examined the metal lift. "It appears to raise and lower on some kind of pulley system."

"Can we make it work?" asked Brigga Lin.

"Yes, but it looks like one of us will have to stay below to operate it." She tapped a small bell next to the lift. A thin rope stretched up into the darkness with the cable. "This is probably how we signal that we want to come back down."

"Aren't you glad you brought me along, then?" asked Jilly. "Otherwise one of you would have to stay behind."

"Very true," said Brigga Lin. "We don't have any idea what sort of reception we'll receive up there from those criminals. It could get ugly."

"You do realize that we are most likely considered criminals," said Hope.

"You know what I mean," Brigga Lin said dismissively.

They stepped into the metal cage and closed the door. Jilly began to turn a large crank. The cage shuddered, then slowly began to rise up into the darkness.

As they ascended, Brigga Lin asked, "Have you decided if you will try to recruit these prisoners to the cause?"

Hope was silent for a moment. Something still bothered her about the idea, but now she distrusted that hesitation. Weakness. Fear. Lack of resolve. If she was to be the Dire Bane everyone expected of her, she couldn't let such things fester within her. She had to cut them out, even if it was painful.

"I will give them the opportunity to be a part of something greater than themselves," she said at last.

Brigga Lin nodded approvingly. "Now you're starting to get it."

Soon they reached the top. The lift ceiling hit a thick metal hatch, which opened slowly as the lift continued to rise. Finally the lift jerked to a halt. They had reached the Empty Cliffs.

Hope locked her clamp on her sword and braced herself. She had considered several possible scenarios that included being greeted by hostile guards, hostile prisoners, or perhaps no one at all. But what greeted them when they stepped out of the lift was not any of those things.

The Empty Cliffs were a flat, mostly barren stretch of rock dotted with low shrubs and boulders. The wind shrieked all around them, making Hope's eyes tear up. It took her a moment to clear her view and see what was before her.

Old Yammy stood as if she had been waiting for them to arrive, her arms folded in a ragged cloak. Next to her stood Brice Vaderton, the captain of the *Guardian*. He wore a simple green coat instead of a nice white and gold uniform, his hair was shaggy, and he had the beginnings of a thick black beard, but it was definitely him. Behind the captain and Old Yammy stood a large gathering of men and women, looking tired and hungry, but resolute. There was a strange air of expectancy that hung over them all.

"Dire Bane, champion of the people," said Old Yammy. "Thank you for coming to rescue me. As a token of my gratitude, I have gathered a small group of souls willing to follow you so that they and their families might finally throw off the cruel oppression and fear of the biomancers."

Vaderton dropped to one knee. "Though we have been enemies in the past, I now see the narrowness of my thinking. Dire Bane, you spared my life. I beg you to allow me to repay that generosity by serving under your command."

As Hope looked at the crowd before her, she almost felt like she was floating in the sea once again. Rebellion on such a grand scale had never truly been her intention. She had only wanted to shake the biomancers up enough for them to release Red. But it was as if the world was thrusting this role upon her. Everywhere she turned, people looked to her to lead them. She had taken the name Dire Bane and they wanted Dire Bane. Perhaps they even *needed* Dire Bane. Could she in good conscience deny them? Perhaps it was time to cast aside the humility of the Vinchen, and completely embrace the power and strength she knew dwelt within her.

"Understand, all of you, that it isn't for me you fight," she said loud enough for it to carry over the endless, shrieking wind. "Nor is it for yourself. It is for the good of the empire, which is not limited to the rich and noble, but *all* its subjects. There are dark days ahead, make no mistake. But if you join me, we will face them head-on with courage and resolution.

And when we are finished, the empire will be a better place for *all of us*. Do you swear to this?"

"I do," said Old Yammy.

"As do I," said Vaderton.

An echo of "as do I" spread through the group.

As Hope surveyed her new recruits, she felt an odd tickle deep in her chest. A strangely pleasant bubbling feeling. It took her a moment to understand that it was triumph she felt. Before she could stop herself, a grin split across her face.

"Then let's give 'em all hells!" she shouted, and the newly freed prisoners cheered.

21

Nettles stared down at Filler's body. He had been cleaned up, dressed, and now lay stretched out on a table in a small room in Apple Grove Manor. The curtains were drawn and the only light in the room was a single lantern that hung over him. His body seemed to float in the darkness.

Nettles had put out the word that any true wag of the Circle was welcome to come and pay their respects. People had been coming all day, an endless train of bewilderment, sadness, and anger. Some had left flowers; some had left booze. Some even left small metal items, perhaps something he'd smithed for them. As quiet and unassuming as he'd been, Filler had been known and loved. Mick, in his arrogant ignorance of how things truly worked in the Circle, had made a grave mistake.

Nettles had not been there when people came to show their respects. Handsome Henny had stood by the body, greeting people on her behalf because she was too busy planning what was to come. But now, before she began her retribution, she allowed herself to be with him, alone, one last time, and let the memories come as they will.

She remembered when she'd first met him, along with Red, and got caught up in their slippy plan to rob Deadface Drem on the opening night of the

Three Cups. Filler was Red's roommate at the time and he had volunteered to sleep at Henny's house so that Red and Nettles could toss in private.

She remembered the hours she and Filler had sat together designing and constructing and tweaking her precious chainblade. She'd been so fussy about it, and he'd been so patient. She held it now tight in her hands, the metal links biting into her palms.

She remembered all those times when Filler had been the peacemaker between her and Red. Likely they wouldn't have remained friends if not for him.

And then there was that time Red came to them, begging them to come with him to Hammer Point and see something Big Sig would show them. It had been Filler who convinced her to go along with it. Not because he had a way with words, but because she couldn't look in those big, honest eyes of his without at least giving Red a chance.

There had never been a more loyal wag. Nettles gazed down at him like she was memorizing every line of his face. Burning it into her brains so that she would never falter in what was to happen next.

Gradually, she became aware of another presence in the room. She turned and saw Mister Hatbox in the corner. He held his black top hat respectfully in his hands. His dark, carefully oiled hair gleamed in the faint lantern light and his expression was as bland as ever.

"Well?" asked Nettles.

"We're ready," he said.

She nodded and turned back to Filler. She leaned over and kissed his cold, broad forehead. "At least you made it home, my wag," she whispered.

Where it's cold, and it's wet,
And the sun never gets.
But still it's my home.
Bless the Circle.

She stood back up and clutched at the edge of the table, forcing the tears away. There would be no tears, ever again.

"I swear I won't let him have it, Fill."

Nettles turned and walked out of the room, followed at a respectful distance by Mister Hatbox.

Gavish Gray waited for her in the darkened hallway. He looked worried beneath his mop of prematurely gray hair.

"Hey, Nettles. You sure you don't want to wait a few days? You know, cool off a bit so you have a more level head going into this?"

She regarded him for a moment. She'd known Gray a long time. He was the wag who'd helped her start the whole southending side business at the Slice of Heaven. He spent a great deal of time at sea, as smugglers and pirates were wont to do. But he'd always come back looking for her. If she'd been the marrying type, he'd have been high on her list. Not the top, mind. But pretty far up.

"Smartly said, Gavish." She put her hand on his shoulder. "You're a reasonable wag, and I know you've got my best interests at heart. Trouble is, there's nothing reasonable about what's been done to Filler. And there's something deep inside me that demands I respond in kind."

———

There was a gaf named Donkey Bray who was known to be one of Mick the Sick's boots. He was at the Drowned Rat drinking heavy. Maybe to shut up a guilty conscience, or maybe just because he liked to drink. Either way, he started choking and spitting blood. It was a slow death, but quiet enough, so no one else in the tavern paid it much mind. A curious wag later found tiny slivers of metal in Bray's tankard. Someone remarked casually that Prin the barmaid seemed a bit raw from crying, and that he'd always had a hunch she'd been sotted with Filler.

Another boot named After Atticus went to the Slice of Heaven for a toss. While he stood with his cock in Tosh's mouth, Misandry came up behind and strangled him with a fishing line. Mo's only response was to remind them to clean up after themselves.

All over Paradise Circle, gafs known to work for Mick the Sick started dying. Hangings, drownings, and fire were a few of the more common causes. Nothing quick or painless. The body count was high enough and public enough that the imps should have noticed. But they didn't seem interested in pursuing the matter. Even they understood Paradise Circle justice enough to not get involved in this one.

The smart boots started declaring they were deserting Mick. Soon they were leaving him in droves. He needed to do something as a show of strength, or he'd lose more. So he gathered up what was left of his crew, about forty strong, and they marched on Apple Grove Manor. Perhaps he'd heard stories of the raid on the Three Cups and imagined he would garner similar enthusiasm.

But no one joined in the march. No one even came to watch. In fact, he'd never seen the streets so empty.

He learned why that was when he and his men came in view of the manor and a storm of bullets erupted from the windows. He lost eight men in the first five minutes. There was a pause as guns were reloaded, and Mick urged them to charge. But Nettles must have drilled her people on loading rifles relentlessly, because they fired again in less than a minute. After two more rounds, the men broke in all directions. Fewer than ten stayed with Mick as he fled.

It was pretty clear who was winning the fight for

control of Paradise Circle. It was also pretty clear that was no longer the point. Because those that survived the raid continued to turn up dead.

Finally, Mick and his remaining men were holed up at Gunpowder Hall. It was the largest building in Paradise Circle, and known to all as a safe house or shelter. Again, he showed his poor grasp of the neighborhood. Because the hall was only a haven for true wags of the Circle.

Still, it appeared to be like any other day at Gunpowder Hall. Rows of benches and tables housed gambling and negotiations over drugs, robberies, and assassinations. Open areas offered tents for whores who could afford them, and straw mats for those who couldn't. The place was filled with shouts and laughter, groans of pleasure and pain, things and people breaking, lives beginning and ending. Nothing unusual.

Mick and his men were clustered at a table in the center of the room. It seemed a smart idea, since it would be difficult for anyone to sneak up on them. To be sure, the crowds were thick in the hall and people bustled by constantly, but it was nobody *dangerous*. Just old wrinks, children, junkies, and perfumed whores. And that was Mick's third and final mistake. Because even he should have known that everyone in Paradise Circle was dangerous.

So Mick and his men sat nervously sipping on tankards of ale, their eyes never leaving the entrance. Maybe they thought Nettles and her crew would come bursting in through the front door for a big shootout. After all, he'd learned the hard way that they weren't lacking in firepower.

But if that was what Mick thought, he knew his sister even less than he knew Paradise Circle.

As the day wore on, a strange sort of weariness crept up on Mick and his crew. They found it harder to keep their eyes focused. Their limbs began to feel heavy. Their mouths grew dry and the more they tried to wet their parched tongues with ale, the stronger their symptoms became.

Black rose was a curious sort of drug, with all manner of applications. A large dose of about three drops in a drink would knock a person out within minutes and keep them that way for hours. This was particularly useful for crimp houses selling unsuspecting lodgers to ship captains in need of crew. A medium dose of two drops into a drink would produce an intoxicating effect that might or might not end in unconsciousness, depending on the size of the person and their particular tolerance to narcotics. In either case, the uniquely bittersweet smell was still strong enough to be detected even in the hoppy bite of Paradise Circle's finest ale.

But black rose stayed in the system a long time. If one delivered only a half drop, the smell was undetectable. A single such dose would have a negligible effect on the user. But if it was delivered many times over the span of several hours, the cumulative effect could eventually bring down even a full-sized mole rat (a fact verified and documented ten years earlier by the biomancer Fitmol Bet).

Mick the Sick was a large man with a robust constitution. He was used to being less affected by drink. So he was more annoyed than concerned when his boots began nodding off around him. He only became alarmed when he tried to wake them up and even a sharp slap across the face had no effect.

He was not completely bludgeon, so he immediately put down his tankard. Except somehow he missed the table and it spilled all over his lap. He stood up, and the world wobbled beneath his feet in a way he didn't like at all. That's when he realized just how bad the situation was.

His vision dimmed, and the last thing he saw before he lost consciousness was his sister walking toward him, her face as dark as a thundercloud.

"Rose...," he whispered in both longing and fear.

———

Mick awoke in a small, hot space. The walls appeared to be made of leather with tools and weapons hanging from them in neat displays. He was staked down spread-eagle on the warm dirt. When he lifted his head, he saw a seething blacksmith forge at the other end. A woman with matted hair and a long ragged cloak was stoking the fire. The orange light flickered on her dirt-streaked face. Next to her stood a man in a pristine black suit and top hat. He gazed expressionlessly at the glowing end of a pair of long-handle pliers he held in one gloved hand.

"He's awake."

Mick couldn't see the speaker, but he didn't need to.

"Rose," he whimpered. "Come on, sis, you gave me a good scare. Joke's over."

Nettles stepped into view, the light of the forge playing on her heavy lashes, smooth high cheekbones, and dark painted lips. Mick again felt the old longing, tinged with new fear.

She wasn't looking at him, though. Instead she stared down at a long, thin chain in her hands. It was the thing she'd hit him with that night a few weeks ago. There was a blade attached to one end that was clean and polished, the light reflecting brightly off its metal. Nettles always was careful with her things.

"I'm no expert, but the only lethal wound I saw on his body was the hole in his stomach that you made for your cock." There was something eerily mild about Nettles's tone. As if she was pondering what he'd eaten for breakfast. "So I can't help but wonder if you had your fun before or after he died. It used to be only after, but who knows? We've both changed since then, isn't that right, Mick?"

"You ain't changed *that* much, Rose." He tried to sound confident. In control. "It ain't like you're going to kill your own brother."

She finally looked at him then, and there was something like pity in her eyes. But her voice remained distant. Aloof. "It's true, Mick. I won't kill you. Not even when you beg me to."

"Here we are!" The ragged woman grinned as she pulled a large handsaw out of the forge. The metal teeth glowed almost white. "All ready for you."

Nettles stared at the saw, transfixed. "Can I confess something to you, brother? This began as vengeance for Filler. I guess hanging around a Vinchen rubbed off on me a little. Although maybe not enough. Because what I'm about to do next goes way beyond vengeance. My Vinchen friend wouldn't approve. And neither would Filler. Kind of ironic, I suppose. That the one person who might have stopped me from doing this is the person you killed."

"I'm sorry!" wailed Mick. "I didn't realize he was that important to you!"

She shook her head. "You still don't understand. This isn't about him anymore. What happens next is just for me. The *real* me, I reckon. The one that's been hiding inside all this time, just waiting for a reason to be let out. The me that's more like you than I ever wanted to admit."

She looked down at the chain in her hands. "Filler made this for me. And after today, I won't deserve it." She hung it up on one of the pegs fixed to the leather wall. "Not the right tool for the job anyway."

Then she took the still-glowing saw from the ragged woman and walked over to Mick.

"Please, Rose…" His face was twisted up and he was so scared, he could barely get the words out. "Please, you can have Paradise Circle. I'll go. I'll leave right now and you'll never see me again."

"Do you remember all those times Dad raped Mom?" She was so close now that he could hear the quiet hiss of the heated saw. "Do you remember when *you* raped *me*?"

"Just the once!" he said shrilly. "I never did it again!"

"Of course not. Because that's when I finally went to Jix and told him what a monster you were." She paused, as if considering something. "Maybe I ought to thank you for that."

A tiny burst of hope bloomed in Mick's chest. "Sure!"

She shook her head. "Nah. I don't think so."

The screams that came from the smithy tent outside Gunpowder Hall lasted a long time. But no one was bludgeon enough to go near. Not even the imps.

———

Mick the Sick was abandoned outside the Hole, the local name for the police garrison in the center of Paradise Circle. He was naked. His arms had been sawed off at the elbows, and his legs had been sawed off at the knees. All four limbs had been carefully cauterized so he wouldn't bleed to death, and bandaged to reduce the risk of infection. His tongue had been torn out by searing-hot pliers. The word *justice* had been carved into his chest.

He lay there on the front steps of the garrison, staring into space, shaking uncontrollably. The imps did not seem eager to immediately collect him.

Deadface Drem had begun his reign with a series of murders that concluded with Jix the Lift found strangled to death with his own guts. Before him, Jix the Lift began his reign by drowning Yorey Satin in a vat of his own whiskey.

When word spread of what had happened to Mick, every true wag of the neighborhood understood that this was a declaration.

The reign of the Black Rose of Paradise Circle had begun.

22

$\mathcal{L}$ady Merivale Hempist stared down at the unconscious form of Lord Rixidenteron Pastinas. He wasn't wearing his darkened glasses or his charming smirk. He would have seemed almost innocent, if not for the fact that he still held a curious dual-bladed throwing weapon in his hand.

When Merivale blew the whistle she had stolen from him the day before, he had stumbled into a large trunk full of Nea's clothes and personal effects before he fell. The ruckus had woken Nea, and she was now battering Merivale's ears with semi-coherent yet very insistent questions. Merivale ignored her and continued to look between Rixidenteron and the whistle. Far more interesting than any of Nea's questions was the one Merivale currently pondered. Why would he purposefully create something he knew was harmful to him? She knew that's what he had done even before she had used the whistle on him, based on the combined information she had gleaned from Nea and Hume. This curious choice of his was something she had been thinking about for some time, yet still did not have sufficient information to answer yet. It was an enigma that kept Lord Pastinas alive, at least for now. Merivale was not one to make irreversible decisions before she had full command of all the pertinent facts.

Leston burst into the room, his white dressing gown flapping around his bare legs. "What in all hells is going on?"

Questions from Nea could be safely ignored, but questions from her prince must be answered. And yet, she was not authorized to tell him most of what he would need to know in order to understand what had just transpired. This might be a compelling enough reason to finally bring him into the fold.

"I'm afraid I can't divulge the details at this time, Your Highness," she said calmly. "For which I sincerely apologize. Suffice it to say, the ambassador's life was in danger. I have mitigated that danger, at least temporarily."

"Danger from whom?"

Merivale nodded to the unconscious Lord Pastinas.

"No, that can't be right. There must be some mistake or misunderstanding." Leston's eyes narrowed. "And what do you mean, you can't divulge the details? On whose orders?"

Finally the right question. "One who outranks you, Your Highness."

"But my father has hardly spoken to anyone in years," objected Leston.

"That is true, Your Highness."

His eyes widened for a moment, then narrowed. "Mother." He spun on his heels and left the room.

Merivale turned to Nea. "If you'll excuse me, Ambassador."

"Lady Hempist!"

She once again ignored Nea as she stepped out into the hallway, where she found Hume patiently waiting for her. "Please find some means of securing Lord Pastinas. I'm afraid it remains to be seen whom we will encounter when he wakes."

"Yes, my lady."

She began to walk down the hallway after Leston.

"Lady Hempist, please wait!" Nea had come out into the hallway. She wore a long yellow robe that was just transparent enough to show the outline of her lithe form in the gaslit hallway. Merivale hoped she could introduce some Aukbontaren fashion into the palace. Once political tensions had begun to ease, of course.

"Yes, Ambassador?"

"What happened here?"

"I'm afraid this is an internal matter, Ambassador. I hope you understand."

"But it was *my* life in danger."

"My sincerest apologies," said Merivale. "Although I feel compelled to point out, it was I who saved your life. So if you would be so kind as to now indulge me for a short time, I promise I will work diligently to get you at least a portion of the answers you seek. Now, I'm afraid I really must be going."

She bowed and left the ambassador staring after her. Things were unraveling quickly. Her cover was blown to both the prince and the ambassador. It was unlikely they would believe her to be a simple scheming lady of the court now. Merivale felt that the appropriate response to this notion was probably chagrin, or frustration, or even panic. But all she felt was a quiet delight, as she always did when a dark secret came boiling to the surface.

She found Leston at the door to the empress's chambers. Kurdem stood blocking his way with an expression at once regretful and resolute.

"Drown it all, Kurdem, I must see her at once!" said Leston.

"I'm afraid the empress is asleep and not to be disturbed," said Kurdem.

Merivale swept into the space between them. "Now, Kurdem, you and I both know that isn't true.

Why, it's only shortly after midnight. The empress never sleeps more than a few hours a night. It's much too early for her to have retired."

"Lady Hempist..." Kurdem looked hesitant.

That was all the opening she needed. "Come now. Any disagreeable results, I will claim full responsibility."

He pursed his lips for a moment, then nodded. "As you wish, my lady." He opened the door and stepped aside.

"Now, Your Highness," began Merivale. "I suggest that you not just—"

But Leston had already stormed past her through the doors.

Merivale gave Kurdem a wry smile. "Impulsiveness is part of his charm. So I'm told." Then she followed after him.

They found Empress Pysetcha seated at a large writing desk, a stack of papers spread out in front of her. As soon as Leston's footsteps sounded in the room, she smoothly gathered them up and slid them into a drawer without turning around.

"Now, Kurdem," she said as she began to turn. "I asked that I not..." She trailed off when she saw her son and Merivale standing before her. She made no show of surprise, however. "Good evening, Leston. It's rather late. I'm surprised to see you up." She nodded to Merivale. "And good evening to you, Lady Hempist."

Merivale curtsied in her dressing gown, but Leston was too worked up for courtesies.

"You have been keeping things from me, Mother!" he said.

"Yes, dear," she agreed. "Parents do that."

"I'm no longer a child."

"Is that so?" she asked. "And other than age, what makes you believe this to be true?"

"What?" He was brought up short. "Well..."

"As far as I can tell, you have done very little to indicate that you have any interest in the adult concerns of running the empire."

"But Your Majesty," Merivale chided gently. "What about his bold alliance with the ambassador of Aukbontar?"

Pysetcha sniffed. "One look at his face when he introduced her made it clear to me that he was motivated more by schoolboy ardor than progressive political strategy."

"But what else motivates a man except money and sex, Your Majesty?" asked Merivale. "They are simple creatures with simple wants."

"Nonsense, Merivale," said Pysetcha. "They can be motivated by loyalty, honor, and a sense of righteousness, just as easily as a woman."

"That has not been my experience, Your Majesty," said Merivale cheerfully. "But of course, I defer to your wisdom in this, as in all things."

"Oh?" A dangerous edge came into the empress's voice. "And is that why you chose to ignore my wishes concerning the safety of my son, and brought him here?"

"An event has transpired, Your Majesty, which I believe necessitated it."

"Such as?"

"The Shadow Demon has revealed himself."

"And?" Pysetcha looked at her intently.

"It is as we feared, Your Majesty."

A look of genuine sorrow broke through the empress's calm exterior. "I am sorry to hear that."

Throughout this exchange, the prince had been looking back and forth between the two women with a bafflement that slowly transformed into exasperation. "Will one of you please tell me what's going on?"

Merivale raised an eyebrow questioningly at Pysetcha. The empress returned her gaze for a moment, then looked at her son.

"I have kept things from you for your protection. But now it seems we are reaching the stage where your ignorance could prove more dangerous than the truth."

"What dangerous information could you possibly know all the way out here, this far from the palace?" asked Leston.

"People assumed I left the palace because I couldn't take the stress of politics. I let them think that because it was advantageous to do so. The real reason I came out here was to work away from the watchful eyes of the biomancers."

"You're afraid of biomancers?" Leston looked genuinely puzzled. "I mean, they're creepy, yes. Especially that Chiffet Mek. And I've learned from Lord Pastinas that they have done unspeakable things. But ultimately, they still *serve* us."

The empress shook her head. "They serve the *emperor*, and him alone, for better or worse. Long ago, when he fell in love with me, he commanded them to make him younger so he could father a son with me. They knew what it would do to him. What he would eventually become if they meddled with his lifespan in such a way. But biomancers rely upon the emperor for their moral compass, having long ago abandoned their own during the course of their dark studies. So they did not question the commands of the emperor, even at the detriment to his own health and the health of the empire. Now the emperor is a lost and feeble thing, and without his guidance, the biomancers are more bold and reckless—more paranoid and power hungry—than they have been since the time of the Dark Mage."

"I hadn't realized it was that bad," admitted

Leston. "But what does any of this have to do with Rixidenteron?"

"Lady Hempist, if you would kindly fill him in while I finish this paperwork. I'm afraid it can't wait." She then took the stack of paper from her drawer and began to work on it once again.

"We still don't have all the facts yet, Your Highness," Merivale told the prince. "But what we *do* know is that the Council of Biomancery were the ones who set Rixidenteron as the legitimate heir to the Pastinas estates. Then his grandfather died under suspicious circumstances. That made me take notice. Since Rixidenteron's arrival at the palace, he has met with several of the council members on a regular basis. After watching him then work his way into your confidences, I began to suspect a plot against you. That is when I involved myself directly."

"So your whole pursuit of marriage was a ruse?" asked Leston.

"Flirting with Lord Pastinas has been one of the more enjoyable tasks I've been assigned in recent years, and should a more intimate relationship have been feasible, I wouldn't have any compunctions about it. But you are correct in saying that I had no intention of actually marrying him."

"But... you thought the biomancers might want him to kill me? That seems like a bit of a leap."

"Well, I first assigned Hume to watch him, and—"

"Wait, Hume works for you?"

"For Her Majesty." Merivale nodded to the empress, who continued to work intently on her stack of paper.

The prince shook his head, as if to clear it of something, then turned back to Merivale. "Go on."

"Thank you, Your Highness. Hume reported that Lord Pastinas was sometimes missing from his bed at night, and would return just after dawn, looking dazed and exhausted before falling back to sleep. As I began tracking these events, I noticed they coincided with a string of brutal murders that had begun plaguing the city. The so-called Shadow Demon murders. All the victims were commoners. Artisans, farmers, barkeeps. The only common link between them was that they were all members of an organization I had been working with called the Godly Naturalists."

"An organization of commoners?" asked Leston. "Like a guild?"

"More like a political movement," said Merivale. "They believed the biomancers were perverting the natural world too much and that Emperor Martarkis was too old and weak to stop them. The aim of the Godly Naturalists was to replace the existing emperor with someone they deemed had the moral fortitude to put the biomancers back in their place."

"You aligned yourself with traitors to the imperial throne?" asked Leston.

"I suppose." Merivale shrugged. "Although they were not traitors in the strictest sense because the person they deemed most worthy is you. In their minds, your father's reign has been unnaturally extended by the biomancers and it is time for you to take the throne."

"So they wanted my father to abdicate?"

"Don't be naive, my son," said Pysetcha, putting her papers away. "The biomancers would never allow such a thing. They have grown fond of their power and freedom to pursue their experiments in any way they see fit. They will maintain the current status quo for as long as they can."

"And how long is that?" asked Leston. "How long can they keep my father alive?"

Merivale gazed steadily into his eyes. "We have no idea, Your Highness."

"So..." Leston looked from Merivale to his mother, then back to Merivale. "These people, these Godly Naturalists, want to assassinate my father so that I can take the throne."

"It *is* the most expedient option, Your Highness," said Merivale.

Leston's forehead furrowed, as if he was in pain. "Then, to protect my father, Rixidenteron was sneaking out at night and killing them?"

"That's what I thought at first," said Merivale. "But as usual with biomancers, the truth was far more complicated. You see, the more I got to know Lord Pastinas, the more I began to suspect that he was acting under duress. I wondered if perhaps they had some leverage over him. And I *do* think that's true. But now I think it's even more complicated than that. Because either Lord Pastinas is better at playing the fool than anyone I've ever met, or he isn't actually aware of his own nocturnal activities."

"You think the biomancers are controlling him somehow while he sleeps?"

"It's only a theory," said Merivale. "One I began to consider after Nea confided in me the details of their encounter with the biomancer assassins at the Call to Arms Inn, and in particular the conversation between Lord Pastinas and a man named Brackson. During this exchange, Brackson admitted to working with the biomancers and intimated that they had even more control over Rixidenteron than he knew. This Brackson then blew on a whistle that Nea claimed she could not hear but that brought Rixidenteron to his knees. That final detail, at least, has now been verified, since it was how I subdued Rixidenteron and saved the ambassador's life."

Leston was rubbing his temples now. "So your friendship with Nea is also a ruse?"

Merivale sighed and gave him a patient smile.

"Your Highness, hopefully it has not escaped your attention by now that I am chief spy in service to Her Imperial Majesty—a position not without some prestige, I might add. I don't have the luxury for things like friends or lovers, which are so frequently used as leverage against people. The woman you have known as Lady Merivale Hempist is no more than a facade. A performance, if you like, which allows me to work unfettered within the palace."

"So you're not actually Lady Hempist?"

"Oh, I am," she said. "But the *real* Lady Hempist is not some doe-eyed, marriage-hungry schemer. This is the real me."

"And you should be thankful for it," said Pysetcha. "Lady Hempist has saved your life and mine several times over already in her brief tenure as chief imperial spy."

By then, Leston was starting to look like a lost little boy. "You, my mother, my best friend. None of you are who I thought you were."

"I'd wager that Nea has not been entirely truthful either."

Merivale liked to play rough. Now and then she forgot how fragile some people were. But this was not one of those times. When she suggested that Nea might be deceiving the prince, it was a calculated move that would tell a lot about the prince's state of mind. Disbelief would indicate he did not trust her. Anger would indicate that he believed her but was so smitten that he was unwilling to accept what she said. She knew that immediate acceptance, the most desirable outcome, was unlikely. But she was pleased that the second most desirable outcome came to pass: pitiful acquiescence.

Prince Leston began to cry.

"I fear I may have broken him, Your Majesty," she said, not without some small tone of contriteness.

"It seems you were right. He's not mature enough to handle the hard truths."

That brought him up short. He glared first at Merivale, then at Pysetcha, biting his lip until the tears stopped.

"Well, my son?" asked the empress. "Will you wallow in self-pity? Or will you do whatever you can to help your friend?"

"Help him?" asked Leston. "How?"

"We question him," said Merivale. "If, through his responses, I am able to determine that he truly is a victim of the biomancers, then we will try to break their hold over him."

"What if we can't break their hold?"

"Then obviously we'll have to kill him," Merivale said flatly.

It had the desired effect. The prince blanched. "It won't come to that. We *will* free him."

"Then I suggest we get started, Your Highness," she said crisply. "Hume should have him chained up, so when he comes to, if he's still *our* Rixidenteron, he will be quite confused and upset."

"Yes, of course." Leston turned to go, then stopped and turned back. He bowed to the empress. "Your Majesty."

"Good luck, my son," said Pysetcha. "I do hope your friend can be saved. And I promise we will talk more soon."

Once Leston had left, the empress turned to Merivale. "You never disappoint me, Lady Hempist."

Merivale curtsied. "It is satisfying to serve someone who appreciates my talents."

"I feel that was about all he could handle right now," said the empress.

"Yes, I suspect it will be a little while before we can tell him the rest," agreed Merivale.

———

The painful rays of sunlight wormed their way past Red's eyelids and jolted him awake. He winced and tried to move out of the light. That's when he realized he was chained up to something.

"Piss'ell!"

The wind on his face suggested he was outside. He felt wooden planks beneath him. The smell of the sea suggested he was near the water. Had he been captured in his sleep and taken somewhere? That seemed unlikely. Light sleeping was a survival trait in Paradise Circle. A year of palace life couldn't have made him *that* soft. Could it?

He forced himself to open his eyes against the glare. It was painful, but he was able to make out five shapes looming over him.

"What's going on?" he demanded.

"Look, Rixidenteron." It was Leston's voice. He sounded deeply concerned about something. "I know this is a little—"

Then Merivale's voice cut in, sharp as a blade. "You're working with the biomancers."

He should have known she'd work it out. In a way, it was almost a relief. "I didn't have a choice. Honestly. They promised they wouldn't go after Hope if I let them train me to be some weapon for them. So I've been putting up with it. Biding my time until I can figure out a way to turn the tables on them."

"I can't believe it..." Leston sounded horrified.

"Look, I know it's a piss situation, and I'm sorry I couldn't tell you. But it's not like I've actually hurt anyone."

"You nearly killed Nea!" the prince burst out.

Red felt an icy twist up his spine. "What are you talking about? I would *never* hurt Nea."

"Last night, you snuck into my room," said Nea. Red couldn't quite make out her expression in the glare of the sun, but her voice sounded strained. Like she was afraid of him. "You were holding these... blades in your hands and there was no humanity in your eyes. If Lady Hempist had not been there..."

Red shook his head. "No, that can't be how it is." But there was no strength in his voice. Flickers of memory began to surface, like dimly recalled nightmares.

"I'm sorry, Rixidenteron." This time, Merivale's voice was a little more gentle. But not much. "*You* are the Shadow Demon."

"What?" He felt sick.

"You are the one who murdered all those innocent people."

"No. Oh, God..."

Red liked to think he didn't believe in God. But deep down, he did. Sometimes the only way his life made sense was if there was some cruel, capricious power lording over it. He thought back to what Ammon Set had said to him when he first arrived at the palace. That by the time they were finished with him, he wouldn't even be a man anymore.

"How is that... even possible?"

"I'll need to gather more information before I know for certain," said Merivale. "But I suspect that they can give you a target while you're conscious. Perhaps there is a key phrase they use as a trigger. Then, when you go to sleep that night, the Shadow Demon takes over."

Red had been so sure of himself. So confident he would find a way to slip out of the biomancers' grasp just like he'd slipped out of trouble his whole life. Even when he'd found out about the whistle thing, it had seemed like just another obstacle. A puzzle to figure out for his escape. Now he understood

that they had been laughing at him this whole time.
There was no escape, because they had already made
him a twisted, unnatural thing. They had made him
one of them.

"You should just...kill me," he said.

"Come now, Lord Pastinas." Merivale's voice had
just a hint of its old playfulness. "I'm quite clever,
you know. With your cooperation, I may be able to
find a slightly more agreeable solution."

———

Everyone was quiet that day, since they'd been awake
half the night—except Etcher, who had apparently
slept through the entire ordeal and decided to go
look for local wildlife around Sunset Point. Merivale was tempted to go with him. There was still a
lot of information to gather regarding Nea and the
intentions of Aukbontar. Etcher seemed like an easy
mark. But she had gotten no sleep the night before
and did not intend to sleep the coming night either.
So she let the opportunity pass this time, and instead
took a much-needed nap.

As darkness fell and people began to prepare
for an early sleep, Merivale placed guards at both
entrances to Nea's room. She put Etcher in her bed
next to the ambassador. Propriety would have to lan-
guish tonight, because she wanted an audience with
the Shadow Demon.

Rixidenteron had been subdued all day, hardly
speaking at all. No doubt the shock of learning you
were a puppet of the Council of Biomancery was not
something you got over easily. He glanced uneasily
over at Merivale when he thought she wasn't looking. She was always looking, of course. She had
honed her peripheral vision to the physical limit, so
unless the person was directly behind her, she could

not only see their general shape, but get at least some idea of facial expression. It was a skill that had saved her life on more than one occasion.

Finally, it was time for bed, and a strange dread hung in the room between them. Merivale sat on top of her bed, smoothed her skirts, and waited.

He eyed her as he slid under his covers. "You're going to watch me all night?"

"Yes," she said. "I'm curious to see if the Shadow Demon emerges again, since he was unable to fulfill his mission last night."

They were silent for a moment.

"You knew the whole time, didn't you?" he asked.

"I *suspected*."

"So your whole idea about flushing out the assassin and forcing them to testify against the biomancers was just a con?"

She gave him a reproachful look. "Did you honestly think that's all it would take to dislodge the biomancers from power after decades of wrapping their tentacles around the throne? Charging them with murdering some common folk and a foreigner?"

He sighed. "I guess it was a bit bludgeon to think so. So why the con, then?"

"To see how you reacted. Because while I was fairly certain that you were the Shadow Demon, I needed to verify whether you knew it or not. Were you an enemy or a victim?"

"And now?"

"At this point, I strongly suspect you to be a victim of biomancery. But I am not yet certain. Meeting with the Shadow Demon will likely convince me one way or the other."

"What'll you do if he comes back?"

She held up the silver whistle.

He gave her a wry smile. "You cut my pocket and

palmed that in the carriage yesterday. When you were pretending to get leaky."

"*Leaky* means sexually attracted, doesn't it?"

"You learned that from Thoriston's book, I reckon."

"I did. And I assure you, my feelings of attraction were no pretext. Especially compared to my usual targets."

"Meaning you mostly manipulate nasty old wrinks?" he asked.

She nodded. "If it's any consolation, not only was it pleasant to flirt with you, I also had to actually utilize my intellect in order to manipulate you. Normally all it takes is a few clever quips and a flash of cleavage."

"I'm not surprised. Both the quips and cleavage are sunny."

"Under different circumstances, perhaps I would have invited you to explore the sunniness of my cleavage further," she said. "But I'm afraid you and I have other business tonight."

"You are a remarkable woman, Lady Hempist." A hint of the old flirty rogue crept in, but it was so labored that it was more pitiful than charming.

"I'm pleased you recognize that fact, Lord Pastinas. Now, if you would be so kind as to fall asleep, we can begin."

Rixidenteron nodded, extinguished the small lamp beside his bed, and laid his head down on the pillow.

There were a few minutes of silence. Then he sat up again. "It's a bit hard to relax with you watching me like this."

"Would you like me to sing you to sleep?" she asked.

"Really?" She couldn't see his expression in this dim lighting, but he sounded surprised.

"Really," she said.

"Sure, it might help."

"Very well. Lie back down and close your eyes."

Once he had done so, she began in a gentle, lilting voice:

> *There was a girl of Lesser Basheta,*
> *Whose beauty shone just like the sun.*
> *She loved a boy from Greater Basheta*
> *Who vowed to be her only one.*
>
> *But then one day the storm came rolling in,*
> *And her sweet boy was called to war.*
> *She made a vow to wait for him,*
> *And kept her vigil by the shore.*
>
> *The darkness spread to all the lands,*
> *And death grew mighty on the sea.*
> *The blood soaked in the very sands*
> *That girl did stand on patiently.*
>
> *At last her love came home to her,*
> *Now a man, and not a boy.*
> *He kissed her hand and married her.*
> *She thought the dark had turned to joy.*
>
> *But war had made him hard and cruel.*
> *Her life had no more happy days.*
> *So heed this well, you pretty fool:*
> *The darkness never goes away.*

It was a song Merivale's chambermaid sang to her as a girl, and she had always been mindful of its lesson. Even now, as she sat and watched the sleeping form of a man who might be the closest thing to an equal she would ever find, she felt the warmth of desire kindled within herself. Rather than succumb to it or tamp it down, she examined it carefully, as one might a specimen of poisonous insect, noting the beautiful coloring and elegant designs, while being careful not to let it sting.

The melody continued to play in her head as she watched over Rixidenteron. Then, a little after midnight, he began to stir. She pinched herself hard to chase off the drowsiness that had begun to creep in, and watched him carefully.

He sat up abruptly. His eyes snapped to her, and even in the dim lighting, she could see he recognized her from the night before.

"You...," hissed the Shadow Demon.

She blew the whistle and his eyes rolled back into his head. But this time she stopped before he passed out. While he was still stunned, she grabbed the chains she'd hidden beneath her bed and secured him to his bed frame. Then she moved back to her own bed and waited.

Once he regained his senses, he strained against the chain, grunting wordlessly. After a few minutes, he gave up. She watched him, fascinated. Everything about the man was different. His movements. The harsh scrape of his grunts. He even looked different, as if his facial muscles were contorted into a different shape.

"So," she said at last. "You came back."

"Of course," he said in a voice like sandpaper. "I have been given permission to kill a person. I will continue to return until I have done so."

"Who gave you this permission?"

"The ones who made me. Their names are unimportant."

"What *is* important?"

"Death is the only thing of true importance. It is the only thing that lasts."

"Are you permitted to kill anyone other than the ambassador?"

"Anyone who directly interferes with this goal."

"Such as me."

He looked at her then, and there was no hunger, or anger, or malice in his eyes. In fact, there was nothing at all. It was like staring into a red-rimmed void.

"Yes," he said. "I will kill you."

She blew the whistle until his eyes rolled back in his head and he passed out. She watched as his face shifted back into the familiar countenance of Lord Pastinas.

She regarded the whistle thoughtfully. If only all men came with one, she might have considered marriage ages ago.

PART THREE

I never intended to do harm. Even in my darkest hour, I thought that what I was doing was for the greater good. But that is the problem with darkness. It makes things so difficult to see.

—from the secret writings of
the Dark Mage

23

The best thing Brice Vaderton could call the *Kraken Hunter* was "controlled chaos." But if anything, he was surprised it wasn't worse. Fifty grateful refugees from the Empty Cliffs, none of them well behaved, all packed into a two-masted brig meant for a crew of twenty.

"I suppose this makes it a proper pirate vessel," he said to Captain Bane as they surveyed the milling, unwashed crowd on her decks.

She nodded. "My first encounter with true pirates was a tiny, one-masted sloop, suitable for a crew of perhaps eight, and there were at least thirty men on it. Their tactic was to get in close as quickly as possible and overwhelm the prize with sheer numbers."

"Not a bad strategy," he said. "But such an over-burdened ship leaves idle hands. And those tend to make mischief."

"Our crew won't be idle, Mr. Vaderton," said Bane.

"Oh? I thought you said we might be anchored here a little while longer. Don't you have people in Paradise Circle gathering ships and crew?"

"Yes," said Bane. "That should give you ample time to get the landlubbers among this crew seaworthy."

"Me?" asked Vaderton.

"Until such time as a commission worthy of your talents presents itself, I name you bosun of the *Kraken Hunter*."

Vaderton gave her a long look, just to be certain she knew what she was asking of him. He thought he detected a slight smile tugging at the corners of her mouth and decided she did.

"Aye, Captain," he said finally.

Her grin came all the way out. "Idle hands are to be avoided, Mr. Vaderton. Including yours."

He smiled ruefully. "I did just say as much, didn't I?"

Captain Bane generally carried herself with a quiet confidence and a calm presence, but a roguish sense of humor would occasionally bubble up at surprising moments. The old Vaderton would have found that in poor taste for a captain. But now he found he was inordinately pleased with himself that he was able to elicit such a response from her. It was, he realized, comforting to see that the person in charge was only a person after all.

So Vaderton began his first commission under Captain Dire Bane with the intent of keeping his own humanity to the fore. Old habits died harder than he expected, however, and many of the people from the Empty Cliffs were woefully inexperienced with both sailing and the sea. Most couldn't even tie a square knot, and the very idea of going aloft terrified them. By the end of the first day, he was barking scathing orders as bad as any naval bosun and wondering if perhaps he might find a lash stored somewhere on board.

Thankfully, he now had friends to keep him in check. Both Kismet Pete and Biscuit Bill were seasoned sailors, and knew him well enough to offer a calming pat on the back when he needed it. Bane's helmsman, an older, one-eyed Paradise Circle man named Missing Finn, was also a stolid, stabilizing presence. And Jilly (it took some effort not to call her Jillen) was there to goad the more cowardly crew members as she scrambled fearlessly among the shrouds and yards. But when the frustration and anger took their toll and he began to truly despair, it was Yammy who brought him back.

Vaderton didn't have his own cabin anymore, of course. He bunked with the rest of the crew. So when he felt like strangling them, he went to one of the few places he knew most of them wouldn't venture: aloft.

"Drown it all, they're hopeless," he growled into his cup of grog one night as he and Yammy sat on the small platform by the foresail yard. It was only the first level up from the deck, but even that was enough to dissuade many of the new crew.

"Then hope is what you must give them," said Yammy. "Just as I gave it to you."

"I refuse to coddle them or lie to them about their abilities," he said.

"You don't need to. These people know they aren't very good. You've made that clear enough." She gave him a hard look and he shrank back slightly. Yammy had never shown true anger, but Vaderton could tell it would be a fearsome thing. "Show them that *you* are a good enough seaman to turn them into good seamen as well. What's more, assure them that you won't simply give up on them."

"Abandon my commission? Not as long as I still draw breath."

"But they don't know that," she said. "These people have been given up on so many times, it's what they expect."

Vaderton considered this as he took another swallow of grog. "That is a poor way to live."

"Then show them a better way."

—

When Hope first assigned Vaderton to train the new crew, she kept a careful eye on him. Even if he was honorable and brave, she worried that his naval background had made him too rigid and narrow-minded.

Her fears were not unfounded. His temper would grow short with anyone who lacked his obsessive attention to detail. But Old Yammy always happened to be nearby. When she saw him start yelling at a hapless crew member who struggled to understand the intricacies of a particular knot, Yammy walked past and whispered something in Vaderton's ear. He stopped a moment, took a breath, and resumed instruction with markedly more patience. After a week of these gentle corrections, his attitude gradually softened to the point where, while he was certainly not lax in his instruction, he at least wasn't cursing at them when they made a mistake.

Hope and Yammy stood on the quarterdeck and watched him explain the finer points of the rigging to a small group of new sailors on the main deck.

"Your effect on him has been remarkable," said Hope.

Old Yammy smiled. "I give him a nudge now and then, but he's been doing all the work. A person is capable of astonishing transformation when something precious is taken from them. Some grow bitter from the loss. But some allow the suffering to instruct them. To help them grow."

Hope's hand strayed automatically to her forearm. Her fingers touched the cold metal of the clamp.

Yammy nodded to her prosthesis. "You know that better than most."

"I suppose I've made that choice a few times now."

They watched Vaderton work with the new recruits for a little while in silence.

"Did you know what would happen to Red?" Hope asked. "That he would be captured by the biomancers?"

Old Yammy shook her head. "It's rarely as clear or specific as that when I look so far ahead. The last time I saw him, I had a sense that he would make a choice which would prevent me from seeing him for a long time."

"What do you see when you look at me?" asked Hope.

She smiled. "I see a determined young woman who is beginning to awaken to her full potential."

"Potential for what?"

"I'm not sure," admitted Yammy. "But I'm very much looking forward to finding out."

"Well now." Sadie strolled up to them, a gleam in her eye. "Looks like I got me some competition for the ship's wisewoman."

"Don't worry, you old goat," Yammy said fondly. "I'll be on my way soon enough."

"Oh?" Sadie narrowed her eyes.

"Don't let her push you out," Hope told Yammy. "You're welcome to sail with us as long as you like."

"A person might even think she'd feel *obliged* to help out," said Sadie. "What with us rescuing her and all."

"I did give you a reformed naval captain and enough crew to sail a ship for him," pointed out Yammy. "And I have...other ideas that will help with the coming struggle. Perhaps things you haven't considered yet."

"I hate when she gets all mystical like this, Captain," said Sadie. "Permission to throw her overboard."

Hope failed to keep her smile at bay. "Permission denied."

Sadie sighed. "Guess I'll just have to drive her off,

then." She leered at Yammy. "So, you bent the cock of that navy tom of yours yet?"

Old Yammy rolled her eyes. "No, Sadie."

"Why not? Couldn't have been much else to do up there on them Empty Cliffs. And I seen him walking around in them tight naval breeches of his. Not bad on the gander at all. Wouldn't be because you've gotten too *old* for such things, would it?"

Old Yammy gave her a level gaze. "If you're going to insist on this topic right now, I think I'll find other company."

"You don't need to do that," Hope said quickly.

"Sadie's mentorship is more what you need right now, anyway," said Yammy. "Our time will come."

Hope and Sadie watched Old Yammy head across the deck toward the bow.

"Heh," Sadie said quietly. "I won that round."

"It's not a competition," said Hope.

"It surely is, my girl. And has been for a very long time."

———

Brigga Lin stood as far from everyone else as possible, up at the very front of the ship, practically leaning on the bowsprit. She wasn't used to so many people around. Especially when she wasn't killing them. The air was saturated with their pheromones and other scents. It was like she could *taste* their emotions in the air. Some were tangy or bitter; some were spicy, some sweet. All of it was more than she wanted.

"Don't worry." Old Yammy walked over to her. "You'll acclimate."

"What do you mean?" Hope might trust this woman, but Brigga Lin hadn't quite made up her mind yet.

"All the stimuli." Yammy waved her hands around. "All the people. They can become exhausting if you let them."

"How would you know?"

"Because it bothers me as well."

"Are you saying we're alike?" asked Brigga Lin carefully.

Old Yammy shook her head. "Alike? Not really. I don't think there's been anyone like you for quite some time. But we have qualities that overlap."

"Such as?"

"You sense the edges of perception that I am completely suffused in."

Brigga Lin's eyes widened. "You're telling me there's *more*?"

Yammy nodded. "I can't affect it directly like you, however. *That* is your biomancer training. I need to resort to what people call blood magic, or else herbs and medicines. Neither are as impactful as what you do."

"But still," said Brigga Lin. "What is it you can perceive?"

"It's difficult to explain, exactly. I feel the connectedness of all things, as you are beginning to do. A bit more strongly, but I've had more practice at it. I also feel this connectedness not just as it is now, but as it was, and as it might be."

"The past and future?" asked Brigga Lin, stepping closer. "You can divine what is to come?"

"To some degree."

"Could..." Brigga Lin swallowed, her mouth suddenly dry as she contemplated the potential. "Could you instruct me to do it as well?"

Yammy's eyes narrowed. "Once you open the doors of perception that widely, you will never be able to close them again. You would be reaching into the unknown with no guarantee of what the end result would be. It might very well be something counter to your current goals."

"I have always reached boldly into the darkness," said Brigga Lin. "I see no reason to stop now." She curtsied low to Old Yammy. "Please train me as your pupil."

Old Yammy smiled broadly, her eyes suddenly glittering with eagerness. "I've been waiting for you to ask that since I came on board this ship."

———

Vaderton, Finn, and Hope continued to train and drill the crew in seamanship as much as they could without going on a voyage or engaging in a real battle. That included drilling them on loading and aiming the cannons, without actually firing them.

"I really don't see why this is necessary," Alash said to Hope with a certain amount of sullenness as the two of them watched the crew perform the actions over and over again at Vaderton's command.

"Because soon Nettles will be contacting us to say she's convinced whoever is running Paradise Circle to give us a few ships. And those ships won't have your firing system in place. You'll still man these cannons during the assault, but we need to get the crews for the other ships ready."

"I suppose," Alash said grudgingly.

Later that day, she stood with Vaderton and Finn and watched the crew raise and strike the fore and main sails again and again.

"Starting to look a bit smart," said Finn.

"They're better than they were," said Hope, "but I wish we could test them under more realistic conditions."

"They'll get those soon enough," said Vaderton.

"This time of year, the course between here and Dawn's Light is rife with storms. Might as well build their confidence a little now while we can."

"Aye," said Finn. "Before the sea knocks it right out of them."

The two men grinned at each other.

Hope shook her head. "Couple of salty old wrinks."

"Old?" Vaderton winced. His hand strayed to his hairline, which Hope guessed was a little further back than it used to be.

"Don't worry, my wag." Finn patted Vaderton on the shoulder. "Old Yammy's still got many years on you."

"She can't really be *that* old," Vaderton said firmly. Then he looked at them uncertainly. "Can she?"

"You've seen what the biomancers are able to do," said Hope. "Do you think she's any less capable?"

"Well, no. But..." Vaderton glanced around, as if worried Yammy might overhear. It wasn't a completely unfounded concern, Hope thought. Wherever Vaderton was, she was usually lurking nearby. Although that had become less frequent, now that she seemed to have taken Brigga Lin under her wing.

"To give you some idea," said Finn. "Sadie told me she looks exactly the same as when they first met over twenty years ago. Not even one extra gray hair." He grinned at Hope. "Maybe that's why Brigga Lin has been spending so much time with her lately. To learn the secrets of ageless beauty."

"I think it's a little more than that," said Hope.

Finn's smile faded. "You think she's learning how to use the Sight?"

"Perhaps."

"Begging your pardon, and I know you two are wags, but do you think a molly with that kind of... *temper* is someone we want seeing the future?"

Hope laughed. "Perhaps it will give her a broader, more gentle perspective."

"Or maybe she'll go as mad as the Dark Mage," said Vaderton.

Hope shot him a hard look. "That's not a joking matter."

Vaderton didn't flinch from her gaze. "With all due respect, Captain, I wasn't joking."

———

Days went by and the crew started to get restless. Hope calculated it had been nearly a month since they'd last been to Dawn's Light. That meant the monthly shipment of innocent girls would soon arrive for the slaughter. But there was still no word from Nettles and Filler. Hope decided if they didn't hear back within a few more days, she would have to go check on them. What would they do if Nettles had failed to get them ships?

But the next evening, Jilly gave a shout from her perch on the foreroyal yard. A lantern had been lit in the old temple bell tower in Paradise Circle. Hope and Nettles had chosen that as the signal, partly because it was the highest point in downtown New Laven, and also because it was the place where Hope, Nettles, and Filler fought side by side for the first time. As soon as Hope saw the tiny flickering light at the top of the bell tower through her glass, an eagerness welled up inside to see her friends again.

She turned to Vaderton with a tight grin. "Mr. Vaderton, if you please, I would like to see us docked at Paradise Circle well before the sun rises."

"Aye, Captain." Vaderton stepped smartly to the main deck and bellowed, "Listen up, you babies of the sea! This is not a drill! All hands, make ready to sail!"

Hope turned to Finn, who already held the wheel and looked at her expectantly. "Mr. Finn. I believe you know the way."

"That I do, Captain." Finn gave the wheel a spin toward starboard.

They had a light, favorable wind and made good time as they rounded the south coast of New Laven. They reached the docks shortly after midnight. As soon as they were secured, Hope leapt to the gunwale and scanned the decks for Nettles and Filler. She didn't see them, which made sense. It was late, after all. They would probably come by after sunup.

But then she saw Handsome Henny sitting in the driver's seat of a small black carriage. She wondered if things had gone badly and the two were hiding out in the carriage.

Henny waved up to her. "Ahoy! Captain Bane, is it now?"

"It is," Hope called back.

"However we call you, welcome back to Paradise Circle."

"Thanks, Henny." Hope paused for a moment, deciding the best way to ask in public like this. "Where are *they*?"

"Apple Grove Manor. I'm to take you there." There was a strange tone to Henny's voice as he said it. Like that wasn't all there was to say about it. Maybe he would say more once they were in the carriage.

"I see." Hope still couldn't tell if she should expect trouble or not. The safest bet would be to assume that things had gone wrong somehow. "How many can I take with me in the carriage?"

He shrugged. "I reckon you could fit three or four in there, including yourself."

"We'll be down in a few minutes." Hope dropped back to the deck.

"A'course I'll be going with you," said Sadie. "I

missed this festering cunt of a neighborhood more than I expected. It'll be nice to see it again, if only to remind myself why I left. And besides, my good name might help recruit more wags."

Hope nodded. "Thank you."

"Can I come, too, teacher?" Jilly shinnied down the ratlines and landed next to her. "I ain't seen the Circle in five whole years."

"What would Brigga Lin say about your choice of words?" asked Hope.

"I *haven't* seen it," Jilly said quickly.

"I suppose you can come," said Hope. "And I think I'll ask Brigga Lin to come along as well."

"You think there's trouble?" Jilly's hand went eagerly to her knife.

"A warrior doesn't seek trouble," said Hope.

Jilly bowed her head. "Yes, teacher."

"Don't worry, Little Bee." Sadie ruffled the girl's hair, which had grown out somewhat from her boyish naval cut to a ragged mop. "You stick with us, you won't ever have to go seeking trouble. It always seems to find us. Ain't that right, Captain?"

"Bold choices have a tendency to bring conflict," Hope said.

"Ah, is *that* the reason?" Sadie nodded with mock gravity.

Hope smiled. "Wait here, I'll go find Brigga Lin."

She moved quickly below deck and found the hairless crew member named Kismet Pete standing outside the officers' quarters.

"Begging your pardon, Captain," he said as soon as he saw her. "Old Yammy wanted me to tell you that she's sorry, but that she and Brigga Lin are in the middle of something that shouldn't be interrupted." He glanced back at the door nervously, then said more quietly, "I think they're doing some kind of *magic*, Captain."

"She knew I'd be coming, then?" asked Hope.

"Seemed that way, sir."

Hope decided there were no such things as coincidences where Old Yammy was concerned. Apparently, this was something she wanted Hope to do without either of them.

Hope returned to Sadie and Jilly on deck. "Alright, let's go."

"No Brigga Lin?"

Hope shook her head. "Mr. Finn, you have command of the ship."

"Aye, Captain," he called back from the helm.

"Mr. Vaderton."

"Yes, Captain?"

"I want us ready to sail at a moment's notice. Just in case."

"Aye, sir."

Hope set her hat on her head and walked briskly down the gangplank to the dock, the tails of her captain's coat swirling around her legs. Sadie and Jilly followed quickly behind.

As Hope neared the carriage, she noted with some surprise that it was very nice. Black lacquered wood with silver trim. When she opened the door, she found that the seats were padded with soft leather. Hope wondered if Nettles and Filler had stolen the carriage. Or maybe they'd borrowed it from the current ganglord. That would suggest that things did go well after all. So why did they send Henny to get her, rather than meet her themselves?

Hope and Sadie settled into their seats. Jilly started to climb in after them, but Hope stopped her.

"You're not riding."

"Why not?" asked Jilly.

"You remember where Apple Grove Manor is?"

"I suppose..."

"Good. You're going by rooftop. Let's see you

apply those climbing skills of yours in a different setting."

Sadie chuckled but said nothing.

Jilly looked like she wanted to protest, but Hope gazed down at her until she bowed her head. "Yes, teacher."

"And hurry. Don't make us wait for you."

Jilly winced. "Yes, teacher." She dropped back down to the wooden planks of the dock, hurried toward the nearest building, and immediately scrambled up the side.

"We're ready, Henny," Hope called to the front.

Henny cracked the whip at the horses without responding and the carriage began to move through the grimy, narrow streets of Paradise Circle.

Hope and Sadie exchanged a glance, wondering at their cool reception.

———

Paradise Circle hadn't changed at all, and yet it felt completely different from the first time Hope had arrived here. She had looked with such a hard, judgmental eye on these streets before. As if she'd somehow been privy to a "right" way of doing things and the people who lived here had been doing it "wrong." It was a strange idea to her now. She supposed she'd been trained to that lofty arrogance by the Vinchen. An idea that the world was merely a binary of right and wrong, good and bad. That idea had begun to erode during her two years at sea with Carmichael, but it was here on these streets that she'd really begun to understand that the world was not so simple.

"It's good to be back," she said.

Sadie turned from the window, and Hope was surprised to see tears in the old woman's eyes. "That it is, my girl."

They sat in silence except for the rattle of the carriage wheels as they watched the buildings roll past.

"What do you think it's all about?" Sadie nodded her head to indicate the carriage and Henny.

Hope wasn't sure how much Henny could hear, or if it mattered. "I don't know. But I'm glad Jilly's on that training exercise. Just in case." If this was some sort of trap, she'd be outside of it, and able to report back to Finn what happened.

"Oh." Sadie smiled, understanding. "You get more clever all the time."

Hope shrugged. "Good teachers."

———

The carriage passed the Rag and Boards, a dingy chaotic theater that showed more burlesque acts than plays. It was at that theater Red had incited the beginning of what would eventually be a full-scale riot. She and Nettles had been onstage with him, and Filler backstage working the flies.

Before that "performance" at the Rag and Boards, they had made their plans in the strange submerged basement of Apple Grove Manor. As the manor came into view, Hope noticed the outside had changed considerably. All the balconies and windowsills had been given a fresh coat of paint. Curtains had been repaired or replaced. The muddy weed patches had been cleaned out and flowers planted in their place. It was nearly morning, and the predawn light made everything seem strange and luminous.

"I ain't seen the place look this nice since Jix the Lift lived here," said Sadie.

The carriage stopped in front of the manor. Henny came around and opened the door for them.

"The Black Rose said to see her as soon as you got here. Didn't matter what time," he told them.

"The Black Rose?" asked Hope. "Is that the new ganglord of the Circle?"

"It is." Again it seemed that Henny was holding something back. "You best go in."

Hope and Sadie exchanged another uneasy look, then turned toward the manor.

"I'm here! I made it!" Jilly came staggering over.

Hope had wanted to get in before Jilly arrived rather than bring her into this potentially deadly situation. But when she looked at the girl, she couldn't help but smile a little. Jilly was panting, her face red and sweaty. She had cuts and scrapes all down her arms and legs, and her feet, once again bare, were a bloody mess. But there was a crazy grin on her face. "I did it!"

"Well done," said Hope. Then she turned back to the manor entrance. "Now, let's find out who this Black Rose is, and what she's done with our friends."

Henny led them into the foyer and down a dim, candlelit hallway. Hope had only seen the basement before and she was struck by the stately grace of the old building. Intricately carved baseboards and doors. Murals of ocean life on the ceiling. She found the preoccupation with seals a bit unnerving, but she remembered that before she'd been attacked by a pack of them, she'd found them somewhat fascinating as well.

At the end of the hallway was a large, ornate door. Henny opened it and gestured for them to enter the sizable parlor room beyond. At one time it had probably been a place to host parties, but now it was dark and mostly bare. The only light was cast from the roaring fireplace in the back wall. In front of the fire was a high-backed chair facing them like a throne. The chair was flanked on one side by a woman in a ragged cloak and long, matted hair, and on the other side by a tall, thin man in a neat black suit and top hat. The person who sat in the chair was someone Hope recognized immediately and yet suddenly wasn't sure she knew.

"Nettles?"

"It's the Black Rose now." Nettles's voice was distant. "You took a new name, thought I might as well take one, too. Although Rose is actually the name I was born with, so maybe it's not all that new."

"*You're* the one running Paradise Circle now?" asked Sadie.

"It was that, or let someone worse run it."

There was a resignation in Nettles's voice that worried Hope. "I think you're an excellent person to run the Circle," she said in a way she hoped sounded encouraging.

"Do you?" Nettles looked mildly surprised for a moment, then settled back into her distant look. "Of course. Because you don't know yet."

"Know what?" asked Hope.

"Filler's dead." She said it dully. As if echoing something someone else said. For some reason, that made it land on Hope even harder. It felt like an actual knife in her gut, cold and sharp. She imagined she tasted the blood. Then she realized she *was* tasting blood, because she'd bit her lip hard enough to break the skin. The iron tang filled her mouth and the pain gave her some relief, but not enough.

"How?" she asked hoarsely.

"Tortured to death by my brother." Nettles's voice was still distant. Almost toneless. Hope wondered if she might be in shock. As much as Hope loved Filler, she knew Nettles loved him more. Nearly as much as Red.

Thinking his name brought another stab of pain. Poor Red. He would be devastated when he found out. Hope could picture the look of agony distorting his cheerful face.

"Where..." Hope cleared her throat. "Where is your brother now?" An old hunger for vengeance boiled up into her chest. Perhaps she was not as far past such things as she'd thought.

"No idea." Nettles's hand strayed to her side. Hope noticed that her chainblade was gone, and there was a large bone saw leaning against the chair next to her. "But he won't hurt anyone ever again. I cut off his arms and legs. And I tore out his tongue, although that was more because I was tired of hearing it."

Hope struggled to grasp the enormity of what Nettles said so calmly. "You...tortured and mutilated him?" She tried to keep the horror out of her voice, but knew she was failing. "And you didn't even put him out of his misery?"

"Can't kill your own brother," said Nettles. "Some things just aren't done."

"Nettie, I—"

"Nettles is dead. She died with Filler." The ganglord of Paradise Circle leaned over and lightly touched the teeth of her bone saw. "Or maybe she was never real to begin with. Just a made-up name for a made-up person who played at being good. But see, it was nothing but balls and pricks. Only bad can come from bad. And that's where I came from. Took me a while to grow up and accept it. I am the Black Rose. This is my Circle. And I'm never leaving it again."

Hope remembered as a little girl, Hurlo telling her that darkness begat darkness. But rather than seeing it as an unchangeable fate, he had presented it to her as a grand challenge. She didn't know if it was possible for Nettles to come back from whatever darkness she'd succumbed to. But it was clear that, at least for now, her friend wasn't up to the challenge.

"That's how it is now?" she asked finally.

"It is," agreed the Black Rose.

They stared at each other across the empty space like two people who didn't know each other. And perhaps they didn't anymore. Hope and Nettles had been friends. But Dire Bane and the Black Rose... what were they to each other?

"Don't worry about your crusade, though," the Black Rose said. "Handy thing about running all of Paradise Circle, I got plenty of ships now. Not as many people, though. I had to kill quite a few to get where I am, so I'm a bit short on those at the moment."

"We have people," said Hope. "We cleaned out the Empty Cliffs and quite a few wanted to join my crew."

The Black Rose's mouth quirked into something that almost looked like a smile. "Of course you did. Getting to be more like a proper champion of the people every day. Things may have changed between us, but you and me got history and I won't forget that. Nor do I want an army of the pissing dead marching into the streets of Paradise Circle. So I'll give you what I can spare. Besides, I promised Filler I would."

Hope stared at her for a moment, so many conflicting emotions rolling around within her.

"I gain a fleet, but lose my friends?" she asked.

The Black Rose nodded. "That's about the length of it. Nothing in this world is free, Dire Bane. You should know that by now."

"That doesn't make the loss any easier," she said quietly. Then she slowly turned and left, with Sadie and Jilly following silently behind.

Handsome Henny was waiting by the carriage when Hope, Sadie, and Jilly emerged into the morning light. He stood there for a moment, nervously shifting his weight back and forth, his eyes darting around. Then he abruptly looked her in the eye. "I'll try not to let her fall too far down the hole."

Hope gave him a tired smile and nodded. "Thank you, Henny."

"Can I give you a ride back to the docks?"

Hope nodded. "Nettles was the one who set us on this course. Now we must make sure her sacrifice, and Filler's, were not in vain."

24

$\mathcal{M}$erivale loathed sailing and ships and everything to do with them. She realized that in an empire composed of more water than land, this attitude was bordering on unpatriotic, so she kept it to herself. But she hated the cramped cabins, the stink of old fish and tar, and the way the world rocked sickeningly beneath her feet. A lesser person might have succumbed to seasickness, but Lady Merivale Hempist would never do something as unsightly as vomit, no matter how much her body urged her to do so.

The only relief was staying topside in the open air as much as possible. This was generally not something ladies of noble birth did on a ship, but the crew of the empress's private yacht, the *Great Endeavor*, were accustomed to her eccentricities. The captain, an old salt by the name of Beverman, even provided her with a seal fur cloak so that the cold sea air wouldn't give her a chill. She wrapped it tightly around herself now as she stared out at the frothy gray sea, only wanly lit by the early morning sun peeking now and then behind a low cloud bank.

"How many more days do you think it will take us to reach Lesser Basheta, Captain?"

Beverman scratched at his bushy white beard, his other hand resting on the wheel. "Two more days, my lady. Three if we run into bad weather."

"I see." These single-masted yachts were pain-fully slow, but anything larger would have drawn too much attention. It was vital at this stage that the bio-mancers not know their cargo or intention.

"It won't be as bad on the return trip, my lady," said the captain. "We're fighting the prevailing cur-rent on the way there. On the way back, she'll help us along."

"That's good to know," said Merivale. "We may need to return in a hurry."

"As you say, my lady." The captain nodded, his eyes cast out to sea. Then in her peripheral vision, she saw him glance nervously at her. "Eh, how is our...guest faring?"

"About as well as one might expect for someone locked in the cabin of a ship for two days straight."

"And you're sure he's...safe, my lady?"

She turned the full weight of her gaze on him. "As sure as you are that the ocean is safe, Captain. You worry about sailing, I'll worry about our guest."

The captain flinched. "Yes, my lady."

———

Later that morning, Merivale had Hume load up a tray of food. She accompanied him down to the cab-ins on the lower deck. The yacht didn't have much of a cargo hold because most of that space had been chopped up into small cabins so that the empress could go on long pleasure cruises or visits of state with guests when the need arose.

Naturally, Merivale had taken the largest cabin, the empress's, for herself. The second largest had been given to Rixidenteron. She'd had a lock put on the door before they'd departed Stonepeak, but that was largely a formality. She had no doubt he could pick the lock if he wanted. But as a show of good faith, she didn't chain him to the bed during the day, and he didn't try to leave the cabin. They had both agreed, however, that it would be prudent to chain him up at night.

Even with the freedom to move around the cabin during the day, Merivale couldn't imagine a less pleasant way to spend a four-day voyage to Lesser Basheta. She thought it likely that the hell waiting for her after death would look a great deal like that. If it had been her in that cabin, she would have been in a murderous mood by now. But when she and Hume reached his cabin door, she was surprised to hear laughter coming from the other side.

She rapped on the door with her knuckles. "My Lord Pastinas, is everything all right? Have you become hysterical?"

"No, no, Merivale. I'm fine. Come in." There was still a lingering mirth in his voice.

She opened the door, curious to see what was so funny it could cheer up a man in his situation. She found him sprawled out on the narrow bunk with her copy of Thoriston Baggelworthy's biography of Lady Gulia Pastinas in his hand.

"Is *that* what's making you laugh?" She nodded her head to the book. "I thought it rather heartbreaking."

Rixidenteron put the book down and accepted the tray from Hume. "Thanks, Humey, old pot."

Hume bowed slightly and left the cabin.

"It certainly reads like a tragic tale," agreed Rixidenteron, a mischievous sparkle in his eyes as he turned back to Merivale. "Probably because that's how I told it to him." Then he began eating.

"Am I to take it you were somewhat cavalier with the truth of your mother's life?" she asked dryly.

"What can I say?" He took a bite of salted fish and chewed reflectively for a moment. "Anyone who takes a subjective recounting of events from someone who was only a child at the time, and doesn't bother to verify or corroborate such a source, deserves to get duped."

"Why didn't you just tell him what really happened?"

"Because the truth is *mine*." He shook his salted fish in her direction. "It's all I've got left of my parents and I'll be damned to every hell before I let the whole world take it from me. Especially for free."

"And that is why you were laughing?" asked Merivale. "Because you got away with your deception?"

Rixidenteron shook his head as he stuffed a hunk of bread into his mouth. He held up the book again as he chewed. Once he'd swallowed, he said, "I was laughing at the bit at the end where old Thoriston tries to understand how wags talk in Paradise Circle."

"Is it that off the mark?"

"Even when he gets the meaning right, his theories on the origins are downright fanciful. And the best part is that it had nothing to do with me. He did it all on his own."

"I take it you don't particularly care for Mr. Baggelworthy?"

"He helped me out in a pinch once, and at least he has some interest in what's going on with the lower classes. So he's okay, I guess. For a lacy."

"And what of me?" asked Merivale. "Am I a lacy uninterested in the lower classes?"

Rixidenteron's smile faded. "I don't know what to make of you anymore."

"Rest assured, the feeling is mutual."

He ate in silence for a moment. "You really think this friend of yours can...cure me? Or free me? Or whatever we're calling it?"

"I'm not particularly knowledgeable in this area,"

said Merivale. "But even if Casasha can't break the biomancers' hold on you, she should be able to at least help us understand and perhaps control it."

Rixidenteron's expression grew bleak. "I'd rather just get rid of it."

"Understandable," Merivale said as kindly as she could. "But that option may not be open to us."

Rixidenteron stabbed moodily at the food on his tray, all traces of humor now gone. "Yeah. I guess I need to prepare myself for that. Like it's some kind of pissing disease I need to manage."

"I'm sorry. I truly am," Merivale said quietly. "I hope the woman you rescued by taking this curse upon yourself was worth it."

Rixidenteron said nothing, but only continued to push his food around on his tray, as if his appetite had fled with his mirth.

—

Merivale kept Rixidenteron company for a little while, but she could only stand to be below for short periods of time. Then she returned to her habitual spot on the deck near the helm. She was reluctant to call it a quarterdeck on such a small vessel.

As the sun began to set, she instructed Hume to go down and chain Rixidenteron to his bed before he changed. Meanwhile, the captain gave the order to light lanterns fore and aft.

The captain hadn't been pleased when Merivale informed him they would sail straight through to Lesser Basheta without stopping. She'd even enlisted enough sailors to have two full shifts. Granted, it made the small craft even more crowded. But Merivale was more concerned about the dangers of having such a potentially dangerous person aboard any longer than necessary. The captain had only agreed to night sailing if they could at least light lanterns. Merivale worried it made the yacht too easy for pirates to spot in open waters, but on that point Beverman wouldn't budge.

"In these well-traveled waters, we're more in danger of crashing into a merchant vessel in the dark than getting attacked by pirates," he said.

Merivale had to admit he had a point. The stretch between Stonepeak and New Laven, which they would spend a large portion of their trip sailing, was the most heavily trafficked sector in the empire. No sane pirate captain would even attempt it.

But it was the damned ocean and she should have known it wouldn't let them through unscathed. Because while pirates might not dare a raid in this sector, they were not the only dangerous things drawn to bright lights in the dark.

Merivale stared out at the black water, her elbows on the port gunwale. She dreaded the queasy, fitful sleep ahead of her, so she hadn't gone to her bunk yet. She wished there was at least some starlight to pretty the view up a little, but a bank of purple clouds hid them from sight, and only the faintest outline of the moon shone through.

There was a dull thud against the port side of the hull that made the yacht shudder.

"What was that?" she demanded of the first mate, Tybel, who manned the helm during the night shift.

Tybel was not much older than Merivale, and didn't seem nearly as knowledgeable as Beverman. "I...I'm not sure, my lady. There's not a reef for leagues, according to the charts, so I don't know what we might have hit." He nodded to one of the sailors. "Mavic, go check it out. Make sure there's no damage to the hull or something clinging to it." He turned back to Merivale. "Perhaps we've just bumped into some flotsam in the water."

Mavic leaned over the port side, his eyes squinting in the dark.

"What in all hells is going on?" demanded the captain as he climbed onto the deck, his coat and hat pulled on over his nightshirt.

"Something bumped into us, Captain. Mavic is checking for damage." Tybel pointed to Mavic, who was still leaning over the side.

Then a goblin shark burst from the water, purple-gray skin gleaming in the lantern light. Its needle jaws stretched past the tip of its nose, opened wide, and twisted Mavic's head off in one bite before plunging back into the dark water.

They all stared in shock for a moment as the headless body gave a twitch, then began to pitch forward.

"Don't let it hit the water!" yelled the captain as he dashed toward it. But everyone else only stared in mute horror as the corpse dropped with a heavy splash into the sea.

"That much blood'll bring the whole pack down on us!" said the captain.

"I'm not sure I see much danger, Captain," said Merivale. "As long as we don't lean over the side, they can't reach us."

"Depends on how much bigger they get," he said grimly.

"They get bigger?" Merivale's eyes widened. That goblin shark had easily been over ten feet long. "How *much* bigger?"

The captain looked from bow to stern, then to Merivale. "Bigger than this ship." He raised his hands to his mouth and shouted, "All hands! Rouse the whole crew! We need to put as much distance between ourselves and this area as we can. Give me full sail and raise the jib. Anything we don't need goes overboard!"

The ship suddenly teemed with activity. Both shifts of crew were out at the same time, making twice as many hands, but also making it hard for them not to trip over one another. Merivale knew now was the time for her to get out of the way and let the sailors do their work, but the only place not packed with men was below deck.

Even as she made her way down, she had to press up against the side of walls or doorways to let sailors by carrying cooking utensils or dishes to be thrown overboard.

She intended to go to her own cabin, but at the last moment, changed her mind and headed for Rixidenteron's cabin. A moment before she opened the door, she remembered it wouldn't be Rixidenteron in there right now. It was the Shadow Demon.

"Something is amiss," he observed calmly as he lay chained to his bunk.

Merivale listened to the panicked shouts and stumbling footsteps on the deck above them. "Really? What gave you that impression?"

The Shadow Demon seemed immune to humor, however. "The crew has become frantic and disorganized, and you stink of fear."

"Of *course* you can smell fear," she said acidly. She had no problem with fear. It was a useful emotion that promoted survival. But she felt more exposed knowing her fear was showing than if her bosom was showing. Her breasts, after all, were quite attractive. Fear, on the other hand, was never pretty.

There was another dull thud against the hull. It sounded louder this time, although Merivale thought that might be because the cabin was near the waterline. Either way, the floor lurched beneath her feet so she had to steady herself. She peered out the tiny portal, but couldn't see much in the darkness except spray from the ship's wake glittering in the lantern light.

Then the portal went dark. Merivale jerked her head back instinctively as the jaws of a goblin shark scraped against the glass.

"You should keep away from there," the Shadow Demon said mildly. "Or you'll draw more of them and they will eventually break through."

"Through the portal?"

The demon only shrugged awkwardly beneath his chains.

"I need to know what's going on. How can I do that if I can't even look out the window?" she said.

"You want to know what's going on?" He shimmied beneath his chains so that he could press his ear against the wall of the ship. He closed his eyes and listened for a long time. "Several large shapes in the water. I can't tell exactly how many because they're moving so fast. But I would guess at least five now."

Merivale wasn't sure if this was an act intended to increase her fear, or if he truly could hear the vibrations of movement at that level of detail.

"There is one that is slower and bigger than the rest on the way. The pack leader, I would imagine."

As fear squeezed up her throat, she reminded herself that this could all be a trick designed to panic her.

"It's coming," he said.

But there was also a chance he wasn't faking it. "I need to warn the captain."

She took a step toward the cabin door but then he said, "Too late."

Something slammed into the ship so hard it sent Merivale sprawling across the room. Her knees banged against the edge of the bunk and she fell on top of the demon's chained body. She lay there for a moment and stared into the demon's eyes. She wouldn't have believed something so red could look so cold.

Outside the cabin she heard one—no, two sailors screaming. They had been knocked overboard by the impact and now were getting torn apart by the smaller goblin sharks.

"It's going away," said the demon, his ear still against the wall.

"It's leaving?" she asked as she climbed back to her feet.

"No, it's making room for the final charge."

"Final?"

"Judging by the impact, the pack leader is large enough to grip the waist of this yacht in its mouth and use the goblin shark's unusual jaw rotation to slam it back and forth against the surface until the ship breaks apart."

Calm finally descended on her. The worst had arrived, which at least took the mystery out of the equation. Now she just had to discover all the factors and make her final calculation.

She opened the door of the cabin. Two soldiers were in the passageway. One was bleeding from a head wound. He had probably slammed it into something during the impact. The other sailor was trying to bandage him, but his hands were shaking so badly he couldn't tie it off. Merivale elbowed him aside and quickly finished the knot before heading up to the deck.

It was true chaos up top. A few sailors were running around trying to secure things, but others seemed frozen by the shock and only stared at the distant hulking form that cut sheets of water to either side as it made a slow arc back toward them. The captain was screaming at his crew to brace for impact, but they didn't move. Along the sides, the regular-sized goblin sharks continued to launch themselves into the air, straining to reach crew members. And off in the distance, she saw the dark purple fin of the pack leader complete its turn and head back toward them.

"How bad is it, Captain?" she shouted to him.

Beverman's eyes were so wide, they looked ready to pop out of his skull. "How bad is it?" he shrieked. "How *bad*? We're all pissing dead! That's how bad!"

Merivale had been looking for a status report on the damage done to the ship, but clearly they were well past that point. The captain, and by extension most of the crew, were now useless. That left precious few options and only one with any great chance of success.

She hurried back down below deck to the Shadow Demon, who still lay in chains, his expression still calm, but also a little smug, as if he'd known it would come to this.

"Can you kill it?" she asked.

"I can kill anything," he said.

"If I let you out, will you swear on your honor as a servant of the emperor that you won't kill me or any other people aboard this ship?"

"I swear on my honor that I will only kill goblin sharks this night if you set me free."

She didn't know if she believed him, but she also couldn't think of another plan anywhere near as likely to succeed. She clenched the whistle between her teeth and unchained the Shadow Demon.

He shook himself free of the chains and stood up slowly, luxuriously. They stared at each other for a moment. In a strangely detached way, Merivale wondered if she could even get in the breath to blow the whistle before he killed her.

But then he said, "I will need whatever weapons are available. Guns, knives, spears. Whatever you have."

Merivale kept the whistle clenched in her teeth as she gestured for him to move into the passageway. Once they were out of his cabin, she pointed to her own cabin a few doors down. When he opened the door, he didn't smile exactly, but his eyes crinkled with pleasure as he saw his own travel trunk. He opened it and pulled out a revolver and several of his throwing blades. Then he turned to her.

"A spear or pike for the big one?"

She pointed up to the deck. She was certain she'd seen one up there.

He nodded and the two of them moved back into the passageway. She made him go first up the ladder to the deck. She wondered what the captain's reaction would be to seeing him, but once she reached the deck herself, she saw he'd hardly noticed.

She took the whistle from her mouth and shouted to the captain. "We need a pike!"

He stared back at her uncomprehendingly.

"I found one," said the Shadow Demon, holding up the long metal pole with a point on the end.

"Here it comes again!" screamed one of the sailors. "Brace!"

While everyone else, including Merivale, scrambled for something to hold on to or threw themselves to the deck, the Shadow Demon quickly climbed the mast until he perched precariously at the top.

Moments before impact, the giant shark opened its mouth and latched on to the side of the boat. Even braced, people were thrown overboard as the shark carried the boat sideways with its momentum. There was a thunderous *crunch* as the shark bit down even further on the hull. Then it began rotating its mouth just as the Shadow Demon had described. It slammed the bow hard against the surface of the water, then the stern, like a seesaw back and forth. The hull of the ship groaned under the strain, and more people were flung overboard to the smaller sharks.

Merivale looked up and saw that the Shadow Demon still clung somehow to the top of the mast, carefully watching the giant shark below him. The shark paused for a moment to rest, and that's when he jumped straight down on it, plunging the pike into its head.

He planted his feet on the shark's back, using the embedded pike to keep him from falling off the slippery, purple surface. The giant shark shuddered, then released the boat and began to sink.

As the water rose above his ankles, several smaller sharks leapt for him. But they dropped away when he threw his blades down their throats.

The ship had begun to drift away from the sinking giant shark. The Shadow Demon took a few steps back, then ran forward, used the pike as leverage, and vaulted across the gap before the dead giant sank completely out of sight. He caught the ship's gunwale in one hand, while firing a bullet into the face of another of the smaller sharks. He shot one more as it leapt for him, then pulled himself onto the deck.

There was a moment of silence as the surviving crew wondered who this man was, while also realizing he had just saved their lives. They looked at each other, smiles of relief on their faces, and began to cheer.

The cheer was cut short by the sound of gunfire as the demon emptied the remaining four chambers of his revolver, killing the captain and three other crew members in the time it took Merivale to bring the whistle to her lips.

"I am death," he told her, tossing his empty gun on the deck. "And death has no honor."

Then she blew the whistle and he dropped to the ground.

25

*B*leak Hope, called Dire Bane by many, gazed out at the great blue sky and sparkling green sea that stretched endlessly before her. Loose tendrils of blond hair whipped against her neck beneath her hat, and her red captain's coat snapped in the wind. The air had a biting chill, but the sun shone down on her with a warmth and generosity rarely seen at this latitude.

"It's a good day to be at sea, Captain," said Missing Finn at the helm of the *Kraken Hunter*.

"It is, Mr. Finn." She turned and looked back at the three ships following in their wake.

She had given the *Glorybound*, a two-masted brig even bigger in size and firepower than the *Kraken Hunter*, to Vaderton. Old Yammy had remained behind on New Laven, but Hope felt she could trust Vaderton by now. She still wasn't sure their political and social values aligned, but she knew him to be a man who needed to be part of something bigger and more important than himself, and that was something she understood well. Saving innocents from the grip of necromancy was sufficient reason for him to sail under her command.

The *Rolling Lightning* was a smaller, one-masted schooner built for speed, and most likely smuggling, but it had a few swivel cannons for close fighting.

She was captained by Gavish Gray. It had been the Black Rose's only condition on giving them the ships, that Gray retain command of the *Rolling Lightning*. Hope had spoken with Gray and he seemed like a solid, dependable wag. A pirate, but a thoroughly professional one. He'd been sailing most of his life and clearly knew his way around a ship, so Hope wasn't worried about his competence. She just hoped his loyalty would hold. If not to the cause or her leadership, at least to what the Black Rose was paying him.

The third ship was a nasty little sloop called the *Devil's Your Own* that had clearly been fitted for hit-and-run piracy. The hull had been patched up so many times, Hope wondered if any of the original wood remained. But it bristled with a surprising number of swivel guns for such a small ship, and instead of a figurehead, there was a vicious-looking two-pronged battering ram fixed to the prow. Hope had wanted Missing Finn to captain it, but he begged off, saying he wasn't cut out for giving orders. She had to admit that his quiet, contemplative demeanor didn't make for the most commanding presence. After some thought, she gave it to Sadie. That pleased Finn and delighted Sadie. And the more Hope thought about it, the more she realized that the *Devil's Your Own* was a perfect ship for the old woman.

"Surveying your fleet, Captain Bane?" asked Brigga Lin as she stepped onto the quarterdeck in her customary white hooded dress.

"Technically speaking, wouldn't you be *Admiral* Bane now?" asked Alash, following in Brigga Lin's wake.

"I'm not sure four ships constitute a fleet." Hope turned to Brigga Lin. "I'm sorry Old Yammy chose not to come with us."

"So am I. But she's not much interested in violence, and she said there was something she needed to do that would ultimately help us more than her presence at this battle would."

"Naturally she was terribly sly and cryptic about it."

Brigga Lin smiled. "Of course she was. I don't think it was even necessary. She just enjoys doing it."

"Should I expect you to become that perverse in the future?"

Brigga Lin arched an eyebrow. "Oh, I think I'm probably already perverse enough."

Jilly emerged from the lower deck, her mop of hair even more unkempt than usual. There were dark circles under her eyes and she walked over to them with heavy limbs.

"Did you finish that chapter?" Brigga Lin asked her.

"Yes, master," she said sleepily.

"You look ready to fall over," observed Hope.

"I feel like it, teacher," she said.

"I know what will wake you up," Hope said brightly. "Up and down the mainmast ten times. I'll time you."

Jilly looked crestfallen, but nodded. "Yes, teacher."

As Jilly began climbing the mast, Brigga Lin turned to Hope. "Speaking of perverse..."

"She can handle it," said Hope.

They watched her climb to the top, then drop quickly down from one yard to the next, using the ropes only occasionally to steady herself.

"Someday, she will be incredible," Hope said quietly.

"Yes," said Brigga Lin. "Let's make sure she doesn't die before then."

"You have something in particular in mind?"

"I do. Something that will help us in the battle *and* keep her out of the worst of it at the same time."

"I'm listening," said Hope.

———

Captain Brice Vaderton sat at the small table in his modest quarters. It was a far cry from the spacious cabin of the *Guardian*, but he was far more content than he ever was before. And although he sat at the table with quill in hand, he wasn't writing meticulous logs this time. Instead, he wrote a letter:

Dearest Yammy,

You said I would be a captain once more, and here I am, beyond all hope, in a hat and coat again. What can I say except that you were right? And not just about me. You were right about Dire Bane as well. I'm sorry you had to miss her address to the fleet at the docks of New Laven before we set sail. I found it so moving, I will try to describe it to you here. Hopefully my dreadful penmanship won't detract from the inspiration I so desperately wish to convey.

The crews from all four ships gathered on the docks, upwards of sixty men and women, all waiting expectantly to hear from the woman we have all sworn to sail under. When the time came for her to speak, she vaulted up to the bowsprit of the Kraken Hunter *and stood on her precarious perch as easily as you or I would stand upon the ground.*

I hope you will forgive me, my dearest, if I

cannot resist setting down some description of her. So lithe a form I have never seen in male or female. The imperfection of her lost hand only serves to emphasize her exquisite grace. Her hair and skin, so startlingly pale, truly brings to mind old stories of the angelic warriors called forth by Emperor Cremalton in his quest to unite the empire. Her elegant neck and fine features make it difficult to believe that she was born to the rude peasantry of the Southern Isles. Yet all these pretty details are mere ephemera when compared to her eyes. They make me think of a day, long ago, when, as a boy, I first gazed out at the endlessly majestic expanse of the ocean and decided that I would dedicate myself to knowing its dark mystery. That was the feeling I had as I looked into her eyes.

She spoke about the dangers that lay before us. Horrors almost impossible to conceive. An army of dead children created by a necromancer and led by not one, but a group of biomancers? My mind reeled at such an abhorrence, and I grew afraid. But I had only to look into those fathomless blue eyes again and my courage returned.

Since then, my resolve has only grown stronger. I think back to how the navy betrayed me after my many years of service. I think back to those months spent on the Empty Cliffs and the poor victims of biomancer experiments. And I think back to all my past crimes, when I was an instrument of such biomancer cruelty myself . . . I know you said I should not be too hard on myself and try to forgive myself. But if it serves to strengthen my resolve in the coming battle, then I will use this burning shame and

*regret to atone for my past sins and stop others
from doing what I have done.*

*If I die in this endeavor, my only regret
is that I will no longer be able to drink in the
gentle beauty of your face. While I do love Dire
Bane, it is as a soldier loves his emperor, at a
worshipful distance. But my love for you is of
a sort I have never known before. I yearn to be
near you, to close this terrible distance between
us as quickly as possible. I know you have your
own part to play in all of this and my meager
imagination can hardly conceive of what it is.
But I do pray nightly that we might win through
this nightmare eventually, and in doing so, that
I become a better man than I am now. One
deserving of your love and affection.*

> *Yours until my final breath,*
> *Brice*

Vaderton put down his quill and carefully blotted
the final page. Then he let out a sigh and leaned back
in his chair.

There was a respectful knock at his door.

"Yes, come in," said Vaderton.

Biscuit Bill opened the door. "The *Kraken Hunter*
is signaling the fleet, Captain. I think we're coming
up on the Breaks."

"Thank you, Bill." Vaderton rose from his chair.
"I want to take the helm myself for this."

Captain Gavish Gray was an idiot. He knew that well
enough. All he had to do was assess his current situation, which involved sailing his schooner, which was
fitted only for night raids and smuggling, in a battle

fleet that included ex-naval officers, ex-Vinchen, ex-biomancers, and ex-prisoners through the Breaks, known to be some of the most treacherous waters in the empire, to an island reportedly populated by walking corpses. Why in all hells had he said yes?

He knew the answer, of course. Because Nettles— the Black Rose—had asked him to do this for her. And if there was one thing you could say about Gavish Gray, other than that he was an idiot, it was that he hadn't been able to say no to that woman since he met her at age fourteen.

He'd been between ships then, eking out a living on the docks until he could find a new crew. She'd been Nettles back then, of course, and she'd recently started working security at the Slice of Heaven. She'd already gotten a bit of a reputation by then as someone not to cross. He'd been trying to flirt with her and she'd been having none of it until she learned he was a sailor. Then she asked him if he was interested in a potentially lucrative arrangement. The two of them had cooked up the scheme to make the Slice of Heaven a part-time crimp house. He'd been the one who negotiated with the captains, while she handled things on the brothel side. Soon, they'd made enough money for him to afford his own little ship, and he'd been off to seek fortune and adventure. Worst mistake of his life. When he came back, expecting to sweep her off her feet with thrilling tales of his exploits (somewhat embellished), he found she'd gotten herself involved with Red. That pissing cock-dribble of a tom was so inhumanly charming, Gavish knew he hadn't stood a chance. All pissed and peppered, he'd set sail again, that time for nearly two years. When he came back, he learned that she wasn't with Red anymore. In fact, Red was completely sotted with some Vinchen molly, and a Southie to tack. Gavish thought this

was his chance. He and Nettles started tossing, and
everything seemed to be going in the right direction.
But then all hells broke loose when the neighborhood
found out Drem had sold them out to the biomancers, and a full-scale riot erupted in Paradise Circle.
Gavish waited out the insanity from the safety of his
ship. Then when things finally started to settle back
down, Nettles disappeared. Tosh said she'd gone with
Sadie and Filler to help out Red and that Vinchen
Southie of his. That time, Gavish decided he wasn't
going to run or hide. He waited it out, getting whatever work he could find smuggling along the coast
of New Laven. She'd be back eventually. A molly
like her could never leave the Circle for good. And sure
enough, a year later she came back with a vengeance.
And he swore he wouldn't lose her this time.

Except here he was, halfway across the empire,
about to get swallowed up in someone else's hell,
being led by that same Vinchen Southie, who had
somehow become the dread pirate Dire Bane. And
all because the Black Rose had a favor to ask him. A
big favor, she'd said. One she couldn't trust with anyone else. He wasn't sure he even thought that what
she wanted him to do was right. But by this point,
that didn't matter. He knew he'd do it for her anyway.

All this went through his mind as he stared at the
tall, ragged reef-heads of the Breaks that loomed
before them.

"Captain, the *Kraken Hunter* is signaling for us to
slow down," said Fisty.

"Slow down?" Gavish frowned. It seemed more
prudent for them to continue apace, letting their
momentum help carry them through the dangerous
currents that swirled around the Breaks.

"That's the signal." Fisty pointed to the small
flags flying from the foremast of the *Kraken Hunter*.

"Give the order, then," Gavish said curtly. The

Black Rose had told him to follow Bane's orders without question. Right up until it was time for that favor.

———

Sadie the Pirate Queen was back, and this time in a proper pirate vessel with swivel guns and a battering ram. Before they'd left Paradise Circle, she'd even had one of her crew roll a merchant captain for his coat and hat. Now she once again stalked the deck of a sloop in ill-fitting clothes and barked orders at a crew of dangerous wags from downtown New Laven. Granted, her old bones didn't move so well as they used to, and after a few minutes, she had to take a rest. But this time, the prize was far more grand than some petty thievery.

To think, only a year ago, Sadie had been at death's door with tunnel lung shutting down her throat like a tavern at closing time. She'd known the end was coming, and she'd made peace with it. After all, she'd already lived an unnaturally long time for a true wag of the Circle. But then that angel slice had come waltzing into their lives and knocked it all askew. She'd saved Sadie's life and won Red's heart without even breaking a sweat. But she wasn't finished even then. What started as a riot in Paradise Circle was now shaping up to be a full-scale rebellion, the likes of which the empire had never seen. Oh, it would be glorious, no matter how it ended.

There was nothing Sadie liked more than proof that a single person's actions could still change things. It was easy to forget something like that in Paradise Circle, where no matter what you did, it always seemed to come back around. Being old and poor and ground down under years of sorrow tended to do that to a person. But here she was, on top one last time. And she'd be damned to every hell there was if she wasn't going to make it count for something.

"Captain, the *Kraken Hunter*'s giving the caution signal," said Ruby Raw, a nervous girl they'd rescued from the Empty Cliffs. "Should I give the order to slow down?"

"Not just yet." Sadie squinted at the *Kraken Hunter*. It had pulled in some sail and slowed down as it crossed the northern tip of the Breaks. Sure, caution was important here. She remembered seeing all the wrecked ships on the eastern side of the Breaks when they'd come this way the month before. But slowing down didn't make a whole lot of sense, unless there was something else going on. Something maybe they weren't even sure of. She knew Brigga Lin could sense things from afar. Maybe she'd caught a whiff of something. But what? It didn't look like there was anything around.

"Captain," said Ruby Raw. "If we keep this pace and line, like as not we'll cut pretty close across the *Kraken Hunter*'s wake."

"I can see that, baby slice," Sadie said absently, but didn't give the order to slow down. Something was nagging at her...

She found herself staring at a strange ripple in the water past the Breaks. Something that didn't match the prevailing current. Sadie was no true salt like Finn, but she knew enough to recognize that it wasn't natural. It was as if there was an object in the water that was fighting against the current. But she couldn't see anything.

Then it hit her. This was the same kind of sneaky biomancer trickery that Brigga Lin had used more than a few times when they were plundering naval ships. Bending the air to make a ship look as though it wasn't even there. The *Kraken Hunter* was on course to come within firing range of an invisible ship in a few moments.

When Sadie thought about it, this whole last year had been something she'd stolen from right under God's nose. In that year, she'd found love and seen the world, all the while hardly doing a thing to earn it besides a few wise words to young people who would've come to it on their own eventually anyway. She reckoned now was the time to pay up for this stolen extra year of life. Nearly every reason Sadie had to keep living was on that ship. She'd be damned if she let it be blown out of the water.

"Give me every inch of canvas we've got!" she roared as she gripped the wheel and aimed her battering ram at where she judged to be the center of the invisible vessel. "And then anyone who wants to live past the next couple of minutes better abandon ship."

"What do you mean, you don't know what it is?" demanded Hope.

"*Something* is out there," said Brigga Lin. "I can feel it. Or, rather, I can feel the absence of something. Like it's being hidden from my senses."

"Biomancers, then." Hope scanned the horizon with her glass. She could make out the shore of Dawn's Light far to the southeast. "You're sure whatever this is, it's not on the island?"

Brigga Lin shook her head. "Whatever is hidden, it's close. *Very* close."

"What in piss'ell is Sadie *doing*?" muttered Missing Finn. His one good eye glared at the *Devil's Your Own*, which had apparently ignored the signal to slow down and was speeding full tilt across their wake toward the gap between the *Kraken Hunter* and the Breaks.

Hope trained her glass on Sadie's ship and saw forms falling off the back. "People are jumping ship. Jilly! Throw some floats aft to them!"

"Aye, Captain!" Jilly leapt down from her perch in the mainmast and popped open the storage hatch that contained some float rings.

"What is she pissing *doing*!" Finn's face was pinched with fear.

Hope turned her glass back to the *Devil's Your Own*. Sadie held the wheel, an exultant grin on her face. "What *is* she doing?"

Then the empty space between them and the Breaks flickered. There was suddenly a three-masted naval frigate with its guns trained on the *Kraken Hunter*. Thick chains stretched from the ship to the water, anchoring it against the strong currents so it wasn't pulled into the reefs.

"Ambush!" said Hope. "Everyone brace for impact!"

But before the frigate fired, the *Devil's Your Own* smashed into her side. The frigate's cannon shot went wide and Sadie's battering ram tore into the hull like it was paper. The impact also ripped the anchors free. The frigate and the *Devil's Your Own* spun wildly around and around, locked together like they were dancing. It was strangely beautiful, with flickers of light as the naval sailors fired on the nearly empty deck of the *Devil's Your Own*.

Hope watched through her glass as a bullet struck Sadie in the temple. Her manic grin faded away, and she toppled over.

"Sadie...," whispered Missing Finn, tears streaking from his one eye. He could not possibly have seen her die without a glass. But it was like he'd felt it all the same.

The two ships continued their dance for a few more seconds, then came to an abrupt stop when they smashed into the frothing, jagged reefs. The ships began to break apart, the hulls cracked and taking on water.

Hope continued to watch as the frigate's crew jumped ship, only to be swallowed up by the relentless current themselves. Over a hundred men drowned within minutes, but even combined, she did not think their deaths outweighed the loss of Sadie the Pirate Queen.

"There's only one person who could hide a ship so well from both sight and my sense," said Brigga Lin. "Progul Bon, one of the chiefs of the Council of Biomancery."

Hope turned to her. "Could he have been on the ship?"

She shook her head. "It's unlikely. Bon is not one to put himself in danger, and he could have easily camouflaged the ship before it disembarked from Dawn's Light."

"But he is at least on the island, then?" pressed Hope.

Brigga Lin nodded.

"Then we owe it to Sadie to make sure he never leaves."

26

Red let them chain him up for the remainder of the voyage to Lesser Basheta, even during the day. He didn't remember what he'd done, but the look of fear on the surviving crew's faces and the grim expression on Merivale's face as she described the events were all he really needed. Even Hume seemed nervous in his presence.

The only one who didn't seem afraid was Merivale. He really had no idea what to make of her now. She had more layers than anyone he'd ever met. He suspected she was carrying around all the secrets of the empire in her head, and yet it never seemed to weigh her down. Now Red's biggest secret had been exposed, yet he felt heavier than ever.

After two days, they arrived at the small village on Lesser Basheta. The island seemed mostly composed of dense forest with the occasional rocky mountain peak jutting out. Even those peaks were dotted with spindly trees that were oddly twisted and almost bush-like in their thickness. As they sailed into the harbor, Merivale brought Red up onto the deck. The surviving crew insisted he be immediately chained to the mast, but at least he was on his feet and breathing fresh air.

The villagers eyed the damaged yacht warily as it glided up to the dock. But the moment they saw

Merivale standing on the deck, they hurried over to help the sailors secure the ship.

"Thank you for your assistance, Mr. Owens," Merivale called to an older fisherman as he tied one of the ship's lines to a cleat. "I'm afraid we ran into a significant amount of trouble along the way."

"The honor's mine, my lady," he said without quite looking at her. The rest of the villagers reacted to her similarly, as if they were too awed to make eye contact. "Will you be wanting your luggage taken to the manor?"

"Yes, thank you, Mr. Owens, that would be appreciated." Merivale turned to Hume, who stood patiently nearby. "Hume, would you let my parents know I won't be heading directly there? Lord Pastinas and I have an urgent need to call upon Casasha first."

"Very good, my lady." Then Hume hesitated and for the first time, Red saw struggle on his usually inexpressive face. "Will you be all right without an...additional escort?"

Merivale gave him a level gaze.

He bowed his head. "Yes, of course, my lady. My deepest apologies. I will make certain everything is prepared for your arrival."

"Thank you, Hume," she said.

Hume hurried over to Mr. Owens and the two began to direct the unloading of the ship.

"Mrs. Mackis," Merivale said to an elderly woman with a scarf wrapped around her head. "Please tell Casasha we have arrived and will be calling on her shortly. We all know how she dislikes surprises."

"Yes, my lady." Mrs. Mackis hurried off.

Merivale turned to the surviving ship's crew. "Gentlemen, my sincerest condolences for the loss of your captain and fellow crew. I fear we don't have adequate means here on Lesser Basheta to fully repair the empress's yacht. But you are welcome to stay as long as you like at my expense before you continue on to Greater Basheta for repairs."

The sailors glanced fearfully at Red, then at one another.

"If it's all the same to your ladyship," one said, "we'll just continue on to Greater Basheta for repairs now."

"I understand perfectly," she said. "Once you have completed repairs and found additional crew, please return with all haste to Her Majesty."

"You won't be needing us to come back for you?" the second one asked.

"We'll be fine, thank you."

The sailors looked relieved. "As you wish, my lady."

Merivale gave them a gracious smile. "Good luck to you."

"Thank you, my lady," said the first.

Merivale turned and uncoiled Red's chain from the mast. "Come along, my lord," she said lightly as she gave a tug on the chain that was still attached to his wrists, pulling him down the gangplank as if it were a leash.

"Those sailors would rather pass up free food and a soft warm bed than be in the same place as me," he said morosely as they walked through the village.

"You can hardly blame them," she said brightly. "If I didn't know you as well as I do, I'd be just as frightened."

"You're not making me feel better."

She stopped and turned to him, giving him that steely gaze he'd come to realize in the last few days was her truest expression. "It was not meant to make you feel better. I don't have the luxury of coddling you. We need this fixed immediately, and I want to make certain you remain properly motivated to do so."

"You think I want to stay like this?"

"Of course not. But the Shadow Demon cannot continue to run amok in the empire as the biomancers' conscienceless killing machine. If we cannot fix you, we must kill you."

"Fine by me," he said, and he still meant it. Better to be put out of his misery than continue life like this.

She assessed him for a moment, then nodded. "I'm glad we are of the same mind. And incidentally, I do have a good deal of optimism that we can fix this."

Red wasn't so hopeful. The biomancers had probably been turning him into this thing for months. Maybe since he got to the palace. Had they snuck into his room while he slept? Or had they done things to him during training sessions, then made him forget? Either idea made his skin crawl.

What would his friends think of him now? What would Hope think? She'd probably be horrified, and with good reason. He'd become everything she despised. An honorless tool of the biomancers.

During the voyage, Merivale had suggested that this all happened as a result of Red making the deal to set Hope and Brigga Lin free. For a day or so, he'd even started to think that way himself. But he knew this wasn't about her. This was about that pissing coral spice experiment. This was something he'd been marked for since birth. It almost felt inevitable that it had come to this. Maybe he would have been better off dying young like all the other coral spice babies. Hells, at least his parents would have had a better shot at living longer, less miserable lives.

They continued to walk through the muddy village streets. The buildings were all one level and made from a rich, dark wood. It was a simple place.

Humble was the word that came to Red's mind. But everything was well cared for, with neat little gardens and stone pathways.

"So this is all yours?" Red asked.

"My family was granted stewardship over Lesser Basheta nearly three hundred years ago."

"The whole island?"

"I would have held the title of archlady, but our population is too small to qualify. Which is just as well, since I'd have to fend off even more unwelcome marriage proposals than I do now. Anyway, it's just this village and the manor house, for the most part. The rest is given over to forestry, our primary export."

"Lumber?"

"In a sense," she said. "We are careful to control it so that we never cut down more than we grow. It makes for a small export, but the quality and maturity of our wood is renowned throughout the kingdom, and best suited for high-end woodwork like furniture and decorative pieces, rather than standard building lumber."

The mention of furniture made Red think of that poor artisan that Leston had commissioned. He'd been awkward, but nice enough. And he'd been a serious talent, one that Red had silenced forever. Thinking of that twisted in his gut like a knife, and he let it. He *wanted* to feel that way. Maybe to punish himself? Or maybe to strengthen his resolve for whatever was coming.

Finally they reached a small house a little set apart from the rest at the outskirts of the village. The building itself was undecorated, with a plain wood finish and closed, unadorned shutters. But the garden that surrounded the house easily rivaled the palace cliff gardens in its neatness and complexity.

Merivale stopped and began to unlock Red's

chains. "Before you meet Casasha, I should warn you that she is rather…well, *eccentric* isn't quite the right word, but it's the closest I can think of."

"Who is she? How do you know her?" asked Red.

"She was my chambermaid originally, when I was a girl. And it must be said, she was not a very good one. I didn't mind, though, because she was strange and mysterious and she told me that I would help change the empire. And what entitled child who is constantly ignored by her parents doesn't want to hear something like that? The difference was, she was right. But perhaps it was a self-fulfilling prophecy, since it was largely thanks to her that I have become the person I am."

"So, she's like a wisewoman?" Red thought of Old Yammy.

Merivale smiled faintly as she dropped the chains on the stone path. "I'm not sure *wise* is the word I would use. But she sees the world in a way you or I never could. Not without cost, I might add. Her actions and words may seem surprising to you. Perhaps even…hostile. But I have learned that it mostly stems from managing the enormous amount of information that comes to her which you and I are deaf and blind to."

"I doubt she's much worse than my old mentor Sadie," said Red.

"We shall see." Merivale stepped up to the front door and knocked quietly.

"Who is it?" asked a harsh female voice.

"You'll have to guess," said Merivale in a mischievous tone.

"I *hate* guessing," the voice said peevishly.

"I know," said Merivale.

There was a pause, then, a little less harshly, the voice said, "If you know that, then you must know me."

"True," agreed Merivale.

"And if you know I don't like it, but you want me to do it anyway..." There was another pause. "That means you are *teasing me*."

"I am."

"There is only one person who teases me," the voice said triumphantly. "Meri-kitty! Come in, Meri-kitty!"

"Meri-kitty?" asked Red.

Merivale shrugged. To anyone else it might have been unnoticeable, but Red's keen eyes saw the slight blush creep into her cheeks.

The inside of the house was one open room, free of furniture. The floor was covered in a mat of soft reeds. The room was dim, since the shutters were closed, and the only light came from a crackling stone fireplace set in the wall on the left side with a kettle suspended over it on an iron hook. Off to the other side was a washbasin, and in the back was a pile of blankets and pillows.

An older woman sat in the center of the room, her legs folded under her. Her hair was a ragged white curtain across her forehead, as if her bangs had been impatiently hacked off with a knife. She wore a large men's jacket, but it was on backward. Her expression was distracted, as if she were listening to some distant music. She glanced at them briefly when they came in, but didn't get up or acknowledge them in any other way. Instead she went back to staring at an empty corner of the room. Her hands fluttered around on her lap like trapped birds, and her lips moved as if she was silently talking to herself.

Merivale didn't seem surprised by the indifferent reception. She left Red by the door and walked toward her. She leaned over and examined a blank canvas, paintbrush, and jars of paint that were laid out next to the old woman.

"Casasha, are you taking up painting?" she asked.

Casasha made a disgusted face, although she still didn't look at Merivale. "I *hate* painting. It gets everywhere. So messy." She wiped her hands against each other for a moment before letting them flutter again.

"So what are these for?" asked Merivale.

"For the *artist*, obviously." Casasha pointed at Red, her eyes never leaving the corner of the room.

Merivale looked curiously at Red.

He shrugged, a feeling of unease growing inside him. It reminded him of Yammy predicting the future. He never liked the idea of his fate being fixed like that. "I'm not really an artist."

"You're not really an assassin either, but that didn't stop you from killing all those people," snapped Casasha. She glanced at Red for the first time, looking him right in the eyes for just a moment. He was glad it was only a moment, because her eyes felt as if they were tunneling into his brain like a hungry mole rat. Then she broke her gaze and turned back to her corner.

"Casasha," said Merivale. "I need your help."

"Wrong," Casasha said absently. "You need *his* help." She pointed again at Red without looking. "And *he* needs my help."

"You're right," said Merivale.

"Say what you mean, Meri-kitty."

"I'm sorry, Casasha," Merivale said with a simple humility Red had never heard from her before.

"Save your double-meaning spy talk for your spies. It gives me a headache."

"I will."

"Right here." She jabbed at her own temple with one finger. "It hurts me right here when you don't say what you mean."

"It's been a little while and I forgot," Merivale said patiently. "I remember now."

"Good." Casasha glared at her for an instant, and Merivale flinched. But then she turned back to her corner again. "Lying Artist."

Merivale looked over at Red.

"She means me?" asked Red.

"Of course I mean you," said Casasha. "You're an artist. You said you're not an artist. So I'm calling you Lying Artist. Now get your paint stuff. It's smelly."

Red walked over to them, unable to shake the tension creeping up his back. There really was something unnerving about this woman, which he couldn't quite put his finger on.

He picked up the canvas, brush, and paints. "What do I do with them?"

"Paint, *obviously*." Her tone was withering.

Red took a deep breath, trying to match the patience Merivale had shown. Supposedly, this woman could help him. "Okay...is there anything specifically I should paint?"

"Yourself." She pointed to the small washbasin off to one side. "You can use that as a mirror, if you don't remember what you look like."

Red walked over to the basin and found it was already filled with water, so that his reflection glimmered back at him in the firelight. How could she be so prepared for him? Again, he felt that uneasiness.

"Why am I doing this?"

"So you *understand* what you look like."

She said it with such scorn, he had to take another deep breath to keep his temper in check. "And that will...help me?"

She glanced at Merivale. "Is he always this stupid?"

"You forgot to tell him the fee," said Merivale.

"Oh." She pursed her lips and gave Red a

flickering look with just a hint of apology. "You have to pay my fee, or I can't help you."

Red's uneasiness grew. "And what's the fee?"

"Trust."

"Trust?" He looked at Merivale helplessly.

"You have to trust her," she said. "Even though you don't know her. Even if that trust feels completely unearned, you have to give it to her. I know that probably feels as unnatural to you as it did to me, but this is what I meant earlier about making sure you were motivated to do what needs to be done. You must give yourself over to this fully, or it won't work."

"I don't know how to just...give trust."

"You can start by shutting up and doing what you're told without asking stupid questions," said Casasha.

Merivale gave him a wry smile. "There you go."

Red managed a very faint smile in return. "I guess so."

"Fine," said Casasha. "Meri-kitty, time for you to leave. Lying Artist, time for you to paint."

———

Red took his time with the painting. He assumed this was not something to rush, and that whatever the actual point of this was, the details were important. He hadn't picked up a brush since he'd painted Hope over a year ago, but he found himself sliding right back to that place of focus. It was even pleasant to push all his worries and fears aside and just paint.

When he was finished, he had a little bit of the creative afterglow, despite the pressure and strange situation. He even felt a quiet surge of pride when he showed it to Casasha.

"Wrong," she said flatly.

"What do you mean *wrong*?" demanded Red. "How can art be wrong?"

"It's not scary enough," said Casasha. "Does this look like someone who could kill eight people in four seconds? No way. Fix it."

Red glared at her, his temper beginning to rise again. But she had already lost interest and went back to staring at the wall, flicking her hands, and silently muttering.

He stalked back to the basin and his paints. He added some harder lines until his red slitted eyes really did look demonic. He also hardened the corners of the mouth. He didn't even know if he did that as the Shadow Demon, but it felt right for some reason. He added a few more details until finally he felt that his portrait was indeed scarier. When he looked at it, an unmistakable chill of recognition ran through him. That's when he knew it was done.

"Okay, did I fix it?" He showed it to Casasha.

"Nope, still wrong."

"What?" Any show of patience was gone, but she didn't seem to notice. "I made it scarier!"

"It's not *fun* enough," she said. "Does this look like someone who tells good stories and tricks people into crazy adventures?"

"No, but you said—"

"Fix it."

"You want me to start over?"

"No one gets to start over. Just fix it."

Red went back to his paint. He worked on the eyes, giving them a mischievous slant. He turned up the corners of the mouth into that grin he was always trying to perfect. The painting was getting messy, but he couldn't help that. The only way to keep those changes from bleeding into the previous changes was to let the original ones dry first, but Red was pretty sure the sun would set soon, and with it, the Shadow

Demon would be free to come out. So he just kept working, letting the paints begin to smear.

As he worked on the grin, he had to show it in the water a few times on his own face. He realized it had been a while since he'd really used that grin. He had to admit, it felt good on his face and strangely enough, by doing it, he felt a little better. He'd had dark times before, hadn't he? And he'd always laughed it off, knowing he would find a way to the other side. That was part of the fun, after all.

By the time he was finished, he even had a little spring in his step as he walked over to Casasha.

"Alright, how about now?"

"Still not right yet," she said.

"You're kidding me."

"Does this look like a painter? Someone who can take a jar of colors and a brush, and create something unique and beautiful that moves people to tears? Someone who has art hanging up right now in big important galleries? Does it look like an *artist*?"

He stared down at her wordlessly. All his cockiness and cheer drained away.

Her eyes drilled into him for a moment as she said, "You *have* to fix it." Then she turned away again.

Red walked slowly back to his paints, his chest filling with dread. He looked down into the water and let his reflection soften. Let it open. Nettles used to make fun of him when he got that "artsy ponce" look. Sadie used to try to slap it right off his face. Even Filler would get uncomfortable around him in those rare moments when Red let it out. And yet, as he thought of how hard they had been on him, he suddenly missed them so much. The longing welled up inside him like it was a physical need. He hadn't let himself truly miss them, always telling himself he'd see them again. He'd find some way out of this like he always did. But what if he didn't see them

again? There would be holes in his heart that he'd
never be able to fill. Pain that he'd never be able to
quell.

Except, maybe when he was painting. He'd always
known that. It would quiet the pain and loneliness
and confusion, at least for a little while. He'd always
wanted to believe he didn't need it. But right now, he
did. So he stretched out on the floor like a child, and
he painted. It was even messier now, but he didn't
care anymore. This wasn't about neatness or detail.
It was about letting the truth come out. Letting that
scared little boy out of his cage, if only for a little
while, so that maybe he could find some peace and
not hurt quite so much.

Red painted until his hands shook. Until his
vision became blurry. Until the world around him
spun and time had no meaning. He painted until he
could no longer keep his eyes open and exhaustion
swept over him like a heavy blanket.

———

He dreamed of being a child. Of lying on that old
couch with his mother in their cozy little apartment
in Silverback. The two of them were bundled up
under a blanket to ward off the cold winter winds
that slipped in through the cheaply made window
frames. The room was dark and they stared out the
window up at the night sky, which they could just
make out as a dark blue sliver between building tops.

"Do you know why I named you Rixidenteron?"
his mother asked.

He shook his head.

"Rixidenteron the Third was one of the greatest
painters who ever lived. What I love most about his
work is that he found the beauty in even the darkest moments. Once, when I was a girl, I saw his

masterpiece, *The Storm Brings Change*. It was so violent, with ships breaking against coastal reefs, people dead and dying... it terrified me. But I couldn't stop looking at it because it was also the most beautiful thing I'd ever seen."

They were silent for a moment. He savored the peace of it. Lately, his mom had been more difficult. Losing patience, yelling, hitting. His dad said it wasn't her fault. That she was just getting sicker. His dad was out now, secretly having sex with people for money so he could pretend to be an anonymous art collector and buy all the new paintings that nobody wanted.

This secret weighed heavily on the boy. It hurt to feel this wedge of separation between himself and his mom. To fight against it, he snuggled in closer to her, savoring her kindness and openness, even if it was only temporary.

She smiled and ran her fingers through his messy hair.

"You were born in dark times," she said. "And I'm worried you'll have more dark times ahead. I know..." She hesitated and he could hear a faint constriction in her voice, like she was fighting back emotion. "I don't know how I will be able to help you. So you must always be like your namesake. You must find the beauty in the darkness. That is what we artists must always strive to do."

"Am I an artist?" he asked.

"Of course you are," she said.

He woke up in Casasha's house, with the shutters still closed and only the flickering light of the fireplace. Casasha sat by the fire, sipping a steaming mug.

He stood up, feeling strangely light. How long had

he slept? He picked up his painting and brought it over to Casasha.

"Well? Did I fix it?"

She stared at her mug, not looking at him or his painting. Her voice was unexpectedly soft and weary. "Why don't you go outside and see for yourself?"

He wasn't exactly sure what she meant, but he was more or less used to that now, so he obediently walked over and opened the front door. He looked out at the trees and the sky overhead. The breeze felt good after being in the stuffy room so long. It took a few moments before it dawned on him he was looking up at the moon and stars. It was night, and he hadn't changed.

Or had he?

He looked down at the self-portrait in his hands. It was all over the place, with parts that looked like the Shadow Demon, parts that looked like Red, and parts that looked like Rixidenteron. It really was a mess. But maybe it was a beautiful mess.

"How did you expect to tame the darkness," asked Casasha from her spot by the fireplace, "if you refused to accept the light?"

He turned back to her. "It was always in me, wasn't it? The Shadow Demon."

"To some degree. So was the artist. The biomancers strengthened the one, so I strengthened the other."

Red looked at her and tapped his chin thoughtfully. "Do you have any more canvases?"

"No, but I have some parchment and charcoal."

"That'll do fine," he said.

"For what?"

"For me to sketch your portrait." Then in the most scathing tone he could muster, he said, *"Obviously."*

She looked over at him, and there was surprise in her expression. Then she suddenly laughed—a rich, unfettered sound that echoed through the room.

Red sat on the small porch, his smoked glasses firmly in place as he watched the first rays of the sun. His fingers itched to paint it. But they itched to paint everything now. It was a little annoying, but it was also a nice reminder, whenever he started to worry that he'd imagined everything that happened the night before.

"My Lord Pastinas," called Merivale as she rode up to the house on a beautiful golden mare. "How are you feeling on this lovely morning?"

"Like a perfect mess," he said.

She smiled. "Was Casasha able to help you sort things out?"

"Yeah." He jerked his thumb at the closed door behind him. "She just kicked me out, though. Said she was tired of me thinking so loudly."

"She does that," said Merivale.

"I owe you, Meri-kitty," he said. "A lot."

"Yes, I'm glad you bring that up. And I'll need you to address me as either 'Lady Hempist' or 'my lady' from now on."

"Oh?"

"It won't do to have you getting so familiar, now that you're working for me."

"Me?" asked Red. "Working for you? Since when?"

"I hope you didn't think I was going through all of this simply because I'm fond of you. As the chief spy to Her Imperial Majesty, I hardly have the luxury of such idle indulgence."

He gave her a wry smile. "I guess not."

"And you did just say you *owe* me, didn't you?"

"I did."

"Fortunately, I know exactly how you can repay me, as well as the empress, who so kindly allowed

you to keep your head on your neck, even after you
nearly killed the ambassador."

"And what, exactly, do you want me to do?" he
asked apprehensively.

"To become a spy in Her Majesty's service, naturally. You are hereby charged by Her Imperial Majesty with utilizing your existing connections to the
biomancers, as well as your astonishing abilities and
undeniable charm, to assist in rooting out corruption within the empire once and for all."

His eyebrows slowly rose above his dark glasses.
"That sounds...ambitious."

She smiled at him, a twinkle in her eyes. "Don't
worry. It'll be fun."

27

The fleet of Dire Bane anchored a good distance from Dawn's Light to await nightfall. Bleak Hope sat in her cabin, alone, and let herself be swallowed up by Sadie's loss. None could equal that old woman in her bold, irreverent wisdom. It was more than just Hope's loss. It was the world's. Hope longed for some sort of comfort, but when she realized that the person she would have been mostly likely to seek it from was Filler, her sense of loss only deepened.

But Hope had fought through pain before. Whether physical or emotional, she would not allow it to stop her now, so close to her goal. So as the sun began to set, she steeled herself against the grief, and went topside to greet the darkness.

The island was called Dawn's Light because it was the first island in the empire to touch the sun every morning. That also meant it was the first island to lose the sun every evening. Before she completely lost the sunlight, Hope trained her spyglass on the fortifications that had been put in place since her last visit. Cannon trenches had been dug across the sandy shore, built up with sandbags. Two massive frigates lay anchored nearby. They clearly thought they were ready for her. Hopefully they were wrong.

The plan was to come at Dawn's Light from three

different directions just as the sun rose. The *Glory-bound* would attack from the northwest, where the dock was located. It was the biggest and most heavily armed of the three ships, and that was the most fortified side of the island. The *Rolling Lightning* would attack from the northeast, and the *Kraken Hunter* from the south.

Since the *Kraken Hunter* had to circle all the way around the island to reach the southern shore, they set sail while the other two were still getting ready.

As they took the long arc around the eastern side of Dawn's Light, they gave it as much distance as they could without getting caught in the massive and unpredictable currents of the Dawn Sea. It wasn't likely they'd be spotted in the gathering dark, but she was taking no chances.

She stood next to Missing Finn on the quarter-deck as usual, but she felt a distance between them that she wasn't sure how to bridge.

"I'm sorry about Sadie," she said at last.

He smiled sadly. "I spent more years missing her than being with her."

"It seems unfair," said Hope. "That she would be snatched away just when things were finally working out for you two."

"That's life for you," said Finn. "Never does seem much concerned with being fair."

"The Vinchen believe that life is fair, ultimately. That all things equal out in time."

"Of course *they'd* say that," said Finn. "Justice comes more often to the strong than to the weak."

"Then it is up to the strong to *make* things fair," said Hope. "I promise you, Finn. Her death will be avenged."

Missing Finn remained silent. Hope couldn't tell if her words gave him any comfort.

The Kraken Hunter *is in position!* Jilly's voice chirped in Brigga Lin's head.

"Jilly, please don't shout."

Was I shouting? Jilly's voice came more gently. *Sorry, master. I didn't realize. That probably means I was shouting in teacher's head, too.*

"Probably," agreed Brigga Lin. "I will tell Captain Gray that everyone is ready. Stay focused so I can let you know when he thinks we'll be within firing range."

Yes, master.

Brigga Lin moved to the quarterdeck, where Gavish Gray gazed out through the darkness at the distant northeast coast of Dawn's Light. She wasn't sure what to make of this captain. He certainly seemed knowledgeable about sailing, bringing his own ship and crew, all of whom worked together with the smoothness of experience. But he had a strange sort of resigned air mixed with bitter amusement. She worried his attitude would make him a less than ideal ally in the coming battle. Nettles had been very insistent on sending him, but Brigga Lin wasn't sure what to make of her anymore either.

"Captain Bane is ready to proceed," she told Gray.

He gave her an uneasy look. "They sent their thoughts to you through that girl, then?"

"Roughly speaking, yes."

"Is she, like, your biomancer in training, then?"

"I'm not sure it would be accurate to call either of us biomancers at this point," said Brigga Lin.

Gray shrugged. "If you say so."

"How long before we're within firing range?"

"We can be there in under ten minutes, but the *Rolling Lightning* is a far sight faster than the

Glorybound, and I know Bane wanted Vaderton to strike first, so we should give him a head start. You tell me when he's starting, and we'll start a short time after that."

"I'll check back with them," said Brigga Lin. "It's nearly dawn. If we wait until full light, we'll lose what little element of surprise we might still have."

———

"So how does it work?" asked Vaderton.

Jilly was aware that he was giving her a curious look as she sat on top of a barrel and tried to keep her breath even and thoughts flexible, just like Brigga Lin had taught her.

"I'm not really sure," she admitted. "There's still so much to learn. Brigga Lin says it's going to take *years*."

"I believe most biomancers study for ten years before they are granted their robes."

"I don't want one of those bludgeon robes. Nothing pat about them," said Jilly. "Anyway, I think this mind message thing has something to do with electricity."

"Really? Like lightning?" asked Vaderton.

"Apparently it's inside our heads all the time and that's how we think." She frowned. "Or... something like that."

"So it's like you're sending tiny lightning bolts back and forth to each other?" he asked.

She shrugged. "I guess. Although one of us has to be the central node, or the whole thing falls apart."

"And that's you," said Vaderton.

"Or maybe they just wanted an excuse to keep me out of the action."

Vaderton's eyes widened. "Out of the action?

seemed able to coax every last bit of speed out of her. She sliced through the water like a knife, heading directly for the shore. The northeast wasn't as heavily fortified, but it had more than enough artillery to sink their small ship.

She saw a puff of orange and smoke from the artillery wall.

"Incoming!" yelled Gray. "Prepare to jibe!"

He hiked the wheel hard and the *Rolling Lightning* cut to one side, the sails rattling for a moment before snapping taut again. A moment later, a massive splash erupted off the port bow.

"That was close," said Brigga Lin.

"We're more nimble than that great lumbering brig of Bane's," said Gray, looking mildly insulted. "Besides, at this range, we can take a few hits."

"What about when we get closer?"

"Well, now." Gray licked his lips. "That's when it'll get interesting."

———

"Both the *Glorybound* and the *Rolling Lightning* are engaged," said Bleak Hope. "Time to move in."

"Aye, Captain," said Missing Finn.

"Let's hope they're drawing enough fire to get us close."

The *Kraken Hunter* opened its sails and surged forward. The southern coast of the island was the least fortified of the three sides, probably because it was tucked in near the Breaks, so it would have been a challenge to get a full fleet on that side. Even so, the fortifications were more than enough to stop the *Kraken Hunter* if her plan didn't work.

Smoke bloomed in a line on the coast.

"Incoming!" called the watch from the royals.

"Take cover!" yelled Hope.

A series of shrieking whistles filled the air. Most hit the water, but one tore through the jib and another shattered the starboard gunwale. Hope knocked a knife-sized splinter out of the air with her clamp. Most of the sailors found cover in time, but a man went down with a thick chunk of wood in his calf.

"Get him below and bind his wounds," she told two of the crew. Then she closed her eyes. "Jilly, are you there?"

Right here, teacher!

"Tell Vaderton he needs to draw more fire or we'll be torn to pieces before we reach the coast!"

"What does she mean, draw *more* fire?" Vaderton shouted over the roar of cannons and the hiss of incoming projectiles.

"She said you have the biggest and most heavily armed ship and that you'd figure it out." Jilly decided not to repeat the rest of the message, which had been *unless twenty years in the navy has turned him into a spineless wretch.* She knew that in the middle of a bombardment, sometimes people said things they didn't mean.

"She wants us to move in close and present a credible threat," said Vaderton. "Only then will they start pulling resources over from the other two sides of the island."

"How long can we last at closer range?" she asked.

"As long as we must, I suppose."

He gave the order and the *Glorybound* took a deep arc toward the shore until they were close enough to see the cannon muzzles. At that range, the *Glorybound*'s cannons had enough force to start knocking down the walls. But the enemy cannons were more dangerous as well.

As they swept across, they took several hits to the hull, but those weren't low enough for them to start taking on water. Then one shot whistled overhead, followed by a thunderous crack as the foremast began to fall.

"Cut the lines!" shouted Vaderton.

Crew grabbed axes and swords and hacked at the rigging that threatened to take the mainmast down with it.

"You stay focused!" Vaderton snapped at Jilly, pulling her attention away from the men desperately trying to free the broken mast. "I need to know the *second* that Bane has cleared the beach, so we can pull out of here."

———

"Looks like that navy gaf is finally starting to take the heat off us," said Gavish Gray. "Only half the cannons are firing now."

"Good," said Brigga Lin as she smothered a small fire that had sprung up after a cluster of shot had struck a pile of rope nearby. "I'm getting tired of—"

An image opened in her head of a cannonball headed directly toward her.

"Hard to port!" she yelled.

Gray moved instinctively, spinning the wheel with his whole weight. The ship twisted and several crew members staggered around to keep their footing. But a moment later, a cannonball struck the water where the quarterdeck would have been.

Gray's eyebrows rose. "How did you see that coming so fast? You weren't even looking in that direction."

"I saw it before it was fired," said Brigga Lin.

Gavish Gray grinned as he leveled them off and

pointed them toward the shore again. "I'm suddenly glad to have you aboard!"

She regarded him coolly. "You weren't before?"

———

Bleak Hope watched many of the soldiers that had been manning the cannons on shore hurry off toward the north end of the island. Vaderton had done it. Now only half the cannons were in use.

"Time to head for the shore," she told Finn.

He winced. "Are you sure about this?"

"We don't have much choice," said Hope. "And I promise, fixing her will be our top priority."

He patted the wheel and nodded glumly. Then he pointed the bow directly at the shore. The advantage to a head-on charge was that it offered the smallest possible target. Many ships, including the *Kraken Hunter*, also had the most reinforcement on the bow.

As they approached, cannonballs splashed down on either side. Occasionally, one glanced off the bow hard enough to slow down the charge, but they had a strong quartering wind, so the ship quickly recovered her speed.

The crew were all under cover to keep casualties down. Hope had her sword drawn and fended off debris that threatened both her and Finn. He held the wheel with tears in his eye as they closed in on the shore.

"Brace!" he yelled.

Hope grabbed the rail, but it still wasn't enough. When the *Kraken Hunter* slammed into the beach, the impact knocked her over the railing. She barely managed to land feetfirst on the main deck.

Her ship cut a deep wedge into the shore. When she heard the wooden ribs groan under the sudden weight, she felt its pain.

"Add it to the rest," she muttered, and leapt over the bow onto the wet sand.

———

Brigga Lin stood leaning over the base of the bowsprit as the *Rolling Lightning* bore down on the fortified coast. Cannon shots sang past. Occasionally one of them threatened the ship, but those she felt a premonition about and called out to Gavish Gray.

It was just as Yammy promised. They had worked together for days without stop and Brigga Lin hadn't felt even the slightest ripple of foreknowledge. She had been so frustrated. But Yammy had assured her it would come in time, probably in a heated moment of self-preservation. It was still not totally under her control, but when she was threatened physically, she could feel it as one feels the wind on her face. Yammy had called it the Breath of Destiny.

"Are we close enough for you to do your thing with the cannons yet?" Gray shouted up to her.

Brigga Lin squinted at the fortifications, but she still couldn't see the cannons themselves. "Not yet."

"I'm not running my ship aground like Bane. This is my whole livelihood and I'd sooner die."

"We might need to fall back on that other idea of yours, then. Is your crew in place?"

"Of course they are, my Lady Witch."

"Lady Witch?" asked Brigga Lin as she hopped down from the bow and walked back to the quarterdeck.

"Well, you said not to call you a biomancer."

She nodded. "I suppose Lady Witch is preferable, although I'll never understand the New Laven compulsion to give everything multiple names."

"Call it a sign of admiration if you like," said Gavish.

"I see. Well, let's begin your reckless plan, then, Captain Gray."

"Not reckless. *Daring*." He turned to his first mate. "Fisty, take the wheel."

"Sir." Fisty hurried over.

"Give it about fifty yards to impact before you drop anchor," said Gavish. "But then do it quick."

"Aye, sir."

Gavish held out his arm to Brigga Lin. "Shall we, Lady Witch? Your carriage awaits."

She had to suppress a smile as she took his arm. "This hardly seems the time for idle flirtation."

"Clearly you haven't been doing piracy properly," he said.

They hurried over to starboard, where the lifeboat had been hung over the side, suspended by ropes on pulley arms at either end. The small boat was packed with sailors, all of them armed with guns, swords, and knives. There was barely enough room for Brigga Lin and Gavish Gray to fit as they all hunkered down low. Brigga Lin leaned over the side and stared at the water that streamed past directly below.

"You're sure this will work?" she asked Gray.

"Sure and we've done this a few times, haven't we, wags?"

They all grinned and nodded.

As they neared the shore, a billow of cannon fire was followed swiftly by the sound of breaking wood coming from the deck of the *Rolling Lightning*.

Gavish winced. "That's going to be an ugly one." Then he turned to the men who sat next to the lines that held the lifeboat suspended. "On my mark."

They each drew a knife and held it against their rope.

"Drop anchor!" they heard Fisty call from the helm.

Two massive anchors were flung off the stern.

"Now!" said Gray.

The men cut the lines to the lifeboat just as the anchor chains went taut and began to drag along the sandy sea bottom. The *Rolling Lightning* jerked back and the lifeboat shot forward, skipping along the surface of the water.

Brigga Lin stood up as the cannons came within view. This was something she couldn't do sitting down. But the boat was still bouncing and she fell backward. Gavish's hands shot up and steadied her, each of his large palms finding a firm grip on her butt.

She snarled at him and he replied with a mockingly innocent look. But she didn't have time to eviscerate him right then, so she turned and let the anger out on the cannons. The microorganisms around the gunpowder combusted all at once, and the entire line of fortifications went up simultaneously.

She turned slowly back to Gray. The chain of fiery explosions that continued from the powder stores framed her silhouette as she glared down at him.

"It was an accident, I swear!" he said.

"You're lucky I need you alive," she said. "For now."

As she turned back to examine her handiwork, she heard him mutter to one of his crew, "A *happy* accident."

———

"They're clear!" Jilly shouted over the bombardment. "We can pull back!"

"Swing us around!" Vaderton said to Biscuit Bill at the helm. "Fly whatever canvas we have left. Let's get the hells out of here!"

The ship began its slow turn away from Dawn's

Light and the endless roar of cannons. Those crew that weren't wounded set every last bit of sail that hadn't been punched full of holes, and even some that had.

Jilly wished she could help, but Brigga Lin and Dire Bane might need her to coordinate their rendezvous at the center of the island.

"Piss'ell," growled Vaderton. It took Jilly by surprise because she'd never heard him swear like that. He had his glass trained back toward the coast. "I was afraid of that."

"Of what?" asked Jilly.

"They're giving chase. Both frigates, looks like sixty gun each."

"*Sixty*? Can we outrun them?"

"Normally, I'd say it was possible, what with our head start and a favorable wind. But with only one mast up, we don't have a prayer."

Jilly scanned the waterline in front of them. To the north, off the starboard bow, was the open sea. To the west, off the port bow, rose the Breaks.

"Could we hide?" she asked. "Maybe in there?"

He frowned thoughtfully. "Hide? Probably not. But they'd have to be suicidal to follow us into the Breaks with ships that large." He turned to the rest of the crew and raised his voice. "All hands, throw everything we have overboard. Anchors, cannons, shot, anything that'll go!" He gazed back at the approaching frigates for a moment, then said, "*Except* the gunpowder!"

"Sir?" asked Jilly. She wondered why he'd want to keep the most volatile thing on the ship if there was a chance the frigates would fire on them before they reached the Breaks.

"You just focus on keeping that connection with Bane and Lin," he snapped to her. "We might need it after this."

———

Bleak Hope hit the sand running. She didn't have Brigga Lin here to disable the cannons for her, so she had to reach the artillery line before they reloaded. She could see them in shallow trenches behind a low stone wall.

As she sprinted toward them, she watched them swab the cannons. She could hear the hiss and crackle as the cotton touched the hot metal bore.

She was closer as they primed and loaded the barrel.

She was closer still as they tamped it down.

She could see their faces as they rolled the cannons into position and locked them in place. Those faces suddenly turned to fear as the canoneers took aim, only to realize that their deaths were already upon them.

Hope leapt over the wall. Two cannoneers died before her feet hit the bottom of the trench. She ran down the line, the Song of Sorrows humming its terrible tune as it flashed back and forth, killing soldiers still fumbling for their pistols.

Once they were all dead and her arm ached with the grief of their passing, Hope climbed up on top of the wall and waved back to the beached *Kraken Hunter*. A cheer rose up from within and her crew spilled out onto the surf, armed and ready for battle.

They ran up the beach and clambered over the wall past Hope as she stood and gave the *Kraken Hunter* one last look. She'd asked Missing Finn to stay behind and begin assessing the damage. She didn't know what pained her more, seeing the ship leaning on its side like that, or knowing that Missing Finn's heart had been broken twice in as many days.

"Are you ready, Captain?" asked Alash.

"You're sure you want to come with us?" asked Hope. "You could have stayed behind with Finn."

"I realize you don't normally consider me a combat asset," he said with such resolve that she wondered if he'd actually rehearsed this speech to himself. "But Sadie was in our crew and one of the most treasured people in my cousin's life. I cannot sit idly by." He held up his strange rifle. "Besides, I think with this I might be of some use to you."

"Yes, your... *repeating* rifle," said Hope. "I really hope it doesn't blow up in your face."

He looked genuinely insulted. "Have a little faith in my design, Captain. I've been working on this for months."

She inclined her head. "My apologies, Mr. Havolon. Let's go test it out. And remember, the evidence we found in the tents suggested the only way to stop these living corpses is a shot to the heart or the head."

Alash blanched slightly, but nodded.

Hope put her hand on his shoulder. "These are the moments we show our true worth, Alash. No matter what happens next, you have come a long way since cowering in your grandfather's mansion."

He smiled. "Thank you, Captain. That means a great deal coming from you."

Bleak Hope turned away from the ship and the sea and began the march into the interior of the island with a small but determined group of true wags at her back. The sun was high overhead now, but a cold wind blew up from the south, drying the sweat on the back of her neck and tugging at the bottom of her coat.

The terrain was fairly level, so it wasn't long before they could see the circle of tents in the distance.

"God, there they are." Alash pointed to the entrance of the large tent. A steady stream of walking corpses was already shambling out at a quick, uneven gait.

"I see them." She turned to her crew, all of whom stared wide-eyed at the growing swarm of living death not more than fifty yards away and closing in fast.

"Today, we are not killers, or warriors. Today, we are angels of mercy, putting these suffering creatures to proper rest. Today, we are deliverance for the girls still alive waiting to be slaughtered. Today, we are vengeance for all of our friends and comrades that have been taken from us." She held the Song of Sorrows aloft. It didn't just hum; it sang in that hard southern wind. The blade flashed like lightning in the midday sun. "Today, we are the storm!"

The crew cheered and Bleak Hope felt the glory of it fill up her heart. She smiled fiercely as she turned to face the nightmare that bore down on them.

———

"Here they come." Brigga Lin watched as a mob of the dead rushed toward them. It mostly comprised girls that had been taken from small rural islands. Many of them were not even full grown. But they were not frail or weak. These had been peasant girls who had probably done manual labor since they could walk. And now they were fearless, perhaps even mindless, with only the command of their necromancer echoing in their slowly rotting heads.

"I been hearing about this for weeks now," Gavish Gray said quietly. "First from the Black Rose, and then from you and Bane. And it wasn't like I didn't believe you, but..." He trailed off, his hard, weathered expression unreadable beneath his thick mop of gray hair.

"Seeing it for yourself is another matter," finished Brigga Lin.

He nodded.

"Bane will be confronting a much larger group at the compound," she said. "So we need to get through this as quickly as we can."

"Then we best get started." Gavish drew his cutlass and turned to his crew. "This ain't pretty work, but it's got to be done. The only sure way to put 'em down is to take off the head. Mind that you do. Now let's go show them our own special type of hell."

They charged forward while Brigga Lin hung back, as she usually did, to cast from afar. She wasn't sure what would work on these creatures, however. As they drew closer she tried a few things. She burst open a rib cage, but the girl continued to shamble forward, her guts flopping in front of her like an apron. She tried turning one's insides to boiling pitch, but the girl kept running, even as smoke billowed from her eyes, nose, and mouth. She tried a few other ideas as well, but nothing worked. What could she do? She was a master of the living, not the dead. When she'd expressed this concern to Yammy, the woman had said in that insufferably superior tone of hers: "You make too much of it. Life, death. It's all part of the same cycle."

The crew of the *Rolling Lightning* hit the wave of dead, hacking desperately at their blank expressions. Gavish was a sight to behold. A model of ruthless efficiency. He had already gotten past the shock of attacking dead little girls and hewed to either side with his thick-bladed cutlass, hacking off moldy little girl heads. But many of the other crew were not faring as well. The dead weren't armed, but instead overwhelmed people first with fear, then with sheer numbers, driving them to the ground and tearing them apart, one limb at a time. Screams filled the air, and for once, it was Brigga Lin's allies, not her enemies, who were suffering. The sound twisted up inside her as she watched with impotent fury.

But something nagged at her. She stared at a girl's head, which had rolled to the edge of the battle. The girl's eyes stared wide, her mouth slack, and her mottled skin shiny like wax. Brigga Lin noticed the fine green crust of mold that lined the girl's temples. And then she finally understood what Yammy had been saying. Life, death, and life again. As anyone who had given serious study to the living processes knew, within hours, tiny organisms were already beginning the decomposition process. These brought other organisms, such as mold and fungi. All biological matter was ultimately nothing more than food for other biological matter. And where there was a food source in nature, there were living things to consume it.

She reached out and found the tiny spores of mold within every dead girl on the field. She called them forth, encouraged them to grow, to propagate, to dominate the host on which they lived.

The dead stopped moving forward. Their swaying, jerky bodies grew rigid, sometimes at odd angles. The battle suddenly came to a halt. Gray's surviving crew looked uneasily at the posed corpses all around them.

Then great plumes of fungi burst forth from the mouths of the dead in blues, yellows, reds, and purples. The crew watched in astonishment as Brigga Lin brought forth a rainbow fungus garden in the middle of the barren field. She'd cast that much before, but never had it been such a pure act of creation. The call to life rang from her like a bell. And it felt glorious.

But then a dizziness swept through her. She felt the blood gush from her nose. Her mind was wrung out like a dishrag. The world around her dimmed and the ground rushed up to meet her.

"Whoa now, Lady Witch," said Gavish Gray as he caught her moments before she hit the rocky soil. "Let's not spoil that dress of yours." He lifted her up and began carrying her, one arm under her knees and one cradling her shoulders and neck. "We still gotta meet Captain Bane, and I'd rather not face her wrath showing up without you."

"You better not…make another grab…at my ass," she muttered weakly.

"The thought's already crossed my mind several times," he admitted. "But in your current condition, it wouldn't be very sporting. I do like a bit of danger, you know."

———

Once Vaderton's men had thrown everything overboard, the *Glorybound* gained enough speed to reach the Breaks before the frigates caught up with them.

From a distance, the Breaks looked like a solid line of reefs, but if you were reckless enough—or desperate enough—to get close, it became clear they were actually grouped in tight, uneven clusters, with pockets and gaps that a nimble ship and a skilled helmsman might slip through. Although Vaderton had been captain of the *Glorybound* for only a short time, his compulsive need for order had driven him to inspect every inch of it before he'd set sail, and already he knew it better than the palm of his own hand, which truth be told, he really only looked at when he was washing it.

He found a long corridor between two lines of reefs. As he entered, he turned back to see if the frigates might abandon the chase. But his faint hope evaporated when he saw them continue apace, shortening sail to give themselves some maneuverability.

"They're following us in?" asked Jilly. "I thought you said it would be suicide for them!"

"It is," said Vaderton. "There's only one reason those captains would throw their ships into something like this. There must be a biomancer on board making them do it."

"So what are we going to do?" asked Jilly.

"*I* am going to my fallback plan. *You* are going to continue concentrating so you can keep contact with Captain Bane. We'll be needing her for certain now." He raised his voice. "I want all the gunpowder moved to the poop deck, quick as you can!"

Then he returned his attention to navigating through the narrow, treacherous corridors of the Breaks. As he yanked the wheel back and forth, he scanned ahead for a likely spot.

"That one." He turned to Biscuit Bill the helmsman, who stood anxiously by. "I need you to gather the entire crew on the quarterdeck."

"The *entire* crew?"

"That's what I said. And find among them the best shot and have that person ready with a rifle loaded." He gestured to Jilly. "And take her with you, but don't let her *do* anything. She needs to maintain her focus and stay alive, or else no matter how this plays out, we won't survive. Keen?"

"Y-yes, sir." He took Jilly firmly by the shoulder and led her to the quarterdeck. Then he began shouting to the rest of the crew, herding them back as well.

Vaderton steered the ship further down the corridor. All the sails had been struck, but he moved on the hard currents that coursed between the reefs. His arms ached as he spun the wheel first one way, then the other, trying to keep her on an even keel toward his goal.

At last he saw it. A passageway where the corridor narrowed too much for the *Glorybound* to get through. He pointed her bow at the sweet spot right between the two reefs and shouted, *"Brace!"*

The *Glorybound* smashed into the narrow crevasse. The air filled with the sound of rending, cracking timber as the front section of the ship folded like a book all the way to the waist, leaving the tail end of the ship where the crew huddled poking out from the reefs.

"Everyone, climb onto the reefs!" shouted Vaderton. "Get around to the far side as quickly as you can!" Then he turned to Bill. "Where's my shooter?"

"Oh, uh..." He shook his head as if to clear the shock out of it. "Kismet Pete!" He pointed to the bald man.

Vaderton grinned. "Sunny. Now, Pete, you're with me. The rest of you, get windward of that reef quick as lightning if you want to live. And Bill, you mind Jilly, 'cause she can't mind herself right now."

"Aye, sir!" Bill started hustling the rest of the crew and Jilly over to the starboard side, where they all began to climb over the gunwale and onto the reef. It was ragged enough at this height that there were plenty of hand- and footholds.

Vaderton watched them, and nodded with satisfaction once they were all clear. Then he turned to Pete. "Alright, we're last."

"I think I'm starting to see what you have in mind," said Pete as he gazed down the corridor of reefs.

The frigates were coming single file, barely fitting in the tight space. In fact, on closer inspection with his glass, Vaderton noted that they had both already sustained some hull damage. Even the best captains in the empire couldn't maneuver those massive warships through a space like this. They had to know by now that no matter how this went for them, they probably weren't getting out of this alive. But they were just following orders. Like Vaderton used to do. He felt a pang of sympathy for them. But then he looked back at his crew huddled along the reef. Most of them were men and women that had come with him from the Empty Cliffs. Some he'd befriended; all he'd trained. He cared more about this crew than any other he'd ever had. These were *his* people, and he'd be damned if he let them die today.

He turned to Pete. "Let's get into position."

They climbed up onto the reef, but didn't move around to the windward side with the rest of the crew. "It's going to get hot."

Pete grinned. "I ain't got no hair to get singed off, and anyway, it'll be worth it to see how this idea of yours plays out firsthand."

"On my mark, then," said Vaderton.

He watched the frigates draw closer. The bow chasers, twelve-pounders just like the *Guardian*'s, moved into position. Like as not, they couldn't see the reefs at the end of the corridor behind the wrecked *Glorybound* and hoped they could blow the ship to pieces and make it to the other side of the Breaks. Of course, Vaderton couldn't let them drown all that gunpowder he'd left on the quarterdeck, but he had to wait until the front frigate was as close as possible. He watched with his glass as the cannoneers prepared to fire the bow chasers. Just before they struck their powder, he said, "Fire!"

Pete's rifle went off loud in Vaderton's ear, making it ring. A moment later, the powder cache on the *Glorybound* went up in a single explosion. With nowhere else to go, it vented backward down the corridor. The front frigate was completely engulfed in the blaze. Its masts caught fire and the sailors screamed as they burned alive. The ship's hull flickered with fire, and staccato bursts of gunpowder explosions went off from unfired cannons. The frigate careened to the side and smashed into a reef, then bounced off back into the narrow channel at an angle.

There was no worse fate for a sailor than to be burned alive. It was universally dreaded. In his panic, the captain of the second ship gave the order to drop both anchors to stern in a desperate attempt to stop before they crashed into the flaming wreck in front of them. But rather than drag along a sandy bottom to slow the ship down, the anchors hooked sharply on the smaller reefs below the waterline, pulling so hard they tore holes in the hull.

As they desperately tried to keep the second ship afloat, the fire on the first ship finally found the powder room. As Vaderton well knew, the powder room for a ship with so many cannons was very large. This second explosion was twice that of the first, swallowing both frigates in an inferno.

Even at his distance, Vaderton felt the heat of it on his face.

Kismet Pete turned to him, his face black with soot. His expression was grave as he said, "Well, Captain. I do believe we gave 'em the slip."

———

Bleak Hope felt that same icy prickle up her arm as she cleaved into the hordes of the dead. She couldn't have said whether it felt better or worse, but while she usually had to fight against the weight of the grief, the coldness kept her sharp. Her movements were quick and brutal. Unfortunately, her entire arm was slowly growing numb.

Then the soldiers appeared, led by a group of biomancers. To Hope's mind, this was an act of desperation. She must be gaining enough ground on the dead army that Progul Bon, or whoever was in charge, felt reinforcements were needed. But some of her crew lost heart merely at the sight of the white-hooded figures emerging from the tent in a long line. Hope had almost forgotten how ingrained that fear was for most people. She had to get over to where the biomancers were so she could show them that even this enemy could be beaten.

But there were so many living dead between them, it would take her a long time to hack her way through. And all the while, *her* people were crumbling or igniting or melting at the touch of biomancers. She slashed and spun, the ice crawling through her veins as she fought harder than she'd ever fought in her life. But it was like moving through tar.

Then, all at once, the dead jerked to a halt. They shuddered, their mouths opened, and colored stalks of mushrooms sprang from their mouths. Hope stared around at the strange forest that suddenly surrounded her.

Between the rainbow trunks, she saw Brigga Lin on the other side of the battlefield. She was pale, and a river of blood poured from her nose. She leaned heavily on Gavish Gray's shoulder. And yet there was a beatific smile on her face. She had somehow found a way to neutralize the necromancer's work.

But screams continued to ring out on the battlefield. The biomancers were still killing her people.

Bleak Hope turned and barreled through the frozen dead, knocking them over like stalks of wheat. She reached her prey seconds later, the Song of Sorrows held overhead. The biomancers saw the flashing blade and fell back. Clearly they recognized it, and feared it. It was just as Jilly had said when they embarked on this cause. It was about time *they* were the ones who were scared. She *wanted* them to be afraid of her. As they reached hands toward her in what they probably knew was a pointless effort to protect themselves with biomancery, she struck

them down with a savage satisfaction she had never
known before. It was for Filler. It was for Nettles. It
was for Sadie. It was for Red. It was for her parents
and her village and all the little girls who had died
on this island. The biomancers were a sickness in the
empire, and *she* was the cure.

The shots of grief came again, but she welcomed
the pain. It burned away the cold numbness that had
been growing within her. It felt like when she plunged
cold hands into hot water. It was a good pain. She
didn't stop until every soldier and white robe had
fallen and she was soaked in their blood.

A stillness fell over the field. To one side were the
surviving members of her crew. She was relieved to
see Alash among them. But easily more than half her
people had been killed.

The colorful fungus forest had grown even taller
now, nearly ten feet in places. The corpses at the base
had begun to blacken, as if the fungus had turned
weeks of decomposition into minutes. One could
almost forget that they had once been innocent children. Almost.

Beyond the rainbow forest she saw Brigga Lin.
She seemed unable to stand without Gavish Gray's
help now. The lower half of her face and the front of
her gown were stained with blood. There were precious few survivors from Gray's crew as well.

Hope turned to the large tent. The girls from the
latest shipment were in there. And so was the necromancer. Dimly she was aware that her body ached
with exhaustion. But the burning, hungry grief had
spread from her arm and lodged itself in her chest.
It gave her the strength to move forward at a slow,
deliberate pace toward the entrance.

When she drew back the flap and looked inside,
it was like her village all over again. The dim, stuffy
interior of the tent was scattered with dead bodies.

No living girls. In the middle of the carnage stood the necromancer in his brown hooded robe, grinning at her with yellowed teeth. In his hand was a sickle covered in blood.

It had happened *again* and she had been unable to prevent it. Was she really a cure? Or just a bandage? That old darkness coiled up inside her and fused with the burning grief of the sword. Her entire body seemed to vibrate with the force of it, but it didn't give her any strength this time. Instead, the feelings seemed to fight each other, pulling her down with them.

"You...killed them all." Her voice was hard and grinding, and sounded unfamiliar in her ears.

"I wasn't about to let anyone else have them," he said in his piercing whisper. "Not even a fellow kinsman."

"We're not kinsmen."

"Of course we are. Look at your skin and hair. Deny it all you like, but we are both children of the Haevanton Triumvirate."

The twisting conflict inside her grew stronger, threaded through with new doubt. "I've never heard of such a place."

"That doesn't surprise me. But perhaps it is destiny that we meet. It may be that my defeat here today is merely a necessary step in the larger victory. My name is Vikma Bruea, last of the Jackal Lords."

Hope lifted the Song of Sorrows and pointed it at the Jackal Lord. She had made this gesture so many times, and never had the point of her sword quivered as it did now. Was it exhaustion? The growing conflict and doubt within her? She took a deep breath and forced the blade to grow still.

"Vikma Bruea, you are guilty of slaughtering the innocent. I will be their vengeance."

"I know who you truly are," he said in a mocking

tone. "But who is it you *think* you are, that you should bear this responsibility?"

"I am..."

Was she Dire Bane, champion of the people? Was she Bleak Hope, vengeful warrior? Was she *either* of those things? After all, neither of those names were truly hers. But try though she might, she could not remember what her real name was. The name her mother had called out just before she died. It now seemed like a failure on her part. Why could she not remember?

"Don't you know?" Vikma Bruea's voice taunted her.

"Who I am doesn't matter," she said finally. "You must die for your crimes."

"Do you think a Jackal Lord fears death?" He sounded almost amused now. "When the biomancers released me from my prison on Height of Lay so that I could do this work for them, I had no illusion that I would live beyond my usefulness. And I far prefer death at the hand of a kinsman than that vile brood, or any of the foul, subhuman vermin that make up the majority of this empire." He lifted his arms out to his sides and dropped his sickle to the ground. "So kill me, if it pleases you. But someday, you'll see. The Jackal Lords will return with the might of the Haevanton Triumvirate to end the line of the betrayer and crush this pathetic empire of savages. And where will your loyalties lie then, fair daughter of Heaven? Will you still side with these foul mongrels, or will you finally accept your true lineage as a warrior of the supreme Haevanton Triumvirate?"

There was a moment where she was tempted to ask him more. What did he know about the people of the Southern Isles? What were these things he spoke of? But she knew if she began to unravel that thread, it might never stop. So she hardened her expression and said, "Your words have no meaning to me."

He suddenly grinned. "Someday, they will. Then you will know who you truly are, and why—"

She thrust her sword into his chest. His pale eyes narrowed and his lips peeled back from his stained teeth in a grimace. He clutched at the blade and shuddered for a moment. When he slid lifelessly to the ground, there was almost no blood.

A new influx of grief brought the turmoil that was already boiling inside her to a level so excruciating, she fell to her knees. Every muscle in her body seized up as she stared first at the dead necromancer, and then at the dead girls. One did not in any way correct the other.

"Captain, did you find them?"

It was Alash, tentative as he peeked into the tent.

"Oh, God," he whispered. "We were too late. They're all dead."

Hope remained on her knees, her hand pressed to the cold earth.

"Are...you okay?" he asked.

"No."

He paused for a moment, then said, "Listen, I think you better come out here."

"Why?"

"They've found the last biomancer. The one Brigga Lin calls Progul Bon. They're all waiting for you to decide what to do with him."

That name brought some strength back to her limbs. One more act of vengeance. She would confront the man responsible for Sadie's death.

She slowly got to her feet, and turned to Alash. "Show me."

They had tied ropes to the biomancer's hands and were pulling them in opposite directions so his arms were stretched as far as they would go. He couldn't touch anyone, including himself. His hood had been pushed back and they had tied a rope around his neck. His face looked like melted wax, although there were cuts on his forehead and cheeks that suggested the crowd had been throwing rocks at him. Now they were screaming at him, their voices mixed with hate and fear. The only exceptions were Brigga Lin and Gavish Gray, who stood off to one side. Brigga Lin was now strong enough to stand on her own again, but she still stood close to Gray.

"There she is!" said a wiry young woman Hope recognized as one of the crew they had fished out of the water from Sadie's ship. "Captain Bane, what should we do with him?"

Hope stared at Progul Bon. She would have to kill him. She knew this. Not long ago, this would have kindled a fierce satisfaction within her. Now she had to steel herself for the act.

"We will get nothing from him," she said bleakly.

She lifted the Song of Sorrows.

"Wait, that's not true!" he shouted, his voice like bubbling oil. "If you still value your Rixidenteron, don't kill me!"

She paused, her blade hovering. "What do you mean?"

"Let me go and I'll tell you how to cure him."

"*Cure* him?"

"I have done things to his mind to make him more pliable. You would hardly even *know* him if you saw him right now. Kill me, and you might never get him back to the way he was."

Hope's jaw clenched, her stomach tight with anger that rose up even now from some previously hidden reservoir. Brigga Lin had warned her something like this might have been done to Red, and she hadn't let herself believe it before. But she knew that biomancers were incapable of lying. If he said it, she knew it had to be true.

She took a slow breath. "If I spare you—"

A single shot rang out. Progul Bon looked surprised as a line of red ran down from the hole in his forehead. He pitched forward gracelessly onto the ground.

"Sorry, Captain," said Gavish Gray, holding a still-smoking pistol in his hand. He didn't sound sorry. "Last order from the Black Rose. She said Red was your one weakness, and if anyone tried to use him against you, I was to kill them before they got the chance."

She stared at Gray for a moment, then the dead biomancer. Then she turned and looked around at the field of battle as if for the first time. There was so much death. More, even, than the massacre of her own village. And she was the one who had brought this about. And for what? Her precious cause? Back on Stonepeak, she had decided she would no longer fight for the dead. But how can one fight for the living by bringing more death?

"Come on, Captain," said Gray, his tone almost chiding. "You couldn't let him live. Dire Bane would never let a biomancer live, no matter what."

"I am...no Dire Bane," said Hope. "Perhaps he would've happily killed this biomancer, but he also wouldn't have brought so many innocents to their death." She closed her eyes and thought back to the smug glory she'd felt when she'd led these people into battle. She had been so sure of her cause. So sure of *herself*. She remembered how good it had felt as they chanted the name Dire Bane. The triumph she'd felt when so many had sworn their allegiance to her on the Empty Cliffs. She had said over and over again that it wasn't for her, but for the empire. But she knew, deep in her heart, that somewhere along the way it actually *had* become about her.

Now even Red was beyond her reach. And perhaps that was for the best. After all, rather than truly grieving for the loss of the two most important people in his life, she had used the deaths of Filler and Sadie as justification for her cause.

"I dared to call myself a champion of the people," she said: "But who am I to claim such a thing? Who am I to throw away all those lives? Now when I look upon the many good people who lay dead because of me, my own arrogance and entitlement sickens me."

She pulled off her captain's hat and coat and dropped them on the ground. The icy wind cut through her thin shirt, drying the sticky blood of other people that marked her so clearly.

"Hope...," said Brigga Lin.

Hope shook her head, her face pinched as she fought to maintain some composure. "I'm not a Vinchen. I'm not a pirate. I'm not a champion. I...I don't know what I am."

She turned slowly as she regarded all the people around her.

"I am sorry that I brought you here. That I brought death to your companions and to my own. I wish I had more to offer you than that, but I..."

Her throat closed up. What words were there anyway? Could anything lessen the grief in her heart or theirs? Could anything ease her shame?

She looked down at the Song of Sorrows. Perhaps it had been trying to tell her all along. Maybe each pang up her arm had been the sword's way of saying, *You are wrong. You are not worthy.* If only she'd been able to understand. But perhaps she hadn't been willing to understand. Until now.

She took the sword—not in her clamp, but in her hand. It felt strange in that hand. Awkward and muted. She walked away from the people into the thickest part of the rainbow forest of dead girls. Then she thrust the Song of Sorrows into the earth.

It sank easily all the way to the hilt, as if it wanted to be there.

She straightened slowly. Laboriously. Then she kept walking. Away from the sword. Away from the people. Away from everything.

28

I must say, Rixidenteron, your mood has improved dramatically since returning from Lesser Basheta," said Leston as the two sat on a bench in the cliff gardens. Far below, the beige buildings of Stonepeak were turning a gentle pink in the setting sun.

Red leaned back and stretched his long legs out in front of him. "And how could I not be feeling sunny, what with that huge weight finally off my shoulders?"

"Honestly, the idea of being under the control of the biomancers makes my skin crawl. Especially that Progul Bon."

Red frowned thoughtfully. "You know, I haven't actually seen him since we got back. Maybe if we're really lucky, something bad happened to him. But it doesn't really matter, because now *I'm* the one who has the power," said Red. "They still think I'm under their control, and that gives me an advantage."

"I'm not sure how much *power* you actually have if you're working for Lady Hempist."

Red shrugged. "A temporary alliance. And I *do* owe her one. Besides, I thought you'd be pleased for me, princey. It's a *job*. I've become a productive member of your society."

"How self-sacrificing of you."

"Well, I must admit I *am* getting paid rather handsomely for my services."

"Oh?" asked Leston.

Red patted his friend's shoulder. "Let's just say that the next time we go into the city, we can take *my* coach if you like."

Leston smiled. "The imperial tax collectors will be so pleased to have some additional income."

Red gave him a look of sincere regret. "I'm sorry, Your Highness. Did I forget to mention that the deal I worked out with your mother is that all my fees are nontaxable? You know, since it's for the good of the empire and all."

Leston laughed. "You really are a rogue, you know."

Red sighed happily. "I know, but it's music to my ears to hear you say it. I was starting to worry this place was making me *respectable*. Thankfully, now I'm more corrupt than ever." He looked earnestly at the prince. "I think perhaps politics suits me."

"Maybe a bit too well," said Leston. Then he frowned. "And you're sure the biomancers don't suspect?"

"Not so far."

"But the fact that you didn't kill Nea . . . wouldn't that tip them off?"

"When we got back, I just made a big show of being tired, like I'd unknowingly been trying and failing every night. I also made sure to mention how much security the empress has. Even then, I'll admit I was a bit worried they'd swallow it. But they've seemed so preoccupied, I think I could have blamed it on mole rats and they would've just nodded."

"Preoccupied? Should we be worried they're hatching some new plan?"

"The opposite, actually," said Red. "According to Merivale, they'd been secretly working on some big experimental weapon down on Dawn's Light and someone went in and completely destroyed it.

Sounds like they lost everything. The experiment subjects, the research data, and a whole pissing lot of soldiers and ships besides."

"My goodness," said Leston. "I'm not sure that allays my concern. If there's a seditionist movement strong enough to cause that much damage, we've got a whole new set of problems to worry about."

Red thought of all those Godly Naturalists he'd unknowingly murdered and felt a stab of guilt. "Come on, Your Highness. You have to admit, the empire would probably be better off in your hands."

"I'd like to think so," said Leston. "But we can't just run roughshod over generations of tradition and government policy. That makes us no better than the biomancers or seditionists."

It occurred to Red that this might be one thing he and the prince would never agree on, so he bit his lip and remained silent. He wished Hope were there right then. He would have pointed this out to her as a moment that proved he was maturing.

"There you are, Your Highness."

Nea walked through the cliff gardens toward them. She didn't come out here very often. She hadn't said so, but Red wondered if the height made her nervous.

"My lord." She nodded to Red.

She also seemed uneasy around him since that night at Sunset Point. Not that he blamed her. Willingly or not, he had tried to kill her. He wasn't sure their friendship would ever completely recover from that.

"Were you looking for me, Nea?" Leston asked.

"Yes, Your Highness." Her smile was not her usual polished ambassadorial smile, but instead a genuine flash of triumph. "I wanted you to be the first to know. Merivale just informed me that thanks to your mother's influence, the emperor has finally granted me an audience one month from today."

"That's wonderful news, Nea!" Leston looked relieved.

"Congratulations, Ambassador," said Red.

"At long last," said Nea, "we can begin the vital process of building an alliance between our two peoples."

———

Red met with Chiffet Mek for firearms training the next day. But he could tell Mek was barely paying attention. He didn't even notice when Red beat his previous record for long-distance target shooting. They practiced in a narrow rectangular room thirty yards long. Red had his back to the wall when he hit the bull's-eye on the target on the other side of the room three times in a row.

"You need to make me a longer room," he told Mek.

"Hm? Oh, yes, I suppose we'll have to think of something." He frowned distractedly. "I think we're done for today."

"Alright." Red took apart the rifle and laid the pieces on the table next to him.

Before he could leave, however, Mek said, "Come here a moment."

Red walked over, a bit of nerves jangling through his limbs. There was something in Mek's tone that seemed off. Did he suspect?

Mek put his hand on Red's neck, touching the exposed skin above his collar with his fingertips.

"It is essential for the safety of the empire that you attend the council meeting tonight at midnight."

Red felt a surge that was both strange and familiar. Flickers of memory came to him. Something like this had happened many times before. Not just from Chiffet Mek, but Ammon Set and Progul Bon as well. This is how they did it. The touch of bio-mancery that buried itself deep within him. Or it used to. Now it found no purchase in him and dissipated after a few moments.

He blinked, as if disoriented, then gave Mek a confused look and said, "What?"

He was pretty sure that was how he had responded in the past, but he couldn't be certain. If he was wrong, if Mek figured it out right now, he was dead. So he waited, holding that confused look on his face as every nerve inside him screamed to run.

"Never mind," Chiffet Mek said curtly. "You may go."

———

Red asked Merivale to come watch over his bed one last time. Not that he was really worried he would turn into a mindless killing machine again, but... just in case he did.

Merivale swept into his apartments in one of her finest and lowest-cut gowns.

"That's not for *my* benefit, is it?" he asked.

She smirked. "I was just coming from an important intelligence-gathering mission and didn't think I had time to change. But if you feel it will make it difficult for you to get to sleep, I suppose I could cover up with a cloak or something."

"I think I'll be alright," he said. "As long as you sing to me."

"*This* again." She sat down on a chair next to his bed. "You're such a child, you know."

"Another of my many charming flaws," he agreed as he lay down in his bed. "I know you have a list somewhere."

"I do, in fact," she said. "I'm quite fond of making lists. Now, get comfortable, something I know *you're* fond of, and I'll begin."

She sang the same song she had the week before on Sunset Point. He wasn't sure why he liked it so much. Maybe it was the song itself, or maybe it was the keen sorrow in her voice as she sang it. Or maybe it was this moment shared just between the two of them. Now that he was no longer one of Merivale's missions, and only her employee, he'd seen significantly less of her, and he found that he missed her quite a lot.

He wasn't aware of falling asleep, but suddenly his eyes snapped open and he could hear Chiffet Mek's voice in his head, telling him again to come to the council meeting at midnight.

He sat up and Merivale immediately went for her whistle.

"No, it's okay...," he said. "It's still me. But I can also...feel him in me. What he would be doing right now. What *I* would be doing right now, I guess. It's coming to me in little flashes. I remember..."

He walked over to a trunk and found a gray shirt and pants. He put them on slowly as more memories came spilling back into his head. He had done this many times. There was a scarf, too, which he knew he wrapped around his head so that only his eyes were visible. If it was meant as a way to hide his identity, it was a terrible idea, because it left open his most identifiable feature. Then he put revolvers at his hips and lined his shirt with throwing blades.

"How do I look?" he asked Merivale when he was dressed.

"Passably terrifying," she conceded.

"I better get going, then."

"Good luck."

"Never something I need," he told her.

"Don't have *too* much fun," she chided him.

"Yes, boss."

She knew him well, though, because underneath his scarf, he was grinning like a fool. His heart was pounding in his chest, and his entire body buzzed with excitement.

He made his way down to the tenth floor, where the biomancer council chambers were. He hadn't been in that room since the awful night when he'd lost Hope and his freedom all at once. The memory of that dampened some of his enthusiasm, but sharpened his focus. That was probably a good thing, since he was fairly certain that the Shadow Demon was never supposed to be giddy.

He pushed open the door to the chamber and saw the entire council standing in a line against the far wall, their hands joined, just as he'd seen them that first night. He knew they were able to communicate with one another silently as long as their hands were linked, and that their power was greatly magnified. He noted that Progul Bon was still absent.

"Good, you're here," said Ammon Set. "Stand behind us and be ready for any physical violence to our persons that might arise."

"Yes, masters," he said, remembering as he said it that he'd done so many times before.

Except as he took up position directly behind Ammon Set and Chiffet Mek, he had no memory of standing in on a council meeting as a bodyguard. This was something new. He wondered what had them so worried that they felt the need for extra protection.

He got his answer a few minutes later when the doors opened again and this time a group of forty men entered. They moved as one body and displayed a smooth confidence that Red had seen from only one other person. And they all wore black leather armor.

The forty Vinchen warriors stopped and turned to face the biomancers in unison. Then one of them stepped forward. He was a short, powerfully built man, and his armor had accents of gold trim.

"I am Racklock the Just, grandteacher of the Vinchen order."

"I am Ammon Set, chief of the order of biomancery. Why have you and your order left your seclusion on Galemoor to seek audience with us?"

"Hurlo the Cunning believed in the seclusion, but his time is over, and I believe the Vinchen should come out of the shadows and once again stand side by side with the biomancers to serve the emperor and the empire."

There was a long silence as the biomancers silently discussed this through their hands. Racklock waited, his face impassive.

"It is fortuitous that you come to us at this time," Ammon Set said finally. "Perhaps it is the work of God's destiny."

"How so?" asked Racklock.

"The most immediate threat to the stability of the empire comes from one of *your* people."

Racklock's eyes narrowed. "One of mine? Are you certain?"

"A woman dressed in Vinchen armor and clearly trained in your ways. She also carries with her the fearsome blade, the Song of Sorrows."

Racklock's face went almost purple with rage. "I know of whom you speak. She is not one of mine. She is a pet of Hurlo's and was the root of his undoing."

"She has cost us dearly," said Ammon Set. "For months she has been raiding our ships under the name Dire Bane, sowing dread in the navy and unrest among the common people. Then quite recently she destroyed our most promising experiment and slew its chief architects."

Racklock looked surprised. "I had not realized she'd taken to her training so well. And you have been unable to kill her yourselves?"

"For reasons I am not at liberty to discuss right now, we are not permitted to attack her directly."

"My men and I would have hunted this abomination down eventually, even if you did not ask us to. She is a blight on the order and has no right to wield the Song of Sorrows. Her very touch is an insult to such a sword."

"There is...something else you should know," said Ammon Set. "Her chief companion is a female biomancer."

Racklock smiled coldly. "Then we are not alone in our shame."

"Her name is Brigga Lin," said Ammon Set. "And you will find her a difficult opponent, especially since you do not yet have the Song of Sorrows."

"We will kill our own abomination, then use the sword to strike down yours."

"See them both dead, and we will welcome you once again as the mighty right hand of the emperor," said Ammon Set.

Racklock drew his sword, and the thirty-nine Vinchen behind him did the same.

"I swear on my honor," said Racklock the Just, "that the blasphemers Bleak Hope and Brigga Lin will not see the end of another year."

Red stood behind them, almost invisible for all anyone was paying attention to him. And that was a good thing, because otherwise they might have seen the rapid rise and fall of his chest. Feelings for Hope that had begun to fade over the last year sprang suddenly back with full force. She was hitting the biomancers hard enough to actually hurt them. *She* was the setback to their latest plans. His heart soared with pride.

But then he looked at the Vinchen before him. Forty men, all as strong and quick and fierce as her. He'd never really worried about her before, because, well, she was a pissing Vinchen after all. But what good would that be to her now?

29

*B*rigga Lin stood on the quarterdeck of the *Rolling Lightning* with Jilly, Finn, and Alash. They were all that was left of the original crew of the *Kraken Hunter.*

Rather than looking ahead, as she had so often in the past, Brigga Lin found herself watching the place they'd come from as it shrank slowly into the horizon. They had left so much behind on Dawn's Light.

"Where do you think she's going, master?" Jilly asked quietly.

"You said that you saw a ship heading south, didn't you?" Brigga Lin asked.

Jilly nodded. "Just a little boat with only one mast. I saw it while me and Captain Vaderton and the rest of his crew were waiting for you to pick us up at the Breaks."

Brigga Lin considered correcting her grammar, but couldn't quite muster up the necessary conviction. Instead, she turned to Finn.

"What's her likely destination?"

"The only thing south of here is the Isles," he said. "Most folks crossing that much water in such a small vessel, I'd say it's unlikely they'd make it. But you know how she is, our Bleak Hope. Somehow, she'll find a way."

Brigga Lin nodded, but said nothing. It made a

certain amount of sense that such a crisis of conviction would send her back to where she came from.

"What about us?" asked Alash. "Where will *we* go?"

"Captain Gray has kindly invited us to join his crew," said Brigga Lin. "I'm not sure any of us are particularly suited for smuggling or true piracy, but I can't think of anywhere else where we would be welcomed. It's difficult to say how much information Progul Bon was able to convey to the council before his death. It's possible we have become the most wanted criminals in the empire. So perhaps this is best. For now, at least."

Finn sighed. "That sounds a lot less fun than it should."

They all stood there silently for a moment.

"Do you think she'll come back?" asked Jilly.

Brigga Lin raised one thin black eyebrow. "Of course she will. But how long it will take, or what she will be like when she returns, I have no idea."

———

Bleak Hope was an experienced enough sailor to know that when her tiny boat ran aground on the black, rocky shores of Galemoor, it was as much luck as skill that got her there. Or perhaps fate, if she was inclined to believe in such things, which, at the moment, she wasn't. One bad storm is all it would have taken to drown her, or send her too far out on the Dawn Sea to ever return. One storm, which had been just as likely to strike as not. Not fate, then, but chance.

She had not eaten in over a week. She hadn't had a drop of fresh water in days. Her body shivered from the cold, but her skin was red and peeling from sunburn. Her lips were cracked and dry, and she couldn't quite focus her eyes. She tried to climb out of the boat, and fell face-first in the black, gritty sand, the lower half of her body still caught up on the edge of the boat. The coldness of the sand felt good on her burning cheek, so she lay there in that awkward position for a moment. Then she reached out with her hand and clawed at the sand, while kicking her legs free of the boat. Finally, she lay stretched out on her stomach, facedown in the sand. She paused for a moment to catch her breath. Then she slowly rolled over onto her back.

She looked up into the sky, which was bright blue and hard as steel. Tattered wisps of clouds skittered across with surprising speed.

Why was she here? Of all the places in the world, why had she come back to Galemoor? She couldn't quite remember, but it felt right. She began here; she would end here. The Vinchen would discover her down on this beach. Eventually. If she was still alive by then, they would kill her. Perhaps they would even do it mercifully, since she'd come back of her own volition to face judgment. Either way, it didn't much matter. She would die in the place where Grandteacher Hurlo died. The man who had given her so many gifts that she had squandered unforgivably.

"I am Bleak Hope," she muttered aloud, her voice little more than a wheeze. "You gave me a name when I had none, and I rejected it. You gave me a purpose, and I abandoned it. You gave me honor, and I sullied it. And why? For a pretty boy? For selfish glory? For *fun*?"

Even now she remembered those feelings. And she could not pretend she had not enjoyed them, or that she would not enjoy them again.

"I am beyond redemption," she said. "Nothing remains for me but death."

"Not so, child."

Bleak Hope squinted up at the face that now gazed down at her. It was old Brother Wentu in his long black hooded robes. He looked ancient, and sad, but he smiled at her.

"There is still one more thing you must do for your teacher."

"Hurlo...," she said. "Is he alive?"

Wentu shook his head. "No. But he left something for you in my care, should you ever return to this island. Come, let us get you indoors. Then I will give you your inheritance."

"My...inheritance?"

"Come, Bleak Hope. You must stand up if you want to claim it."

The world wobbled, and strange spots trailed across her vision as she forced herself slowly to stand. Then, with old Brother Wentu supporting her, she walked up the beach to the monastery. The familiar black walls loomed before her. As a child they had always seemed so foreboding. Now they seemed as safe as a mother's arms. But of course, she knew they weren't really.

"The other brothers," she said weakly. "They'll kill me."

"Not here, they won't," said Wentu. "They left some time ago."

"Left?" She remembered Broom telling her the brewery had shut down, but she hadn't believed him. "How could they do such a thing?"

"It was Hurlo that kept us here, away from politics and corruption. When Racklock became grandteacher, he abandoned all of that."

Hope looked around as they entered the open gates of the monastery. On closer inspection, she saw the walls had been scored with fire and damaged with blunt instruments. The buildings within the walls were now only charred husks. Only the temple itself remained whole.

"It was a statement," said Wentu sadly. "That they were finished with this place forever and would never return."

"Where did he lead them?" asked Hope.

"Stonepeak. To rejoin the biomancers as servants of the empire. But come, we can talk about that more another time. First we must get you well."

He brought her inside the temple, since it was the only building that still had a roof. The inside was even more of a comfort than the outside. Somehow it still smelled as it did when she was a child, of wood and dust and jasmine-scented prayer candles. The large altar was still in the center, with the prayer mat where she had knelt more hours than she could possibly calculate. The only differences were a small bedroll off in the corner, and a small iron stove that had been brought over from the kitchens. One of the windows had been broken to accommodate the metal pipe of the stove's chimney. An orange light flickered inside the stove, and a small pot simmered merrily on top. The smell of fish stew reached her, bringing with it memories of watching the brothers cook at that stove, and a sudden hunger she hadn't felt in days.

Wentu helped her over to the bedroll. "We'll get you a place to sleep of your own, but for now, you can use mine. You rest while I get you some food."

He hurried over to the stove and ladled out stew into a wooden bowl. He brought it back to her, and she accepted it with a shaking hand. She tried to show some restraint in front of Brother Wentu. But after the first sip, she just guzzled it down.

She gave him an embarrassed look, but he laughed delightedly. "No one has enjoyed my cooking in a very long time. Let me get you another."

After several bowls of stew, Hope was feeling much more like a person. Even if she didn't know who that person was.

"There now," said Wentu, as he sat down next to her on a cushion. "Feeling better?"

She nodded. "Thank you."

He smiled at her for a moment, then the sadness returned. He looked up at the higher windows of the temple. "Damn my old bones, I wasn't able to replace the glass you broke when you escaped all those years ago. Racklock couldn't be bothered."

"As soon as I'm recovered, I promise I will fix it, Brother Wentu."

He nodded, but didn't turn back to her. "Several days before that night, Hurlo came to me. He'd heard rumblings. The other brothers were starting to figure out that he was secretly training you. He hadn't deigned to train a Vinchen in nearly two decades, and here he was wasting years of his time and energy on a *girl*. I think the sting of their pride was more what drove them to action than a loyalty to the code."

"Did *you* know?" asked Hope.

"I figured it out after a few years. He and I had known each other for a very long time, and I could tell something had given him renewed purpose. Something had given him…" He smiled wryly. "Hope."

"And you didn't object to what he was doing?"

"I didn't understand it at first," he admitted. "I thought it might even be impossible. But he was my oldest friend. How could I object to something that clearly gave him such joy?"

"Joy?" asked Hope.

"You were his joy, child. Like no other. And when he came to me just before the end, he entrusted something to me. He said if you ever returned to this island, I was to give it to you."

"I am unworthy of anything he intended for me," said Hope. "He entrusted the Song of Sorrows in my care, and I abandoned it."

"I never much cared for that sword," admitted Wentu. "A brooding and resentful thing, if you ask me."

Hope stared at him. She had never heard anyone speak so disrespectfully and dismissively of one of the greatest Vinchen artifacts ever made.

He grinned impudently at her. "It's true. I can tell by your face you agree with me. Anyway, what I have is much better. At least, *I* think so."

Hope wanted to protest again, but she couldn't resist finding out at least what it was. "Okay. What is this thing that is even better than one of the greatest swords ever forged?"

His eyes twinkled gleefully. "A book."

He handed her a thick, unmarked book. She felt its weight in her hand for a moment. Then she placed it on her lap and opened it. Inside was page after page of diary entries written in Hurlo's spare, elegant handwriting. A single loose sheet of paper lay on top of the first page.

To my dear Bleak Hope,

If you are reading this, then you have returned to Galemoor in spite of the unfriendly welcome you might receive. Perhaps you seek answers to questions that you have not found elsewhere. Perhaps you are angry with me for turning you into something the world is not yet ready or willing to accept. Perhaps you are desperate and alone and despairing. Regardless of your circumstances, first let me say how happy I am that you are still alive. That alone will bring me comfort beyond

*the veil of death. What's more, you are still
seeking. And that is a joy to contemplate. That
you have stayed true to your namesake and not
given up.*

*If you came seeking instruction, however,
I have none to give you. A dead man cannot
be a teacher. What follows is a record of my
thoughts and feelings over the many years I
trained you. I beg you to read it not as a pupil
reads the words of a teacher, but as one reads
the work of a kindred spirit. As equals, each
of us seeking some truth of the world in our
own way.*

*For the last twenty years, I have become
steadily more concerned with the state of
the empire and the direction of the Vinchen
order. I believe there must be a better way.
A more noble path. One that doesn't involve
inflexible prejudice or wanton death. I
thought, perhaps, that through training you,
I could redeem myself, and thereby come to
understand what that more noble path might
be. But at the end of eight years, I feel I am
only beginning to grasp it. Perhaps if we had
more time... However, I am almost certain we
do not.*

*So I must leave this unfinished task to
you. Read this journal so that you can better
understand where I have come from. Take these
humble ruminations and use them as a starting
point down a new path for the Vinchen order.
One that we can both be proud of.*

*I am sorry to lay this burden on you, my
child. But I fear that if you do not find this
new path for us, Racklock will drag the order
to a level of disgrace it has never known, and
countless innocents will die along the way.*

You must be bold enough to dream of a better future, and strong enough to defy the present. Remember that every storm begins with only a breath.

Hope looked up at Wentu, tears in her eyes.

"I am not worthy of this task."

He smiled down benevolently on her. "Worthy or not, you are the only one left to do it. So perhaps the first step is *making* yourself worthy."

THE STORY CONCLUDES IN BOOK THREE OF THE EMPIRE OF STORMS

Keep reading
for a sneak peek!

An Unbiased Overview of the Reign of the Dark Mage

By Progul Bon, Chief Strategist for the Council of Biomancery

There have been many so-called historians who have written about the Dark Mage. Few have known the full story, and none have told it without being clouded by the prejudice of their time. While it is true that a great many lives were lost during the reign of the Dark Mage, the supposition that it was mere wanton slaughter is patently absurd. Every life that was lost, on either side of the conflict, was known by the Dark Mage, and felt deeply. That is the true measure of his greatness. For anyone can kill without thought, but someone who kills knowing the price, and does so anyway because it is for the greatest good, shows a strength of will few of us could match.

Little is known about the man who became the Dark Mage. None of our primary sources, including his own private writings, suggest he spoke or even thought much about his life before he became the Dark Mage. Physical descriptions are scarce, but there is a general consensus that he was not a physically imposing man. Several accounts even describe him as "bookish" and "reserved." Certainly he was a biomancer of great skill and boundless intellect. But there was no record of indoctrination into the order of biomancery in those days, as there is now, so we cannot even ruminate over a list of potential names.

What we *do* know is that he reached the shores of Morack Tor roughly 350 years ago. The island of Morack Tor was of course named after one of the great biomancers of ancient times, a man who lived long before Burness Vee and Selk the Brave aided Cremalton in uniting the islands into the great Empire of Storms. It was said that much of Tor's knowledge was buried with him in his tomb beneath the temple—aspects of biomancery unknown to us even today. Those aspects were lost forever when Burness Vee destroyed the temple at the urging of Selk the Brave. Several historians have suggested Selk had some ulterior motive, but I doubt that. Unlike today, biomancers and Vinchen in that era were comrades, with strong ties of loyalty and common purpose. In particular, Burness Vee and Selk the Brave were known to not only be companions, but close friends. No, I think it far more likely that both Burness Vee and Selk the Brave saw the tremendous amount of power that could be gained from these more dangerous aspects of biomancery, and decided the potential threat posed too great a risk to the newly formed empire.

Not all of Morack Tor's knowledge was lost, however. When the Dark Mage arrived on the island several hundred years later, he discovered a scroll that had somehow escaped the fires set by Burness Vee. What he read that day changed not only his own life, but the very shape of the empire. No one since has ever laid eyes on that scroll, because the Dark Mage destroyed it immediately after he finished reading it. He had come to the remote island seeking knowledge and power, but what he found was apparently so horrifying, he wished to renounce it immediately. It is widely known that any aspect of biomancery takes years to perfect. By destroying the scroll so quickly, he should have ended any chance of learning what it had to teach. But this particular scroll is said to have burned itself into his brain the moment he read it. No matter how much he tried, he could not forget it.

And he did try. He once confided in his chief lieutenant that before he finally accepted his fate, he spent years drinking, whoring, and taking drugs in a desperate effort to rid his mind of the words that whispered endlessly in his head. He spent all of his family's considerable fortune in the attempt, but it did him no good. In the end, even the famous hedonism of Vance Post's Shade District could not wipe away the words that had been seared into his mind. Eventually, he ran out of money, and was left with nothing but those words and their dark power.

In his private writings, the Dark Mage speaks of entering an altered state, similar to a fever dream, from which he could not awaken. He finally regained consciousness weeks later and found he had been abandoned to a sick house—a place where the poor bring their dying loved ones to live out the short remainder of their lives in relative comfort. What was worse, even though he was again aware of his surroundings, the edges of that fever dream state still clung to him, as they would for the remainder of his life. Years later, he wrote that from that day forth, nothing ever felt quite real to him. Instead, it felt like he was trapped in a paper world, surrounded by paper people. Most historians suggest that this was the root of his madness. But I cannot help wondering if perhaps it was instead a sign of a previously untapped and nearly untenable level of sanity.

Gift or curse, this was the birth of the man we call the Dark Mage—a man who was able to bend all but the strongest to his will. It was said that hearing him speak was like hearing your own thoughts, so that it was impossible to tell if the opinion was yours, or his. Knowing what I do of cognitive biomancery, my hypothesis is that his commands bypassed the conscious mind entirely and embedded themselves in the dark and primal aspect that lives deep within our minds.

With such power, commandeering a ship in Vance Post was child's play for him, as was recruiting a crew to his cause. Peasant and noble alike fell under his sway. He moved from one island to the next, taking every able-bodied man and surprisingly, even some women. In a year, his single ship had become a fleet, and his small crew, an army.

During that year, the Council of Biomancery and the Vinchen order watched with increasing alarm as the Dark Mage gathered his horde. When it became clear that his goal was the very crown itself, they knew something must be done. But in the centuries after Burness Vee and Selk the Brave, the relationship between the Vinchen and the biomancers had become strained. Emperor Kelwaton was notoriously cruel to the peasantry, and while the biomancers obeyed his commands, as they obeyed every emperor's commands, many of the older Vinchen were troubled by His Imperial Majesty's disregard for his humblest subjects. That the Dark Mage was recruiting so many peasants only added to the tension. The biomancers argued for swift and decisive action against the growing army, while the Vinchen insisted that those under the Dark Mage's sway were victims rather than traitors and should not simply be slaughtered as if they were voluntary enemies to the crown.

While the biomancers and Vinchen bickered, the Dark Mage completed his preparations for conquest. Nearly half the islands in the empire were under his command when he began his march on Stonepeak. The loyalty he inspired in his troops—or perhaps forced upon them—was without equal. They landed on the west coast of the island and marched inland on foot, not stopping for food or rest until they reached the city walls. Then, over a dozen men and women gave their lives when the Dark Mage turned them into living bombs that sundered the Rain Gate.

Once inside the city, any other army might have been slowed by the temptation to rape and pillage the defenseless townsfolk. But the Dark Mage commanded his troops to immediately continue their march through the city to the palace, and so they did. The imperial soldiers put up a fierce resistance, of course. Lines of cannon roared down the wide thoroughfares, killing hundreds in minutes. But the Dark Mage was not concerned with losses, and the imperial soldiers soon realized they faced an enemy who did not fear death. Some soldiers fled. Others buckled to the will of the Dark Mage and turned their cannons on their own comrades. Over a thousand men died in a single afternoon.

While the Council of Biomancery and the Vinchen order had been locked in furious debate, one biomancer and one Vinchen had decided to take the matter into their own hands. Xunera Ray and Manay the True were not yet the leaders they were destined to become, but they saw the absurdity of their respective orders arguing ideology while the Dark Mage amassed his army. Even though neither was particularly fond of the other, Xunera Ray and Manay the True put aside their animosity for the sake of the empire. They reasoned that if the Dark Mage was slain, those under his sway would be released, and the army would disperse of its own accord. So they began work on a weapon of tremendous power that would be able to counteract the Dark Mage's power and any biomancery he might use in his defense. Like many Vinchen swordsmen, Manay was a master blacksmith. Xunera Ray specialized in aspects of biomancery that dealt with metallurgy. Together, they forged the sword known as the Song of Sorrows. It took them months to complete. Indeed, the handle had not even been properly wrapped yet when the Dark Mage and his army stormed the Lightning Gate.

There are countless bards who will sing of how Manay the True slew the Dark Mage. Needless to say, most of their tales are more fancy than fact. In reality, the fight was short and ugly. With the handle still unwrapped, every blow cut into Manay's hands. Some say he wept as he hewed through the Dark Mage's guards, though from pain or the grief at killing those under the Mage's sway, we will probably never know. By the time he reached the Dark Mage, Manay's hands were a bloody mess, the steel handle sunk down to the bone.

There is one thing the bards sing of that *was* apparently true by all witness accounts. The moment the Song of Sorrows entered the Dark Mage's heart, the Mage's expression was not of agony, but of relief.

But the death of the Dark Mage was not the end of the damage his actions caused the empire. Although his army willingly dispersed, Emperor Kelwaton still hungered for reprisal. Xunera Ray was able to convince His Imperial Majesty to pardon any noble-person who had been a victim of the Dark Mage's power, but that meant the emperor brought his full wrath to bear upon the peasants. A thousand people may have died on the day the Dark Mage stormed the palace gates, but as many as ten thousand died in the weeks that followed.

The biomancers followed the will of the emperor, as they were sworn to do. The Vinchen, however, spoke out against what they considered to be the needless and unjustified slaughter of innocents. A direct confrontation between the two orders seemed inevitable. But Manay the True realized that such a conflict, especially following the reign of the Dark Mage, would tear the empire apart. So he took his Vinchen into seclusion down in the cold, savage Southern Isles. Xunera Ray generously allowed him to keep the Song of Sorrows as an acknowledgment of the sacrifice the Vinchen order was making for the good of the empire. And there the Vinchen have remained ever since, becoming more out of touch and inconsequential with each passing generation, while the Council of Biomancery has remained steadfastly loyal to every emperor who has come since.

During my introduction, I proposed that the Dark Mage's actions, though volatile and treasonous, were for the greater good of the empire. Many historians believe that controlling the will of people was the Dark Mage's most fearsome power. But that was not so. Over a century later, the great scholarly biomancer Yornel Kiv uncovered the Dark Mage's writings on the island of Walta. Among the more personal entries, he found a series of prophecies. One of those predictions was his own death at the hands of Manay the True. Since then, several more of his prophecies have come true, and none have yet proved false. Most disturbingly, there is a prophecy that one day, the Empire of Storms will be lost to a conflict incited by a country far across the sea. That country could only be Aukbontar, whose technological advancements far surpass our own. This is why Emperor Martarkis wisely shut our borders to them, and authorized the Council of Biomancery to use any means necessary to develop weapons that will ensure our supremacy in the inevitable war to come.

I believe that we have a chance to prevail over our enemy. But I cannot help but wonder, if the Dark Mage had taken control of the empire, could he have truly united the hearts of all his subjects? If so, how powerful might we have become? Strong enough to defeat Aukbontar? Perhaps even strong enough to rule the world? This is of course merely idle speculation. What's done is done. But there may come a time when we find ourselves longing for someone with the unyielding will of the Dark Mage.

Acknowledgments

My friend Eve passed away from cancer while I was writing this book. She and I went to college together back in the late '90s, and remained friends ever since. She was there for me at a difficult time in my life, so when she was diagnosed with lung cancer, I tried to be there for her. Her battle with cancer was long and painful, but through it all, she never gave up. Only months before the end, she and I were still making plans for my sons and me to come visit her and her husband in the mountains. It's difficult to parse out how something like this affects your writing, but there is no doubt that both the grief I felt at her loss, and the inspiration I found in her courage, were a profound influence on this book.

I would like to thank Stephanie Perkins, Libba Bray, Diana Peterfreund, Jessica Spotswood, and Holly Black for providing insight and encouragement at times when I desperately needed it. To my editor, Devi Pillai, for always asking the hard questions (although she *still* hasn't made me cry). And of course to my agent, Jill Grinberg, and the whole JGLM team for their boundless and steadfast support.

I did quite a lot of research for this book, mostly in terms of naval culture and tactics. In particular, *Master and Commander* by Patrick O'Brian and *The Sea Rover's Practice: Pirate Tactics and Techniques* by Benerson Little were a tremendous help.

extras

orbit

meet the author

JON SKOVRON is the author of *Hope and Red*, as well as several young adult novels, and his short stories have appeared in publications such as *ChiZine* and *Baen's Universe*. He lives just outside Washington, D.C., with his two sons and two cats. The Empire of Storms is his first adult fantasy series.

introducing

If you enjoyed
BANE AND SHADOW,
look out for

THE EMPIRE OF STORMS:
BOOK THREE

by Jon Skovron

1

"They say he comes from the blackness of night itself."
Old Turnel the mason put down his tankard of ale and
wiped the foam from his bushy mustache. "And that he
oozes in and out of the dark like he was part of it."

The other three wags at the table nodded into their
own tankards. They'd all heard similar things. The
Wheelhouse Tavern was especially crowded that night,
as it had been nearly every night the last few weeks.
Folks in Stonepeak didn't feel safe lately, so it was natural for them to gather. And yet they couldn't stop talking
about the thing that filled them with such dread.

"Someone told me that he makes no sounds and has
no mouth," said Mash the ink maker. Most people in his

trade could be easily spotted by the dark purple stains on their fingers. But Mash always wore gloves while he worked, so his hands were unusually pale and soft.

"No, I heard he had *three* mouths," disagreed Trina the cobbler. She had short hair for a woman. She said she didn't like the feel of it when it was tied back, and she couldn't wear it loose or it would get in her eyes while she hunched over her work. So instead she just cut it off. "One mouth spits acid, one spits poison, and one screams so loud, it makes your ears bleed."

"Regardless of whether he's got three mouths or none at all," said Old Turnel, "it's a fact that he's killed a great many folk in the last month. I seen some of his handiwork myself, and them poor gafs weren't burned or poisoned or anything like that. Every last one of them had the life choked out of them, but without no finger marks on their necks."

The people had given this new killer the nickname Stonepeak Strangler. His victims had been turning up every night, from Artisan Way all the way down to the docks. Not just men, but women and children, too. Unlike the Shadow Demon, who had always targeted dissidents and troublemakers, this Stonepeak Strangler seemed to have no motive or pattern. And he was all the scarier for that. Parents had started keeping their children indoors at night, and even the mildest mollies carried a knife with them when they were about town. Over the last month or so, the capital city of the Empire of Storms had become gripped in a fear that seemed very close to boiling into citywide panic.

"I heard he can't abide the sun, though," said Mash. "That's something, ain't it?"

"If it's true," said Trina.

"My tom heard a funny thing down at the docks," said Hooper, the dressmaker. He was a quiet wag, but greatly respected by the others as the most successful among them. He'd even made gowns for Archlady Bashim and Lady Hempist, two of the most fashionable noblewomen in the empire. "You know that old warehouse along the west bank of Trader's Fork?"

"The one slowly falling in on itself these past ten years?" asked Trina.

"That's the one," said Hooper. "Anyway, my tom was down there bartering with Jacklow the fisherman. You know him?"

"He's my cousin!" Mash said, always eager to impress Hooper any way he could.

Hooper gave the youngest member of their group a steady look, then said, "Be that as it may, my tom and I have known Jacklow to be a truthy wag who always speaks crystal. And he said someone's been lurking down in that warehouse for the last month or so. Someone who ain't entirely...natural."

"That's about the same time these killings started," observed Old Turnel.

Hooper nodded gravely as he drank from his tankard.

"How does he know someone unnatural's been lurking?" asked Trina. "He seen 'em?"

Hooper shook his head. "He only *hears* him, just around sunset, crying and moaning like some kind of beastly thing. Happens nearly every night, he said."

Mash shuddered. "Like to give me nightmares, we keep talking in this direction."

"Don't be a ponce," said Hooper.

Mash turned to Trina with an appealing look. "Don't you think so, Trin? This one's even worse than that Shadow Demon we had a while back."

Before Trina could reply, a new voice cut in:

"You think so?"

The speaker sat at the next table over, leaning back in his chair, his arms crossed. He wore the fine jacket and cravat of a lord, which made him a little out of place in the Wheelhouse. But even stranger, he wore glasses that were tinted so dark they hid his eyes. "And who would win in a fight, do you think?"

The artisans all looked at one another.

"Between the Strangler and the Shadow Demon?" asked Hooper.

"Personally, my money would be on the Demon," said the newcomer.

"Why would they fight?" asked Mash.

"Like as not, they'd be in league," agreed Trina.

The newcomer shrugged. "I suppose that's possible."

"But see now," said Old Turnel, finger and thumb rubbing his mustache thoughtfully. "They could be *competing*, you know. For territory."

"Could be," said the newcomer. "Or *maybe* they'd fight because the Shadow Demon has seen the error of his ways and wants to make amends for his past crimes."

They all looked at one another again.

"Ain't seen you around here, stranger," said Old Turnel finally. "You got a name?"

The man grinned. "You can call me Red."

———

Red went down to the docks the next evening. The sky had that peculiar gold color of twilight that made things seem not quite real as he walked past ships being loaded and unloaded. He wore the soft gray clothes the biomancers had given him when they'd forced him to be the Shadow Demon. His lacy clothes would have stood out in the dockyards, and if he ran into trouble, they would have hindered his movement.

He'd always considered the docks of Paradise Circle big, with over twenty piers, and upward of fifty ships coming and going at any given time. But the docks of Stonepeak stretched all the way down the Burness River from the heart of the city, through the remains of the Thunder Gate, to the coast. There were even piers built up on some of the larger tributaries that fed into the Burness. And where the Burness met the sea, the largest docks in the empire stretched for miles along the southern coast. All told, there were nearly eighty piers and over a hundred warehouses. Red couldn't even guess the number of ships that came and went.

Thankfully, Trader's Fork was one of the smaller, less populated tributaries, mainly used as a trading post between artisans for items unrelated to the needs of the nobility. That meant it wasn't well policed or nearly as crowded. It was, Red decided, a perfect place for a monster to hide. Red hoped that Jacklow the fisherman had been right about hearing something "unnatural" coming from the abandoned warehouse down there. Lady Hempist had assigned this mission to him weeks ago, and this was his first promising lead.

He made his way along the riverbank, skirting the people still working on the docks. There were more than he'd expected this close to sunset, and that worried him a little. Merivale had made it crystal that this mission was to be carried out unobtrusively, like a proper spy mission should be. He wasn't supposed to draw any unnecessary attention or increase the panic of a city already on edge. He also had to hide his identity by wearing a gray scarf over the lower half of his face. Apparently, it wouldn't do if anyone recognized the lord of Pastinas Manor out hunting monsters. At first it had seemed silly to keep his mouth and nose covered, yet leave his eyes visible. They were by far his most distinguishing trait. But Merivale had pointed out that, as Lord Pastinas, he was hardly ever seen without his tinted glasses, so most people didn't even know his eyes were red.

Red finally reached the warehouse around sunset. That cobbler hadn't been exaggerating when she said the place was collapsing. Most of the roof was gone, and the walls were beginning to cave in on one another. There were two entrances. One at the riverbank, where goods had likely once been loaded into the warehouse directly from boats. The other entrance was on the opposite side, where those same items might have been loaded onto wagons for transport into the city. Given the fact that all of the victims had been inland, Red thought it likely his prey was better on land than sea. He decided to approach from the landward entrance, cutting off the easiest escape route.

As he drew closer to the warehouse, he heard an unsettling keening sound from inside. Somewhere between the cry of a child and the whine of a wounded animal. Red had been trying to formulate an image of what this creature might look like in his mind, but the various descriptions he'd heard had all been so conflicting, and he still had no idea what he would find inside. The only thing he was fairly certain about was that it had been made by a biomancer, with their usual lack of compassion or basic decency.

He saw a large window above the entrance. The glass had already been broken, and he decided it would be a little better than just walking in through the door. He climbed up the wall, his heightened sense of touch allowing his fingers and soft-shoed toes to find any crack or edge that would help his ascent.

He perched on the window ledge and surveyed the inside of the warehouse with his red, catlike eyes. It was a large, open space cluttered with rusted boating equipment, coils of rotting rope, and chunks of roofing that had already fallen. There were windows near the ceiling that let in the last faint rays of sun, drenching everything in crimson.

The painful cries came from beneath an upturned rowboat by the wall. There was enough space under that boat to allow for a fairly large creature, but whatever it was would have to flip the boat over to get out, which would leave it vulnerable for a moment. That's when Red would strike.

But when the last rays of sunlight disappeared, the boat didn't flip. Instead, Red watched with sick fascination as something pale and veiny began to ooze out through the small gap between the boat and the floor. It spread out across the wooden floorboards like a lumpy pool of flesh, only occasionally pushing the edge of the boat up as one of the larger chunks passed through.

Once it was completely free of the boat, Red realized that it wasn't a blob or pool exactly. There was a shape to it. A *human* shape. But it was malleable, as if all the bones had been turned soft and pliable. This person lay on their belly, drooping and heavy, arms and legs bowing out to the sides like rubbery insect legs. Then Red saw the mashed-in face.

"Brackson?"

Red remembered Progul Bon casually mentioning that Brackson had been punished after prematurely revealing Red's vulnerability to high-pitched sounds. Brackson and Red had clashed more than a few times back when they'd both been rash young toms in Paradise Circle. So when Brackson showed off his whistle that night, Red knew it was just a bit of payback. Indulgent, sure, but understandable.

Biomancers were not the understanding type.

The thing that used to be Brackson turned sluggishly when Red called out his name. Instead of walking, or even crawling, he had to squirm and undulate across the floor like some kind of human-octopus hybrid. With such a soft rib cage, the weight of his own flesh must be pressing down on his innards. Red guessed it had to hurt like all hells. And the way Brackson's head sagged to one side like a deflated pastry suggested his brain wasn't getting much protection either.

"Brackson, can you speak?" Red had always hated the gaf, but *nobody* deserved this. He pulled down his scarf to show his face. "Do you recognize me?"

Brackson made a grunt that didn't sound particularly friendly. His mouth flapped around. Maybe he was trying to speak, but his jaw was too soft to form the words.

"Listen. I know we ain't ever been wags, but what's been done to you is wrong as wrong can be. Let me help you." He had no idea how, but he knew the prince and the empress. There had to be *something* he could do.

Brackson shuffle-slithered toward the door like he was ignoring him. Or maybe there'd been so much brain damage, he didn't understand. Either way, he seemed intent on getting out of the warehouse, probably back into town where he could mindlessly strangle anyone he came across with his rubbery arms.

Red sighed and pulled his scarf back up. "I should've known you wouldn't make things easy for me even now." He jumped down from the windowsill, blocking Brackson's exit. "Sorry, old pot. Your murder spree ends tonight."

Brackson's rubbery face stretched into something that might have been a frown, and his grunt stretched out into a gurgling growl.

Red drew a throwing blade in each hand. Brackson paused when he saw the gleaming steel, scrunching back into himself.

"There, now," said Red. "You may not understand much, but you still know danger when you see it. Maybe we can settle this peacefully after all."

Brackson scrunched even further into himself. Then he shot forward like a spring, slamming into Red's chest and knocking him over.

Brackson trampled over him, and would have escaped, but Red plunged one of his blades into the creature's soft shoulder and used it as leverage to get on the creature's back as it passed him. He then stabbed his second blade into the other shoulder and held on tight. He was grateful he still wore his fingerless leather gloves, or the blades might have cut right through his palms.

As Red tried to straddle him, Brackson made a warbling sound of protest and took off faster than Red thought possible. It was a strange sort of lurching gait in which Brackson compressed himself, then shot forward, his rubbery arms and legs scrabbling at anything in reach for additional purchase. Red wanted to put a blade or two in Brackson's soft skull, but at their current frantic speed, it was all he could do to hang on.

Red and his unwilling ride smashed through the door and down the wagon path toward town. But town was the last place Red wanted this to go, so he leaned hard on the blades in Brackson's shoulders, steering them in a wide arc through tall grass back toward the small docks along the west bank of Trader's Fork. Brackson had some trouble moving in the grass, and Red thought he was about to get his opening. But before he could take advantage of it, they reached the docks. Brackson's rubbery fingers and toes hooked onto the widely spaced planks of wood, and they lurched forward with even greater speed.

"Clear the way!" yelled Red as they neared a group of dockhands unloading something from a small sloop that, at this hour, was probably smuggled goods.

The dockhands dodged to the side and Brackson smashed through the crates, sending the fine pink powder of coral spice into the air.

"No loss there," muttered Red. He still held a grudge against the drug that had claimed his mother and nearly killed him. He was sentimental that way.

The dockhands stared incredulously as the bizarre pair raced past them. The dock stretched along the banks of Trader's Fork for a quarter mile or so. Red saw that there were four or five other groups of workers ahead of them, all blocking the way.

"How much smuggling goes *on* here?" he groaned.

He had to end this before every drug runner in Stonepeak saw it. It was time for some risky, and possibly ostentatious, acrobatics.

Red jerked his blades out of Brackson's shoulders and jumped straight up. In midair, he threw the blades, which both sank into the base of Brackson's soft skull. Red landed in a crouch on the dock and winced as the lifeless monstrosity was carried forward by momentum into another stack of crates on the dock. The angry shouts of the workers quickly turned to yelps of alarm when they saw what it was that had knocked over their cargo.

Red hurried over and shoved Brackson's body off the edge of the dock into the water, where it quickly sank out of sight.

A proper spy probably would have slipped away right then, silent and mysterious. Well, a proper spy probably wouldn't have allowed themselves to get into this mess in the first place. But seeing as how he was already in the muck of it, Red couldn't resist a little flourish.

"Well, my wags," he said to the smugglers, his red eyes gleaming in the moonlight above his gray mask. "I think that about takes care of your Stonepeak Strangler problem!"

He gave them a quick bow, and ran off, his laughter trailing into the night.

introducing

If you enjoyed
BANE AND SHADOW,
look out for

THE DRAGON LORDS:
FOOL'S GOLD

By Jon Hollins

**Guardians of the Galaxy meets The Hobbit in this
rollicking fantasy adventure.**

*It's not easy to live in a world ruled by dragons.
The taxes are high and their control is complete.
But for one group of bold misfits, it's time to band
together and steal back some of that wealth.*

No one said they were smart.

1

Will

It was a confrontation as old as time. A tale begun back when the Pantheon of old first breathed life into the clay mold of man and set him down upon the earth. It was the tale of the untamable pitted against the master. Of the wild tearing at the walls of the civilized. It was man versus the beast.

Will placed each foot carefully, held his balance low. He circled slowly. Cold mud pulled at his feet. Sweat trickled down the crease between his eyebrows. Inch by inch he closed the distance.

The pig Bessie grunted at him.

"Five shek says she tips him on his arse," said Albor, one of Will's two farmhands. A strip of hairy gut was visible where he rested it upon the sty's rickety old fence. It was, Will had noted, significantly hairier in fact than his chin, which he scratched at constantly. Albor's wife had just departed the nearby village for a monthlong trip to help look after her sister's new baby, and Albor was three days into growing the beard she hated.

"I say it's face first, he lands," said Dunstan, Will's other farmhand. The two men were a study in contrasts. Where Albor's stomach swayed heavily over his gut, Dunstan's broad leather belt was wrapped twice around his waist and still flapped loose beyond the buckle. His narrow face was barely visible behind a thick cloud of facial hair, which his wife loved to excess. She had a tendency to braid sections of it and line it with bows.

"You're on," said Albor, spitting in his muddy palm and holding it out to Dunstan.

Will gave a damn about neither beards nor wives. All he cared about was his father's thrice-cursed prize sow, Bessie. She had been his dancing partner in this sty for almost half an hour now. He was so coated in mud that if he had lain upon the sty's floor, he would have been virtually invisible. He briefly considered this as a possible angle of attack, but the pig was as likely to shit on him and call it a good day's work as anything else. There was an uncanny intelligence in her eyes. Still, she was old and he was young. Brute force would win the day.

He closed the distance down by another inch.

Bessie narrowed her eyes.

Another inch.

Bessie squealed and charged. Will lunged, met the charge head-on. His hands slammed down hard against her sides.

Bessie flew through his mud-slick palms and crashed all of her considerable weight into his legs. The world performed a sprawling flip around Will's head, then hit him in the face.

He came up spluttering mud, and was just in time to hear Dunstan say, "That's five shek you owe me then."

Bessie was standing nonchalantly behind him, with an air of almost studied calm.

Will found his resolve hardening. Bessie had to die. With a roar, he launched himself at the pig. She bucked wildly. And yet still one of his hands snagged a bony trotter. He heaved upon it with all his might.

Bessie, however, had lived upon the farm longer than Will. She had survived lean winters, breeched piglets, and several virulent diseases, and was determined to survive him. She did not allow her limb to collapse under Will's weight, advanced years or no. Instead she simply pulled him skidding through the mud. After several laps, he appeared to be done. With her free hoof, she kicked him in the forehead to emphasize the lesson, then walked away.

"I think you almost got her that time," Albor called in what might be generously described as an encouraging tone.

Will did not respond. Personal honor was at stake at this point in the proceedings. Still, there was only so much mud a man could swallow. He clambered to his feet and retreated to consider his options.

Dunstan patted him on the shoulder as he collapsed against the fence. Bessie regarded him balefully.

"She's too strong for me," Will said when he'd gotten his breath back.

"To be fair, you say that about most girls," Albor told him.

"I have to outsmart her."

"That too," Dunstan chipped in.

"Don't usually work, though." Albor chewed a strand of straw sagely.

"This," said Will, his temper fraying, "is not so much helpful advice as much as it is shit swilling in a blocked ditch. That pig has to become crispy rashers and if you have nothing helpful to add you can go back to picking apples in the orchard."

For a short while the only sound was Bessie farting noisily in her corner of the sty.

Above the men, thin clouds swept across a pale blue sky. The distant mountains were a misty purple, almost translucent.

Will softened. None of this was Albor's or Dunstan's fault, even if they did not want to see old Bessie taken to the butcher's block. Deep down—deeper perhaps now than at the start of his ordeal—neither did he. Bessie had been part of this farm as long as he could remember. His father had sat him upon her back and had him ride around the sty, whooping and hollering, while his mother stood clucking her tongue. Dunstan and Albor had been there, cheering him on. Even old Firkin had been there.

But now Will's parents were gone to an early grave, and Firkin had lost his mind. Bessie was old and would not sow anymore. And Will was the unwilling owner of a farm on the brink of ruin.

"Look," he said, voice calmer, "I want Bessie dead no more than you do, but I am out of options. The Consortium increased taxes again, and paying them has left my coffers bare. If I am to have a hope of surviving another year, I need to put her to the knife and sell her pieces for as much as I can get. Next winter she'll be blind and hobbled and it will be a kindness."

Another silence.

"You can't wait a little, Will?" said Albor, straw drooping in the corner of his mouth. "Give her one last good year?"

Will sighed. "If I do, then there won't be anyone to slaughter her. This whole place will be gone to the Consortium and I'll be in a debtors' jail, and you two will be in old Cornwall's tavern without any sheks to pay for his ale."

At that threat, the two farmhands looked at each other. Finally Dunstan shrugged. "I never liked that fucking pig anyway."

Albor echoed his sad smile.

"That's more like it," said Will. "Now let's see if together three grown men can't outwit one decrepit pig."

Slowly, painfully, Will, Albor, and Dunstan hobbled back toward the farmhouse. Albor rubbed at a badly bruised hip. Dunstan was wringing muddy water out of his sodden, matted beard.

"It's all right," said Will, "we'll get her tomorrow."

Later, the farm's other animals locked away for the night, straw fresh on the barn's floor, Will stood in the farmhouse, heating a heavy iron pot full of stew over the hearth. A few strips of chicken roiled fretfully among vegetable chunks.

He never bothered naming the chickens. It was easier that way.

He sighed as he watched the stew slowly simmer. He should be checking the cheese presses, or scooping butter out of the churn and into pots before it spoiled, or possibly even attempting to tally his books so he could work out exactly how much money he owed folk. Instead he stood and stared.

The nights were long out on the farm. It was five miles through the fields and woods down to The Village. The distance had never seemed far when he was a child. But that was when his parents were alive, and when Dunstan and Albor, and even Firkin, would all have stayed to share the supper, with laughter, and jokes, and fiddle music lilting late into the night. That was when performing the chores around the house had never seemed exactly like work, and when stoking the fire so it warmed the whole room had never felt like an extravagance.

The firelight cast the heavy wooden cabinets and thick oak table and chairs in guttering light. Will tried to focus on that, not the shadows of the day. Maybe Bessie did have one more litter in her. Maybe he could give her one more year. A good litter would bring in enough coin. Or near enough, if the taxes didn't go up again. And he could scrimp and save in a few places. Maybe sell a few of the chairs. It wasn't like he needed more than one.

Yes. Yes, of course that would work. And Lawl or some other member of the Pantheon would manifest in the run-down old temple in the village below and shower them all with gold. *That* was what would happen...

His slow-bubbling thoughts were interrupted abruptly by a sharp rap at his door. He snapped his head to look at the thick oak slats. Outside, rain had begun to fall, tapping a complex undulating rhythm against the thatch roof above his head. It was over an hour's walk from The Village. Who would bother dragging themselves out here at this hour?

He had half-dismissed the sound as a loose branch blowing across the yard when it came again. A hard, precise rap that rattled the door latch. If it was a branch, it was a persistent one.

Removing the stew pot from the fire, he crossed the room quickly, unlatched the door, and opened it onto a cold and blustery night.

Four soldiers stood upon his doorstep. Their narrowed eyes stared out from beneath the shadows of their helms, which dripped rainwater down onto their long noses. Swords hung heavily on their large belts, each pommel embossed with an image of two batlike wings—the mark of the Dragon Consortium. Sodden leather jerkins with the same insignia were pulled over their heavy chain-mail shirts.

They were not small men. Their expressions were not kind. Will could not tell for sure, but they bore a striking resemblance to the four soldiers who had carried off most of the coin he'd been relying on to get through the winter.

"Can I help you?" asked Will, as politely as he was able. If there was anything at which he could fail to help them, he wanted to know about it.

"You can get the piss out of my way so me and my men can come out of this Hallows-cursed rain," said the lead soldier. He was taller than the others, with a large blunt nose that appeared to have been used to stop a frying pan, repeatedly, for most of his childhood. Air whistled in and out of it as he spoke.

"Of course." Will stepped aside. While he bore the guards of the Dragon Consortium no love, he bore even less for the idea of receiving a sound thrashing at their hands.

The four soldiers tramped laboriously in, sagging under the weight of their wet armor. "Obliged," said the last of the men, nodding. He had a kinder face than the others. Will saw the lead soldier roll his eyes.

They stood around Will's small fire and surveyed his house with expressions that looked a lot like disdain. Large brown footprints tracked their path from the door. The fourth guard looked at them, then shrugged at Will apologetically.

For a moment they all stood still. Will refused to leave the door, clinging to the solidity of it. Grounding himself in the wood his father had cut and hewn before he was born. As he watched the soldiers by the fire, his stomach tied more knots than an obsessive-compulsive fisherman.

Finally he crossed to them, the table, and his stew. He began to ladle it into a large if poorly made bowl. He wasn't hungry anymore, but it gave him something to do. These soldiers would get to their business with or without his help.

As he ladled, the lead soldier fiddled with a leather pouch at his waist.

"Nice place this," said the fourth, seeming to feel more awkward in the silence than the others.

"Thank you," Will said, as evenly as he was able. "My parents built it."

"Keep saying to the missus we should get a place like this," the guard continued, "but she doesn't like the idea of farm living. Likes to be close to the center of things. By which she really means the alchemist. Gets a lot of things from the alchemist, she does. Very healthy woman. Always adding supplements to my diet." He patted his stomach, metal gauntleted hand clanking against the chain mail. "Doesn't ever seem to do any good." He looked off into the middle distance. "Of course my brother says I'm cuckolded by a drug-addled harpy, but he's always been a bit negative."

The guard seemed to notice that everyone was staring at him.

"Oh," he said. "Sorry. Obviously none of that is related to why we're officially here. Just wanted to, well, you know…" He withered under his commanding officer's stare.

The lead soldier looked away from him, down to a piece of browning parchment paper that he had retrieved from his pouch. Then he turned the gaze he had used to dominate his subordinate upon Will.

"You are Willett Altior Fallows, son of Mickel Betterra Fallows, son of Theorn Pentauk Fallows, owner and title holder of this farmstead?" he asked. He was not a natural public speaker, stumbling over most of the words. But he kept his sneer firmly in place as he read.

Will nodded. "That's what my mother always told me," he said. The fourth soldier let out a snort of laughter, then at the looks from the others, murdered his mirth like a child tossed down a well.

The lead soldier's expression, by contrast, did not flicker for an instant. Will thought he might even have seen a small flame as the joke died against his stony wall of indifference. The soldier had the air of a man who had risen through the ranks on the strength of having no imagination whatsoever. The sort of man who followed orders, blindly and doggedly, and without remorse.

"The dragon Mattrax and by extension the Dragon Consortium as a whole," the officer continued in his same stilted way, reading from the parchment, "find your lack of compliance with this year's taxes a great affront to their nobility, their honor, and their deified status. You are therefore—"

"Wait a minute." Will stood, ladle in his hand, knuckles white about its handle, staring at the man. "My lack of *what*?"

For a moment, as the soldier had begun to speak, Will had felt his stomach plunge in some suicidal swan dive, abandoning ship entirely. And then, as the next words came, there had been a sort of pure calm. An empty space in his emotions, as if they had all been swept away by some great and terrible wind that had scoured the landscape clean and sent cows flying like siege weaponry.

But by the time the soldier finished, there was a fury in him he could barely fathom. He had always thought of himself as a peaceable man. In twenty-eight years he had been in exactly three fights, had started only one of them, and had thrown no more than one punch in each. But, as if summoned by some great yet abdominally restrained wizard, an inferno of rage had appeared out of nowhere in his gut.

"My *taxes*?" he managed to splutter. He was fighting against an increasing urge to take his soup ladle and ram it so far down the soldier's throat he could scoop out his balls. "Your great and grand fucking dragon Mattrax took me for almost every penny I had. He has laid waste to the potential for this farm with his greed. And there was not a single complaint from me. Not as I gave you every inherited copper shek, silver drach, and golden bull I had."

He stood, almost frothing with rage, staring down the lean, unimpressed commander.

"Actually," said the fourth soldier, almost forgotten at the periphery of events, "it was probably a clerical error. There's an absolutely vast number of people who fall under Mattrax's purview, and every year there's just a few people whose names don't get ticked. It's an inevitability of bureaucracy, I suppose."

Both Will and the commanding officer turned hate-filled eyes on the soldier.

"So," said Will, voice crackling with fire, "tick my fucking name then."

"Oh." The soldier looked profoundly uncomfortable. "Actually that's not something we can do. Not our department at all. I mean you can appeal, but first you have to pay the tax a second time, and then appeal."

"Pay the tax?" Will said, the room losing focus for him, a strange sense of unreality descending. "I can't pay the fucking tax a second time. Nobody here could afford that. That's insane."

"Yes," said the guard sadly. "It's not a very fair system."

Will felt as if the edges of the room had become untethered from reality, as if the whole scene might fold up around him, wither away to nothingness, leaving him alone in a black void of insanity.

"Willett Altior Fallows," intoned the lead soldier, with a degree of blandness only achievable through years of honing his callousness to the bluntest of edges, "I hereby strip you of your title to this land in recompense for taxes not paid. You shall be taken from here directly to debtors' jail."